"Will you agree to cease pursuing me and instead treat me as you previously have?"

He held her gaze for a moment, then sat back. "No."

Her eyes widened. "What do you mean, *no*?"

"You'll do perfectly well warming my bed."

"What?" Thunderstruck, she stared at him.

"Madeline." He waited until her eyes met his. "What did you imagine that kiss was about?"

"I . . . haven't the faintest notion. Why don't you tell me?"

"That kiss was intended to reveal whether or not we are compatible." He held her gaze. "In case you aren't sure how to interpret the result, let me assure you we are."

"Compatible . . .

"Aft . . . . ly sane, rationa . . . . . nd vis-à-vis y . . .

"And . . .

"I wan . . . will have you in my bed."

Enter the World of Stephanie Laurens

The Bastion Club Novels

The Cynster Novels

Also Available the Anthologies

Each and every Stephanie Laurens book is always available in stores and online. For details of these upcoming Cynster and Bastion Club novels visit *www.stephanielaurens.com*

ATTENTION: ORGANIZATIONS AND CORPORATIONS
Most Avon Books paperbacks are available at special quantity discounts for bulk purchases for sales promotions, premiums, or fund-raising. For information, please call or write:

**Special Markets Department, HarperCollins Publishers,
10 East 53rd Street, New York, New York 10022-5299.
Telephone: (212) 207-7528.   Fax: (212) 207-7222.**

Laurens, Stephanie.
Beyond seduction : a
bastion club novel /
2007.

STEPHANIE LAURENS

Beyond Seduction

A BASTION CLUB NOVEL

AVON

An Imprint of HarperCollins*Publishers*

This is a work of fiction. Names, characters, places, and incidents are products of the author's imagination or are used fictitiously and are not to be construed as real. Any resemblance to actual events, locales, organizations, or persons, living or dead, is entirely coincidental.

AVON BOOKS
An Imprint of HarperCollins*Publishers*
10 East 53rd Street
New York, New York 10022-5299

Copyright © 2007 by Savdek Management Proprietory Ltd.
Excerpt from *The Taste of Innocence* copyright © 2007 by Savdek
Management Proprietory Ltd.
ISBN: 978-0-06-083925-3
ISBN-10: 0-06-083925-2
www.avonromance.com

All rights reserved. No part of this book may be used or reproduced in any manner whatsoever without written permission, except in the case of brief quotations embodied in critical articles and reviews. For information address Avon Books, an Imprint of HarperCollins Publishers.

First Avon Books paperback printing: September 2007

Avon Trademark Reg. U.S. Pat. Off. and in Other Countries, Marca Registrada, Hecho en U.S.A.
HarperCollins® is a registered trademark of HarperCollins Publishers.

Printed in the U.S.A.

10 9 8 7

If you purchased this book without a cover, you should be aware that this book is stolen property. It was reported as "unsold and destroyed" to the publisher, and neither the author nor the publisher has received any payment for this "stripped book."

Beyond Seduction

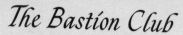

The Bastion Club

"a last bastion against the matchmakers of the ton"

MEMBERS

Christian Allardyce,
Marquess of Dearne

#2 ~~Anthony Blake,~~
~~Viscount Torrington~~

Alicia
"Carrington"
Pevensey

#5 ~~Jocelyn Deverell,~~
~~Viscount Paignton~~

Phoebe
Malleson

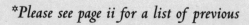

*Please see page ii for a list of previous

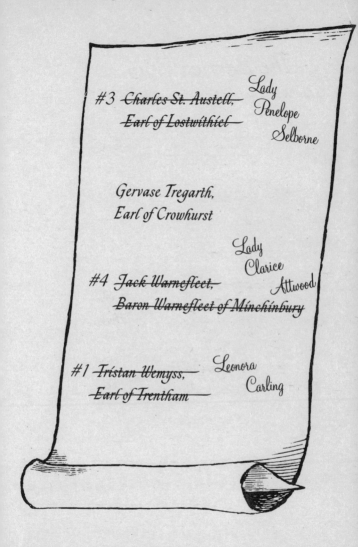

#3 ~~Charles St. Austell, Earl of Lostwithiel~~ Lady Penelope Selborne

Gervase Tregarth, Earl of Crowhurst

#4 ~~Jack Warnefleet, Baron Warnefleet of Minchinbury~~ Lady Clarice Attwood

#1 ~~Tristan Wemyss, Earl of Trentham~~ Leonora Carling

titles in the Bastion Club series.

Chapter 1

Early July 1816
Crowhurst Castle, Cornwall

"*How the devil did they break the mill?*" Gervase Tregarth, 6th Earl of Crowhurst, paced before the hearth in the elegant drawing room of Crowhurst Castle. The exasperation of a man driven to the limits of frustration colored his face, tone and every long-legged stride. "And am I to surmise that they were also behind all the rest? The broken fences, the damaged boats, the mix-up with the grain, the unexplained ringing of the church bells at midnight?"

Swinging around, he pinned his stepmother, Sybil, with a sharply interrogatory, hard hazel gaze.

Seated on the chaise, a silk shawl about her shoulders, Sybil returned his stare with a blank look, as if she hadn't fully comprehended his meaning.

Gervase knew better. Sybil was wondering how to answer. She knew he was one step away from losing his temper, and would much rather he didn't. He narrowed his eyes even further. "They *were*, weren't they? Of course they were."

His voice had lowered to a growl; the past months of futile traveling to London only to be summoned back within a few days to deal with some inexplicable calamity flashed across his mind—and frayed the reins of his temper even more. "*What in all creation do they think they're about?*"

He wasn't shouting, but the force behind his words was enough to overset a more robust female than Sybil; he drew in a breath and tamped down his welling fury. The "they" he and she were discussing were her daughters—his three halfsisters—currently featuring as the bane of his life.

Belinda, Annabel and Jane took after their father, as did he, which was why Sybil, mild, sweet Sybil, fair-haired and gentle, was entirely unable to control them. Or comprehend them; all three were more intelligent, clever and quick than she. They were also more vigorous, bold and outgoing, altogether more confident.

He, on the other hand, shared with the three the affinity of character. They'd always been close; as their adored older and only brother, he'd grown accustomed to them being on his side.

Or at least operating on some form of Tregarth logic he could understand.

Instead, over the past six months they'd apparently transformed from lovable if mischievous hoydens of whom he was deeply fond to secretive, demon-inspired harpies whose primary focus in life was to drive him demented.

His last question had thus been rhetorical; if he couldn't fathom what had possessed his dear sisters to stage what amounted to six months of guerrilla mayhem designed to overthrow his sanity, he didn't imagine Sybil would.

Yet to his surprise she looked down, and picked at her shawl's fringe. "Actually . . ." She strung the word out, then glanced up at him. "I think it's because of what happened to the Hardesty girls."

"The Hardesty girls?" He halted, frowned, struggling to place them. "The Hardestys of Helston Grange?"

Sybil nodded. "Robert Hardesty—Lord Hardesty now his father is dead—went to London last September, and came home with a wife."

Gervase's recollection of Robert Hardesty was of a wet-behind-the-ears whelp, but that memory was more than twelve years old. "Robert must be . . . what? Twenty-five?"

"Twenty-six, I believe."

"A trifle young for marriage perhaps, yet if, as I suppose, he has his sisters to establish, a wife seems a sensible addition to his household." *His* sisters' futures rated as one of the many reasons he himself felt compelled to wed. Gervase tried to recall the Hardesty girls, but drew a blank. "His sisters are about Belinda's age, aren't they?"

"A year or two older—eighteen and seventeen. Everyone *thought* Melissa and Katherine would be presented this past Season, and with Robert marrying . . . well, we all imagined that the new Lady Hardesty—a young widow said to have been a London beauty—would, naturally, take the girls under her wing."

From Sybil's tone it was clear the generally held expectations hadn't been met. "What happened?"

"Robert brought his lady home just before Christmas." Sybil's rosebud lips tightened into an expression of severe disapprobation. "In January, with the snows still blocking the roads, Robert dispatched Melissa and Katherine to visit their aunt in York. It seemed his new wife wanted time to settle into her new life without the distraction of having to deal with the girls. However, it's now July and the girls are still in York. Meanwhile, Lady Hardesty spent the Season in London, then returned to the Grange a week ago with a bevy of London friends in tow. I understand she's told Robert that it would not be wise to have the girls return home while they have so many London gentlemen under their roof."

Gervase stood before the fireplace staring at Sybil while he grappled with the implied connection. Then he blinked. "Am I to understand . . ." Lifting his head, he looked past Sybil, trying to see the Hardesty story from his sisters' perspective. "They can't possibly be equating me with Robert Hardesty."

His tone made it clear he found the notion inconceivable. He refocused on Sybil's face in time to meet her widening eyes.

"Well, of course they are, dear. The parallels are rather obvious."

He felt his face harden. "No. They're not." He paused, then growled, "Good God! They can't seriously imagine—"

He broke off and looked toward the main door as it opened to admit his halfsisters. He'd sent for them the instant he'd stalked into his front hall, having been met in the castle forecourt by Gregson, the local bailiff, with the news that the three had been discovered creeping away from the mill just after midnight. Subsequently, it had been discovered that the mill was no longer functional.

Despite the best efforts of the miller, it still wasn't.

In the wake of the string of strange accidents that had plagued the estate for the past six months, Gervase and Gregson had set up a secret watch. But the very last culprits they'd expected to catch were the three schoolgirls who marched into the room.

Belinda, the eldest, led the small procession. At sixteen she was already taller than Sybil and bade fair to turn men's heads with her lustrous light brown hair and long, long legs. But if the expression on her heart-shaped face was any guide, any man would have his hands full with her. Defiant determination oozed from every pore and flashed in her hazel eyes.

She lifted her chin as she halted behind the chaise, facing Gervase, meeting his hard gaze with her own Tregarth stubbornness.

Annabel, fairer in coloring, with almost blond hair and blue eyes, ranged alongside Belinda. There was less than a year between them, and barely an inch; while Belinda had started to wear her hair up, Annabel was content to let her long pale tresses ripple over her shoulders in a romantic veil.

Gervase met Annabel's eyes, and saw the same trenchant purpose infusing Belinda repeated there.

Increasingly wary, he shifted his gaze to the third and youngest of the three, lowering it to her sweet, delicate face, still very much that of a child. Jane was barely ten, and had always been devoted to him. Confined in neat plaits on either side of her small face, her hair was a darker brown than the others', more his coloring, but her eyes were Sybil's blue.

Meeting those usually innocent orbs, Gervase was faintly stunned to encounter unwavering, resolute determination—further accentuated by the set of her little chin.

Keeping his own expression impassive, he glanced again at the other two, mentally at sea. What on earth had changed them? Why . . . why had they lost faith in him?

He suddenly comprehended that he was treading on ground that wasn't as firm as he'd thought. He had to go carefully.

Where to start?

He let the silence stretch, but while Sybil fidgeted, her daughters were made of sterner stuff. They just waited for him to speak, their gazes locked on him.

"I've just heard from Gregson that the three of you were caught leaving the mill last night, apparently after sabotaging it. The mill is still out of action, and John Miller is in danger of losing what little hair he has left. I'll admit I'm having trouble believing that the three of you could be so unthinking as to deliberately cause Miller and all those who rely on the mill so much unnecessary trouble for no

good reason. So I assume you have an excellent reason for
what you've done—I hope you'll share it with me, so I can
explain your actions to the rest of the neighborhood."

Belinda's chin tilted a fraction higher. "We do have an excellent reason—for the mill and all the rest." She briefly
scanned his eyes, confirming that he had, indeed, guessed
about "all the rest." "However," she continued, "you might not
wish to make that reason public. We had to find ways to bring
you back from London, and preferably keep you here, although as of yet we haven't managed the latter."

"We thought we'd be able to make you stay by creating
a mystery by ringing the bells," Annabel said, "but you just
took away the ropes. So we had to think of something
else."

"None of the other things we did kept you at home." Jane
looked at him severely, as if that were his fault. "You just
came home and fixed them, and then left again—back to
London."

It *was*, apparently, his fault.

He was starting to feel a little disoriented. "Why do you
want me to stay at home?"

Belinda shifted, lips pressing together; he could see she
was hunting not for just words but for how to explain. The
other two looked at her, deferring to her. Eventually she met
his eyes. "We asked you to stay, each of us every time, but
you always just smiled and insisted that you had to go back
to town. We suspected—well, everyone in the neighborhood knew—that you were going there to find a wife. We
didn't want you to do that, but we couldn't just say so, could
we? You wouldn't have listened to us, that was obvious. So
we had to find some other way of stopping you."

He stared at her. "You don't want me to find a wife?"

"We don't want you to find a wife in London." Belinda
capped the statement with a definite nod—repeated by the
other two, one after the other.

It was, indeed, as Sybil had guessed. Compressing his lips, he battled to shore up a patience that six months of mayhem—let alone all the futile racing back and forth—had worn wafer-thin. "Sybil has just told me about the situation with the Hardestys." He managed to keep his tone even, his diction not so clipped that it would cut. He was still very fond of them, even if they'd temporarily turned into bedlamites. "You can't seriously imagine that I would marry a lady who I would subsequently allow to send you away."

Yes, they could. Yes, they did.

They didn't say the words. They didn't have to; the truth was writ large in their eyes, in their expressions.

He felt positively insulted, and didn't know what to say—how to defend himself. The idea that he needed to was irritation enough.

"I'm older, and wiser, and far more experienced than Robert Hardesty. Just because he's married unwisely is no reason whatever to imagine I'll do the same."

The look Belinda bent on him was as contemptuously pitying as only a younger sister could manage; it was mirrored to an unsettling degree by Annabel and Jane.

"Gentlemen," Belinda stated, "always think they know what they're doing when it comes to ladies, and they never do. They think they're in charge, but they're blind. Any lady worth the title knows that gentlemen, once hooked, can be led by the nose if the lady is so minded. So if an attractive London lady gets her hooks into you, and decides like Lady Hardesty that having girls like us to puff-off isn't a proposition she wants to take on, where will that leave us?"

"Living in the North Riding with Great-Aunt Agatha," Annabel supplied.

"So it was obvious we had to take action," Jane concluded. Her eyes narrowed on Gervase. "Drastic action—whatever was necessary."

Before he could even think of a reply, Belinda went on, "And there's no use citing your age as any indication of your wisdom in such matters. You've spent the last twelve years out of society—it's not a case of your skills in this regard being rusty so much as you've never developed the relevant skills at all."

"It's not the same as if you'd spent those years in London," Annabel informed him, "watching and learning about choosing a wife."

"This is not a battlefield on which you have any experience," Jane declared in her most serious voice. "In this theater, you're vulnerable."

She was obviously reciting arguments they'd discussed at length; just the thought was horrifying. Trying to assimilate their unexpected and peculiarly female point of view was making Gervase giddy.

He held up a hand. "Wait. Just stop. Let's approach this logically." He cast a glance at Sybil, only to surmise from her attentive expression that however much she might deplore her daughters' actions, she didn't, materially, disagree with their assessment. No help there. He drew breath, and stated, "You're worried that, like Robert Hardesty, I'll fall victim to some fashionable London lady who will take a dislike to you and convince me to send you to live with Great-Aunt Agatha."

All three girls nodded.

"To prevent such an occurrence, you made sure I had no time in the capital during which to meet any such lady."

Again three definite nods.

"But you know I need a wife. You understand that I have to marry?" Not least to secure the title and the entailed estate, given he was the last male Tregarth.

"That's obvious," Belinda informed him. "Aside from anything else, you're never going to manage the social obligations adequately on your own, and Mama can help only so far. Once we wed, she'll live with us, so you should marry as soon as possible so your countess can learn the ropes."

"Besides which," Annabel put in, "you having the right lady as your countess will make it much easier for us to make our come-outs properly. We're now titled ladies, and poor Mama is going to have a time of it if she has to manage our come-outs on her own."

"And, of course," little Jane continued, her voice lighter than the other two, "there's the fact you need to sire an heir, or else when you die the estate will revere . . ." She stopped, frowned.

"Revert," Gervase supplied.

She thanked him with a serious little nod. "*Revert* to that disgustingly fat, dissolute reprobate, the Prince Regent." She met Gervase's gaze. "And no one would want *that*."

Gervase stared at her, then glanced at the other two. Clearly he didn't need to explain the facts of his life—familial or social—to them. "If you understand all that, then you must see that in order to find the, as Annabel put it, right lady to be my countess, I need to go to London—"

He broke off as all three vehemently shook their heads. It wasn't just the action, but the look in their narrowing eyes, and the set of their firming lips and chins, that stilled his tongue.

"No," Belinda stated. "*No* London ladies. Now that you understand our position, you must see that we can't allow you to simply swan off and search by yourself in London."

"If you do," Annabel prophesied, "you'll be caught."

"Some London harpy will get her claws into you, and we won't be there to drive her off."

That last came from Jane. Gervase looked into her eyes, hoping to see that she was joking, or to at least detect some comprehension that she was overextrapolating, some indication that she understood that he had no need of their protection, especially in such an arena. Instead, all he saw was that same dogged, unbending purpose. One glance at the other two confirmed that they, too, saw her words as a simple statement of fact.

He stared at them, feeling like he'd strayed into a reality he no longer recognized. He really couldn't believe he was having this discussion. One part of his mind was convinced he must be dreaming. "But"—he seemed to have no alternative but to ask the obvious—"if I can't go to London and find a bride there, where do you imagine I'll find a suitable lady to be my countess?"

That earned him a three-pronged look that suggested he was being deliberately obtuse.

"You need to look around here, of course," Belinda informed him.

"In the neighborhood and nearby towns," Annabel clarified.

"So you can bring her home and show her the castle, and us," Jane added. "*Before* you marry her."

He suddenly understood—or rather, his brain finally accepted what his intellect had deduced. "You want to vet my choice?"

All three blinked at him; Sybil did, too.

"Well, of course!" Belinda said.

His expression set like stone. "No."

That should have been the end of it. He should have said not one more word and stalked from the room. Should have realized from what had already passed that in the last ten years his sisters had grown even more like him—until he was no match for the three of them together.

They could talk rings around a philosophy professor.

The one peculiar talent he'd brought to his decade and more as a covert agent operating primarily on foreign soil, slipping in and out of the ports of France during the final years of the wars, was his ability to persuade. It wasn't charm; it owed nothing to a smile or a glib tongue. It was more a matter of being able to twist arguments, of having the sort of mind that could see possibilities and frame connections in such a way that they seemed plausible, causal and direct. Even when they were in no way linked.

He was an expert in persuasion, in the art of framing the reasonable suggestion.

Yet every point he made, his sisters attacked. From three sides. At once. He knew where he stood, knew the rational ground beneath his feet was solid, yet no matter how hard he fought, he couldn't seem to defend his position.

He was driven back, step by step. Onto a slippery slope that he suddenly realized led straight to abject surrender.

"Enough!" Running a hand through his hair, only just suppressing the urge to clutch the close curls, he ignored their pressing, leading questions designed to send him sliding down that slope and forced them to return to the single central point. "Regardless of anything and everything, as there *is* no lady anywhere near who might be suitable, I have to go to London to make my choice."

"No," Belinda said.

"Not without us," Annabel belligerently declared.

"If you try to return to London alone," Jane warned, "you'll force us to do something *terrible* to bring you back."

Gervase looked into all three pairs of eyes, each brimming with a determination equal to his own. They weren't going to budge.

But this was his life. *His* wife.

And he was so tired of the mounting frustration of not being able to even start his search for her.

All, it now seemed, because of his sisters.

His temper, already tried beyond bearing, quietly slipped its leash.

"Very well," he said.

All three girls straightened. They'd never, ever, seen him lose his temper, but knew him well enough to sense the change.

His tone cold, even and uninflected, he stated, "As you're so convinced a suitable lady exists hereabouts, and that any such local lady will pose no real threat to you, I'll make a bargain with you. I won't return to London for the next three months, not until the Little Season commences. And I swear on all that's holy that, from this moment on, I'll marry the first suitable lady I meet—suitable on the basis of age, birth and station, temperament, compatibility and beauty. In return, you three will accept that lady *without question*." He held their gazes, his own as hard as stone. "And you will not, again, indulge in any behavior designed to influence my decisions, or my life, in any way whatever."

He paused, then said, "That's the bargain. Do you accept it?"

They didn't immediately answer.

All three studied him, then Belinda asked, "What if you don't meet a suitable lady over the next three months?"

He smiled, a chilly gesture. "Then when the Little Season starts and I return to London, I'll have to look there."

They didn't want to take the risk; the wariness in their eyes said so.

He pressed his advantage. "If you're so sure that a suitable lady lies waiting in the neighborhood, then you should be prepared to let fate take her course and arrange for her to cross my path. You should be prepared to accept my bargain."

The three looked at each other, wordlessly communing, then faced him once more. Belinda spoke. "If you promise on your honor to seriously look for, and then actively pursue, any suitable lady, then . . ." She hesitated, glanced one last time at the others, then looked back at him and nodded. "Yes—we accept your bargain."

"Good." He didn't want to say more, much less hear any further words from them on his inability to choose his own wife. He glanced at Sybil, a silent observer throughout, and curtly nodded. "If you'll excuse me?"

Another rhetorical question. With a last, raking glance over his sisters' faces, he turned and strode to the door.

He had to get out—somewhere he could stride so he could let the coiled tension, the inevitable outcome of suppressing his fury, free.

By the time he reached the drawing room door, manifesting temper had infected his movements. Jerking the door open, he swung into the corridor—and nearly ran down Sitwell, his butler.

A paragon of his calling, Sitwell stepped back quickly to avoid a collision. Gervase inwardly sighed. Closing the door, he arched a brow in query.

"Miss Gascoigne has arrived and is asking to see you, my lord."

The Honorable Miss Madeline Gascoigne. He was going to have to swallow his ire. "Where is she?"

"In the front hall, my lord. She intimated the matter wouldn't take long and she did not wish to disturb Lady Sybil."

Thanking Heaven for small mercies, Gervase nodded. "I'll go to her."

He strode down the corridor, leaving Sitwell in his wake.

His bargain with his sisters didn't worry him; he knew beyond doubt that there simply wasn't any suitable lady anywhere in the vicinity. He'd looked about the locality first before accepting the need to look in London. The notion that he'd *choose* to run the gauntlet of the London marriage mart was absurd; London was simply his only field of choice.

Which meant that for him finding a wife was postponed

until the ton returned to the capital in late September. Given he'd had no intention of putting himself through the excruciating ordeal of countless house parties—the summer hunting grounds of the matchmaking mamas—that would have been the case regardless.

So his bargain with his sisters had cost him nothing he hadn't already surrendered, namely the next three months. The point that seriously exercised his temper was that he'd had to make such a bargain at all.

Indeed, the entire subject of his wife—or more specifically his lack of same—had become a sore point, a mental bruise that throbbed every time he thought of it. Let alone spoke of it.

Turning a corner, he looked ahead, and saw a tall figure waiting by the round table in the center of the castle's great front hall. He inwardly grimaced. No doubt Madeline had come to ask about the mill.

The daughter of the previous Viscount Gascoigne, only child of his first marriage, she was the older halfsister of the current viscount, Harold, known to all as Harry, still very much a minor at fifteen. The Gascoignes held the estate of Treleaver Park, situated above Black Head, the eastern headland of the same wide bay on which the castle stood overlooking the western cove. Gascoignes had been at the Park for very nearly as long as Tregarths had been at the castle.

The two families were the principal landowners in the area. As, under the terms of her late father's will, Madeline was the primary guardian of her three brothers, including Harry, it was she who was the de facto Gascoigne. She ran the estate and made all necessary decisions. As she'd been groomed by her father for that duty, and had performed in the role since before his lingering death eight years ago, the neighborhood had long grown accustomed to treating her as her brother's surrogate.

Indeed, for the exemplary way she conducted her brother's

business and for her devotion to the difficult role of her brothers' keeper, she had earned the respect of every person on the peninsula, and far beyond.

Gervase approached; hearing his bootsteps, Madeline turned, an easy smile lighting her face. Courtesy of his years abroad, he didn't know her well, but as he'd been born at Tregarth Manor outside Falmouth, not that far away, and had spent many months throughout his childhood visiting his uncle and cousins at the castle, he'd known of her existence for most of her life.

Since his unexpected ascension to the earldom three years ago, and even more since he'd sold out the previous year and personally taken up the reins of the estate, he'd dealt with Madeline frequently, although busy as they both were, they most often communicated by letter.

She was considerably taller than the average, only a few inches shorter than Gervase. As usual when riding about the county, she was gowned in dark colors; today's gown was a sensible rich brown. A wide-brimmed hat dangled from one hand, worn to protect her fair skin from the sun, but even more to help confine the mass of her hair. Fine and plentiful, no matter how tightly she restrained it in a knot on the top of her head, strands escaped, forming a halo of spun copper filaments about her face, rather like a Russian madonna. Her hair, however, was the only element of her appearance beyond her control; all the rest was deliberately and severely restrained, strictly business.

As Gervase neared, she held out a gloved hand.

He grasped it, shook it. "Madeline."

Retrieving her hand, she returned his easy nod. "Gervase." Her expression turned rueful. "Before you say anything, I'm here to beg your pardon."

He blinked, frowned. "I thought you'd come about the mill."

Her smile widened. "No, although I did hear of your

problem. It seems quite bizarre that your sisters were involved. Have you discovered why they did it? Or, as is the case with my brothers, was it simply a matter of 'it seemed a good idea at the time'?"

He managed a rueful smile. "Something like that. But what's your apology for?"

"In light of the mill, you'll understand. I'm afraid my hellborn three's latest interesting idea was to put your bull in among your dairy herd. Don't, pray, ask me why—their logic escapes me. I've already had them out to see your herdsman to apologize, and I supervised them in recapturing the bull and putting him back in his field. He didn't seem any the worse for his adventure, although I'm afraid your milk production might suffer a trifle due to the excitement."

She paused, a frown in her gray-green eyes. "I should, I suppose, have expected something. They're home for the summer, of course, but I had hoped they would have outgrown such schoolboy exploits."

Gervase raised his brows, falling into step beside her as she walked slowly back to the front door. "Harry's fifteen, isn't he? He'll stop his schoolboy tricks soon enough, but when he does, you might well wish he hadn't. In this season a slight disruption to our milk production won't even be noticed, and if that's the worst he and your other two get up to this year, we'll all think ourselves lucky."

"Hmm . . . be careful what you wish for?" Madeline wrinkled her straight, no-nonsense nose. "In that you might be right."

They paused in the shadow of the front porch. She glanced at him. "When do you expect the mill to be fixed?"

They chatted for several minutes, about the mill and the coming harvest, about the local tin mining in which both estates had an interest, about the latest local business news. Like all the neighborhood gentlemen, Gervase had learned to respect and rely on Madeline's views, drawn as they were from a much wider pool of information than any of them could tap.

There wasn't a local merchant, miner, laborer or farmer who wouldn't readily talk to Miss Gascoigne about his enterprise. Likewise his wife. Madeline had a much deeper understanding of anything and everything that went on on the Lizard Peninsula and in surrounding districts, one no mere man could hope to match.

She glanced up at the sun. "I really must be going." She met his eyes. "Thank you for understanding about the bull."

"If it helps, you can tell your brothers that I was not amused. I'll be going out to the mill shortly."

With a smile, she held out her hand. Gervase shook it, then went with her down the steps to the forecourt, where her horse, a tall, powerful chestnut few other women could hope to control, waited, alert and ready to run.

Lifting her hat, she settled it on her head, then reached for the front of her saddle. Gervase held the horse's bridle, watching without a blink as Madeline planted her boot in the stirrup and swung up to the horse's broad back.

She always rode astride, wearing trousers beneath her skirts for the purpose. Given the miles she covered every day watching over her brother's interests, not even the most censorious dowager considered the fact worth mentioning.

Madeline lifted her reins. With a smile and a brisk salute, she backed the chestnut, then wheeled and trotted neatly out of the walled forecourt.

Gervase watched her go, idly aware that her peers in the district were the other male landowners; in their councils, she was never treated as a female—as someone of different status from the men. While no one would actually treat her as a man—thump her on the back or offer her brandy—she occupied a unique position.

Because, in many ways, she was unique.

Thinking of his sisters, Gervase considered that a little of Madeline's uniqueness could, with benefit, rub off on them. Turning back to the castle, he remounted the front steps. And turned his mind back to his temper . . . only to discover that it was no longer straining at the leash.

He no longer had anything to suppress. He felt calm, in control once more, confident and able to deal with whatever might come his way.

His conversation with Madeline—sane, sensible and rational—had regrounded him. Why couldn't his sisters be more like her?

Or was that one of those things he should be wary of wishing for?

He was still pondering that point when he reached the drawing room. Opening the door, he walked in.

Belinda, Annabel and Jane turned from the window overlooking the forecourt, through which they'd obviously been observing him and Madeline. Sybil, swiveled on the chaise, had been watching her daughters, no doubt listening to their report.

Before he could frown at them, all four looked at him, their expressions identical, eager and expectant.

He stared at them. "What?"

As one, they stared back.

"We thought perhaps you might invite her in," Belinda said.

"Madeline? Why?"

The look they bent on him suggested they were wondering where he'd left his wits.

When he didn't spontaneously find them, Belinda deigned to help. "Madeline. Isn't she a suitable lady?"

He stared at them, and couldn't think of an answer. Not any answer he wanted to give. Oaths, he suspected, wouldn't shock them.

He let his face harden, let his most impenetrable mask

settle into place. "I have to go and unjam the mill. I'll speak with you later."

Without another word, he swung around and stalked out.

That evening, Gervase entered his library-cum-study and headed directly for the tantalus. As he poured himself a brandy, the latter events of the day scrolled through his mind.

Reaching the mill, he'd discovered the frustrated miller about to commence the laborious task of dismantling the grinding mechanism to see why "the damned thing won't budge." Asking him to wait, Gervase had gone outside to where the huge waterwheel sat unmoving in the narrow stream. His sisters knew nothing about gears and axles; there was no evidence they'd even entered the mill. Whatever they'd done to cripple the mechanism had been simple and ingenious—and something three schoolgirls, two of decent height and strength, could physically achieve.

The stream had been bubbling and gurgling along, covering the lower third of the wheel. After squinting into the rippling water, Gervase had called the miller and his sons to lend a hand; they'd managed to turn the wheel—enough to expose the gaps where three paddle blades ought to have been, and the anchor, doubtless purloined from the castle boathouse, that had held the wheel so that the jostling of the stream hadn't shifted it. With the three blades missing, the water rushed freely through the gap, providing no force to turn the big wheel.

John Miller had stared at the gaps, at the anchor, and had sworn.

They'd found the blades, which for ease of replacement simply slotted into grooves in the wheel's inner sides, tucked out of sight among some bushes. A matter of minutes had seen the anchor removed and the blades replaced—and the millstone grinding once more.

His sisters' latest misdeed righted, he'd returned to the castle and had closeted himself in the library until dinner-time.

He'd contributed little to the dinner table conversation; the few exchanges had been of a general nature, of local affairs and local people. No one, however, had mentioned Madeline Gascoigne.

When, with Sybil, his sisters had risen and retreated to the drawing room, he'd watched them go, and then come here. Lifting his glass, he carried it to a well-padded arm-chair, sank down into the cushioning leather, and sighed.

He sipped, then put his head back and closed his eyes.

Despite their careful silence, his sisters were watching him like hawks. Demanding creatures. He'd made a prom-ise, and they expected him to keep it.

And, of course, he would.

Opening his eyes, he raised his glass again, and refo-cused on the issue never far from his mind, his principal and continuing problem—his lack of a wife.

When he'd resigned his commission late last year, he'd had a vague notion that now peace was established and he was free to become the Earl of Crowhurst in more than name, then getting himself a wife ought to be his next step.

When a group of close comrades—six others who like him had spent the last ten and more years working behind enemy lines under the orders of the secretive individual they knew only as Dalziel—had proposed banding together and creating a private club to guard against the marauding mamas of the ton, he'd thought it an excellent idea. The Bastion Club had indeed proved useful in facilitating the search for suitable wives—for most of the others.

So much so that as of a day ago, there were only two of the original seven club members still unwed. Christian Allardyce, Marquess of Dearne, and Gervase himself.

Christian, he'd realized, had some secret that was holding him back. Some reason why, despite, of them all, having spent the most time in the ballrooms and being the most comfortable in that milieu, he seemed unable to summon any interest in any lady, not even in passing.

There was some story there, some excuse for Christian remaining detached and consequently unwed.

He, however, had no excuse. He wanted to wed, to find the right lady and establish her as his countess. As his sisters had so bluntly enumerated, there were multiple reasons he should, not least among those being them and their futures. He'd set out to find his bride in February. Nearly six months had passed and he'd achieved precisely nothing.

The failure nagged. His was a nature that thrived on achievement. He was constitutionally incapable of accepting failure.

News of the trouble with the mill had reached him just after he'd arrived at Paignton Hall in Devon to witness the nuptials of one of their small band, Deverell, and his Phoebe. So afterward, rather than returning to spend a last week or so in London in the hope that among the few tonnish families lingering in the capital he might discover his future wife, he'd had to hie back home instead. The continuing frustration, even if it had been entirely outside his control, had only exacerbated his already abraded patience—and an irrational sense of time running out and him still not having found his bride.

Courtesy of what he'd now discovered to be his sisters' machinations, he'd spent no more than a few consecutive days in London, not since the Season had commenced, but rather than making his failure to find a wife easier to accept, the knowledge that he'd had no real time to look had only given his restless dissatisfaction a keener edge.

Six months, and he'd got nowhere. He hadn't even managed to develop any, as Annabel had termed them, relevant skills.

And he wouldn't get anywhere in the next three months, either.

Draining his glass, he forced himself to face that fact. To accept it, set it aside, and turn to the matter at hand, the one he could actually do something about.

The Honorable Miss Madeline Gascoigne.

He'd made his bargain with his sisters but, of course, he'd left himself an escape route. He'd slipped the loophole in between "temperament" and "beauty." The other criteria he'd listed were ones others—his dear sisters, for example—could judge for themselves, but "compatibility" was entirely his to define.

Just as well he'd been so farsighted; Madeline qualified on all other counts.

She was, he'd calculated, twenty-nine or close to it; her father had died eight years ago and she'd been twenty-one at the time, that much he knew. A trifle long in the tooth perhaps, and she doubtless considered herself well and truly on the shelf, but as he was thirty-four, her advanced years weren't something anyone would hold against her.

Indeed, he'd prefer a wife with more rather than fewer years in her dish, one who had weathered a little of life. God knew, he had. A *young* young lady would be extremely unlikely to fix, let alone hold, his interest.

And as the daughter of the late Viscount Gascoigne, Madeline unquestionably possessed birth and station appropriate to the position of his countess; there was no fault to be found there.

Although he hadn't stipulated fortune, she was possessed of that as well, having inherited a sizable sum from maternal relatives, and the Gascoignes were wealthy, so she'd doubtless be well dowered, too.

As for temperament, he couldn't imagine any lady more competent, more calm and capable, one less likely to enact him any tragedies or fall into hysterics. Indeed, he couldn't imagine any occurrence that might throw Madeline into hysterics, not after some of the exploits she'd dealt with in bringing up her brothers.

His last stipulation had been "beauty." Considering that point, he frowned. Although he had an excellent visual memory, especially for people, when it came to Madeline . . . he knew she was handsome and striking rather than pretty, but beyond that it was hard to decide how he rated her appearance. How he reacted to her as a woman—because he didn't, because he didn't think of her in that way. The years of dealing with her as a surrogate male, as the de facto Gascoigne, had dulled his senses with respect to her, yet he suspected she'd pass any "beauty" test.

Which left "compatibility" as the one criterion on which he could rule her "not suitable."

He'd promised on his honor to actively pursue any suitable lady, and the girls would expect to see him doing just that. So he would; he'd spend a little time with Madeline, enough to establish just why he and she weren't compatible, enough to make his declaration of incompatibility credible.

Time together shouldn't be difficult to arrange. Now he was fixed for the summer at the castle, there were any number of issues on which his and Madeline's paths would cross—or could be made to cross.

He felt the brandy working its way through his system, relaxing, warming, easing as it went.

His next steps didn't seem too onerous. Not even vaguely problematic. He'd just spend some time with Madeline, and all would be well.

Or as well as things could be, until he could return to London and find himself a wife.

Chapter 2

$\mathscr{M}$adeline was cantering westward along the bridle path that followed the clifftops around the bay when she saw Gervase Tregarth riding toward her. Drawing her mind from her mental list of all she hoped to accomplish that day, she smiled and thanked fate; she really didn't have the time to spare had she been forced to search for him.

He was still some distance away, but the vivid green cliffs were devoid of trees or other cover. The instant he'd come into sight she'd recognized him; there were few other males in the area with quite his build, the broad shoulders and long rangy frame that seemed so at home in a saddle, especially with the sky wide above and the sea crashing on the shore below. His hair, a dark mousy brown, was, as always, uncovered, his fashionably cropped curls rippling in the breeze.

As he neared, she pondered the oddity of hair that appeared so soft yet did nothing to gentle the austere, aristocratic planes of his face. Well-set eyes beneath a wide brow, a strongly patrician nose and squared chin all contributed to the aura of strength, solidity and power that habitually clung to him.

They met midway between the Park and the castle. Slowing, they drew rein; their horses pranced, danced. Subduing her big chestnut, Artur, Madeline nodded a smiling greeting. "Gervase—the very man I was seeking."

His brows rose; his sharp hazel eyes—a pale hazel more amber than green—passed over her face. For an instant she sensed he was studying her, but then he asked, "Is there some problem?"

She laughed. "Not of my brothers' doing, thank Heaven, but I received a note from Squire Ridley asking me to call. He wants to pick my brains on the subject of the local mines, but I confess I'm not aware of any recent developments. I thought perhaps you might have heard something to account for his query."

Gervase's face was always difficult to read; expressions rarely rippled his surface, leaving one to guess at his thoughts. Yet in this instance, his blankness suggested he knew no more than she.

He confirmed that. "I've heard nothing recently—indeed, for some time. All goes well as far as I know."

She nodded. "That's my understanding, too." She picked up her reins. "Nevertheless, I'll ride to the manor and see what's troubling Gerald."

"I'll come with you."

As Gervase circled her, turning his huge gray, she glanced at him. "By all means—but weren't you on your way somewhere?"

His head came up and he met her eyes—and again she sensed that he was looking at her more intently than usual. "I was just riding—no specific destination in mind."

"In that case . . ." With a grin, she tapped her heels to Artur's sides and the big gelding surged.

Within ten strides, the gray drew alongside. She flicked

Gervase a laughing glance; he smiled back, then gave his attention, as did she, to the clifftop path.

She didn't often get the chance to ride freely in company; when she rode with her brothers or their aged steward, one part of her mind was always on guard to identify any potentially lethal rabbit hole or hidden ditch. It was an unexpected pleasure to ride before the wind—or into it, as was the situation that day—without any such care clouding the simple pleasure of the fresh air on her face, the regular tattoo of Artur's hooves, the exhilaration of their speed, and the strangely shared moment.

A sidelong glance at Gervase confirmed that he was enjoying the ride as much as she. Neither of them held back, but let their hacks—both seventeen hands plus, powerful and strong—run freely, using the reins only to guide them when they angled off the clifftop path and struck inland, over the windswept downs, going north of Kuggar Village with the hamlet of Gwendreath to their right, then over a section of the Goonhilly Downs to the village of Cury.

As they rode under the cloudless summer sky, with larks dipping and swooping high overhead, the only occurrence to ruffle her serenity was the occasional piercing, penetrating glance Gervase directed her way. Not that she saw them; whenever she glanced at him he was looking ahead, transparently at ease, no sign in his inscrutable face that he'd been looking at her.

But she felt those glances, lancing sharp and . . . examining. She'd been right; he was looking more closely at her, studying her.

She couldn't for the life of her imagine why. She'd glanced into the hall mirror on her way out; there was nothing odd about her appearance. Her hair, of course, would be doing its best to escape its confinement, but that was nothing new.

Ridley Manor lay just beyond Cury; they slowed and

clattered into the cobbled yard before the old stone house. Hearing the racket, Gerald, Squire Ridley, came out to greet them, leaning heavily on his cane. He was over sixty, with a thick shock of white hair; he'd started to develop a stoop, but his blue eyes were still shrewd and there was nothing whatever amiss with his mind.

A smile wreathing his lined face, he stumped forward as they dismounted. "Madeline, my dear—I knew I could count on you." He shook her hand, then turned to Gervase. "And I see you've brought the prodigal with you."

Gervase grinned; handing his reins to the groom who'd come running, he clasped Gerald's proffered hand. "Madeline mentioned your query—I was curious, as is she, to learn what occasioned it."

"Aye, well." Gerald beckoned them to follow him inside. He led the way into his front parlor. Waving them to armchairs, he sank into his own, angled beside the hearth. "I would have sent to you as well, but I thought you were off to London again."

Gervase's smile was perfunctory. "I was, but this latest business with the mill brought me back. I expect to remain here over the summer."

Madeline saw that it was on the tip of Gerald's tongue to ask about the mill and Gervase's sisters' antics, but then the older man thought better of it and turned to the business that had brought them there.

"Well, as to why I asked whether you've had any recent news about the mining, there's a London gentleman making offers for mining leases hereabouts."

Gervase frowned. "A *London* gentleman?" Puzzling if true; the tin mining leases in the area were, by and large, held by locals. Estates such as Crowhurst and Treleaver Park, as well as local landowners like Squire Ridley, had made it a tradition to absorb any leases that might be offered for sale. They were a small community and had seen the wisdom of keeping control of the extensive tin mining in the locality in local hands. In addition, the royalties from the mining provided a welcome cushion against the vissicitudes of fortune to which farming enterprises were so vulnerable.

Gerald nodded. "Supposedly, but it's his agent doing the rounds. Polite young man, not quality but neat, knows his place. He called here day before yesterday. I'm not sure where he—the agent—is staying, and he didn't give me his master's name. Just asked very nicely whether I was interested in parting with any of the leases I hold. I told him no, but then I got to thinking." Gerald fixed his faded eyes on Gervase's face. "Perhaps this London gentleman knows more than I do, and thinks there's some reason why I might want to sell?" Gerald glanced at Madeline. "That's why I sent to ask whether you'd heard any whisper—of a downturn, or a glut, or . . .?"

Madeline shook her head. She looked at Gervase; in her eyes, he saw the same puzzlement he felt. "I've heard nothing at all—indeed, what little I have heard recently is entirely in the vein of all going on as before, with, if anything, the outlook being brighter."

Gervase nodded. "That's my understanding, too—and I've spoken in the last month with my London agents and they said nothing about any change in the wind."

Gerald frowned. "Wonder what's behind this, then? Not often that we have interest from outside the area."

"No, indeed." Gervase caught Madeline's eye. "But now you've alerted us, we can keep our ears to the ground and pass on anything we learn."

Madeline nodded and rose. "Indeed." Gervase and Gerald rose, too. Pulling on her gloves, she headed for the door. "I have to get on, Gerald, but rest assured I'll let you know if I hear anything at all relevant."

At the front door, Gervase and Gerald shook hands. Already outside, Madeline waved. Gerald raised his hand in salute, waiting by the door as his groom ran to fetch their horses.

Gervase strolled to where Madeline was waiting. One glance confirmed there was a frown in her eyes.

Without looking at him, she said, "I think I'll send to Crupper in London and ask what he knows, and there are a few others locally who might have news."

The groom approached leading their horses. Gervase caught her chestnut's bridle. "I'll send a query to my London agent, and I have a few friends in other tin mining areas who hold leases. It's possible they might have heard something we haven't."

Mounting, Madeline picked up her reins; he swung up to Crusader's back while she rearranged her skirts. Then she looked at him. "I'll let you know if I hear anything to the point."

He met her gaze. "I'll do the same."

She smiled then, a gesture that lit up her face, transforming it from serenely madonnalike to glorious. She didn't see him blink as she wheeled her horse. "I'll race you back to the cliffs."

An hour later, Gervase returned home—sometime over the past three years Crowhurst Castle had become "home"— and sought refuge in his library-cum-study.

Sinking into his favorite armchair, he let his gaze travel the room. It was a comforting masculine precinct devoid of flowery touches, all solid, highly polished dark woods, leather in deep browns and greens, dark patterned rugs and mahogany paneling that seemed to enfold any occupant in welcoming shadows. It was a soothing place in which to ruminate on his progress—or, in this instance, the lack of same.

He'd thought getting to know Madeline would be a simple matter of spending a little time in her company.

Unfortunately, the three hours he'd spent with her riding the downs had demonstrated that the reason he and all the other men in the locality, like Gerald Ridley, didn't see her as a female was because she constantly kept a mask—no, more a shield—deployed between her and them. Although he'd looked, and damn carefully, he hadn't been able to discern the female behind the shield at all.

All he'd seen was a lady focused on business—on her brothers' business, to be precise.

Admittedly, the speed at which they'd ridden had rendered conversation impossible, yet he was accustomed to being able to read people more or less at will. Even those who employed social masks and veils; he could usually see past them, through them. But not with Madeline; it seemed a cynical twist of fate that the one female he actually wanted to get to know was the one not even he could readily read.

Naturally, he viewed that as a challenge; he knew himself well enough to understand his response. Yet as he did need to get to know her, his instinctive reaction happened to coincide with his rational plan—so he would, definitely, press harder, and find some way past her shield.

He'd also been somewhat disconcerted to discover that her appearance, which he'd categorized as handsome and striking, was—now he'd actually *looked*—more along the lines of alluring. Although it was difficult to judge a woman's figure when it was disguised in a loose, mannishly cut riding dress, especially with trousers adding padding to her hips, he'd seen enough to have developed a definite curiosity; he was looking forward to examining Madeline's attributes more closely when he caught her in more conventional attire.

He was curious—and just a little intrigued. He rather liked tall women, but more than that, Madeline possessed a certain vitality—an open, honest and straightforward appreciation of life—that he found attractive in a surprisingly visceral way.

She'd enjoyed their ride, and he'd felt drawn to her in that, as if the fleeting moment had been a shared illicit joy.

The memory held him for some minutes; when his mind circled back to the present, he realized a smile was curving his lips. He banished it and refocused on his goal: how to get to know the Honorable Miss Madeline Gascoigne, the woman, rather than her brothers' keeper.

It had been a very long time—more than a decade—since he'd actively pursued a lady, but he presumed the facility would return to him easily, somewhat akin to riding a horse. The clock on the mantelpiece ticked and tocked as he evaluated various strategies.

Then a knock on the door heralded Sitwell.

"Luncheon is ready, my lord. Will you be joining the ladies in the dining room, or would you prefer a tray brought to you here?"

Perfect timing. "Thank you, Sitwell. I'll join the ladies." Rising, Gervase strolled to the door. "I believe it's time we did some entertaining."

If his sisters and Sybil were so keen for him to cast his eye over Madeline Gascoigne, they could do their part and be useful.

Later that afternoon, Madeline was ensconced in her office at Treleaver Park, steadily working through the most recent accounts from the home farm, when Milsom, their butler, appeared in the open doorway carrying his silver salver.

"A letter from Lady Sybil, miss."

With a smile, Madeline waved him in. Milsom was one of the few who persisted in calling her "miss," rather than "ma'am." Presumably because he'd known her since birth, her advanced age of twenty-eight didn't yet qualify her for the appellation normally accorded older spinsters in charge of a house. Her brothers had wagered with each other on how old she would be before Milsom changed his tune. She

privately agreed with the youngest, Benjamin: Never—
Milsom would die rather than be absolutely correct in the
deference he accorded her.

He offered his salver and she picked up Sybil's letter. Her
brows rose as she realized it contained a card; breaking the
seal, she unfolded the sheet and read the neatly inscribed
lines, first on the sheet, then on the enclosed card.

Lowering the invitation, she hesitated, then asked, "Have
my brothers returned yet?"

"I noticed them riding around to the stable, miss. I daresay they'll be in the kitchen by now."

"I daresay." Her lips softened into a smile she shared
with Milsom. "They're no doubt fortifying themselves as
we speak. Ask them to attend me here, please—they can
bring their biscuits and scones if they wish."

"Indeed, miss. Immediately." Milsom bowed and withdrew.

Madeline read the card again, then laid it aside and returned to her figures.

She was shutting the ledger when a commotion in the
corridor warned that her brothers were approaching.

Harry led the way into the office, his brightly burnished
brown hair windblown, his rogue's smile lighting his face.
At fifteen, he was on the cusp of adulthood, poised between
the carefree delights of boyhood and the responsibilities
that awaited him as Viscount Gascoigne.

Edmond followed at his heels. A bare year younger, he
was Harry's shadow in all things. A trifle quieter, more serious perhaps, but the Gascoigne temperament—indomita-
ble will and courageous if sometimes reckless heart—showed
in his stride, his confidence as, alongside Harry, he grinned
at Madeline and obeyed her waved command to settle in the
chairs facing her big desk.

The last into the room was Benjamin, Ben, the youngest
of the family and a favorite of all. Madeline held Ben espe-

cially close to her heart—not because she loved him any better than the other two but because he'd been a babe of mere weeks when Abigail, their mother, Madeline's step-mother, had died, taken from them all by childbed fever.

With a tight grin for Madeline—his mouth was full of buttered scone—Ben, ten years old and with much of his growing yet to come, hiked himself onto a straightbacked chair and wriggled back, feet swinging.

Smiling—trying not to appear too obviously fond and doting—Madeline waited while they finished the last of their snack; she knew better than to try to compete with food for the attention of growing boys.

Her gaze rested on them, on the three faces alight with undimmed happiness, with the simple joy of living, and as she always did, she felt an overwhelming sense of rightness. Of conviction, of vindication. Of satisfaction that she'd done what she'd needed to do and had succeeded.

This—they—were her life's work. She'd been barely nineteen when Abigail had died, leaving Ben to her care, with Harry a lost little boy of five and Edmond a confused four-year-old. Harry and Edmond had at least had each other, and their father. For virtually all of his life, Ben had known only her as a parent.

She and her father had been close; she'd been the older son he'd never had. Knowing he was ill, with Harry, his heir, so very young, her father had trained her to be the intermediary, a de facto regent—he'd taught her all she'd needed to know to run the estate, and left her to pass that knowledge on to Harry.

Struck down only months after Abigail's death, her father hadn't, as many people described it, lingered; he'd fought and clung desperately to life for nearly two years—long enough for Madeline to attain the age of twenty-one, and the legal status, backed by his will and their family solicitor, to become the boys' coguardian.

It was no coincidence that her father had died a week after her twenty-first birthday.

Their solicitor, old Mr. Worthington, indeed a worthy man, was the boys' other guardian. He'd honored his late client's wishes to the letter and dutifully been nothing more than a cipher, approving any request or instruction Madeline made. She had nothing but fondness for Worthington. Then again, he'd been dealing with the Gascoigne temperament for long enough to acknowledge that the only person capable of dealing with her three brothers was another Gascoigne, namely herself.

She understood her brothers and they understood her. The bond linking them ran much deeper than mere affection, carried in blood and bone. They would all be, like her and their father, tall, strong and vital. Confident, too, masters of their lives, with a streak of open honesty that, on occasion, set others back on their heels.

She'd devoted the last ten years of her life to ensuring they were as they were, that nothing would dim their potential, that they would have every opportunity to be the men they might be, the best men they could be.

What she saw before her pleased and reassured. She'd never consciously questioned the decision she'd taken long ago, foisted upon her by fate perhaps, yet she'd never doubted that being the boys' guardian was the right path for her. And if sometimes, in the quiet of the night when she was alone in her room, she wondered what might otherwise have been, the question was irrelevant, the thought behind it fleeting.

She'd made a decision, and she'd been right. The proof sat before her, licking crumbs from their fingers.

"The Crowhurst bull." Her words brought all three boys instantly alert; her expression impassive, she watched them quell the impulse to glance at each other. Instead, they fixed their gazes, limpidly inquiring, on her.

"I spoke with his lordship yesterday," she continued, "and smoothed things over. However, he said to inform you that he wasn't amused."

She made the last words sound ominous. Harry opened his mouth, but she held up a hand, staying his comments. "Be that as it may, you'll have an opportunity to make your apologies in person. Or at least Harry will."

"I will?" Harry looked taken aback.

She held up Sybil's white card. "This is an invitation to dine at Crowhurst Castle this evening. For Aunt Muriel, me"—she looked at Harry—"and you."

Their father's older sister, Muriel, a widow, had come to live with them on their father's death. Built on the same generous lines as all Gascoignes, although now elderly, she was still spry. While she used her age as an excuse to avoid any social gathering she did not choose to attend, Madeline didn't need to ask to know that Muriel would be dressing tonight; while she was fond of her nephews, she doted on girls, and looked on Sybil's daughters as de facto nieces. As Muriel had often told Madeline, albeit with amused understanding in her eyes, as Madeline had refused to give her a wedding to think about, she had to find her pleasures where she could.

Harry frowned. "Do I have to—"

"I suspect from what Lady Sybil has writtten—that she's holding an impromptu dinner to spread the word that his lordship is home from London and expecting to remain at the castle through summer—that the other local landowners will also be present." She met Harry's gaze. "So, yes, as Viscount Gascoigne you should attend."

Harry wrinkled his nose, then heaved a put-upon sigh. "I suppose I'll have to start attending such events."

Madeline felt a whisper of relief. "You may be only fifteen, but it's better to start to learn the ropes now, little by little, and while your elders will be ready to excuse any blunders you might make."

Harry shot her a twisted grin. "True enough."

"I expect Belinda will be there, too, so you'll have some-one your own age to talk to."

She fully expected Edmond and Ben—if not Harry himself—to make some sneering comment about girls; in-stead the boys exchanged swift looks.

Edmond nudged Harry. "You can ask how they broke the mill."

"And about the lights on the headland." Ben leaned for-ward. "If that was them."

"Did his lordship manage to fix the mill?" Edmond asked.

Inwardly frowning, Madeline nodded. "Apparently. I heard from John Miller that all was well." She'd assumed that any interaction between her brothers and Gervase's sisters would result in his sisters exerting a civilizing influence on her often barbarian-brained brothers, but of that she was no longer so sure.

Until the incident of the mill, and the implied suggestion that Belinda, Annabel and Jane had been behind the other odd occurrences, too, she'd always thought Gervase's sis-ters were eminently sane and sensible young women.

She wondered again what had given rise to their recent strange behavior.

"Is that all you wanted us for?" Harry asked. When Mad-eline nodded, he rose. "Because if so, we're off to the library."

Knowing she was supposed to, she looked her shock; it wasn't hard to fabricate. "The *library*?"

Both Edmond and Ben had leapt to their feet; flashing farewell grins, they headed for the door. Harry played supe-rior elder brother and let them jostle their way through, then looked back at Madeline and grinned. "You needn't worry—we won't do anything as childish as moving his lordship's bull again. We've found far better sport."

Before she could ask what, he was gone; she heard their

voices echoing in the corridor as their footsteps faded, then the library door closed and silence descended.

What "better sport"? She could ask and demand to be told, but . . . if she wanted Harry to learn to exercise responsibility, that might be counterproductive.

Gervase's observation that Harry would stop his boy's tricks soon enough rang in her mind. All in all, raising Harry to his present age hadn't tried her ingenuity overmuch, yet she knew—could sense—that the years to come were going to be more difficult.

Despite her best efforts to fill her father's shoes, she wasn't a man. A male. She might be a Gascoigne, but she was unsettlingly aware that there were certain interests men of their class developed that ladies neither indulged in nor necessarily understood.

Whether she *could* steer Harry through the next five years of his life was a question that sat uneasily, unresolved in the back of her mind. What she could do, what she vowed to do, was to do all she could to encourage him to take up the burdens of adulthood, and his title, and to accept the restrictions that entailed of his own free will. Perhaps to see his position as a challenge.

In that, his reaction to Sybil's invitation was encouraging. Madeline made a mental note to thank Sybil accordingly.

Meanwhile, why the library? She inwardly snorted, and made another mental note to whisper in a few select ears that she would appreciate a warning should said ears' owners suspect that her brothers were up to anything outrageous.

There was no point expecting them to transform into angels overnight.

The dinner that evening at Crowhurst Castle was a relaxed and relatively easygoing affair. Or rather, it should have been, and seemed destined to be so for everyone else, even Harry, yet for Madeline, from the moment she climbed the castle steps and followed Muriel into the front hall, she found herself subtly, curiously, and largely inexplicably off-balance.

The sensation—as if her world had fractionally tilted, as if its axis had suddenly canted—bloomed in the instant she reached Sybil, waiting to greet them beside the double doors leading into the drawing room.

"Muriel! Welcome." Sybil and Muriel clasped hands, touched cheeks; although much younger, Sybil was very fond of the older lady. "Do go in."

Turning from Muriel, Sybil's eyes lit. "Madeline—I'm delighted you could come at such short notice." Taking her hand, Sybil clasped it between hers. "Just our usual circle, my dear, to spread the word that Gervase is home for the summer, so to speak." Sybil held her hand for a moment longer, her eyes searching Madeline's, then she pressed her fingers. "Naturally, the girls and I are very *glad* he's home."

The emphasis suggested that Madeline should read something more than the obvious into the remark. Nonplussed, she smiled and retrieved her hand. "Of course. His presence must be a comfort." She omitted any mention of Gervase needing to deal with strange difficulties like the mill, and stepped back to let Harry make his bow.

Sybil greeted him with her customary easy and gentle smile—underscoring the unusual way she'd interacted with Madeline, suggestive of something, but as to what Madeline had no clue.

Madeline knew Gervase's father's second wife distantly for many years, but over the past three years since Gervase had inherited the title and, Sybil and his sisters taken up residence at the castle, while Gervase himself had remained largely absent overseas, Sybil had held the fort, and thus had met Madeline regularly, at the very least every week. As the other senior lady of the small community and moreover one born to her rank, it was to Madeline

Sybil had most often turned. They got on well, so Madeline wasn't surprised to be greeted warmly. What she hadn't expected was that peculiarly *meaningful* welcome.

Walking into the drawing room with Harry by her side, she told herself she'd overinterpreted. Either that, or there was something going on with Gervase and his family that she didn't know.

They'd barely crossed the threshold into the long, elegant drawing room when Belinda appeared at her elbow.

"There you are!" Belinda beamed, transparently delighted. "We're so glad you could come."

Madeline studied her curiously. "So your mother said."

"Well, yes! I daresay she did." Belinda's exuberance dimmed not one jot. "Perhaps I can take Harry around to meet the others. Gervase is over there."

Finding herself all but pushed in that direction, Madeline consented to step further into the room. Presumably Belinda had been instructed to ease Harry's way; considering, justifiably she was sure, that from the superiority of her sixteen years Belinda would be able to manage him, she left her to it.

She herself needed no assistance, not in this company; with a smiling nod to Lady Porthleven, holding court on the chaise, and to Mrs. Entwhistle beside her, she strolled into the room.

And saw Gervase.

Standing before the marble mantelpiece, he was chatting with Mrs. Juliard. As if sensing an arrival, he glanced across the room. His eyes met hers; he stopped speaking.

And she stopped breathing.

It wasn't his appearance that snatched her breath away— she'd seen him in settings such as this before, where his height and the width of his shoulders, tonight clad in a superbly cut walnut-brown coat, made him a cynosure for female eyes.

The subtle arrogance and less subtle command that cloaked his every movement, from the idle gesture of a hand to the way he turned his head, the strength and power implicit in the characteristic stillness of his stance—none of these things were responsible for her lungs seizing.

Nor was it his face, the features whose lines even in this company were startling in their lean, chiseled hardness, with aggressive clarity branding him a descendent of warrior-lords.

She'd encountered all these facets of him before, and they'd never affected her, impinged on her. They didn't now, not of themselves.

It was the look in his eyes, the *way* he looked at her, that jerked her nerves tight, then left them taut and quivering.

Before she could draw breath, before she could even think, he turned back to Mrs. Juliard, excused himself, then strolled across the room to greet her.

Or, as her senses reported it, he *prowled* over to demand her hand; halting before her, his eyes on hers, he held out his hand, calmly waiting until, frantically shaking her wits into order, she remembered to surrender hers.

His fingers closed strongly around hers, and more of her nerves quaked. For the first time in her life she understood what being tongue-tied felt like. She managed a nod. "Gervase."

His lips lightly curved. He inclined his head. "Madeline."

She made the mistake of looking into his eyes, searching for some clue as to why he was watching her like a hawk watched prey, like a cat watched a bird—and found herself trapped, unexpectedly caught in the mesmerizing, agatey, green-flecked amber depths.

Gentle heat spread beneath her skin. All sorts of crazed notions flitted through her mind. It took an effort of will to banish them, to sternly reassert control over her wayward wits—and drag them back to reality. "I—" She broke off and glanced around, noting the others present. She cleared her throat. "It seems you've gathered the local elite."

"Indeed. After our encounter with Squire Ridley this morning, I thought it might be wise to make it more widely and definitely known that I intend remaining at the castle for the summer."

Releasing her hand, Gervase turned slightly, so that the group of gentlemen by the windows was in their line of sight. "I haven't yet had a chance to ask if anyone else has been approached about their mining leases."

She leapt on the topic, as he'd known she would. "This seems the perfect time to ask."

Smiling lightly, he strolled by her side as they joined the other gentlemen. In planning the evening, he'd searched his memory, and recalled this as her habit; before dinner she chatted with the gentlemen, who, as now, welcomed her into their midst without a blink, shifting to make space for her, as well as for Gervase.

After the usual brisk greetings, she asked, "Have any of you been approached about your mining leases?"

He stood beside her, his interest implied, but let her do the interrogatory honors; as it transpired, Lord Moreston and Lord Porthleven had both heard of the young man making inquiries, but hadn't yet been approached.

The talk quickly turned to fields and crops, with Mr. Caterham asking Madeline for her predictions on tonnage per acre likely to be achieved this year. While she answered, Gervase watched and learned—not about crops but about her.

She'd detected, all but instantly, his focus on her, but . . . for some reason he didn't yet understand, she hadn't reacted as ladies normally did. He wasn't all that delighted that she'd sensed his interest so immediately, especially as it was likely to prove no more than that—she intrigued him enough for him to want to learn more of her, but once he had . . . Yet her response to his interest had only intrigued him all the more.

She'd seen it, identified it correctly, then dismissed it. As if she'd decided it couldn't possibly be so, that the very idea was simply nonsense.

Confusing though she was, he'd seen enough of her stunned surprise to know that, despite it not being precisely his intention, he had reached her—had penetrated her shield enough for her to notice, at least, that he as a male had some interest in her. But then she'd breathed in, and apparently shaken aside the notion.

As she recounted to the gathered gentlemen—all older than either he or she—the latest prophecies of Old Edam, an ancient whose prognostications on the weather were treated as gospel on the peninsula, he let his gaze, very carefully, trail down from her face.

Perhaps her dismissal of his interest was based on the idea that no gentleman of his ilk could possibly be attracted by a lady in a gown at least three seasons old. He was hardly a fashion maven, but he knew enough of feminine fashions to know her gown wasn't à la mode. However, while women might consider such issues important, men rarely did. The body in the gown was far more relevant, and in Madeline's case, there was nothing wrong with that.

Indeed, now her figure was no longer swathed in yards of twill but sleekly sheathed in plum silk, he felt pleasantly vindicated; he'd been right—she was alluring.

Curvaceous but, given her height, not enough to be buxom. Her breasts, the upper swells decorously veiled by a fine silk fichu, were the definition of tempting, lush but not overripe, the lines of her shoulders, nape and arms were regally graceful, her hips nicely rounded, while the length of leg concealed beneath her silk skirts would fire any male's imagination.

Except, of course, that no man in the vicinity viewed her as female.

Except, now, for him.

He'd distracted her with the mining leases because that was part of his plan. Tonight he intended to watch and learn—and, if he could, discover any weakness in her shield. Until he could undermine it, break through it, or in some way get past it, he wouldn't be able to declare her incompatible. He needed a reason, one he could put his hand on his heart and swear was real, and for that he needed to know her—the woman concealed.

When Sitwell announced that dinner was served, he smiled and offered her his arm. "I believe we're partnered tonight."

She glanced up at him, then inclined her head and placed her hand on his sleeve. "Lead on."

Hiding a wolfish smile, he did.

The dinner table conversation was general and lively. Lady Porthleven was seated on his left, with Mr. Caterham beyond her, opposite Mr. Juliard, who was on Madeline's other side. The five of them swapped stories; Gervase contributed a commentary on the latest London scandal.

Otherwise he listened and watched.

Yet all he learned from the exchanges was that, just as Madeline enjoyed a unique status among the male half of the local gentry, she also held a special position in the eyes of the ladies. Spinsters were not normally accorded such respect, let alone status, in female circles, nor were they so transparently free, and acknowledged to be free, of the customary social constraints. No matter how he steered the conversation, he detected no disapprobation whatever from Lady Porthleven—an old stickler if ever there was one— nor from the other ladies toward Madeline.

Dinner's end saw the ladies retreat, leaving him to pass the decanters with the men. Resigned, he set himself to play the genial host while waiting to rejoin Madeline and continue his campaign.

Unfortunately, when the gentlemen strolled back into the drawing room, he discovered she'd taken steps—deliberately or unwittingly he couldn't be sure—that effectively thwarted him. She'd planted herself on the chaise between Mrs. Juliard and Mrs. Caterham and appeared to have put down roots.

Short of some too-revealing, too-masterful gesture, he couldn't budge her.

From the corner of her eye, Madeline watched Gervase prowl—and tried, yet again, to tell herself she was imagining it. Imagining his focus on her; certainly no one else seemed to have remarked it. But no matter how logically she lectured herself, at some instinctual level, she knew what she knew.

What was the damn man about?

He reminded her of a tiger circling his prey; there was an element in his long-legged, soft-footed stride that reminded her forcibly of a large hunting cat. He hovered, again and again appearing on the periphery of her little circle, but he didn't attempt to intrude on the essentially female discussions while Sybil poured and the teacups were passed.

No. He was biding his time; she knew he was. And she had no clue what he was planning, let alone how best to deflect it.

She was accustomed to being able to command all in her life; be that as it may, she didn't imagine—not in her wildest dreams—that she could command him. There were some beings beyond even her control, not many but he was one.

One she clearly needed to guard against, although what peculiar notion had wormed its way into his brain she couldn't imagine.

It had been a very, *very* long time since any man had thought to, or dared to, look at her in that considering, assessing, quintessentially male way. As if he were considering . . . but he couldn't be, so why the devil was he doing it?

Just to get on her nerves?

Smiling at Mrs. Juliard's tale of her youngest son Robert's exploits, Madeline inwardly admitted that if she could make herself believe that Gervase was behaving as he was purely to rattle her—perhaps because she wasn't easily rattled—she'd feel considerably better, but she knew that idle male whim, the sort that had no real purpose, was unlikely to move him to any action at all. He wasn't that sort of man.

Which was precisely what was tightening her nerves to the point where they were twanging.

He had some goal in mind—and that goal involved *her*.

Not her as the Madeline Gascoigne she'd over the years created, but the real her—the nearly twenty-nine-year-old spinster underneath.

She drained her teacup, and told herself—yet again—that her imagination was running away with her.

"Well!" Mrs. Juliard set aside her cup. "It's been a lovely evening, catching up with everyone, but now it's time we started for home." With a smile, she stood.

Madeline and Mrs. Caterham did the same, just as Mrs. Entwhistle, middle-aged, plump, sweet-natured but rather fluttery, fluttered up. "Madeline, dear, we really need to call a meeting of the festival committee. Time has got away from us, and we need to make decisions somewhat urgently."

Madeline smiled reassuringly. "Yes, of course." She lifted her gaze to Gervase's face as he halted beside Mrs. Entwhistle; he'd been chatting with that good lady for the last several minutes.

His amber eyes met hers. "I suggested that, as this will be the first Summer Festival for which I've been in residence as earl, the committee could meet here." He glanced at Mrs. Caterham and Mrs. Juliard, also members of the committee, a light smile inviting them—beguiling them—to back his plan. "I'd like to attend, to learn more about the festival and what's entailed. Perhaps tomorrow afternoon?"

The ladies delightedly agreed; few of their menfolk willingly attended such organizational sessions. There was nothing Madeline could do other than smile her acquiescence, and in truth if he were to attend, she wasn't averse to holding the meeting there, rather than at the Park, the most likely alternative.

Mrs. Entwhistle, the festival's general, fluttered off to inform the other committee members as everyone rose and prepared to depart.

Gervase didn't move away; there was no reason he should, yet . . . he trailed close behind Madeline as she smiled and exchanged farewells as the company filed out into the front hall. For the first time in her life—certainly that she could recall—she was *aware* of a man; her skin seemed to flicker, her nerves to twitch, reacting almost nervously to his nearness.

But it was the shockingly intense shiver that slithered down her spine when his palm brushed the back of her waist as he ushered her through the drawing room doorway that snapped her patience. The gesture was purely social, a gentlemanly courtesy, yet she knew he'd done it deliberately.

Halting beside the hall's central table, she let the other guests press ahead, then turned and narrowed her eyes on his. "*What* are you doing?"

From her tone, her brothers would have understood she was seriously displeased. Gervase studied her eyes, then his impassive expression eased in some way she couldn't define. The hard line of his lips certainly softened, but it wasn't in a smile. "I intend to get to know you better—much better than I do."

His voice had lowered, deepened; combined with the look in his amber eyes it was impossible to mistake his meaning—what he intended "get to know you better" to convey.

Her lungs slowly tightened; she ignored the sensation and narrowed her eyes even more. "Why?"

His brows rose. "Why?" She sensed—saw in his eyes—a glib response, something along the lines of amusing himself, but then his lids lowered, long brown lashes fleetingly screening his eyes, then they rose and he again met her gaze. "Because I want to."

And that, she decided, was a far more worrying response than any lighthearted quip. She briefly searched his eyes, confirmed the agatey hazel remained as hard—as determined—as ever, then she looked toward the door, saw that most of the other guests were out on the porch and that Harry was waiting by the door with Belinda, with Muriel nearby.

She glanced at Gervase and met his eyes. "I fear you're destined for disappointment. I have no interest in dalliance."

His brows rose again, but this time more slowly. "Is that so? In that case . . . I'll have to see if I can change your mind."

Her eyes couldn't get any narrower. She closed her lips tightly over the words that leapt to her tongue; she knew males far too well to utter what he would inevitably interpret as a challenge. Falling back on chilly dignity, she inclined her head, then started for the door—but she couldn't resist having the last word. "You'll tire of beating your head against that brick wall soon enough."

Sweeping on, she collected Harry and Muriel, took her leave of Sybil on the porch, inwardly relieved that Gervase remained beside Sybil, letting Harry escort Muriel down the steps and into their carriage. She followed.

Once the door was shut, the coachman flicked the reins; she relaxed back against the squabs—and drew what she only then realized was her first entirely free breath in hours.

As the carriage slowly negotiated the local lanes, Harry recounted his conversations; he'd clearly enjoyed the evening more than he'd expected. His chatter and Muriel's answering comments rolling over her, Madeline let her mind drift back over the evening, focusing on Gervase and what she now suspected had been his machinations.

Why? Because I want to.

There'd been truth beneath his words; she'd heard it clearly. Rather than answer with some flippant remark, he'd deliberately given her that kernel of truth to shake her. To shake a response, some reaction, from her. To prod her into reacting.

Into playing his game. But playing that particular game with him, with the sort of male he was, would be . . . like a sensual game of chess. He moving here, then there, maneuvering to trap her, she defending—for how could she go on the offensive without giving him precisely what she wished to deny him?

A conundrum, especially as her nature predisposed her to action rather than stoic defense.

Yet the larger question remained unanswered: What was his ultimate goal—the prize, the queen he sought?

She pondered that for several minutes, swaying in the comfortable dark, then a more pertinent question flared in her mind: Why was she letting herself get drawn into this?

It was nonsense, futile, a waste of time, energy and effort, none of which she had to waste, yet . . . given who and what he was, did she have any choice?

As the trees of Treleaver Park closed about them, welcoming them home, she inwardly sighed, set aside that question and faced what lay beneath. Acknowledged what it was that had had her spending the entire journey home focused solely on the machinations of Gervase Tregarth.

Underneath all lay her besetting sin—the one element in

her makeup capable of tempting her into the reckless acts characteristic of her family. Curiosity.

Aside from all else, Gervase Tregarth had succeeded in stirring that sleeping beast to life. And that, she knew, could be exceedingly dangerous.

Chapter 3

*T*he following afternoon, Gervase welcomed the festival committee—Mr. and Mrs. Juliard, Mrs. Caterham, Squire Ridley, Mrs. Entwhistle, and Madeline—into
the drawing room at the castle. Sybil was there, too, patently pleased that he'd acted to involve himself in local
affairs.

Whether Sybil had realized his motives he couldn't say,
but he felt certain Madeline had; the last to arrive, she
greeted him with a distant civility that was a warning in itself. When, ushering her into the drawing room, he paused
beside her, a fraction too close, she threw him a narrow-
eyed glance, then swept regally forward to the vacant
straightbacked chairs facing the chaise. She chose the one
beside Clement Juliard; as she settled Gervase took the
chair beside her, exchanging an easy smile with the Squire
as Ridley stumped up to claim the chair beside his.

"Now, then!" Mrs. Entwhistle cleared her throat. "We really must discuss the details of our Summer Festival. First,
to confirm the date. I assume we're sticking with tradition

and the Saturday two weeks away. Does anyone see any difficulty with that?"

Numerous comments were made, but no one spoke against the motion.

"Right, then." Mrs. Entwhistle ticked off that point on her list. "That Saturday it is."

Gervase sat back and listened as under Mrs. Entwhistle's leadership the group moved on to considering the various aspects of the festival itself—the booths, the entertainments, the competitions for local produce and wares.

The exercise revealed a side of the rotund little matron he hadn't before seen; she was surprisingly competent. He was well aware that the lady beside him was even more competent—and so was everyone else. On any point of contention, it was to Madeline Mrs. Entwhistle appealed, and her verdicts were accepted by all; while Mrs. Entwhistle ran the show, Madeline was the ultimate authority.

Beside Gervase, Madeline gave mute thanks that she'd delegated the mantle of festival organizer to Mrs. Entwhistle some years before; she wasn't sure she could have focused sufficiently to adequately play the role—not with Gervase alongside her.

Especially not when, as he occasionally did, he leaned nearer—too near—and in his low, deep—too intimate—voice quietly questioned her on this or that.

Despite her adamant determinaton not to allow him to ruffle her feathers, he distracted her in a manner against which, it seemed, she had no real defense.

He—and his distraction—were a nuisance.

Unfortunately, both were unhelpfully intriguing.

Her curiosity had lifted its head and was sniffing the wind—not a comforting development.

On the ride to the castle, she'd attempted to ease her mind by telling herself she'd imagined the entire previous evening's interaction. When that didn't work, she'd tried to convince herself that he'd merely been joking, that his attention would have already wandered, as gentlemen's attention so frequently did.

But the instant she'd met him in the castle front hall, the look in his eyes had banished such delusions. His focus on her had, if anything, grown more marked, even though, given the company, he screened it. His manner easy and assured, he was taking care that no one other than she glimpsed his true intent.

That realization sent a subtle shiver through her; that he was being careful suggested that whatever he had in mind, he was taking this game of his seriously.

Gervase Tregarth seriously intent on her—on learning about her, not the lady but the woman—wasn't a thought designed to calm.

Much less sedate her rising curiosity.

He leaned closer again and quietly asked, "Are there any contests like archery and . . . oh, bobbing for apples—the sort of entertainments that appeal to youths?"

His eyes met hers; at such close quarters, the green-flecked amber exerted a dangerous fascination. She blinked and shifted her gaze to Mrs. Entwhistle. "No, there haven't been . . . but you're right. We should have some contests to keep the older lads amused."

Raising her voice, she made the suggestion, crediting him with the idea.

Mrs. Entwhistle quickly added archery and apple-bobbing to her list of amusements; when she looked inquiringly at Gervase, he agreed to organize the events.

Squire Ridley volunteered to ask his stable lads what other contests they would like to see, then have them arrange the events.

The talk turned to the craft, produce and art contests; Madeline let the chatter wash over her as a potential danger took shape in her mind. She waited until all Mrs. Entwhistle's points had been discussed to say, "One item we haven't considered—the venue."

Everyone looked at her, the surprise on their faces quickly replaced by faint embarrassment as they all realized they'd taken it for granted that she would host the festival at Treleaver Park as she had for the past four years.

Glancing around the circle, she smiled reassuringly. "As you know, the Park has hosted the festival since the late earl was taken ill, but the home of the festival is here, at the castle. Its roots—which are ancient and sunk in our collective pasts—lie at the castle, not at the Park." She turned her gaze on Gervase. "Now the castle once again has an earl in residence, then perhaps it's time for the festival to return to its true home."

Most were nodding; all looked expectantly at Gervase.

His slow, easy smile curved his lips. He inclined his head to them all, his gaze coming to rest on her. "Thank you— I'm sure I speak for Sybil and my sisters, as well as our staff, in saying we'd be delighted to welcome the festival back within the castle grounds."

Murmurs of approval and appreciation rose around them. Holding the festival at the castle would ensure an even better turnout than holding it at the Park, as many in the district were still curious about the castle's most recent acquisition—the earl.

Madeline smiled. Had the festival been held at the Park, organizing various entertainments would have given Gervase an excellent excuse to be forever visiting and getting under her feet. And under her skin.

Feeling smug, she met his eyes, only to see—was that *unholy* amusement?—lurking in the amberish—tigerish— depths.

He knew why she'd so graciously handed back the festival, but he'd seen some advantage in that for him.

Damn! She managed to keep the word from her lips,

managed to keep the linked expression from her face, but her mind raced.

To no avail. She would have to wait and see what he did—how he capitalized on her first offensive move.

Sybil rang for the tea trolley; Madeline set aside her pondering—too dangerous with him so close—and set her wits to avoiding him and his attentions for the rest of the meeting, until she could escape.

She learned how Gervase planned to capitalize on her action the next day; in the early afternoon, Milsom knocked on her office door to announce his lordship, the Earl of Crowhurst.

Surprised, Madeline stared as Gervase entered. After one glance at her he turned his gaze on the room, taking in the many bookshelves filled with ledgers, the huge map of the estate on the wall, the brass lamp poised to shed light over the polished surface of the enormous desk so she could work on papers and accounts at night.

The door closed behind Milsom. Gervase's eyes rose from the open ledger before her to her face. "So this is where you hide."

Where you hide the real you; the insinuation was clear in his tone, in his acute gaze.

She deflected that disconcerting gaze with a bland smile. "Good afternoon, my lord. To what do I owe the pleasure of this visit?" She waved him to an armchair angled before the desk.

He smiled, quite genuinely, and sat. "You owe my presence to your suggestion to shift the festival back to the castle, of course." Sitting back, he met her gaze. "I've come to pick your brains over the details involved."

She kept her all-business smile on her lips. "I'm afraid I know nothing about how the festival was hosted at the castle. My experience only relates to the four years it's been held at the Park."

"Indeed. However, as you no doubt are aware, many of the staff at the castle retired when my uncle died. The current staff have little idea of the logistics involved. I fear that without guidance we'll be hopelessly unprepared."

"Ah." She looked into his eyes, and saw no way out. She'd saddled the castle with the festival; it was only fair that she explain what they'd have to accommodate. "I see. What do you need to know?"

"While Mrs. Entwhistle has supplied a detailed list of the types of entertainments and amusements involved, she was regrettably unspecific about quantities. How many booths, tents and enclosures will we need to set up for the various activities, how many for the produce displays and for the visiting peddlers and dealers?"

She held up a hand. "One moment." Rising, she went to a nearby cupboard. Setting the door wide, she searched through the numerous papers stacked within; finding the packet she sought, she extracted it—or tried to, but the whole two-foot-high stack started to tip.

"Oh!" She tried to hold it back—and would have failed, but suddenly Gervase was there, his shoulder brushing hers as he reached past her; his big hands spanning so much more than hers, he first steadied the stack, then gripped the packets above the one her fingers had closed around.

"Take it now."

She slid the packet out. She stepped back immediately, trying to calm her thudding heart—wondering if she could convince herself it was shock and not his nearness that was making her pulse race. Making her curiosity not just stir, but leap. She slapped it down, and decorously returned to the desk. Sitting once more, she nodded wordless thanks to him as he closed the cabinet, and came back to drop into the armchair.

"The number of booths and so on should be listed in here." Untying the ribbon securing the packet, she rifled through the sheets. "Yes." Pulling out one sheet, she glanced at it, then held it out. "The accommodations we provided last year."

Gervase took the sheet; sitting back in the armchair, he studied it.

And thought of her.

She was too deeply entrenched as "her brothers' keeper" in this room; not even his brushing against her, inadvertent though that had been, had seriously undermined her hold on her damned shield—it had slipped, but she'd recovered all but instantly. Neat figures marched down the page in his hand. How to get her out of here? "What areas are we looking at in total? What was the approximate square footage—or acreage—required?"

Looking up, he prayed she, like most females, had little ability to accurately estimate such things. The blank look on her face, and the frown that succeeded it, confirmed that beneath her shield, she was all female.

"I really couldn't put a figure to it," she admitted.

He met her gaze with unstudied innocence. "Perhaps you could show me the area used last year." He brandished the list. "Together with this, that should give me enough to work with."

She was suspicious; she searched his eyes, but he made very sure she would see nothing of his intent therein. Lips tightening, she pushed back from the desk. "Very well."

Madeline led him out of the office, ridiculously conscious of him strolling with tigerish grace beside her. Quite aside from that novel and irritating sensitivity, there were few men who could make her feel . . . if not small, then at least not a physical match for them. Gervase Tregarth could make her feel vulnerable in a way few others could.

And he did.

On that one point, her instincts and her intellect were as one: He was dangerous. To her. Specifically her. Aside from all else, because he could make her feel so.

Unfortunately, instinct and intellect reacted completely differently to that conclusion.

Shoving her burgeoning curiosity back into a mental box, she swept down the corridor to the garden door. Pushing through—he reached over her shoulder and held the door back, making her nerves quake—she marched into the gardens and headed down the path through the roses. He fell into step beside her, his strides easily matching her mannishly long ones.

Recalling that he'd been overseas with the army for the past ten and more festivals, she waved ahead. "We staged the festival beyond the gardens, in the park itself, closer to the cliffs. People could reach the site by the cliff paths as well as through the estate."

Gervase nodded, idly surveying the gardens she led him through. The further they got from the house, the more he sensed a certain tension rising in her. No matter how she tried to hide it, he affected her, although he was reasonably certain she viewed that effect more as an affliction. She was very conscious of being alone with him.

"Last year we had sixteen local merchants as well as thirteen intinerant vendors who set up booths. We don't need to provide the booths for them—they bring their own—but we do need to set aside specific spaces, and mark each with a vendor's name, or they'll shed blood over the best positions."

"You'll need to give me some indication of who takes precedence." The path they were on continued beyond the garden into the heavily treed park. Although the clifftops and downs were largely devoid of trees, there were pockets such as this where the old forests still held sway. She shivered lightly as the shadows fell over them. He glanced around. "I'd forgotten how densely the trees grow here."

"Only for a little way in this direction." She gestured ahead to a clearing. The path led to it; afternoon sunlight bathed the coarse grass as they stepped out from beneath the trees.

She spread both arms, encompassing the entire clearing. "We needed all this space, and last year we had to put some booths and tents right up against the trees."

Halting in the center of the expanse, Gervase slowly turned, estimating. "I think . . ." He looked at Madeline. "With luck, we should manage with the area between the forecourt gate and the ramparts."

Head tilting, she considered, then nodded. "Yes, that should do."

She hesitated, eyes on him; any minute she would suggest they return to the house. He glanced around again, then pointed to another path that led further from the house. "The cliffs are that way?"

She nodded. "Many came via the cliffs."

"Hmm." He set off in that direction, but listened intently; after a fractional hesitation, she followed. "We might have to open up some of the older gates—we usually only have the main one open, but with lots of people streaming in, the forecourt entry arch might get too crowded."

"If you do"—he'd slowed enough for her to come up beside him—"you'll need to put men—burly ones—on watch at each gate." She grimaced and glanced at him. "After the first year here, we realized that multiple entries also meant multiple exits, and although most of those who attend are law-abiding, the festival is well known and attracts a small coterie of . . ."

"Poachers, scavengers and outright rogues?"

She grinned fleetingly. "Thieves and pickpockets mostly. We found that the best method to discourage them was to have men on watch visible at each entry. That was enough to deter them."

He nodded. "We'll do that."

They reached the edge of the trees; a wide expanse of

clifftop, verdant and green, opened up before them with the sea an encircling mantle of blue slate that stretched to the horizon. Just out from shore, a light breeze kicked up small white horses, sending them rollicking over the waves.

He slowed to an amble, but continued walking; she went with him, reluctantly perhaps but, like him, drawn to the view. To the incomparable sensation of standing just back from the cliff edge and feeling, experiencing, the raw, primal power of the windswept cliffs, the ever-churning sea and the sky, huge and impossibly wide, careening above.

It was an elemental magic any Cornishman responded to. Any Cornishwoman.

They halted, stood and looked. Drank in the sheer, incredible beauty, harsh, bleak, yet always so alive. To their left, Black Head rose, a dark mass marking the end of the wide bay. Far to their right, almost directly opposite where they stood, the castle sat above the western shore, keeping watch for invaders as it had for centuries.

Even as late as the early half of the previous year, there'd been a watch kept from the towers.

Unbidden, unexpected, Gervase felt a visceral tug, a grasping that went to the bone. A recognition. This was the first time since he'd returned to England that he'd stood on the cliffs like this.

And, for the first time, he truly *felt* he'd come home.

He knew she stood beside him, but he didn't look at her, simply stood and gazed out at the waves, and let the sensation of home, the place of his ancestors, claim him.

Madeline glanced at him. He stood to her right, between her and the castle; when she looked his way, she saw him with the distant battlements and towers as a backdrop.

An appropriate setting.

She would have wondered at his absorption, but she knew what had caught him, could sympathize. She came to the cliffs often herself, to the places like this where cliff, wind, sea and sky met, and melded.

It was in the blood, his as much as hers. She'd forgotten that, for not every soul was attuned to the magic, to the wild song the elements wrought.

She followed his gaze, and was content, in that moment, to simply stand and know. And, unexpectedly, share the knowing.

Eventually he stirred, and faced her. His eyes searched hers, and she realized he, too, had sensed the mutual connection, but didn't know how to speak of it.

"It's powerful." She gestured all-encompassingly. "The essence of nature's wildness."

His lips quirked; he glanced out again. "Yes. That it is."

And it lived in each of them.

Feeling the tug of the breeze, she raised her hands to her hair, verifying that it was a tangled mess. She gave a disgusted sound that had his head turning her way. "We'd better get back."

He grinned, but swung to follow as she retreated toward the path.

"I tell you there has to be *something*. It stands to reason."

Both she and Gervase halted and turned back to the cliff edge. The breeze rushed off the sea and up the cliff face, carrying voices—familiar voices—in its current.

"We'll have to search further afield."

"Lots of caves, after all."

The last comment came in a light, piping voice.

Frowning, Madeline started back.

Gervase's hand closed over her arm, staying her.

When she looked at him, he shook his head. "You don't want to startle them."

She looked back at the cliff edge, and bit her lip. He'd spoken softly; when he tugged, she let him draw her further back so her brothers, climbing the narrow, dangerous cliff path, wouldn't see them until they'd stepped safely onto the clifftop.

First one bright head, then a second, and eventually a third—Harry, bringing up the rear—appeared. Madeline breathed a little sigh of relief; Gervase's restraining hand fell away and she walked forward.

"Oh!" Edmond was the first to see her. Guilt—she was expert at detecting it—flashed across his face, but then he saw Gervase. Edmond brightened. "Hello." He bobbed politely.

The greeting was echoed by Ben, who had all but jumped when he'd seen her. Harry, rather more controlled, nodded and said, "Good morning."

Gervase acknowledged the three with an easy smile. "Hunting for something?" he asked, before she could demand.

The younger boys looked to Harry.

"Ah . . . birds' nests," he offered.

Gervase raised his brows. He believed that no more than Madeline. "A bit late in the season."

"Well, yes, " Edmond said, "but we've only just got back from school so we thought it was worth checking."

Three angelic faces smiled at him, looking from him to Madeline.

Gervase glanced at Madeline. Her expression was severe, but . . . although she knew she was being lied to, she was suppressing her reaction.

"It's tea time," Ben stated. "We were going in for scones."

Lips compressing, Madeline nodded; stepping out of their way, she waved them on. "Off you go, then."

They went, with telltale alacrity.

She watched, then sighed. "They're up to something—I know it."

Gervase fell in beside her as she started back more slowly along the path. "Of course they are—they're boys."

"Indeed." She cast him a sharp glance. "You probably understand better than I do."

His lips quirked. "Very likely." After a moment, he added, "You didn't call their bluff."

They walked through the clearing; he thought she wasn't going to respond, but then she said, "If there's one thing I've learned over the years, it's never to force a confession or an accounting. They'll either tell me the truth of their own accord . . . or whatever they tell me won't be worth a damn."

Truer words were never spoken. Gervase inclined his head. They trailed the boys back to the house; he had a strong suspicion about what they were up to, and it had nothing whatever to do with birds.

He'd spoken a little with Harry at the castle two nights before; the lad had reminded him of his cousin Christopher, he who had died of consumption unexpectedly, leaving Gervase as his uncle's heir. Gervase had been a few years older, and like him Christopher had been a child of this coast. He'd been as adventurous as Gervase, yet underneath there'd been a quiet seriousness, as if he'd always known that at some point the responsibility of the earldom would fall on his shoulders.

Gervase had seen the same combination of traits in Harry, adventurousness running hand-in-hand with an acceptance of fate. He couldn't see Harry leading his brothers into any truly dangerous enterprise.

Sometimes, however, danger wore a disguise.

They reached the house; he held the door open for Madeline, then followed her in. She led him into the front hall, then turned to give him her hand. "If you have any further questions about the festival, I'll be happy to answer as best I can."

Closing his fingers about her hand—not shaking it as she'd expected—he smiled. "I'll bear that in mind." Lowering his voice, he said, "I suspect your brothers are hunting for the smugglers' caves."

Her lips tightened. "I think so, too."

"If you like . . . I still have excellent contacts with the local fraternity. I can mention the boys' interest—they're unlikely to come to any harm if the locals know they might stumble on them."

The local smuggling gangs were one arena of male activity to which she would never, ever gain admittance; she would never know who was involved, let alone be invited to join, as every male in the locality, especially those of the major houses, usually were.

Her eyes narrowed as she searched his. "It must be some time since you sailed with any of them."

"On a run? More than a decade." He hesitated, then admitted, "But I had other, more recent reasons for keeping those contacts alive. I know all the leaders along this stretch of coast, and they will all talk, and listen, to me."

He watched her put two and two together, and come up with a revealing answer. Over the years he'd been away "fighting Boney," he'd reappeared now and then, when his father had died, and Christopher, and later his uncle, and then again to install Sybil and his sisters at the castle, and put his agents and stewards in charge of the estate.

Her eyes widened; her lips formed a soundless "Oh." Refocusing on his face, she hesitated for an instant more, then nodded. "If it's no trouble . . . I would like to know that they don't need to fear anything from that direction." Meeting his eyes, she grimaced. "While I would much rather they didn't get involved in such exploits, I might as well try to hold back the waves."

"Indeed." He hadn't released her fingers. Now he raised them; closing his other palm gently over her hand, he lifted the slender digits to his lips and pressed a light kiss to their backs.

Her eyes went wide; her breathing suspended.

A light blush rose to her cheeks.

He smiled, more intently. He lightly squeezed her fingers, then released them. "I'll let you know if I hear anything definite about the boys."

With a nod, he turned and walked out of the front door, entirely content.

Entirely aware that she stood rooted in the hall and stared after him until he disappeared from her sight.

Late that night, Madeline sat before her dressing table brushing out her long hair. The tresses gleamed copper and red in the candlelight, but with her gaze unfocused she didn't see; as she usually did at this point in her night, she was mentally reviewing the events of her day.

Behind her, her maid Ada shook out her day dress, then headed for the armoire to hang it.

Madeline focused on the maid in the mirror as she returned. "Ada, please mention to the rest of the staff that should they hear anything about the boys associating with any of the smuggling gangs, they should pass the information to me—either through you or Milsom."

A local, Ada had been with Madeline since before the boys were born. "Aye, well, they're of that age, true enough. Master Harry and Master Edmond, at least, and no doubt but that Master Ben will inveigle those two into taking him with them."

Madeline grimaced. "That's one activity in which I wish Harry and Edmond weren't quite so good over including Ben."

"Ah, well, you can't have everything." On that stoic note, Ada swept up Madeline's linen, along with her boots. "I'll take these downstairs. Will you be wanting anything else tonight?"

"No, thank you. Good night."

Ada murmured her customary "Sleep well," and left.

Madeline remained seated before the mirror, drawing the brush slowly through her thick hair. Reliving the rest of her day.

Until she'd turned to farewell him in the front hall, she'd thought she'd managed Gervase and his visit rather well. True, there'd been that moment on the cliffs, but she didn't think he'd planned that any more than she had. It had simply *been*, because they were who they were.

Nothing that special or surprising, really. The shared sense of connection had been predictable, had she considered it.

But then he'd understood about her brothers and had offered to help. In the right way—a way she could accept. He hadn't lectured, nor made pompous suggestions of how to deal with them.

She'd known that in accepting his offer of information she'd be giving him another reason to call and see her privately, yet more disturbing than that, her brothers and their lives were not a matter with which she'd previously allowed others to become involved, but she'd bent if not broken that rule for Gervase.

Because he'd offered something she'd needed. And when it came to her brothers, there was little she wouldn't do to keep them safe. Or at least safer.

And . . .

She refocused on her reflection—and pulled a face. Honesty forced her to admit—reluctantly—that, most peculiarly for her, she trusted Gervase, at least on the subject of the boys.

Frowning, she brushed harder, then laid down the brush, gathered her hair and twisted it into a loose knot.

That moment on the cliff—had it swayed her? More likely it had been her noticing how her brothers, usually quite standoffish when it came to gentlemen, had reacted to Gervase. They'd been curious, intrigued . . . rather like their sister.

Perhaps it was her recent realization that Harry needed, and Edmond would soon need, some older male to be, if not an acknowledged mentor, then at least a pattern-card. And in that, they could do a lot worse than Gervase Tregarth.

So she'd accepted his help—and then he'd smiled and raised her hand and kissed the backs of her fingers.

She'd felt that light caress to the depths of her being.

Other gentlemen had kissed her hand and she'd felt absolutely nothing. It was a courtesy, one which perhaps they intended to convey more, but never before had the gesture affected her.

When Gervase's lips had touched her skin . . .

She stared into the mirror, the moment, the sensations, alive in her mind . . . until the guttering candle recalled her. Snuffing it, she rose, and went to her bed—telling herself she'd do much better to ban Gervase Tregarth and all his doings from her head.

Two days later, she attended the monthly afternoon tea at the vicarage. Situated just along the lane from the church at Ruan Minor, the rambling house was set in ample grounds; in summer, afternoon tea was served on the back lawn. Muriel had declared she was too tired to attend; the truth was her aunt had little interest in the wider social round.

Passing among the other guests—all the usual local faces—Madeline kept her eyes peeled, but then realized Gervase wasn't there.

She told herself she was relieved, and embarked upon her customary round of chatting with the other landowners and ladies of the district. The day was warm; she sipped and talked, and forced herself to concentrate on Lady Porthleven's latest tale of her daughter's offspring.

"Albert is a veritable jewel," her ladyship enthused. "Quite the most *gifted* child!"

Madeline found her mind wandering, yet again. She tried

to make herself pay attention, inwardly acknowledging that this—the normal extent of her social life—was, indeed, rather dull.

Excusing herself with a murmured word and a smile, she slipped from Lady Porthleven's circle. She surveyed the crowd, decided to join Squire Ridley, took one step in his direction—and felt her nerves leap.

She glanced to her side and discovered Gervase exactly where she'd thought he was. Beside her, right by her shoulder.

Her gaze had landed on his lips; she saw them curve, felt his gaze on her face.

Rendered breathless again, she determinedly breathed in and lifted her eyes to his. "Good afternoon, my lord. I wasn't sure we'd see you here."

Gervase held her gaze for an instant, then, as she had, looked around. "Not, perhaps, my customary milieu, but as I have, indeed, taken up residence, I thought this might prove a useful venue in which to improve my local knowledge."

He glanced at her. "In return for my scouting on your behalf about your brothers, I hoped you might assist me in this arena." With his head, he indicated a couple chatting with Mr. Caterham. "For instance, who are they?"

"The Jeffreys," Madeline supplied. "They're relative newcomers. They've taken on the old Swanston farm at Trenance."

"Ah." He closed his fingers about her elbow and drew her into an ambling walk. She glanced at him sharply, but consented to move. He smiled. "If we remain stationary, Mrs. Henderson is going to come bustling up and trap me."

She hid a swift grin behind her teacup. "You clearly remember her."

"No greater gossipmonger was ever birthed." Gervase considered, then amended, "At least not this side of Basingstoke."

She shot him an amused glance. "Are there worse in London, then?"

"Oh, yes. Those in London aspire to the epitome of the form."

"If you remember Mrs. Henderson, then there are few others here you won't know."

"Ah, but are they as I remember them? For instance"—continuing to stroll, he directed her attention to a large gentleman of middle years hovering over an older, sharp-featured lady seated on a chair with a cane planted before her—"is George as much under the cat's paw as he used to be?"

"His mother's hold on him only increases with the years—and the maladies she likes to consider herself a victim of."

"She seems in rather robust health."

"Indeed. The general opinion is that she'll probably bury George." Madeline paused, then added, "Of course, she would almost certainly soon join him, for without him she'd have no one to harangue, harry and hound, and that appears to be the sole purpose of her life."

"I would say 'poor George,' but if memory serves he always was one to simply give way."

She nodded. "No spine. And, of course, she's never let him marry."

"So what of local scandals? The Caterhams are still together, I see."

"Yes, that blew over—as it was always likely to. They seem settled these days." Madeline looked further afield. "The Juliards are as devoted as ever, and all others go on much as before—oh, except for the sensation of Robert Hardesty's marriage."

"I heard about that." In response to the steel that had crept into his tone, Madeline glanced sharply at him. He kept his expression scrupulously noncommittal. "What's the new Lady Hardesty like?"

"I really can't say—few of us have met her. The reports from those who have aren't all that complimentary, but as the comments run along the lines of 'London flirt,' I'd prefer to meet the lady before judging her. We don't see many of the London set, for want of a better designation, so her behavior might be no more than what passes for normal in the capital."

Inwardly acknowledging the wisdom of her stance, he glanced around. "Enough of our neighbors. Tell me about local matters in general. I know about the mining—what about the fishing? How have the last few seasons gone?"

As he steered her down the long sloping lawn, he questioned, she answered, and he listened. He'd gleaned bits and pieces from others—his agents, his steward, his grooms—but her account was more comprehensive, more balanced. More what he needed. Her point of view and his were largely the same; she was the de facto Gascoigne, and he was Crowhurst, and that similarity that had shone on the clifftops also impinged, as did her straightforward, no-nonsense way of dealing with the world.

Levelheaded, rational, competent and observant; in those traits she was much like him. More than anyone else he trusted her view of matters enough to act on her intelligence; the truth was she was infinitely better connected with this world he'd returned to than he. It wasn't just his years away that separated him from the locals, but also his quieter, more reserved nature.

While they strolled, others came up and exchanged ready greetings and snippets of information, those last directed to Madeline. She was a person everyone around about knew, and not just trusted but felt comfortable with. His years as an operative had taught him to value that gift of putting others at ease. It wasn't one he himself could employ; he simply wasn't the sort of man others readily confided in.

He recognized her worth in that, perhaps more clearly than she did.

Eventually they reached the low stone wall at the bottom of the vicarage lawn. Pausing, they looked eastward over the cliffs to the sky and the sea. After a moment, she said, her voice low, "My brothers." She glanced at him. "Have you learned anything?"

He felt her gaze, but didn't meet it. He'd spent the last day and a half letting the local smugglers know he was back at the castle, and encouraging them to fill him in on recent developments. "The boys are known to the smugglers—all three gangs. And all know them for who they are. As you're aware, running with smugglers is virtually a rite of passage in this area. The boys will be safe—or at least as safe as they might be."

Glancing at her, he saw she was frowning.

A minute ticked past, then she met his eyes. "If the boys already know the local smuggling gangs, what are they searching for in the caves?"

His lips tightened. He hesitated, then said, "I think they're searching for evidence of wreckers."

Her eyes widened. He went on, "I asked, and the word is that there's been no activity of that kind for months. There won't be anything for the boys to find—no cache, and very likely nothing else."

The smugglers broke the excise laws, but most locals happily turned a blind eye to that. Wreckers, on the other hand, were cold-blooded killers. Along with the wider community, the smugglers regarded wreckers as an unmitigated evil.

"No one knows who the wreckers are. Secrecy is their watchword—you know that. It's unlikely the boys have had any contact with them, equally unlikely that they ever will. They might find a boat hidden in caves close by the Lizard, or up near Manacle Point, but other than that . . ."

She searched his eyes; today, hers were pale green, the color of the sea, serious and unshielded. Then she drew breath, and asked, "Do you believe they're in—or courting—any danger?"

He felt the weight of the question, the importance of it to her. He took a moment to consult his own inner gauge of pending trouble; it had never been wrong—that was why he still lived. "I don't believe they are."

She studied his eyes, then exhaled. Looking again at the view, she grimaced. "Would that I could forbid them to search, to go down to the caves, but that would simply be wasted breath."

He didn't bother nodding, but was conscious of an impulse to try to, if not lift, then at least ease the burden of her brothers from her shoulders. He glanced at the distant sea. "I was wondering if I might interest them in going sailing or fishing." He met her eyes. "If they wish to, would you approve?"

She blinked; eyes wide, she studied his expression, then frowned. "Of course. Why wouldn't I?"

"My background." He paused, then clarified, "My years as a spy. The boys will be interested—they'll quiz me."

He didn't say more; he felt perfectly certain, acute as she was, she'd understand his point. Not everyone considered the life of a spy a suitable subject for polite conversation. He'd broached the subject deliberately, not knowing how she felt. As she stared at him, still frowning, he wondered with an odd sinking feeling whether he'd discovered the incompatibility he'd been searching for.

If she thought his past was less than honorable, she'd be unlikely to entertain any offer from him—and he was even less likely to make one.

Madeline continued to frown; she couldn't believe he'd think she would object to his past, find his service to his country—the manner of it—less than laudable. That she was the sort of silly female who might. She let irritated exasperation seep into her expression—and her tone. "I'd be *relieved* to know the boys were out with you—and of course they'll question you, and you may, with my blessing and even my encouragement, tell them as much as you deem fit—whatever you're comfortable telling them. I warn you they'll ask about anything and everything once they get started."

The words brought home the fact that she trusted him not just over but *with* her brothers. There wasn't a single other gentleman she trusted in that way. The realization was a little shocking, and annoying, too; it would have to be him, of all men, and just now, when he'd decided for some incomprehensible reason to be a thorn in her side.

Not that he'd been all that difficult that day.

He nodded. "I'll ask them, then." He glanced back up the lawn, then offered his arm. "Come, let's stroll back."

To the rest of the guests. Acquiescing, she took his arm.

While he guided her up the gentle slope, she thought of that moment by the stone wall, when he'd waited to see how she would react. In that instant she'd sensed a vulnerability in him, a man she'd imagined hadn't a weak spot anywhere. Yet how she'd reacted had mattered to him.

The truth was she admired him, both as a man and for what he'd done with his life. As far as she was concerned, he could distract her brothers with tales of his past, and her only response would be gratitude.

They rejoined the guests; some had departed, but others had arrived. Gervase remained by her side; reluctantly, grudgingly, she had to admit she was comfortable with him being there. Their occasional private comments, colored by their similar views of their neighbors, enlivened the moments; the predictable conversations no longer seemed quite so dull.

"Miss Gascoigne, I believe?"

She turned to find a gentleman beside her, one she'd never set eyes on before. He was dressed well—too well to be a local—in a blue coat of Bath superfine and a nattily striped waistcoat; she thought it the ensignia of the Four-in-Hand Club. With his air of urbane polish, he almost certainly hailed from town. Still, if he was at the vicarage afternoon tea . . . She raised her brows, inviting him to continue.

He smiled. "Mr. Courtland, Miss Gascoigne." He bowed. "We haven't been introduced, but in this setting I hope you'll forgive my impertinence in approaching you."

He was a personable man; she smiled in reply, still unsure why he was there.

"I came with Lady Hardesty's party." With a nod, he directed her gaze to a group of similarly garbed gentlemen and dashingly gowned ladies across the lawn. "We were starved of entertainment, so thought to come here, to see who else lived in the locality."

There was an underlying tenor to the comment Madeline didn't entirely like—as if having identified her as being a local, he was imagining she might entertain him.

Still smiling, she offered her hand. "I am Miss Gascoigne." She omitted the customary "of Treleaver Park." "And this"—shifting to the side, with her other hand she indicated the looming presence beside her; she'd been aware of Gervase's sharpened attention from the moment Courtland had spoken—"is Lord Crowhurst, of Crowhurst Castle."

Still smiling amiably but with an assessing, even challenging glint in his eye, Courtland offered his hand. "My lord."

Grasping it, Gervase nodded. "Courtland."

Madeline glanced swiftly at him; his lips were relaxed, his expression unthreatening, but the look in his amber eyes was not encouraging.

She looked at Courtland; his expression suggested he was developing reservations about the wisdom of approaching her. As he retrieved his hand, he glanced again at her—with Gervase by her side, yet she no longer had her hand on his arm—then he looked at Gervase and raised his brows. "Do you spend much time in Cornwall, my lord?"

Gervase's reply was cool. "I haven't in recent years, but that looks set to change."

"Indeed?" Courtland glanced around. "I wouldn't have thought there'd be much to hold one's interest hereabouts."

"You'd be surprised." Gervase glanced at Madeline. "Those of us who've grown up in the area naturally have a deeper appreciation of its features."

Madeline caught his gaze. Was he implying she was a local feature, moreover one of sufficient attraction to induce him to remain in Cornwall? Her eyes started to narrow.

Gervase turned to Courtland. "You'll have to excuse us. Miss Gascoigne was about to leave." He offered her his arm. "Come. I'll ride with you to the lane."

Madeline struggled not to glare. But here was a conundrum: She didn't wish to encourage Gervase—to in any way let him believe she approved of such arrogantly protective behavior—yet her instincts had already decided she didn't wish to dally with Courtland.

She compromised, letting her eyes speakingly flare at Gervase as she put her hand on his arm, then she turned to Courtland with a dismissive smile. "I hope you enjoy your time in the district, sir."

Courtland bowed. "A pleasure to make your acquaintance, Miss Gascoigne." Straightening, he smiled into her eyes. "No doubt we'll meet again."

She made no reply, just waited while he and Gervase exchanged curt farewells, then allowed Gervase to steer her toward the house.

They paused on the way to thank their hostess, the vicar's

sister Miss Maple, then continued on. Madeline glanced at the group of London ladies and gentlemen as they passed. Laughing and joking rather too loudly, they didn't quite fit the tenor of the afternoon.

"I'm curious about Lady Hardesty," she murmured, "but not curious enough to bother tangling with them all."

"Do you know which one she is?" Gervase asked.

Madeline shook her head. "Dark-haired, that's all I've heard." There were three dark-haired ladies in the group.

Once they were away from the milling guests, she glanced at Gervase, intending to make her disapproval of his too-protective stance clear, only to see him eyeing—narrowly—something. She followed his gaze to three raffish gentlemen clearly hailing from Lady Hardesty's party. The trio were standing to one side, openly eyeing anything in skirts. Their eyes turned her way; their gazes met Gervase's.

A second passed as over her head some elemental male exchange took place, then the trio shifted almost nervously and all three looked away.

Looking ahead, Madeline canvassed her options. She knew how pigheaded her father used to get, and even Harry occasionally showed signs of that particular male affliction. Of course, both her father and Harry held some claim to the right to protect her, something Gervase didn't.

Regardless, she knew how fruitless it was to argue with a male in the grip of protective delusion; that Gervase didn't have any right to behave so was unlikely to make him more receptive to her protest.

Indeed, quite possibly less, for he'd know himself in the wrong and would therefore argue all the harder.

From her point of view, little would be gained by airing the issue if all that happened was that he dug in his heels and growled; it might serve her better to pretend she found his irritating behavior so ludicrous as to be beneath her notice.

She liked that idea. She was smiling to herself when they

reached the narrow path that ran through the shrubbery to the stable courtyard. The passage was narrow; Gervase stood back to let her go ahead.

Defiantly lifting her chin, she stepped forward.

His hand fleetingly brushed the back of her waist.

She swallowed a gasp as sensation flooded her, searing skin, tightening nerves. She stumbled—

Hard hands grasped her waist, steadying her.

Against a large, hard, hot male body.

Her lungs seized; her knees felt weak. She felt flushed and skittish. At her back, she could feel the muscled solidity of his body all down the length of hers. Her breath strangled in her throat.

Eyes wide, she glanced over her shoulder—and met his amber eyes.

Close, so close, those eyes saw too much; they searched hers, then passed slowly over her face . . . lingered on her lips.

Time stopped.

Stretched.

Her lips throbbed.

The sounds of others approaching reached them.

Gervase glanced back; his hands briefly gripped, enough for her to sense their steely strength, then he urged her on.

Her feet moved, one in front of the other; his hands fell from her.

By the time she reached the end of the passageway and stepped out into the open, she'd managed to subdue her traitorous senses enough to haul in a breath.

There wasn't anything she could say, any comment she wanted to make. His initial action had been nothing more than gentlemanly courtesy—an escort's steadying touch. It was her reaction that had precipitated the rest.

Just the thought of being so susceptible to a man's touch made her mind reel.

She glanced over her shoulder. Gervase was scanning the area around the horses and carriages, his expression the same as when he'd looked at the importuning trio. Forbidding, protective . . . possessive.

She blinked, looked for one last instant, then faced forward.

Protesting that he didn't have the right to behave so over her was, she suspected, no longer even an option.

She was, absolutely and definitely, in much deeper trouble than she'd thought.

Chapter 4

Two evenings later, Madeline followed Muriel into Lady Porthleven's drawing room. By an exercise of will she kept her gaze on her ladyship's face, waiting while Muriel greeted their hostess.

She'd had two days to recover her equilibrium. On leaving the vicarage, Gervase had ridden alongside her gig until she'd reached the lane; she'd deftly turned into it, flourished her whip in farewell and escaped at a good clip, leaving him to ride on to the castle. She hadn't looked back.

In the intervening hours, knowing she'd come face-to-face with him tonight, she'd endeavored to recall what their previous relationship had been—how they'd interacted, addressed each other; as far as she could remember she'd always treated him just as she did the other local gentlemen.

She'd come here tonight girded for battle, determined to get their interaction back on its previous tack, well away from the increasingly personal, increasingly intimate level they'd been broaching.

"Madeline." Turning from Muriel, Lady Porthleven clasped her hand warmly. Her ladyship's protuberant eyes widened as she took in Madeline's gown. "That's a delightful shade, my dear." Raising her quizzing glass, she examined the rich, bronzed silk. "It matches your hair wonderfully, and does very nice things for your skin. You should wear it more often."

Madeline smiled. "Thank you, ma'am." With a nod, she started to move on to make way for the Entwhistles.

Mrs. Entwhistle reached forward and tapped her arm. "Lovely gown, Madeline, dear."

Acknowledging the compliment with a confident smile, head high, she swept into the room. The compliments were welcome; she rarely paid much attention to her gowns—where was the point?—but it appeared she hadn't forgotten how to shine when she wished.

Still smiling, still confident, she made for the circle of older gentlemen she customarily joined before dinner; as usual they stood before the French doors, tonight open to the terrace and the balmy night beyond. At no point did she glance around. She was not going to look to see if Gervase was present; he was just another gentleman to her.

Stationed inside the door chatting with Mrs. Juliard, Gervase saw Madeline sweep by. He blinked, looked again, then had to stop himself from staring, from turning to track her progress as she swept across the room.

With her back to the door, Mrs. Juliard hadn't noticed the Valkyrielike vision. "We'll definitely need a tent for the embroidery displays."

"I'll make a note of it the instant I reach home." Gervase clung to his politely interested expression, although the urge to follow Madeline was a tangible thing. "If you'll excuse me, I must have a word with Ridley about the contests he's organizing."

"Of course." Mrs. Juliard patted his arm. "It's so wonderful that the festival will be back at the castle this year. There's a great deal of excitement brewing, I assure you."

Gervase smiled, bowed and moved away. He hadn't liked the glint in Mrs. Juliard's eyes. Making a mental note to ask Sybil if there was a daughter or niece he should know about, so he could avoid same, he slowly made his way around the room toward Squire Ridley.

Madeline was standing by Ridley's side.

Taking his time, Gervase pondered the blatantly apparent. She had gone on the offensive. He'd expected something—some reaction—but had had no real idea what tack she might take. Even now, with the evidence before him—stunning his senses—he was far too wise to take the message at face value.

She'd clearly made some decision, although he had no clue as to what. Regardless, he had his own agenda for the evening. After those revealing moments in the vicarage shrubbery, learning what made them *in*compatible was no longer the dominant thought in his mind.

"Madeline." He halted beside her as the other men shifted to give him room.

She'd been speaking animatedly to Ridley; as she turned his way, Gervase captured her hand without waiting for her to offer it. He held the slim digits securely as he nodded a genial greeting around the circle, both felt and sensed the tension that gripped her as she waited, wondering if he would dare. . . .

Bringing his gaze back to her eyes, he smiled. For one instant he considered doing what she feared and raising her hand to his lips; instead, he lightly squeezed her fingers and released them.

Her eyes on his, she drew breath, then smiled a fraction tightly and inclined her head. "Gervase. Gerald was just saying his lads have suggested a horseshoe competition."

"Is that so?" Gervase looked at Ridley.

"We'll need an area marked, and a peg of course, but it should be easy enough to manage."

"There's an area near the stable arch that should do," Gervase replied. "I'll have my grooms mark it out."

He turned to Madeline.

She looked across the circle. "Mr. Juliard wanted to ask about the treasure hunt."

Juliard cleared his throat. "I did hear some talk about a hunt for the younger children. I could help with that."

"I believe Sybil and my sisters have that in hand—I'm sure they'll be delighted to have your aid."

And so it went. Every time he so much as glanced at Madeline, she directed the conversation—and his attention—in some other direction. They covered a host of topics, from aspects of the festival to crops and mining, even touching on the weather.

Initially amused, as the minutes ticked by, he felt frustration bloom.

Madeline sensed it—how, she didn't know—but she knew he was getting her message. Buoyed, she stuck to her plan.

"Gentlemen, gentlemen!" Lady Porthleven swept up. "Dinner is served. Crowhurst, if you would take Madeline in? And Gerald, come with me. Mr. Juliard, if you take Mrs. Canterbury? And . . ."

Madeline didn't take in the other table assignments; the first had made her mind seize. What had possessed her ladyship . . .?

She shot a sharp glance at Gervase.

He met her gaze and smiled—intently. "No, I didn't arrange it, but it seems fate is on my side."

He'd spoken quietly, just for her; the low purr of his voice slid along her skin; she fought to quell a shiver.

"Shall we?" Eyes still on hers, he offered his arm.

She reminded herself of her aim, her determined course—and smiled, equally intently, back. "Thank you, my lord." Placing her hand on his arm, she let him lead her to join the procession to the dining room.

"I meant to ask." Gervase caught her eye. "Have you any particular interest at the festival—embroidery, knitting . . . saddlery, perhaps?"

The last surprised a laugh from her. "No. I'm usually so involved in the organization of the day I barely have time to think of the activities."

"A pity. At least, this year, you'll have time to wander and enjoy."

She raised her brows. "I suppose I will."

The thought distracted her; he guided her down the table to her place, then took the chair beside hers.

Conversation was general as the dinner commenced, but gradually became more specific as partners turned to each other and applied themselves to being entertaining. Madeline should have felt relieved when Gervase divided his time equally between her and Lady Moreston on his other side; instead, she viewed his amiability with suspicion.

The tiger's stripes were there, concealed beneath his elegantly cut black coat, disguised by the precisely tied cravat and ivory linen perhaps, but he hadn't lost them.

Yet every time he turned to her, he seemed perfectly content to toe the line she'd drawn, and interact with her purely on their previous social plane.

Perhaps he'd realized the unwisdom of his enterprise—his tilt at changing her mind about indulging in dalliance with him?

The thought gave her pause. When next she turned from Mr. Hennessy, Gervase was turning from Lady Moreston.

"I meant to thank you," she said, voice low. "For taking the boys sailing yesterday."

His lips curved; she saw the smile echoed in his eyes. "I can honestly say it was my pleasure. I haven't had a boat out in years, and the truth is I can no longer so easily call on my grooms to join me. Having your brothers to crew was the perfect answer."

She smiled. "They thought the day beyond perfect, too. Of course, now they're pestering me for a boat of their own."

"No need. Once Harry and Edmond are a trifle older and stronger, they can borrow one of the castle boats. One of the smaller ones, so they won't be tempted to go out too far." He met her gaze and shrugged. "Otherwise the boats are just sitting in the boathouse. The girls will never sail."

She raised her brows, hesitated, then inclined her head. "The promise of that will hold them for now."

He sat back, lifted his wine glass, and sipped.

She glanced at him—and found herself trapped in his eyes.

For one long heartbeat, she stared into those tigerish orbs, then she hauled in a breath, wrenched her gaze away and looked across the table. "I—"

"We have to talk." Beneath the table he closed his hand over hers where it lay in her lap, lifted it when she jumped, long fingers tensing, gripping when she would have twisted free.

Lungs tightening, she again met his eyes. "We are talking." She clung to her mask, her social persona.

His lips curved, the light in his eyes one she'd never expected to encounter, certainly not about a crowded dinner table. Out of sight, his fingers stroked hers, a soothing touch that didn't soothe her at all.

"Not about what I need to discuss with you."

She arched a brow. "Oh? And what's that?"

His smile widened. "I seriously doubt you want me to answer—not here, not now. Not in public." He let a moment pass, then added, "Of course, if you insist . . . far be it from me to disoblige a lady."

She jettisoned all notion of pretending disbelief; the threat in his words was proof enough of his fell intent.

Rescue came from an unexpected source. Lady Porth-leven rose to her feet. "Come, ladies—let's leave the gentlemen to their musings."

Chairs scraped. Madeline seized the moment to lean nearer and murmur, "We *don't* have anything to discuss, my lord—nothing that can't be aired in a public forum." She twisted her fingers and he let them go. She met his amber eyes. "There is nothing of a private nature between us."

She turned from him and rose.

He rose, too, drawing back her chair.

Facing the door, her back to him, she stepped out from the table.

Into the hard palm he'd raised, ostensibly to steady her.

In reality to shake her.

He succeeded, his touch searing through layers of fine silk to set fires flickering on her skin.

She froze, her breath tangled in her throat.

He leaned close, his murmured words falling by her ear. "I believe you'll discover you're mistaken."

She sucked in a breath, decided against any attempt to have the last word. Head rising, she plastered a smile on her face and walked forward, joining the exodus as the ladies left the room.

The gentlemen didn't hurry back to the drawing room, for which Madeline gave fervent thanks. She spent the time ensuring she was adequately protected from whatever machinations or maneuverings her nemesis might employ.

Returning to the drawing room to find her wedged between Mrs. Juliard and Mrs. Entwhistle on one of the sofas, Gervase spent no more than an instant in appreciation of her strategy.

He was running out of time.

Not only had the gentlemen lingered over their port, reminiscing and swapping anecdotes, but a storm was blowing in. He'd felt the elemental change in the air long before he'd glimpsed the thickening clouds beyond the windows.

Until then he'd been content to let Madeline play her hand, but there was only one place at Porthleven Abbey where, during a dinner party, he could speak with her alone.

He needed to get her to himself before the storm hit.

Hanging back by the door, he waited until the other gentlemen had been absorbed into the various groups around the room, then strolled across the floor to halt before Madeline.

With an easy smile for Mrs. Juliard and Mrs. Entwhistle, leaning down he reached for Madeline's hand—trapped it before she, lips parted in surprise, had a chance to pull back. "If you'll excuse us, ladies, there's an important matter I must lay before Madeline."

Straightening, he drew smoothly on her hand; his smile changed tenor as he met her eyes. "It's that matter I mentioned before."

She all but gaped, but then her wide eyes searched his, confirming his determination—confirmed that he wasn't in any way bluffing. "Ah . . ." She allowed him to draw her to her feet. "I . . . perhaps . . ."

He wound her arm in his, nodded politely to the other ladies, then steered her across the room.

She went with him, but . . . "This is ridiculous!" He stopped before a pair of French doors. She faced him as he released her arm. "We are *not* having any discussion—and certainly not here!"

His fingers locking about her hand, he met her gaze as he reached for the doorknob. "Half right." Opening one door, he whisked her through, ignoring the squeak of surprise that escaped her.

Leaving the door open, he put a hand to her back and with barely any pressure kept her moving down the terrace.

They were nearly at the end—out of sight of anyone in the drawing room—when he halted and dropped his hand.

She swung to face him, every inch the Valkyrie, sparks lighting her darkened eyes. "What, precisely, are we doing here?"

Madeline used the tone guaranteed to quell every male she'd ever met. She pinned her tormentor with a fulminating glare—only to discover that neither tone nor glare seemed to have any effect whatever on him.

Worse, he was looking at her hair. The bane of her life, doubtless it had already started escaping from the knot at the back of her head.

But then his eyes shifted; there was just enough cloud-drenched moonlight for her to watch as his gaze slowly swept her face, lowered to linger on her lips, then, at last, returned to meet her eyes.

"We're here"—his voice had lowered, deepened—"to face what must be faced."

His amber gaze remained steady; his tone wasn't forceful, yet neither did it carry any indication of softness. Of uncertainty.

She was reminded, yet again, that he was one of those rare males she couldn't rule. Which left her with far fewer weapons to fall back on; anger and stubbornness seemed her best hope. She lifted her chin, held to her stony glare. "I have no idea what particular worm has infested your brain, but let me make one thing perfectly clear. I am not looking—"

"Precisely." There was nothing—not the tiniest hint—of softness in the line of his lips, either. "That's my point."

She blinked. He continued, "I haven't been looking, and neither have you." He took a step closer. "And you still aren't."

Her entire vision was now filled with him.

But this was a side of him she hadn't before seen, only sensed. She'd locked her curiosity safely away—or so she'd thought—but now it stirred, stretched, pressed forward to look.

She narrowed her eyes on his. "What am I supposed to be looking at?" She lifted her hands, palms up, to the sides. "What is there to see?"

His amber gaze didn't waver. "Not to see." Slowly, his gaze lowered to her lips. "To discover."

His voice had dropped again, to an even deeper, more resonant note. Her lips throbbed; she could feel her own breath passing over them. And knew she had to ask. "What? What is there to find?"

She'd wanted, expected, the words to sound dismissive, derisory; instead, confusion and her damning curiosity colored them.

The heavens answered her. A deep rumble growled through the night, followed by a sharp crack as lightning split the sky. The first flare was followed by others, flashing behind the screen of the roiling clouds, a display of elemental energy.

The light lit his face, every chiseled angle, each rock-hard plane. Gave her fair warning when he moved closer yet, when he raised his large hands and framed her face.

Tipped it to his.

"This." The word feathered through her mind, dark and tempting.

He bent his head; she was so tall he didn't have to bend very far before his lips hovered over hers.

She drew in a breath, held it, every muscle tensed and quivering.

His lids lifted; his eyes trapped hers. "Don't fight." It was a warning. "Don't try to break away."

His lashes lowered as he closed the last inch. "Don't try to pretend you don't want to know."

The last word was a seduction, a whisper staining her lips, a promise—one he instantly fulfilled.

His lips closed over hers, no light caress but a proper kiss—one she'd been waiting for all her life.

Or so it seemed. One part of her seized, grabbed, gloried.

The rest felt stunned, shaken out of her world and into some other.

She was kissing him back before she'd thought. Moving into him in the same instant his hands fell from her face and he reached for her.

Then she was in his arms, locked to him. His lips were hard, demanding; she parted hers, not to appease but to know. To discover. To see.

What she hadn't imagined might be.

There was heat and sensation, from him, of him—and within her. Not fire, not true flame, but a warmth that was every bit as elemental, as potentially powerful, as tangible as the heavy muscles of his chest beneath her hands.

She sank against him, not because she was boneless, helpless, but because she wanted to.

And the heat merged, his and hers, and flowed about them.

His tongue swept her lower lip, then slid into her mouth, touched hers, and she shivered. Sank closer still, her hands fisting in his coat as she welcomed him in and he drank.

Strength surrounded her, to her more potent than any drug, one so few could give her. She counted the world well lost as he wrapped her in his arms and kissed her as if she were not just a drug but the breath of life to him.

He angled his head, deepened the kiss—and hunger burst through. Elemental, powerful, pure. His, hers—one fed the other, quickly escalating, with every heartbeat spiraling higher, spreading, out of control.

Until it roared through them, ravenous, greedy—insatiable.

Gervase had stopped thinking. In the instant she'd moved into his embrace, when his arms had closed about her and she'd offered her mouth, he'd stepped over some edge—into a world ruled by desire.

But not any simple desire he recognized. The heat was familiar, but every touch was heightened, every glow brighter, every aspect keener, deeper, broader, tighter—infinitely more compelling.

Infinitely more addictive.

He had to have more—and whatever he asked for she gave. Surrendered.

Her lips were his, her mouth, her body supple and curvaceous filling his arms.

Cracccccckk!

They both jumped, clutched each other as their senses rushed back and the world returned.

Lightning forked down from the sky; a raking gust swept the terrace, hurling leaves stripped from nearby trees.

"Madeline? Gervase? Are you out there?" Lord Porthleven stood in the open French door, peering down the terrace.

Gervase drew a deep breath, felt his reeling head steady. The shadows hid them. "We're here—watching the storm."

"Ah." Nodding, his lordship looked out at the sky. "Quite something, ain't it? But you'd best come in—there's rain on the way."

Madeline had stepped back, out of his arms. Placing a hand under her elbow, Gervase turned and paced beside her as they strolled—nonchalantly—back along the terrace.

Other guests were pressed to the windows, staring out at nature's show. Madeline paused before the French door.

Halting beside her, he glanced at the sky, then looked at her. "It's . . . mesmerizing. Wild, exciting."

She met his eyes. "And dangerous."

Turning, she stepped through the door. He followed, fairly certain that, like him, she hadn't been talking about the storm.

The following morning, Gervase sank into the leather chair behind the desk in his library-cum-study. Leaning back, raising his legs, he crossed his ankles, balancing one boot heel on the edge of the desk, and gave himself over to the latest reports his London agent had sent him.

Barely ten minutes had passed before the door opened.

"Miss Gascoigne, my lord."

Surprised, Gervase looked up to see Sitwell step back from the open door, allowing Madeline to march into his library.

March, stalk, stride—definitely nothing so gentle as walk.

"Thank you, Sitwell." With a crisp nod, she dismissed his butler.

Sitwell bowed, and glanced inquiringly at Gervase. At his nod, Sitwell slid from the room, closing the door.

Madeline halted midway across the room, tugging rather viciously at her gloves. She was wearing a carriage gown, not her riding dress; she must have driven over. She had to have set out—Gervase glanced at the clock on the mantel—immediately after breakfast.

Swinging his feet to the floor, he rose. "Perhaps the drawing room—"

"No." She shot a frowning glance his way, her eyes the color of a storm-wracked sea. The recalcitrant button finally gave and she stripped off her gloves, then glanced around. "This is your lair, is it not?"

Bemused, he answered, "So to speak."

"Good—so we're unlikely to be disturbed. I do not wish to have to exchange polite conversation with Sybil and your sisters—that's not the purpose of my visit."

She stuffed her gloves in a pocket, then started to pace back and forth before his desk, all but kicking her skirts out of the way as she turned. From what he could see of her face, her expression was set in determined, uncompromising lines.

"Perhaps you should sit down and tell me the purpose of your visit."

She halted, looked at him, then at the armchair he indicated. She shook her head. "I'd rather pace."

Inwardly sighing, he remained standing behind the desk, and watched as she resumed doing just that.

She glanced his way, saw, and scowled. "Oh, for heaven's sake, sit down!" She pointed to his chair. "Just sit and listen. This time it's *I* who have something to say to *you* in private. And I do mean *say*."

He dropped back into his chair. "Discuss." When she threw him a confused look, he elaborated, "Last night I said we had to discuss something in private—and we did."

She blinked, then nodded. "Indeed. Which is precisely why I'm here." She flung around and paced back past the desk. "What we *discussed* last night is not something we are ever going to *discuss* again."

He'd wondered how she would react; now he knew.

Energy poured from her in great waves with every stride. Her fingers, now free of her gloves, linked, twisted, gripping convulsively. Combined with her forceful strides, the signs were impossible to mistake. She was agitated, not angry.

A telling point. One that enabled him to consider her statement with something approaching mild detachment.

"Why?" He kept his tone even, purely curious.

Not that he needed to ask; that was what she'd come there to tell him.

"Let's consider how we came to this point—the events that led to what occurred last night on Lady Porthleven's terrace."

"I kissed you, and you kissed me. And we both enjoyed it."

"Indeed." She paused as if debating whether to modify that acknowledgment, but then she drew in a huge breath and continued pacing, addressing the stretch of carpet before her feet. "But regardless, looking back—correct me if I err, but this started with you taking some nonsensical notion into your head that you needed to get to know me better.

Subsequently, when I informed you I had no interest in dalliance, you decided convincing me otherwise would be a good idea—and one way and another, that led to last night." She shot him a glance that was close to a glare. "Is that correct?"

He debated telling her of the initiating action, the point she didn't know—the reason he'd needed to get to know her better—for all of one second. "That succession of events is materially accurate."

"Exactly." She grew more agitated, but she hid it well; it was only by her hands that he could tell. "So there is absolutely no reason behind what occurred on her ladyship's terrace beyond your whim."

He opened his mouth.

She silenced him with an upraised finger, even though she wasn't looking at him. "No—hear me out. That's all you need to do. Against the worth of your whim stand these facts. One"—she ticked off the point on her finger as she paced—"I am Harry's regent, his surrogate, and will be for six more years. Two, you are Crowhurst, and as such you and I need to do business with each other on numerous issues, on at least a weekly basis. Three, we are, you and I, the principal landowners in the district, and as such hold positions as effective community leaders."

She paused at the end of the track she was wearing in his rug, then swung to face him, eyes narrow, her chin set. "I have absolutely no interest in jeopardizing any of those functions in order to accommodate any more of your whims."

Madeline paused only to draw breath before continuing, "And before you say anything, permit me to remind you I am considerably more than seven. Before you think to even obliquely suggest that dalliance between us might lead to something more, allow me to inform you I am well aware that you couldn't, wouldn't, not in this world or the next, imagine me as your wife."

She cast him a sharp glance—and saw that his expression, until then impassive, had at last changed. Now it was hard—no, stony. His eyes had narrowed; his lips parted—she rode over him again. "For instance, I know perfectly well that your whim to get to know me better was assuredly not driven by any sincere interest in me as a woman—you've known me for years, so why now? Because there *are* no other ladies in the vicinity at present, at least none to your taste, and you are therefore suffering from boredom, if not ennui.

"But I was about, hence your whim. But as we both know, I'm far too old to be considered eligible for the position of your countess. I have none of the airs, graces and aspirations that would be considered right and proper for the position—and am unlikely to develop them, as everyone in the district—even you—knows!"

She barely paused for breath. "Beyond that, my temper and attitudes are entirely incompatible with being your wife." She wagged a finger at him as she swept past his desk. "We are far too alike to deal well on a daily, household basis, not that you ever actually intended of that, of course."

At the end of her track, she swung to face him. "Which brings me to my peroration. Given you're not thinking of marriage, and have no true interest in me—and you needn't pretend you've suddenly been visited by some overpowering urge to make me your mistress—then"—she met his gaze—"as you have no motive whatever beyond satisfying a passing whim, you should cease and desist from this nonsensical pursuit of me."

Gervase stared at her. His initial impulse was to argue—although deciding which ludicrous point to attack first would take some time. However . . . as he held her gaze, looked into the stormy seas of her swirling emotions, heard again her voice as she'd catalogued her virtues—missing most—it occurred to him that arguing would almost certainly get him nowhere.

She believed what she'd said. Absolutely, beyond question.

Her words had been rehearsed, yet had rung with conviction.

She honestly didn't believe he would ever consider, let alone want, her as his wife. And as for desire—she didn't believe she could inspire that either, at least not in him.

Of course, she'd nicely pricked his ego in numerous places, at least one of which he was disinclined to forgive. She'd all but accused him of trifling with her affections, preying on her finer feelings for idle sport. He didn't like that, not at all, yet how the hell was he to deal with her now?

Without completely sinking himself in the process.

She met his stare with one of her own, then uttered a small humph and folded her arms. Tightly. Beneath her very ample breasts. Making it even more difficult for him to keep his eyes locked on hers, let alone think.

Her lips pursed. For half a minute, she actually tapped her toe.

Finally she uttered a frustrated sound, and demanded, "Well?"

"Well what?" She hadn't asked any question, and he certainly had no answers. Not yet.

Her eyes stated she *knew* he was being willfully obtuse. "Will you agree to cease pursuing me and instead treat me as you previously have?"

He held her gaze for a moment, then sat back. "No."

Her eyes widened until they resembled silver discs. The Valkyrie was back. "What do you mean, *no*?"

Had he been less experienced in battle, he would no doubt have cowered and beat a hasty retreat. Instead, he considered her, then evenly stated, "You'll do perfectly well warming my bed."

"*What*?" Thunderstruck, she stared at him. Any doubts he'd had over her complete blindness to her own attractions were slain by the dumfounded look in her eyes. Then she drew herself up; cool dignity fell about her like a cloak. "Stop it," she said. "You know you don't want me—"

"Madeline." He waited until her eyes met his. "What did you imagine that kiss was about?"

She blinked, then frowned at him. "I . . . haven't the faintest notion. Why don't you tell me?"

"That kiss was intended to reveal whether or not we were compatible." He held her gaze. "In case you aren't sure how to interpret the result, let me assure you we are."

Her eyes narrowed. "Compatible as to what?"

He arched a brow; who was being willfully obtuse now? "Leaving aside the subject of marriage—"

"Please don't insult my intelligence by mentioning it."

He considered her raised hand, her contemptuous expression, replayed her words and listened to her tone. No matter what he said, no matter the force of any arguments he advanced, she wasn't going to believe it was marriage he had in mind.

Even though it was. He no longer harbored the slightest doubt on that score, not since he'd followed her from Lady Porthleven's terrace.

But her disbelief—more, her inability to believe—left him few options. "Very well. As I said, leaving that aside, after last night, I have one, perfectly sane, rational, logical and sensible goal in mind vis-à-vis you."

"And that is?"

"I want, and will have, you in my bed." The only woman who would ever warm *his* bed—the one upstairs in the earl's apartments—was his countess.

She stared at him for a long moment. "That's sane, rational, logical and sensible?"

"It is to me." He kept his expression mild but uninformative; they could have been discussing crop rotations.

She studied him, then drew in a huge breath; as her arms

were again folded beneath her breasts, the action severely tried his resolve.

She let that breath out with an explosive, "Lord Crowhurst—"

He rolled his eyes, which made her glare.

"Oh, very well!" She flung up her arms, relieving the pressure on his control considerably. "Gervase, then! But you must see that this nonsense—your ridiculous pursuit of me—isn't going to get anyone anywhere. All you'll achieve is to make me lose my temper, and as my brothers will tell you, you don't want to do that."

He wasn't so sure; in her Valkyrie guise she was undeniably arousing. Of course, she didn't believe she was attractive at all, so telling her so would get him precisely nowhere. He studied her—agitatedly pacing again. If she'd been insulted by his tilt at her, she would have been angry. If she'd been truly uninterested—something he wouldn't have believed after last night's kiss, but if she'd been honestly unaffected—her usual calm confidence wouldn't have been disturbed.

Instead, here she was, wearing a track in his rug, trying to persuade him to stop pursuing her. . . . Why?

Inwardly, he smiled. The right question. The most pertinent question.

He took a moment to assess, then evenly asked, "What if I succeed?"

She halted, stared at him; although he could see her eyes clearly, he couldn't for the life of him decipher her thoughts. Then she swallowed, and said, "That's not the point." Her tone was low. She lifted her chin, and continued more strongly, "The point is why you would want to, and we already know the answer to that."

He held her gaze. "By your estimation, for a whim. Which, by definition, effectively translates to, 'Why not?' So let's consider. Here I am, as you so rightly note deprived of feminine company. And here you are, twenty-nine years old, unmarried and unattached—and expecting to remain so for the next six years at least. We hail from the same circles. We both know there's no social impediment to any liaison in which we might indulge."

He paused, then went on, "I say I want you in my bed—the only hurdle to achieving that is your agreement. The only person I have to convince to say yes is you. And I intend to."

"But you won't!"

"Why?"

She made an exasperated sound. Her hands rose as if she were going to run them through her hair; she stopped at the last moment and waved them instead. "Because you *don't* truly want me—you're *not* truly attracted to me!"

He blinked. "And that kiss last night?"

"Was an aberration!"

"And if I say it wasn't?"

When she looked at him, all he could see, all he could sense, was suspicion; she didn't understand why he was doing this. It was time to close in. "Our situation, correct me if I err, can be reduced to this. I say I want you in my bed—and you don't believe I truly do. Is that correct?"

Madeline compressed her lips. She wished she could read what was going on in his oh-so-male mind, but she couldn't, so she nodded; his statement was true enough.

"If you're correct, then nothing will actually eventuate." He was still sitting back in his chair, the epitome of a gentleman at his ease, except for his eyes, his piercing gaze. "If I'm not serious, I won't actively pursue you—I'll lose interest and turn my attention to something, or someone, else. If you're correct, then I will, indeed, cease and desist, more or less as a matter of course."

Having him put it like that, so simply and succinctly, made her wonder why she'd driven there in such a frenzy—

why she'd spent the entire night talking herself into a panic.

She shifted to face him squarely; she could feel the tension that had driven her to that point draining from her.

Then his lips curved—and all that tension came flooding back.

"If, however, I'm correct, and I am sincerely attracted to you and truly do want you in my bed, then, to my mind, given our current situation, at the very least you should allow me the opportunity to prove that to you."

She stared. How the devil had they got to this point?

"Do consider"—his voice took on a steely edge—"you have, in essence, questioned my word, certainly my honor. It would only be fair and reasonable for you to allow me to clarify the matter—to set you straight."

No, no, no, no, no . . . but . . . she put a hand to her temple. Rubbed. Frowned. "Why—"

"Why should be obvious. All you need to answer is yes or no."

She frowned harder. "Yes or no to what?"

He sighed as if she were a widgeon. "To whether you'll allow—meaning you won't throw unnecessary hurdles across my path—me to prove to you that my attraction to you is entirely real."

She narrowed her eyes on his handsome—and as ever uninformative—face. He continued to speak of his outrageous suggestions as if they were commonplace matters. "What, specifically, do you mean by 'prove'?"

His eyes widened; he paused as if considering the answer, then said, "I suppose I mean that you'll allow me to seduce you."

She refused, of course. At length, in various ways. But he wouldn't budge. He continued to talk her around in circles, bringing her back again and again to his simple, straightforward, transparently reasonable points.

Until, driven to the limit of her endurance, with a headache pounding in her temples, she threw up her hands in defeat. "All right! I *agree*!" Whipping her gloves from her pocket, she started pulling them on, ignoring his measuring gaze.

"Just to be specific . . .?"

She gritted her teeth; she couldn't clench her jaw more than it already was. "Specifically—I will permit you to *try* to seduce me. However"—gloves buttoned, she pinned him with a glance every bit as steely as any of his—"I do *not* guarantee to succumb."

The damned man had the gall to smile, entirely genuinely. He rose. "Indeed. That wouldn't be any fun."

Fun? She nearly choked. Deciding words were not a weapon to use with him, she swung to the door. "I'm leaving."

"So I see."

Although she moved quickly, he was beside her when she reached the door. She paused to let him open it.

"Do give my regards to your brothers."

He opened the door. She stepped forward, then hesitated.

As if he could hear the question in her mind, he said from behind her, "I haven't heard anything more about their interest in the smugglers, or the wreckers—if I do, I'll tell you."

It was the assurance she wanted. She dipped her head in acknowledgment, then stalked down the corridor—away from his lair.

Gervase accompanied her to the forecourt, saw her into her gig, then watched her drive away. When he turned back into the castle, he realized he was smiling; he took a moment to savor the feelings behind the smile.

Life in Cornwall had suddenly become very much more interesting.

Madeline was such a complicated, confusing jumble of female types, just learning them all, every fascinating facet of each of her personas, would keep him occupied for years.

He headed back to the library, replaying the last hour in his mind; it was heartening to know he hadn't lost his knack for successful negotiations. So now, at last, he had a defined goal, a clear target. Dealing with his intended was very like maneuvering on a battlefield; at least now he knew which hill on the field he next had to take.

Chapter 5

The manor house outside Breage was located two miles west of Helston and the Lizard Peninsula, and a mile north of the harbor at Porthleven—not too close yet not too far from the valuable lands between Godolphin Cross and Redruth beneath which ran the rich veins of ore heavily laced with tin from which much of the district's wealth derived.

The afternoon sun struck through the leaded panes of the small parlor as the door opened and the gentleman who had recently acquired the small property walked in, followed by his agent.

Malcolm Sinclair waved Jennings to one of the pair of armchairs angled before the empty hearth, then elegantly subsided into its mate.

Jennings, his fresh round face drawn in a frown, perched rather nervously on the edge of the seat. "None of the rest want to sell." He grimaced. "Those first two must have been just luck. Every other place I've asked, the gents just smile and say no. I don't know what to say to persuade them." He glanced at Malcolm. "Not that I tried—you said just to ask and see."

Malcolm nodded. "Yes—I wanted to get the lie of the land, as it were. Now we know. . . ." He fell silent. After a moment, he steepled his fingers; he continued to stare unfocused across the room.

Jennings waited with not a hint of impatience. Sinclair was a master who suited him—cool to the point of cold, unemotional yet decisive—and their past association had led him to believe any future in Sinclair's service would reward him well.

Eventually Malcolm stirred. "I think we should concentrate on the smaller leaseholders—the farmers, the villagers—rather than the gentry. And as for persuasion, direct arguments won't work. Hard to convince someone it's time to sell an asset when you're there, hot to buy."

"Exactly." Jennings nodded. "Even farmers and villagers have sense enough to be suspicious of that."

"Indeed. Which is why I think it might serve us better to consider what news might convince such people, relatively ignorant and uninformed, that selling their leases to anyone silly enough to offer—not knowing said news—would be the act of a prudent man."

Jennings's frown returned, this time more pensive.

Malcolm eyed it, and waited, watching as Jennings worked through the possibilities himself.

"Rumors," Jennings murmured. "But we can't spread them—not ourselves."

"No, for who would believe that those bearing the very tidings suggesting their leases will soon be worthless would then want to buy those same leases?"

"Aye." Jennings glanced at Malcolm. "But it's rumors we want, isn't it?"

Malcolm nodded. "Rumors—for instance that the local ores are declining in grade, or that the market for tin itself is declining, or better yet, news of a massive oversupply from another region driving down the price for the foreseeable future. Any rumor that suggests that poorer returns are in the wind will do the trick—and 'persuade' those small leaseholders that selling to ignorant and ill-informed Londoners is the clever thing to do."

Jennings nodded. "But it can't be us spreading the rumors."

"No—it'll be necessary for you to find some ears whose owners don't know you, and are unlikely later to see and recognize you. I've heard there's a festival in the offing—itinerant peddlers, troupers and the like gathering for that should be perfect for our purpose. Wait here."

Rising, Malcolm went out into the hall. In its center, he paused, head cocked, listening, but no sound reached his ears. Reassured, he continued to the library at the front of the house.

He'd sent the Gattings, the couple he'd hired to look after him and the house, to spend the day at the markets in Porthleven, a necessary precaution given the Gattings knew him as Thomas Glendower, rather than Malcolm Sinclair. He wasn't entirely sure why he'd decided to buy the manor as Glendower, but as the money for the purchase had come from Thomas Glendower's accounts it had seemed simpler at the time. He'd kept his alter ego separate, free of any taint from Malcom Sinclair's unfortunate past with his late guardian. That scheme had ended badly; he'd always known it would.

Keeping Thomas Glendower and his steadily accumulating investment accounts unconnected with Malcolm Sinclair simply seemed wise.

Entering the library, Malcolm crossed to the desk set before the windows. Finding the right key on his chain, he unlocked and opened the central drawer, and lifted out a heavy pouch. He'd already counted the coins. Hefting the pouch, he relocked the drawer.

Tucking his chain back into his waistcoat pocket, he paused, his gaze drawn to the view beyond the windows. A pleasant prospect of gently rolling lawn undulated southward, then dropped away; beyond, in the distance, he could see the sea.

To either side, the lawn was bordered by well-established trees; the manor stood on ten lightly wooded acres, with stables at the back. There were no formal gardens, but until now a Londoner, Malcolm felt no lack.

He glanced around the room, comfortable yet gracious with its oak half-paneling, then, lips quirking, headed for the door.

He hadn't come to Cornwall expecting to buy a house but the manor had been there—just the right size, in just the right place, not far from a village and close enough to the sea, with a view from all the front rooms, including his bedroom on the first floor, that allowed him to appreciate the storms and drama of the weather that swirled past this stretch of coast.

Entirely unexpectedly he'd fallen in love with the place. He hadn't had a real home, not since he'd been orphaned at age six. Until he'd seen the manor, he hadn't known he wanted one, but the simple house with its quiet grace had reached out and snared him.

As yet he hadn't changed anything; the furniture was an eclectic mix of styles that somehow suited both the rooms and him. He'd wait for a few months and see if anything grated.

The pouch in his hand, he headed back to the parlor and Jennings. The man had worked for him in London until, a month or so ago, Malcolm had suggested a sojourn in the country might be wise. Jennings had taken the hint and gone to visit his aunt in Exeter. On leaving London, Malcolm had decided to investigate Cornwall, not least because of the mines; he'd found Jennings in Exeter and had beckoned, and his erstwhile henchman had followed.

He'd left London not just to escape the heat but to leave behind the cloying stench of his guardian's suicide and the slavery scheme Lowther, a law lord, had run. Malcolm, through Jennings, had been instrumental in arranging the details, but he hadn't been sorry to see the scheme undone. He'd never understood the rationale of acting illegally in order to amass wealth, not when there were so many ways to accumulate funds while remaining entirely on the right side of the law.

Tin mining being one.

Opening the parlor door, he crossed to Jennings and dropped the pouch into his hand. "Try the alehouses and taverns in Falmouth. Any intinerant heading for the Lizard Peninsula is most likely to come through there."

She was never going to try reasoning with Gervase Tregarth again.

The day after she'd been goaded into allowing him to *try* to seduce her, Madeline climbed the castle steps, sternly quelling an unsettling notion that she was walking into a tiger's hunting ground.

The front doors stood wide; she continued into the hall beyond. Gervase was standing by the central table speaking with Mrs. Entwhistle; lit by slanting rays from the afternoon sun, he turned his head and watched as she approached.

She refused to look away, refused to allow any of her very real consciousness to show.

"Claudia." Halting beside Gervase, Madeline nodded to Mrs. Entwhistle, then gave him her hand. "My lord."

His fingers closed about hers; his eyes touched hers, then his lips curved. "Madeline. You're in good time."

He looked past her to where other members of the festival committee were entering.

"I believe that's all of us," Mrs. Entwhistle said, peering myopically toward the door.

Neither she nor the latest arrivals saw Gervase's fingers slide over Madeline's before he released them. Ignoring him and her cartwheeling senses, she turned to accompany Mrs. Juliard into the drawing room where Sybil and Lady Porthleven were waiting.

She'd had every intention of sitting between two other ladies; instead, somehow—and that she didn't know quite how did not auger well—she found herself sitting beside Gervase on one of the small sofas set to form a semicircle before the hearth.

"Now, after the festival is formally opened—Reverend Maple and Lord Crowhurst will do the honors from the front porch—the first display to be judged will be the knitted works. Mrs. Juliard will be in charge there. We'll leave twenty minutes for that, then . . ."

Madeline struggled to keep her attention on Mrs. Entwhistle's tortuously detailed schedule of events, hideously aware of the large male body filling the sofa beside her.

She could feel the heat emanating from him, could sense the hardness of his long limbs, another subtle temptation . . . her mind slid back to those moments on Lady Porthleven's terrace. . . .

That kiss had been . . . something quite out of the ordinary, at least in her limited experience. Perhaps that was the reason her resistance to the notion of allowing him to *try* to seduce her wasn't as strong as she felt it should be. *Trying* meant more kisses, but surely there couldn't be any great harm in indulging her curiosity that far, if nothing else in the interests of her education and ultimate self-preservation; assessing just what, in him, she faced, what temptation he might bring to bear. . . .

"Madeline?"

She blinked. Everyone was looking at her.

"Sorry." She shook her head. "Woolgathering. What did you say?"

Mrs. Entwhistle blinked; several other pairs of eyes widened. Madeline inwardly cursed. Since when did she drift off in meetings? She was usually the one keeping everyone else focused and up to the mark, ensuring all went smoothly and swiftly so she could get on with whatever was next on her schedule.

"The carthorse contest," Mrs. Entwhistle said. "How may entrants do we usually have?"

She dredged the answer from her brain. "Eight, sometimes as many as ten. But over the last four years, there've been at least eight."

"I'll get Robinson to lend a hand with the judging," Squire Ridley put in. "Truth be told, he'd be insulted if he weren't asked."

Robinson was the farrier for the district. Madeline nodded, then looked attentively at Mrs. Entwhistle—and willed her senses away from the distraction beside her.

That took significant effort, but she prevailed well enough that she wasn't caught out again. She avoided meeting Gervase's eye; whether he'd guessed the source of her abstraction was a point she didn't need to know.

Finally all the arrangements had been approved, the schedule decided. Everyone rose and filed out into the hall, chatting and swapping the latest local news. Her mind elsewhere, she hung back, politely letting her elders go before her—only to recall, too late, that that would leave her with Gervase at the rear.

He touched her arm before she could sweep ahead. "I went fishing with your brothers this morning."

She glanced up to see him considering those before them.

Then he looked at her. "Stay a moment—I'll fill you in on what I learned."

She could detect not the faintest hint of predatory intent in his tiger eyes. "All right." She walked into the hall by his side, and hung back by the central table while he farewelled the others. Sybil went out onto the front porch to wave; Gervase turned to her.

By then she'd had time to think. She gestured to the courtyard, to where the ramparts rose. "It's such a lovely day, why don't we stroll outside?"

He glanced back through the doors. "The wind's coming up on that side. The east battlements will be more sheltered." He gestured to a door down the hall.

Inclining her head—ramparts or battlements, both were outside, and thus during the day subject to public gaze—she acquiesced and strolled beside him. Opening the door, he waved her up a narrow spiral stair. Lifting her skirts, she started up; he followed, closing the door behind him.

"Did the boys tell you what they're searching for?"

With difficulty Gervase drew his gaze from her hips, swaying provocatively before him, and forced himself to look at her heels. "In a manner of speaking. They assured me they haven't had any dealings this summer with the smugglers—a fact verified by the smugglers themselves—and then grilled me on all the wrecks I knew of, specifically where debris got washed ashore."

"I trust you led them astray?"

He grinned. "That wasn't necessary. From their questions, they're concentrating on the reefs to the west, off Mullion and Gunwalloe. According to Abel Griggs—he's the leader of the Helston gang—there hasn't been a wreck there since last October, and if anyone would know, Abel would."

She climbed for a minute before saying, "So there's nothing for them to find, but they'll hunt through the coves and caves anyway."

They'd reached the landing before the door to the battlements. He came up beside her; studiously ignoring the perfume that rose from her skin and hair—and its effect as it wreathed through his senses—he reached past her, turned the knob, and pushed the door wide.

She went through, immediately lifting her hands to hold

back whipping tendrils of her hair. Below and before them, stretching all the way to Black Head on the other side of the bay, the sea was pale, corrugated and frothed by the strafing wind. Although much less strong than on the exposed ramparts to the west, the capricious gusts that snaked their way around to the battlements were still strong enough to plaster her light gown to her body, to her legs.

Gervase considered them, then remembered what he'd intended to say just as she swung to face him.

"I suppose searching for treasure, even if they find nothing, will still keep them happy as grigs."

"Actually, I'm not sure about that—at least not in Harry's case." Shutting the door, he leaned back against it.

Still holding her hair, she came closer, the better to hear him. Frowning. "What do you mean?"

"I got the distinct impression that the search is mostly Ben's idea. Edmond's caught up in it, too, but Ben is the primary enthusiast. Harry, unless I'm much mistaken, is going along because of the others, not because he has any real interest in the endeavor."

Her frown remained. "He's usually the instigator—he used to be forever on about joining the smugglers and doing runs."

"Undoubtedly. But that was before." Gervase paused, then asked, "He's fifteen, correct?" She nodded. He grimaced wryly. "I remember being fifteen. I remember Christopher being fifteen." He hesitated, then said, "A word of advice, if you'll take it. The very last thing you want is for a fifteen-year-old youth to grow bored. And unless I read matters entirely wrongly, underneath it all, Harry is bored. There's no challenge in his life."

Her lips tightened; her gaze grew unfocused. For a moment she was completely still, then she blinked and looked at him. Studied his eyes for an instant, then raised her brows. "You have a suggestion."

Statement, no question. "A suggestion, nothing more.

He's Viscount Gascoigne, and fifteen is old enough to start learning the ropes."

Her frown remained etched in her eyes. "He never asks about the estate, things like that. I usually have to push to make him play the viscount, even socially."

He couldn't help a snort. "Madeline, the social aspects are the ones he'll like least. Try him with some of the real work. Take him with you when you ride out, when you visit the farms. Start asking for his opinion—that'll give him an opening to ask you to explain things."

Again he hesitated, searching her eyes, pale, green, today remarkably clear. "Don't wait for him to ask, because he won't—he'll see that as encroaching on your territory. If you're ever going to hand the estate on to him—and yes, I know that's your intention—you'll have to make the first overtures. Always, with each aspect, he'll wait for you to suggest he gets involved. Out of loyalty to you, he won't push for involvement himself."

Her frown had evaporated, initially superseded by puzzlement that now dissolved into revelation. "Oh, I see." After a moment, she added, "Yes, of course." She refocused on him. And smiled—a glorious smile full of happiness and content.

The impact was considerably greater than if she'd boxed his ears.

"Thank you. I hadn't thought of it like that." The power behind her smile faded as fondness crept in. "He's been so intent on rushing off, keeping himself busy out of the house, that I've hesitated to . . . well, rein him in and test him in harness, so to speak. But if in reality he's chafing at the bit, then I will. Thank you for the hint."

"My pleasure." It was easy to smile back.

When he remained against the door, watching her, his smile still softening the hard planes of his face, Madeline felt her instincts twitch. She raised her brows. "Was there something else?"

"No." His smile widened in a way she recognized well enough to distrust. "I'm just waiting for you to thank me."

"I just did."

"Appropriately."

Her lips parted to repeat the word; abruptly, she shut them. She narrowed her eyes. "I am *not* kissing you again."

His untrustworthy smile deepened. "How do you plan to leave here?"

Belatedly, she glanced around.

"The stair beyond this door is the only way down."

She swung away and marched down the battlements; she didn't need to go far to see that there was, indeed, no other exit—no door, not even a dormer window.

Stalking back to where he patiently waited, shoulders against the door, she halted a pace away. Holding back her hair as the breeze swooped past, she glared at him. "You are *so* . . ." Momentarily lost for words, she gestured wildly with one hand.

"Good at this?"

She uttered a frustrated hiss. "*Irritating!*" She felt like stamping her foot. "For heaven's sake—"

Gervase leaned forward, grasped her waist, lifted her to him, then let her fall against him.

With a smothered squeak she did, her long limbs flush against his, her breasts to his chest, her hips to his upper thighs.

Every nerve, every muscle in his body snapped to attention. Including . . .

Something she, plastered against him, couldn't possibly mistake. He saw her eyes widen. He smiled—intently. "Just so."

He bent his head and kissed her.

Her lips had parted in shock; he took immediate advantage and claimed her mouth. Claimed, tasted, plundered just a little before settling to entice.

She didn't physically struggle—her body remained passive in his arms, instinctively accepting his embrace—but she battled nonetheless, fighting doggedly and valiantly to hold aloof.

His lips on hers, his tongue stroking hers, his instincts pressed him to wage war against her—against her will, weakening it so her desire could triumph, and she would surrender and be willingly his. Yet as he angled his head over hers and engaged with her more definitely, he was strangely aware of a dichotomy within, of his warrior's instinct—a primal conviction that he had every right to claim the woman in his arms—clashing with an equally insistent sense that with her he needed to be giving. To persuade and negotiate, not force and insist.

He didn't want to rule her; he wanted her by his side, a willing partner, a helpmate—his wife.

The thought slid through his mind, gentled his approach—and all but instantly delivered a reward. Her resistance wavered; immediately he set himself to tempt her more, to beckoningly tease, to seduce in earnest.

Her lips softened, then returned the pressure of his—more impulse than considered action—but then she realized, froze for a heartbeat—then gave up. Gave in. Stopped fighting and joined him.

Her sudden change of tack—not capitulation so much as embracing the inevitable—left him momentarily adrift, mentally scrambling to adjust his strategy, then her hands, until then pressed against his upper chest, slid up to his shoulders, gripped, then one eased and slid to his nape, then further into his hair, fingers twisting, lightly gripping . . . an evocative urging his instincts needed no help to translate.

He responded, more driven than deliberate, yielding to her demand and letting their mouths meld, their tongues tangle in a more flagrant, more explicit engagement than any he'd planned.

She met him, was with him, through the greedy, heated caress. Urged him on with a small gasp when he broke the kiss, sliding his lips to the hollow beneath her ear while his chest swelled and he dragged in a breath.

But then he returned to her mouth, too hungry, not yet appeased—any more than she was.

Her lips were lush, hot, demanding, the slick cavern of her mouth a sensual haven as she welcomed him back. He sank deep, and she pressed against him, into him.

He no longer needed to hold her to him; releasing his until-then-immovable grip on her waist, he spread his hands and pressed his palms to her back, without conscious thought satisfying his need to learn—of every curve, every long plane, each supple muscle, each delectable swell of female flesh.

Raising his hands to the backs of her shoulders, he cupped them in his palms, then slowly ran his hands down, tracing the long planes of her back, the indentation of her waist, the flare of her hips, the ripe swell of her derriere, sliding down and around to cup one firm globe in each hand.

She shuddered; he felt it, felt the primal thrill of it in his bones, through the kiss sensed her response, her uninhibited, unscreened wanting.

Sensed her desire rise to meet his.

Rise to swirl with, to complement, to mesh with his.

To set fire to passion and ignite sensual need.

Madeline gasped through the kiss. Never before had she felt like this—as if there were some thing, some being within her, within her skin, expanding, taking over, driving her to grasp, to seize, to embrace every second of sensation, of experience.

Of all she'd thought she'd never know.

She felt heated, nerves alive, her breath no longer hers but his—her body wrapped, trapped in his arms and glad, so glad, to be there.

Her rational mind couldn't take it in, but her senses reveled and gorged. And some side of her she didn't know frankly rejoiced in the escalating heat, in the compulsive, burgeoning swell of what even she, innocent and inexperienced, recognized as passion.

Hot, urgent, increasingly explicit.

Their kiss had grown wildly so, infecting his touch.

Infecting him.

And her.

So that she made not the smallest demur when one hard hand swept up her side to palm her breast. To caress, to cup, then to lightly knead.

Sensation, new and novel, flared, grew, spread molten delight just beneath her skin.

And he knew. His hand closed, more possessive; beneath the straining bodice of her walking dress, his fingers found the furled bud of her nipple and tweaked, rolled—and pleasure, sharp and sweet, sliced through her.

Breathing was beyond her. Raising both hands to grasp his head, she gripped, felt the slide of his curls, so much softer even than they looked, over her fingers as she held him and kissed him—hard—then in desperation pulled back.

"Oh, God—Gervase!" Eyes closed, she struggled to breathe. "Someone might see."

"They can't." His voice was deep, gravelly by her ear as his hands, both now ministering to her breasts, continued to play. "No one can see up here, even with a spyglass."

The fact he'd thought even of a spyglass reassured her completely.

Dragging in one last breath, she reached for his face, framed the long planes between her palms and brought his lips back to hers.

She was still hungry, still greedy for his kiss, his lips, and the sensations they wrought. For the reaction they evoked in her, the heretofore unknown side of her that came alive in his arms.

Gervase inwardly groaned, and complied, unable not to, incapable of denying her—yet he hadn't imagined, hadn't dreamed she would be so demanding. So wanting.

So starved.

If he'd known, he would have chosen some other site for this encounter. His apartments, for instance, with the bed he intended her to grace close at hand.

Instead . . . they were on the battlements.

The increasingly wind-strafed battlements.

It took more than effort, more than steely will—it took desperation to drag his hands from her breasts, to grip her waist and shift, turn, so her back was to the door and he was before her.

Even then she merely kissed him again, her mouth a gift he couldn't refuse. It took several minutes of heated engagement before he recalled—again—why he, they, had to stop. Halt. Now. Before . . .

Before matters got entirely out of hand and stopping became impossible.

When he finally lifted his head, Madeline discovered hers reeling. Her lips throbbed, swollen and slick—and still eager.

So damningly willing.

Hauling in a breath, irritated to feel a sense of loss that his hands were no longer on her breasts, she opened her eyes and forced herself to meet his.

They'd never looked more tigerish, their expression more intent.

"Have you changed your mind yet?"

The words, gravelly and low, laden with male desire, nearly made her shiver. Distracted with suppressing the wanton reaction, when she stared at him uncomprehendingly, he clarified, "About warming my bed."

Her mind refocused in a rush. She blinked up at him. "No." Her hands had fallen to rest against his shoulders. She pushed. Hard.

And he budged not one inch.

A very odd sensation skittered down her spine, novel and distinctly startling.

She was helpless, trapped between the door and him, between ungiving wood and the hard muscle and bone of his unyielding body. Never before had any man made her feel captured.

To win free she would need to cede . . . something.

She blinked, inwardly snapped free of that ridiculous supposition. "Let me go."

She endeavored to infuse every ounce of her will into the words; she lifted her chin to give them emphasis.

His expression hardened. But he eased his grip on her waist. "For now."

The warning in the words was every bit as explicit as the kiss had been.

She glared, but it was a weak effort. With one hand, she groped behind her, found and grasped the latch. Stepping to the side, her eyes on his, she opened the door.

He stepped back and let her swing it wide.

Breathing a little more easily, head high, she flashed one last defiant glance at him, then turned and went through. Stepping onto the stairs, one hand on the stone wall, she started down.

It had been just a kiss, a part of his silly game. No matter what he'd said, he wasn't—couldn't be—seriously intent on seducing her.

If she repeated that statement often enough, she might again believe it.

"Fancy forming your own private gentlemen's club in London, just so you have somewhere where society can't bother you." Edmond glanced up the breakfast table at Madeline. "Neat, don't you think?"

"Better'n neat," Ben opined around a mouthful of sausage, relieving her of the need to reply.

Just as well; in her present mood, any response she made regarding Gervase Tregarth and his doings was bound to be laced with frustrated ire.

She sipped her tea, and tried to shift her mind from that irritating gentleman, and his effect on her; unfortunately, in the present company that appeared a lost cause.

Bad enough that the interlude Gervase had engineered on the castle battlements, and all that had transpired there, had laid siege to her mind throughout the previous evening and disturbed her night, but his outing with her brothers and the exploits with which he'd regaled them had been the principal subjects of their conversation ever since.

Normally she could rely on her harebrained trio to distract her from any inner brooding. Instead, their speculation and comments about Gervase only reinforced his presence. Reinforced the reality that he was there, and she was going to have to deal with him.

"Do you really think what Joe and Sam said is right?" Ben turned to Harry, seated at the head of the table. "That there'll soon be lots of men with no work and things will be bad around here?"

Madeline blinked to attention; she looked at Ben, then up the table at Harry.

Who was frowning. "I don't know. It seems strange that if there's such trouble brewing, so few people have heard of it." Harry looked at Madeline. "Have you heard anything? Are the mines at Carn Brea really closing?"

What? was her instinctive reaction; she swallowed it, and frowned. "I haven't heard any whisper of such a thing. Where did you hear that?"

"In Helford," Edmond said. "We went there after we got back from fishing."

"We went down to the docks to watch the boats come in," Harry said. "Sam and Joe were there. Sam's father keeps the tavern in Helford and Joe's dad is the blacksmith. Both Sam and Joe said their fathers were worried about what would happen in the district when the money from the mines dries up."

"Both Sam's and Joe's older brothers work at Carn Brea," Edmond added.

When she stared, gaze distant, down the table, Harry shifted. "Could the mines be closing? It'll be bad for the district if they are, won't it?"

She mentally shook herself. "Yes to the latter question, but I know of no information that suggests the mines are even in difficulties, much less that they're on the brink of closing."

She'd done as she'd told Squire Ridley she would, and had written to her London contacts; she'd heard back only yesterday that all was as she'd thought. She looked at Harry. "I heard from London yesterday that the tin mines, including those locally, are doing very well—in fact, exceeding expectations—and the outlook is rosy."

"Perhaps I could tell Sam and Joe that, so they can tell their fathers. It seemed they were truly worried."

She nodded. "Do. In fact, unless you have something pressing to attend to, I think you should go back to Helford today." She paused, then added, "You"—she tipped her head at Harry—"could drop by and speak with Sam's and Joe's fathers directly. That would be the neighborly thing to do. You may tell them I've checked very recently and everything's as it should be. We don't need rumors of that sort spreading and frightening people."

Harry, his expression unusually serious—much more adult, she saw with a pang—nodded. "I'll ride that way this morning."

"We'll come," Edmond said.

Ben, still eating, merely nodded.

Madeline watched while Harry drained the cup of coffee

he'd recently graduated to, Gervase's words about including him more in estate business whispering in her head.

"One thing," she said. Harry looked inquiringly at her as he set down his cup; Edmond and Ben did, too. "Keep your ears open on the subject of the mines. There might be someone deliberately spreading rumors. We know there's some London gentleman interested in buying up mining leases, and it's possible the rumors are in some way linked."

It took Harry but a moment to see the connection; Edmond was only a heartbeat behind. Ben remained fully absorbed with his last slice of ham.

Harry and Edmond exchanged glances, their features assuming the same expression, one she'd never before seen on their faces.

"We'll listen." Harry nodded, quietly grim. "We'll tell you anything we hear."

Gervase had been right; they were growing up. Despite the pang she felt near her heart, she couldn't help feeling satisfied that both boys—youths, young men in the making—clearly possessed real interest in the district, in the industry and people that were part of their patrimony.

Regardless of Harry's evolving maturity, Madeline did not press him to attend Lady Moreston's ball that evening.

Her ladyship's event was one of the many held over summer through which the local gentry and aristocracy entertained themselves through the long, mild evenings. Gowned in mulberry satin, feeling suitably armored as the Honorable Miss Madeline Gascoigne, she greeted Lady Moreston with her customary assurance and followed Muriel into the ballroom.

The long room was bedecked with summer greenery, rather more to Madeline's taste than ribbons, silks or gilded decorations. Halting at the top of the ballroom steps, she surveyed the room—searching for one curly dark head.

But Gervase wasn't there, at least not yet.

Descending the steps in Muriel's wake, Madeline inwardly frowned—then realized and banished the underlying emotion, whatever it was. She couldn't possibly be disappointed; it was simply irritation at having to remain tense, on guard, until he appeared. Once he was there she would know what he was up to, and she wouldn't feel so off-balance, trying to imagine what he might do.

Might take it into his devilish mind to do.

The man was plainly dangerous, but she wasn't some silly witless girl to allow herself to grow too curious for her own good. She was her own person, in charge of her own life. What decisions she made would be her own.

With that determination ringing in her mind, she set herself to make use of the evening in her customary manner. She circulated through the guests, chatting with the gentlemen, listening for any confirmation of the rumors her brothers had heard; she hadn't yet decided how to proceed on that front.

"I met Penterwell today," Gerald Ridley told her. "He'd been approached by that agent, too. Not that he has any intention of selling, but like me, he's wondering what's behind this."

"I've checked again since we spoke, and everything I hear suggests that all is going well and expected to improve even further. Perhaps this London gentleman simply thinks we're naïve?"

Gerald snorted. "Well, it seems he's had no takers, so he must by now realize he'll need to think again."

Madeline smiled and inclined her head in parting, but the squire's words lingered. The gentry weren't the only ones who held mining leases. She was idly circling the dance floor, pondering that, when Gervase suddenly appeared before her and trapped her hand in his.

He smiled, openly wolfishly—tigerishly—at her, then

raised her fingers and kissed them. She tried to frown, difficult when her eyes had widened.

Shifting to stand beside her, he tucked her hand in his arm. "Sybil cried off and left me to make my own way." He glanced around. "I forgot the country operates on earlier hours."

His gaze returned to her face. "But now I'm here, we can dance."

The musicians had just started up; Gervase drew her toward the floor. Madeline jerked back to reality. And pulled back. "No. I mean, I don't dance."

He raised his brows, but didn't stop leading her forward. "Why not? You can't expect me to believe you never learned."

"Of course I learned. It's just . . ." She blinked as he neatly twirled her, then smoothly drew her into his arms.

And she realized she had to look up a good few inches to meet his eyes. Realized that the hand at her waist and the arm behind it possessed uncommon strength, remembered how easily he'd lifted her off her feet the day before.

She didn't dance—even though she was drawn to the exercise—because most men were shorter than she. Or at least not tall enough, or strong enough, to accomplish what was needed.

Two revolutions in Gervase's arms and . . . when he raised his brows at her, she shook her head. "Never mind."

He smiled, then looked forward, and whirled her through the turn. Literally whirled her; she'd never danced—been able to dance—with such unrestrained ease. Never had she been able to pace her partner as she could him—without having to shorten her stride, limit her movement, rein in her natural flair.

As they circled the room, effortlessly outpacing the other couples yet moving so smoothly there was no sense of speed, only a refreshing freedom, her heart lightened, took flight.

He looked into her eyes, and smiled. "There—you see. You enjoy it."

She closed her lips on the too-revealing answer that had leapt to her tongue. *Only with you* was hardly a wise thing to say, not to him.

He needed no encouragement. Not to whirl her off her mental feet, something he proceeded to do with ludicrous ease. Being so confidently steered around the room was frankly exhilarating. He held her close—enough for her to feel truly secure at the pace they moved—closer than he perhaps should, yet it wasn't so blatant an attack on her senses that she felt compelled to balk.

All she felt compelled to do was follow, to relax and let him lead as he would; her inner self sighed, and embraced the golden moments of unexpected pleasure.

His eyes were on her face, searching. Deeming it wise to distract him, she said, "You must have been waltzing quite a bit this year, what with all the balls in London."

He raised his brows, his expression—mild resignation—for once clear. "Thanks to my sisters' antics, I spent very little time at any balls. I'd reach town only to be called back within a few days."

"So they were behind all those strange happenings?"

The line of his lips turned grim. "Indeed." He met her eyes, hesitated.

She waited, eager to hear more but knowing better than to press him.

His lips quirked. "At least, having dealt with your brothers, you'll understand. Those strange incidents, all of which were expressly designed to bring me hot-foot home, were my dear sisters' reaction to the advent of the new Lady Hardesty."

She blinked, tried to imagine, and couldn't. "I don't see the connection."

"Thank you. I didn't either. They, however, had convinced themselves that like poor Robert, I, too, might succumb to the lures of some femme fatale who would banish them to live with Great-Aunt Agatha in Yorkshire."

She stared at him, confirmed that he was speaking the plain truth. She tried to keep her lips straight, failed entirely and laughed. "Oh, dear."

He merely gave her a resigned look; his lips not curved but relaxed, he continued to whirl her as she struggled to master her mirth.

"I . . ." She paused to draw in a huge breath. "I truly can't imagine you falling victim to any female."

Gervase looked into her face, into her eyes, a shimmery peridot green in the chandeliers' light. He'd thought the same, but was no longer so sure.

The music ended; he swung her to a flourishing halt—which, he noted, she enjoyed. Her unalloyed delight in the dance, something she'd permitted him to see, had to him been a subtle pleasure.

It was also a significant advance from where he had been when he'd first fixed his eye on her; then he hadn't been able to see past her shield. Now . . . in moments like this, he glimpsed the woman behind it clearly.

With every fresh insight she grew more intriguing.

After one swift glance over the heads, he took her arm. "I believe it's time for supper. Shall we?"

Her brows rose a little at his clear expectation of her agreement, but then she inclined her head. Her next words told him why. "The boys told me you'd formed some new gentlemen's club in London. If they had it right, one with a rather unusual purpose."

He smiled. And set about distracting her.

In that he was surprisingly successful; between her questions and his answers, ranging over the Bastion Club and its members, the true nature of his past service to the crown, Dalziel and his office, they progressed through supper in earnest conversation, sufficiently engrossed to discourage others from joining them. As they strolled back into the corridor leading to the ballroom, Gervase couldn't recall a supper he'd enjoyed more.

Why he found her, of all females, so easy to talk to he didn't know, yet her quick wits and the breadth of her understanding had allowed him to speak freely of topics he normally eschewed.

That had been another subtle pleasure, just being able to relax and speak without thought. Without censoring his words.

Perhaps it was dealing with her brothers that had left her so patently unshockable. So calm, so grounded.

Around her he felt anchored in a way he never had, not with any other, not at any time.

"This Dalziel," she said. "You're quite sure he's right, and there is one last traitor somewhere in the government?"

Taking her arm, he turned her away from the ballroom. "Yes. If you met Dalziel you'd understand, but quite aside from the fact he's the last person to invent things, we—the rest of us—have seen evidence that this last traitor exists. Jack Warnefleet got closest—he nearly caught the man's henchman—but the traitor killed his man rather than allow him to fall into our, and Dalziel's, hands."

She walked beside him, looking ahead, puzzling over Dalziel's nemesis and not really seeing. He knew that last was true; she made no demur when they reached a garden room and he opened the French doors giving on to it. Without comment, a faint frown on her face, she walked through.

"This traitor—what is known of him?"

"Another traitor suggested he had some connection with the War Office. Beyond that, the only physical description is of a tall, well-set-up, dark-haired gentleman of the ton."

"Of the *ton*?" She whirled to face him as, having closed the door, he joined her.

He nodded. "He killed his henchman at a royal gala at

Vauxhall. The only people who could obtain tickets were members of the ton, and the young lady who saw him was quite certain of his station." He paused, looking into her eyes. "As Dalziel puts it, the last traitor is one of us."

She looked stern—a severely disapproving Valkyrie. "No wonder he—Dalziel—is so determined to expose him."

"Indeed. But enough of Dalziel." His ex-commander had served his purpose. They stood alone in the garden room, well away from the ballroom. He reached for her.

Madeline blinked and glanced around; before she could do anything beyond register that they had somehow wandered down to Lady Moreston's garden porch—a square room between two others, wall-less on one side and so open to the garden with a pair of slim ivory columns framing the view—she was in Gervase's arms.

Recalling his fell purpose—and her opposition—she braced her hands on his chest and pushed back to glare at him. "You distracted me."

The accusation made him smile. "I did. I admit it." Holding her fast within one arm, he raised his hand, and brushed the pad of his thumb across her lower lip. Leaving it throbbing. Then his eyes, dark in the weak light, lifted to hers. "And now I propose"—his hand shifted; his long fingers framed her jaw and tipped it up as his lips lowered to hers—"to distract you even more."

Chapter 6

$\mathscr{M}$adeline intended to hold firm, to refuse to play his game, but her besetting sin had other ideas.

No matter how much she'd tried to dismiss it, to play down her interest, that more adventurous side of her that she so rarely let loose knew the truth.

Knew how deeply she longed to know more, to learn of desire, and the passion that, with his arms around her and his lips on hers, seemed to hover at the edge of her perception.

It was that need to explore that had her twining her arms about his neck and kissing him back, had her sinking against him in flagrant encouragement entirely deaf to the protests of her rational mind.

Rationality, caution, held little sway as their mouths melded, as the kiss deepened and time spun away.

Simple heat, simple hunger.

And a yearning that welled from her soul. That touched her in a way she'd never felt before, that swelled and grew and drove her.

Drove her to twine her fingers in his hair and clutch as his hand, drifting down from her jaw, feathered over her breast, then closed.

Through the taut satin, one artful finger circled her ruched nipple, and she mentally gasped.

Waited. Poised on a cliff edge of elusive tension, wanting to know yet more.

His lips left hers. From beneath her lashes, she watched him glance down, to where his hand cupped her firm flesh.

His fingers lightly closed, then he glanced at her. After an instant, he closed the distance and brushed his lips over hers again, then drew back.

"You're curious." His tone made it a discovery.

She blinked, breathed back, "How can you tell?"

"I can taste it."

Did curiosity have a taste, a texture?

"You want to know about this." His fingers shifted again.

Her nerves leapt, and she shivered.

"I've a confession to make." His voice was low, a gravelly rumble. "I want to know, too. Want to see where this . . ."—his fingers drew another shuddering response from her—"leads. Yesterday, at the castle, when you insisted on leaving, when you turned and gave me your hand I very nearly seized you, tossed you over my shoulder and carried you off to my bed."

"Oh?" Some totally wanton part of her wished he had.

"Yes." Gervase paused, hand caressing, fingers stroking, then went on, "Just so you know you're not the only one affected, not the only one involved here." *Caught. Trapped.*

By what, he didn't know.

He drew her back into his arms, back into the kiss, steeped them both in the moment, in the spiraling sensation and welling need—as far as he dared. With her and him, and where they were, there was only so far they could go.

With real reluctance, he lifted his head, drew breath—felt

the pounding in his veins, compulsive, insistent, demanding. Sensed the same in her.

Her lashes fluttered, then she focused on his face.

"Have you changed your mind yet?"

She blinked at him, not once, but twice, before comprehension swam into her gaze. Then she snapped out of the spell—theirs, not his alone—and eased back out of his arms. "No."

He hadn't expected any other answer, not yet, but despite the words her less-than-certain, faintly puzzled tone sent his spirits soaring. She was wavering, yes!, but experience warned the time to press was not yet. She had to come to him of her own accord, for her own reasons; she was that sort of woman. An independent lady.

Letting his face set, he coolly stated, "If that's the case, then we'd better get back to the ballroom."

She hadn't wanted to return to the ballroom, a fact that demonstated just how completely her besetting sin had overwhelmed her good sense. Climbing the castle steps the next morning, Madeline sternly lectured herself—yet again—that under no circumstances should she allow Gervase to embrace her again.

The instant his arms settled around her, her besetting sin came to the fore . . . and turned her into some wanton creature who simply had to know more. Far more, she was convinced, than would be good for her.

Striding into the front hall, she saw Gervase's butler gliding from the nether regions to greet her. "Good morning, Sitwell." Halting, she tugged off her gloves, acknowledging Sitwell's bow with a nod. "I'm here to see his lordship. Where may I find him?"

"I'm here." Gervase stepped from the mouth of a corridor. He nodded to Sitwell. "Thank you, Sitwell. I'll ring if I need you."

As the butler bowed and withdrew, Gervase turned to her. He met her gaze, read the determined, businesslike expression she'd plastered on her face. His lips curved, too knowing for her liking. "I was on my way to the library. If you'd care to join me?"

She nodded. "Indeed." She kept her tones brisk. "I have some information you need to know."

His brows rose, but he said nothing more as he strolled beside her down the corridor and ushered her into his library.

She walked to the armchair angled before the desk. Pausing beside it, she glanced back—and discovered him by her shoulder. Felt one hard hand grasp her waist while with his other he tipped up her chin.

So he could kiss her.

A swift, not undemanding yet unforceful kiss, a reminder, a promise.

A complete and utter distraction. When he lifted his head, she blinked at him, dazed, mentally lost.

He smiled and nudged her into the armchair. "Sit. And tell me what brought you here."

She sank down, struggling to marshal her wits. She'd lost them in the instant his lips had touched hers—no, before, when she'd realized he was close.

He rounded the desk and sat in the admiral's chair behind it; the smugness he tried to hide as he looked inquiringly at her broke the spell. She dragged in a breath. "This business of the mining leases."

Once she'd started, it wasn't so hard. Briefly she explained what her brothers had heard, then outlined the information she'd received from London. "Then yesterday when Harry returned to Helford and spoke with Sam's father, he thought to ask who had spread the rumor. It was a peddler in the tap—Sam's father thought the man was most likely heading for the festival. So the boys decided to follow him and see what they could learn—they caught up with the peddler in the tavern at St. Keverne."

She glanced at Gervase. All hint of private emotion had vanished from his demeanor; he was as intent on her tale as she might wish. "The peddler said he'd picked up the rumor in a tavern in Falmouth. He said it was general, a tale doing the rounds. He didn't know of any specific source."

Gervase grimaced. "Falmouth, and the fleet's in. If one wanted to start an anonymous rumor, a few whispers in drunken sailors' ears would do it."

"So I thought. Assuming, of course, that these rumors have no basis in fact but are being spread by this London gentleman or his agent to encourage locals to sell their leases."

He tapped a pile of letters stacked to one side of the blotter. "Like yours, my London contacts confirmed no suggestion of any diminution in the tin trade, but rather an expectation of improved returns. They were puzzled that I should have heard anything to the contrary. Beyond that, I also wrote to St. Austell, the Earl of Lostwithiel, and Viscount Torrington— his estates are near Bideford." He glanced at Madeline. "Both hold tin mining leases and are members of the Bastion Club."

"Your private club?"

He nodded and lifted two letters. "Both replied in much the same vein as all else we've heard. No hint of any problem with tin mining, but rather an expectation of increased profits." His lips curved ruefully. "They, of course, now want to know why I asked." He dropped the letters back on the pile.

Glancing up, he found Madeline's gaze fixed on a point beyond his shoulder.

"It occurred to me," she murmured, "that while most of us—the gentry and aristocracy—are unlikely to sell on the basis of rumor, not without checking if not with London then at least with each other, there are many others who hold leases who are not as well connected, not as well informed."

She met his gaze. "Should this rumor become widespread, if an offer is made to them, small farmers will likely sell."

He nodded.

Looking down, chin firming, she started pulling on her gloves. "I'm going to ride to Helston and see if I can locate this agent, and ask him to explain these rumors. If I can't find him, I intend putting it about that I would like to speak with him concerning selling some leases." She looked up and smiled—icily. "That should bring him to my door." Gloves on, she rose.

Forcibly reminded of his Valkyrie analogy, Gervase rose, too. "I'll ride with you."

She might be her brother's surrogate, but he was the local earl, the senior nobleman in the district. A fact she acknowledged with an inclination of her head, and no argument.

Ten minutes later, they were galloping side by side—riding hard, wild, unrestrained. She had her chestnut again, and he was on Crusader; they pounded north across the golden-grassed downs, an exhilarating run, shared and carefree, before, in wordless concert, they mentally sighed, remembered who they were, and eased back and swung northwest for Helston.

They approached the town from the south, trotting along a newly macadamized stretch of road. "Let's start our search in the northwest quadrant." He glanced at Madeline. "More taverns there."

She nodded. Entering the town, they walked their mounts on.

The next hour saw them, side by side, talk to seven tavern and inn keepers. All recognized the man Squire Ridley had described; all had seen him about town, or in their taps, but none knew who he was or where he was staying.

"Nope." John Quiller shook his head in answer to Madeline's final query. "Ain't seen him with no one else either. Keeps to himself but polite with it. He talks readily enough, will join in a discussion if asked, but o' course no one's been so bold as to ask him outright what he's here for."

Inwardly sighing, Madeline nodded.

"If you see him again, John, tell him I'd like a word." Gervase took her arm. "Tell him it might be worth his while. Send him to the castle."

"Aye." John nodded. "I'll do that."

Steered out of the Cow & Whistle, Madeline considered protesting Gervase's usurpation of her idea, but then dismissed the notion. All the better if he was willing to pursue this troublesome subject; she had enough on her plate with her brother's estate, and her brothers.

And he was the senior nobleman; it was only right and proper that in this she cede to him.

They paused on the pavement; she glanced down the street. They'd tried most of the likely places and had circled back to the center of the town. Sensing Gervase studying her, she glanced at him, then arched a brow. "What?"

He shook his head and retook her arm. "I was waiting for your protest. I expected some snide comment at least."

She sniffed and elevated her chin as they proceeded down the street. "I decided against it."

"Ah."

The gentle humor in his tone robbed the syllable of any offense; indeed, she was rather impressed that he'd realized he'd come close to stepping on her toes.

They turned into Coinagehall Street, the town's main thoroughfare; Gervase glanced around as they walked. "It's lunchtime. Why don't we stop for a bite at the inn?"

He waved at the Scales & Anchor, the main inn in the town, just ahead of them; they'd left their horses in the stable there.

Hungry herself after their busy morning, Madeline nodded. "Alice Tregonning keeps an excellent table."

"Good. I'm famished." Ushering her up the inn's steps, he reached past her and opened the door.

An hour and more later, after a meal as excellent as she had prophesied enlivened by relaxed conversation that neither had had to work to achieve, they left the inn in companionable good humor. Pausing on the pavement, eyes adjusting to the bright sunshine after the dimness of the parlor inside, they looked around, then Gervase touched her arm.

"Let's go down to the river." Coinagehall Street dipped steeply to the banks of the Helford. "If I recall aright, there are two boardinghouses facing the old docks. Perhaps our man is staying at one."

One hand smoothing back her wayward hair, she nodded. "Let's go and see."

Unfortunately, no one at the boardinghouses had sighted their quarry. They were toiling slowly back up Coinagehall Street, heading to the inn to fetch their horses, when carriage wheels rattled on the cobbles behind them.

Glancing back, Gervase saw an open landau with a collection of fashionably garbed ladies and gentlemen—escapees from London, if their studied airs of sophisticated boredom were any indication.

The dark-haired lady in the middle of the rear seat, a frilled parasol shading her fair skin, saw him; she studied him for an instant, then leaned forward and spoke to the coachman.

The carriage slowed, then drew in and halted alongside Gervase and Madeline.

They both paused, turned. Madeline was wearing a dark blue riding dress; unlike a conventional habit it didn't possess a train, but the skirts were still long enough that she'd needed both hands to lift them as they'd climbed the steep street. Consequently, he hadn't taken her arm, but had been walking beside her as if they were mere acquaintances.

Furling her parasol, the lady leaned forward. Her gaze lingered on him, then shifted to Madeline. The lady smiled. "Good afternoon. I'm Lady Hardesty. And you must be Miss Gascoigne." Lady Hardesty held out her gloved hand. "I've been wanting to make your acquaintance, Miss Gascoigne—sadly I missed doing so at the vicarage tea."

"Lady Hardesty." Stepping to the carriage's side, Madeline touched her gloved fingers to her ladyship's. Unsurprised to see Lady Hardesty's gaze flick to Gervase's face, she gestured his way. "I believe you've yet to meet Lord Crowhurst."

"My lord." Lady Hardesty's eyes locked on Gervase's, held as he took her hand.

"Lady Hardesty." His expression coolly distant, he half bowed, then released her.

She immediately gestured to the others in the carriage. "If you'll permit me to introduce . . ."

Madeline exchanged nods and greetings with the other ladies and the two gentlemen, one of whom was Mr. Courtland. The ladies, following their hostess's lead, fixed their attention avidly on Gervase, leaving Madeline to Mr. Courtland and Mr. Fleming, neither of whom were backward in trying to engage her.

Or, as she cynically suspected, attach her.

"Perhaps," Mr. Courtland suggested, "I could call on you?"

She smiled the distant smile she'd relied on for years to quell the aspirations of overly enthusiastic males. "My aunt is elderly. She rarely entertains."

Courtland's smile developed an edge. "It's not your aunt I'd be coming to see, m'dear."

Madeline held his gaze, and slowly, pointedly, raised her brows.

Under her steady regard, Courtland shifted, then an unbecoming shade of florid pink rose from beneath his neck-cloth and spread upward.

Releasing him, she turned to see how Gervase was faring.

He was, she discovered, giving an excellent imitation of a stone wall. Certainly Lady Hardesty's entreaties and entice-ments had made no impression whatever; he looked arro-gantly, superiorly, unmoved.

Good manners forbade him from cutting her ladyship, but now that Madeline had ended her conversation, he glanced her way, then turned back to Lady Hardesty and with cool civility informed her, "I fear we must get on. We have quite a ride before us." He reached for Madeline.

As his fingers closed about her elbow, Madeline saw the flash of annoyance that passed through Lady Hardesty's dark eyes. She wasn't used to being denied.

But she was too wise to press.

With an inclination of her head that she endeavored to make gracious, her ladyship sat back. Her gaze shifted to Madeline; somewhat to her surprise Madeline detected nothing more than residual annoyance in that look.

It was transparently clear her ladyship saw her as no threat, no rival; she'd dismissed her as a woman—or rather as too inconsequential a female to have any chance of at-taching Gervase.

That look was so unmaliciously dismissive, so purely a statement of her ladyship's experienced evaluation and noth-ing more, Madeline was taken aback. But habit stood her in good stead; she parroted the right phrases as she and Ger-vase took their leave of the party, then he drew her back from the pavement's edge.

Lady Hardesty leaned forward to speak to her coachman, then looked back at Gervase. "Until later, my lord."

Her dark eyes holding his, she sat back, then the carriage jerked forward; raising and unfurling her parasol, she looked ahead.

They stood and watched the carriage clatter away.

Madeline glanced at Gervase and found his eyes narrowed on the retreating parasol. She hesitated, then unable to help herself asked, "What's your verdict?"

He glanced briefly at her, then back at the carriage disappearing up the street. "My sisters," he said, urging her on, "were right. Robert Hardesty has made a very big mistake."

Gervase insisted on escorting her all the way back to Treleaver Park. The afternoon was waning by the time they clattered into the stable yard. Grooms came running. Madeline dismounted, gracefully sliding to the ground; she turned—only to discover Gervase beside her.

"Come." He waved ahead. "I'll walk you to the house before I ride home."

She acquiesced with a nod. Side by side, they strode out of the yard, then by mutual accord slowed to a stroll. The path to the house cut through the gardens, a pleasant, wending walk in the golden light of the fading day.

From the cliffs, out of sight to their right, the surf boomed like distant cannon fire dulled by the thick canopies of the intervening trees. The tang of the sea didn't reach this far; as they followed the path, the scents of lavender, roses and freshly clipped grass mingled and swirled around them.

They walked in silence; they'd exchanged few words, all purely commonplace, since parting from Lady Hardesty. But there was little to discuss; while trawling through the taverns searching for their quarry, they'd grasped the opportunity to spread their view of the current prospects for the local tin mines. Beyond that, until they located the elusive agent or he presented himself to Gervase, there was nothing more they could do.

As for Lady Hardesty . . .

Madeline halted beneath the arbor giving on to the formal rose garden. Beyond the roses lay the house, its red brick walls washed by the westering sun, the leaded windows glinting.

The gardeners had finished for the day, their tools tidied away; there was no one about, not a soul in sight. She stood silent beneath the arbor, supremely conscious of the large male who'd prowled the long path in her wake to come to a halt behind her.

Was Lady Hardesty right, or wrong?

Until recently the question wouldn't have bothered her, would have occurred to her only to be derisively dismissed.

Until recently she'd had no interest in attracting any man—and, if truth be known, no real belief in her ability to do so, not once they got to know her.

She was who she was—nearly six feet of twenty-nine-year-old spinster with an uncompromising attitude and a purpose in life that to her mind precluded any dalliance.

She hadn't, until today, felt any less of a woman for that.

Her senses flickered as Gervase stepped closer, and she felt the heat of him against her back. Her lungs tightened; her breathing grew shallow as he shifted, raising one hand to gently, evocatively caress the side of her throat.

She closed her eyes, shivered. Tried to breathe.

He bent closer, and his lips replaced his fingertips. Touched, traced, lightly kissed. The most tantalizing, most provocative caress she'd ever felt.

"Have you changed your mind yet?"

His words flowed across her mind.

Eyes closed, she drew in a deep breath. Scented the lavender, the roses, the grass—and him. Male. The unknown, the dangerous, wrapped in the familiar.

Opening her eyes, she turned and faced him. Met his amber gaze, saw the latent heat in his tiger's eyes. "No, but . . ." She lowered her gaze to his lips. Moistened hers. "I'm open to persuasion."

A risk, but one she couldn't not take, not anymore.

A heartbeat passed, then two; she felt the increased intensity in his gaze, but refused to look up and meet his eyes.

His lips curved, just a little, the line almost wry. "In that case . . ."

He closed the few inches between them, and covered her lips with his.

Kissed her—and welcomed her response when she kissed him back.

And their hunger flared again, more insistent and intense, unsatisfied and growing, evolving and developing, strengthening and deepening.

He angled his head over hers; she locked her arms about his neck. Their mouths fused, tongues tangling, tempting, wild and uninhibited. She sank against him, into him, and felt his breath hitch.

His arms rose and locked around her, and as before she became someone else—or perhaps she became who she really was. She was no longer sure.

She no longer knew anything beyond the moment, beyond the thrill, the excitement, the yearning.

He lifted and turned her, setting her on her feet deeper under the arbor; she understood why—now they stood fully under the foliage, no one could see them. Only if someone approached on the path and came close could they be seen, and as the path was gravel they'd be warned long before.

So when his arms eased and his hands roved her back, then slid low to close over her bottom and lift her against him, she made no demur. Instead, she rejoiced, dizzy with the knowledge that if nothing else he wanted her. She could hardly miss the evidence, pressed low against her belly. When he molded her against him, shifting provocatively, she gasped.

He couldn't have been clearer over exactly what he wanted.

Of her. From her. With her.

She could have pulled back then, Lady Hardesty's view rebutted and dismissed, yet the thought never entered her head. Now she was in his arms, kissing and being kissed, she had other questions, much more burning ones, to address.

Such as whether there was any limit to the heat that rose between them, that like a flame seemed to ignite, flare, then rush through her, and him, through his touch, over her skin, down her veins. How hot could she—they—get? Enough to melt her bones along with her reservations? Enough to cinder all wisdom and cauterize all doubts?

More importantly, more tantalizingly, whether the sharp edge of desire now coloring their exchange, harder, more definite, more real, was his, hers, or theirs.

Regardless, it possessed power enough to drive them, to leave them both gasping when they broke from the kiss. To have her senses reeling when he closed his hand over her breast, and kneaded. To have her breathlessly willing him on when his fingers found the buttons closing her bodice and deftly, expertly, flicked them free.

To have her closing her eyes, head falling back, trapped in a web of expectation when he pressed the halves of her bodice wide and slid one hard hand beneath, with a quick jerk and a tug stripped away her chemise . . . and touched.

Her senses seized. Her lungs locked.

On a strangled gasp, she drew his lips back to hers. She had to kiss him, deeply, passionately; she couldn't breathe but through him and she was desperate. Desperate to know, to feel, to experience . . . the pleasure in his touch. The reverence, near worshipfulness with which his fingers traced, tested, learned. Until at the last he cupped her breast in his palm, hot skin to hot skin, and gave her all she wanted.

All she suddenly needed.

Gervase inwardly shuddered. He wanted nothing more than to taste the firm flesh beneath his fingers, but that couldn't happen, not now, not here. He ached, and knew matters were only going to get worse. Much worse. She was so responsive, so uninhibitedly ardent, so free of all guile in her wanting that all he could think of was appeasing her. Of slaking her sensual thirst, even at the cost of his own.

But he couldn't let matters go any further. Even though they were both on fire, bodies heated and urgent for far more than just a touch—although he knew exactly what they needed to sate the intense hunger that gripped them both, he knew far too well that it couldn't be.

Especially not with her, given what he wanted of her.

Drawing back, reining both of them in and turning aside from the sensual brink they'd been galloping toward far too fast, was a battle beyond any he'd previously waged. He managed it, just, by the skin of his sensual teeth, and only by gripping her shoulders and physically setting her, holding her, back from him, breaking all contact between his body and hers.

She blinked at him, dazed; he was growing accustomed to seeing that sensually stunned look in her eyes, a balm of sorts to his scoriated libido, slashed, wounded, denied what it saw as its rightful prey.

He'd never been more aware of the beast within, of the strength of his own passions. That she awoke something no other had ever touched was both a marvel and a trial.

They were both breathing too fast; he could hear the dull thunder of his pulse in his ears.

She blinked, and confusion and uncertainty swam into her sea-green eyes.

He drew in a breath, and forced his hands from her shoulders. Held her gaze. "This is neither the time, nor the place."

His voice was deep, gravelly, but she made out his words.

She nodded, drew a huge breath, then realized and glanced down, and quickly did up her bodice. She glanced at him again; she tried for cool censure, but her gaze was still hot. She must have realized; she blinked, then, straightening, she inclined her head and without a word turned and walked on toward the house.

He watched her go. With every step she took, he found it harder not to smile; eventually he gave in and did.

She hadn't said anything, because what could she say?

She went into the house. Turning, he headed back to the stable, still smiling, inwardly imagining all her possible ripostes, which only made him smile all the more.

In the darkest hour of the night, Helen, Lady Hardesty, her senses still reeling, her breathing yet to slow, pushed up from the low gardener's bench over which her lover had bent her.

Squinting in the poor light, she brushed her fingers over the pearly skin of her ample breasts, nipples still erect, a darker pink after he'd rolled and squeezed them. Drawing the gaping halves of her evening gown closed, she quickly refastened them. Reaching behind her, she tugged loose the back of her skirts and petticoats from where he'd tucked them above her waist, and shook them down.

She could hear him behind her, cloaked in darkness, righting his clothing. Whenever they met in restricted locations—in this case a rarely used gardener's shed concealed in the thick trees that grew along the riverbank—while he insisted on baring her breasts as well as her legs and bottom, he invariably did no more than open the flap of his trousers to service her.

However, as he did that exceedingly thoroughly, and equally invariably, she wasn't about to complain. Lovers like him did not grow on trees, a fact to which from long experience she could attest.

He drew nearer; she felt him at her back. One long-fingered hand circled her throat, gently stroking, then his lips brushed her temple.

"Meet me here tomorrow night." His voice was deep, dark, edged with that hint of danger that tempted so many ladies to spread their legs for him. She knew she wasn't his only lover, just, at present, the most convenient.

Of course, he wasn't her only lover either, just the most exciting.

She stifled a sigh. "I can't see why you won't join the party. My suite is at the end of the west wing—you could share my bed. I assure you Robert won't be a problem."

Glancing up and back, she saw his lips curve.

"You have to admit he was an excellent choice."

"Indeed." Then, knowing what hint was buried in the words, she added, "I'll always be grateful to you for pointing him out."

"And telling you how to land him."

She nodded. He'd been inspired in that, too. An impoverished gentlewoman, at twenty-eight finding herself the still-youthful relict of an impecunious lord who had gambled away her portion as well as his estates, she'd had little choice but to look for a wealthy protector.

And she'd found one. But in him she'd found a gentleman with a deep comprehension of their world. He'd understood her need for security and position, and had shown her how, in the person of young Robert Hardesty, she might achieve her goals.

For one of her talents, further tutored by him, seducing Robert Hardesty had been child's play, roping him into marriage even easier. The boy doted on her.

As the gentleman who stood behind her could have informed Robert, that was not the way to win her devotion.

Behind her his hand drifted down, passing over her hip to stroke one globe of her silk-clad bottom, idly fondling. Her gaze on the dingy window before her, she caught her lower lip between her teeth; he never did anything idly.

"There are too many guests at Helston Grange."

"You asked me to invite them." He valued his privacy, yet still . . . "You know them all—you chose them."

"Indeed. They're the excuse for me to join you socially, if and when I choose. What more natural than that, while paying a duty visit to an aging relative in the neighborhood, I should join your party for a day or an evening?" He paused, then continued, "No. The arrangements are perfect as they are."

His arrangements. She didn't even know where he was staying, couldn't even guess whether there truly was an aging relative or not.

"If only the rest were going as well."

She frowned. "What do you mean?"

"The ship I'm waiting for. It hasn't come in."

His fingers continued to play, palpating her firm flesh; although his touch had grown harder, edged with suppressed anger, it was his tone, flat, cold, that set her nerves skittering.

"I expected it two or three nights ago, but it hasn't been sighted."

His accents had grown more clipped, quite different to the drawl he usually affected.

He had a temper. She'd only seen glimpses, fleeting at most, yet she knew it was there, formidable and frightening. He was ruthless, entirely devoid of softer feelings, and sometimes his intensity, his *obsession* with his plans, with having them succeed, made her more than uneasy.

She swallowed, kept her gaze on the darkness beyond the window. "Perhaps I could ask around, see if anyone has heard anything?"

He was silent, considering, then replied, "Not yet. But I want what that ship is carrying of mine."

His thirty pieces of silver. His payment—his ultimate reward, also his ultimate triumph. His ultimate revenge.

He wanted it, thirsted for it, could almost taste it. So close, but it wasn't his—in his hands, his to gloat over—yet.

"I want that cargo." He glanced down at her perfect

profile, flexed his fingers more powerfully. "But I don't want to risk any undue attention. Not yet."

The fact that although he'd won the war—his private war waged against a powerful enemy who knew him not, and not for want of trying—that although he'd triumphed, he still had to skulk, plot and scheme to lay his hands on what was rightfully his because, despite all, he was still too fearful to face that enemy, and knew he never could, irked him to his soul.

Face setting, he gripped hard, heard her breath catch, strangle. "Do you understand?"

She nodded. Her "Yes" was breathless.

He held her there, poised between pleasure and pain, let the moment stretch. He could all but hear her pulse thundering, could easily sense her spiraling arousal.

Then he smiled into the dark, eased his grip, and patted her abused flesh. "Meet me here tomorrow night, and then . . . we'll see."

Chapter 7

$\mathcal{T}$he following afternoon, Gervase strode into the front hall of Treleaver Park. He nodded to Milsom, who appeared to greet him. "Miss Gascoigne?"

"In the office, my lord. Shall I announce you?"

"No need. I know the way." With a nod, he headed down the corridor toward the estate office. As he walked, he polished the elements of his plan.

He knew better than to expect Madeline to invite him to further seduce her, *especially* not after that interlude in the arbor. With any conventional lady, their transparent compatibility would have resulted in encouragement, but Madeline would react by strengthening her defenses, rather than lowering her drawbridge.

Yet she was weakening, and now he had her measure. Her curiosity was a tangible force, powerful enough to override her reticence; once engaged, it became a potent weapon, all the more effective because it worked from within.

Her independence—her very unconventionality—was the other ace in his hand. Once she was compelled by her curiosity to experience something new, her independence ensured that considerations of "what was proper" or "how things were done" held little power to deflect her.

Her curiosity and her independence combined had led to that encounter in the arbor; now was the time to press her further, to storm the breach in her defenses.

The office door stood open; he paused in the doorway, lips curving as he took in the sight of her, seated behind the desk, head bent, open ledgers spread before her. Sunlight slanted through the windows behind her, lighting the corona of her hair, as always escaping its restraints to form a gilded fretwork about her face.

He was naturally soft-footed; she hadn't heard his approach. What he could see of her expression said she was absorbed in her accounts. Swiftly rejigging his plan, he stepped into the room and shut the door.

She looked up, blinked, then rose. Behind his back, he turned the key; the click of the bolt fell into the silence.

He smiled, and started toward her.

Eyes widening, she put down her pen. "Ah . . . Gervase. Is there something . . . ."

She turned to face him as he rounded the desk, eyes widening even more when he didn't slow. With his knee, he nudged her chair aside, and finally halted, effectively trapping her between him and the desk.

"What . . .?" She swayed back, then straightened, stiffened, the instinct to lean away from him countered by her will.

He met her eyes, endeavored to keep his expression mild. "You told me that if I had any further questions, you'd happily answer them." He'd let his gaze slide to her lips. Leaning closer, he brushed them with his. Not a kiss—a tantalizing touch.

Enough to distract her, but when he drew back an inch,

she shook off the effect. Frowned. "About the festival—questions about the *festival*."

"Oh." He infused the word with boyish disappointment. "I'd hoped . . ." Again he touched his lips to hers, for longer this time, until he sensed her instinctive response; one hand rising, fingers lightly cradling her cheek, one side of her jaw, he held her—barely—and sent his lips cruising, tracing her jaw, feathering up over her cheekbone, over her ear, dipping down until he breathed in the scent of her, and closing his eyes breathed softly out, lips hovering above the sensitive hollow below her ear.

His other hand had risen to lightly grip her waist; he felt her reaction, the swift indrawn breath, the quiver of fascinated expectation.

Of curiosity awakening, stretching.

Inwardly smiling, he murmured, "I'd hoped . . ."—he drew back just enough to meet her eyes—"to learn the answer to a question that's been plaguing me since last we parted."

Her eyes, peridot-bright, searched his; her lips, lush and ripe, were parted—she moistened them before whispering, "What . . .?"

Feeling his hands move between them, Madeline glanced down. Her lungs seized, her head spun as she watched his quick fingers unfasten the tiny buttons closing the bodice of her day gown.

They stood in her office with the afternoon sun streaming over them and he was baring her breasts, and intended God knew what. She should stop him—could stop him.

But she made no move to.

Unable to take her eyes off his fingers, off the swell of her breasts he was so rapidly exposing, she swallowed. "What was your question?"

"I need to know, I'm burning to know . . ." Her bodice open, her breasts laid bare, he cupped one swelling mound.

Ran his thumb gently, tantalizingly, over the peak. Watched it harden.

Her gaze rose to his face; she couldn't breathe. His features had never looked harder, more rigid. More clearly etched with passion reined.

"What these taste like."

The intent words penetrated her mind only slowly; when they finally impinged, she blinked, went to look down, but he looked up at that moment and kissed her.

Not as he had in the past, so that her wits evaporated and her ability to think dissolved, but lightly, soothingly, enticingly.

Entreatingly, in patent supplication.

So that even while his lips supped at hers, she could feel his hand at her breast, could fully appreciate each evocative caress, feel each touch sink to her bones.

"Will you let me learn the answer?"

His words drifted over her lips, through her brain. There wasn't any answer she could make—other than to let him take what he wished. To, when his lips feathered over her jaw and his head dipped, close her eyes and let it happen. His lips traced down the column of her throat, and she shivered. He paused as if to note it—all the answer, all the permission he needed. Then his head lowered.

Eyes tightly closed, she gasped; with one hand at her waist, he bent her back. Then his lips pressed hotly to the upper swell of her breast and she shuddered. Lost all touch with the world as with lips, tongue and teeth, with the hot wetness of his mouth, he tasted and learned.

And taught her. The sensations he evoked, that he sent whirling through her, that speared her, that wracked her, were more, far more intense than she'd imagined they might be. With his mouth on her breasts, he waltzed her into a new landscape of heat, hovering passion, and a deeper, sharper, more powerful yearning.

Not good, she knew, but oh so addictive. Her senses unfurled; parched, denied for so long, they gloried and wallowed in the bounty of delight he pressed on her.

He gripped, lifted her, then she was on the desk, lying back amid her ledgers and accounts, her knees and thighs spread with his hips between. And he was leaning over her; one of her hands had risen to his head, holding him to her as he devoured.

As he unhurriedly pursued the answer to his question, and flooded her mind with pleasure.

Pleasure that swelled, grew, built, until she was squirming, arching lightly as the heat rose, as passion took hold, and that nameless yearning grew ever more insistent.

He paused; she felt his breath, as ragged and shallow as hers, wash over her swollen flesh, over her sensitized skin. Then his hand closed over her breast, his touch harder, more driven; his head rose and he found her lips—and whirled her into a more heated kiss.

This she knew, this she recognized; she opened her senses and embraced the moment—gathered to her all the sensations he offered—and felt her world quake.

He growled something through the increasingly ravenous kiss, then his hand left her breast, but to her relief not her body, moving lower, possessively claiming midriff and waist, hip and belly and upper thigh. He gripped briefly, then released the taut muscle and moved his hand to the juncture of her thighs.

He touched her through the thin material of her gown, sliding the silk of her chemise against her most sensitive flesh. She shuddered, held him more tightly to the kiss, tempted and challenged with her tongue—sensually reeled when he responded with a devastating invasion that left her trapped, caught, driven to some indefinable peak.

Then she realized it was his fingers, cleverly, expertly caressing between her thighs that were making her feel so.

Making her feel as if her world—the one he'd swept her into—was about to end.

To erupt, to shatter.

Then it did.

Gervase knew the instant her climax overcame her, so powerful, so dramatic that *his* head reeled. Drawing back from their kiss, he watched her—watched passion tighten her features, peak, then fracture, to be erased by a sweeping wave of satiation.

He continued to drink in the sight of her, of the lovely lines of her face as they eased—inwardly victorious at being the first to evoke that particular expression.

Inwardly affirmed that he would also be the only.

He hadn't intended this interlude—this latest step in his campaign—to progress quite so far, yet he was in no way sorry that it had. Her curiosity, her willingness, were the defining aspects; he'd had to adjust his pace to suit.

Which, thank Heaven, meant he was closer to success—and therefore to relief—than he'd been an hour ago.

Her lashes fluttered, then rose. For a long moment, she simply stared, dazed, into his eyes. He hid a self-satisfied smile, but couldn't stop his gaze from lowering, lingering first on her lips—swollen from their passionate kisses—then lowering still further over the expanse of creamy, now pinked skin to her bare breasts, full and bearing the telltale marks of his possession.

It took effort not to allow what he felt at the sight to show in his face. With a sigh he let her hear, he moved back, straightened; taking her hands, he drew her up, until she slid from the desk to her feet.

They both looked at the desk, at the ledgers and papers now scattered in disarray across its surface.

Raising one hand, cupping her nape, his thumb beneath her jaw, he drew her face to his. Met her eyes for a finite moment, then bent and kissed her—long, slow, deeply but with passion well banked, restrained.

Lifting his head, he released her, then brushed his thumb over her glistening lower lip. "We'll meet again tomorrow evening. For now, I'd better leave you to your buisness."

She stared at him, but he only smiled, then turned and crossed to the door. He felt the distracted confusion in her gaze as, transparently struck dumb, she watched him leave.

As he closed the door, his smile took on a grim edge.

Riding when aroused wasn't his idea of pleasure, but with any luck at all, the end of his campaign was nigh.

She wasn't a wanton.

Late that night, when all the rest of the household were long abed, Madeline sat before her dressing table, restlessly, idly, brushing her hair.

Unbidden, her gaze lowered to her breasts, decorously concealed beneath her fine linen nightgown. She'd never thought much of them before, but he'd seemed fascinated . . . he'd certainly been thorough in his studies . . .

She blinked, sucked in a breath—stared at the evidence that just thought, just the memory of what she'd experienced that afternoon courtesy of his expertise was enough to stir her. Again. To make her breasts swell, her nipples pucker.

As for the rest of her . . . .

She pressed her thighs together, and determinedly refocused on the mirror. She might not be a wanton, but when in his arms, she became abandoned, lost to all good sense.

A creature of her senses.

She'd never been that before.

She didn't know what that side of her was like, and didn't know where learning more of it might lead her. But now she knew that part of her existed—an undeniably female, womanly side of her nature that she'd never explored . . . she couldn't imagine not learning more.

Knew in her heart, and in her head, too, that she wouldn't be satisfied until she'd learned more.

Much as falling in with Gervase's stated aim went against her grain, she had no doubt whatever that warming his bed would answer her every question.

"Much as I would prefer not to pander to his arrogance"— she fixed her gaze on her reflection and spoke to it—"who else is there with whom I might learn?"

A telling point. Quite aside from the fact that in her nearly twenty-nine years he was the only male to stir her in that way—to evoke the sensual female inside her—he was also the only man she could imagine trusting enough to venture further. Quite why she trusted him so implicitly she wasn't entirely sure, but that trust went bone-deep, beyond thought or question.

Her brush strokes slowed, halted. She stared into her eyes, then narrowed them. "I've never been missish in my life."

Setting down the brush, she rose. She looked at her reflection, at the long length of her, the rippling mass of her hair, the lush curves of breasts and hips imperfectly concealed beneath the thin nightgown.

She studied the vision, then raised her chin. "Very well, my lord. Tomorrow evening it is."

Bending forward, she blew out her candle, then retreated to her bed.

They'd known they would meet at Caterham House. Madeline arrived first. Garbed in a gown of chartreuse silk, she prowled the drawing room, impatient and restless. Having made up her mind, she wanted to get on. Lady Caterham's party was an annual event, no dancing but with every local family of note summoned to fill her ladyship's drawing room, overflowing onto the terrace, with conversation on every side and supper to look forward to later.

While accustomed to attending such entertainments and chatting with her neighbors with good grace, tonight Madeline felt too keyed up to relax into her usual routine; tonight, discussing tin mining held no allure.

Luckily, with such a crowd, no one was likely to notice such aberrant behavior.

"Miss Gascoigne—we meet again."

Madeline whirled and discovered Mr. Courtland bowing before her. She gave him her hand, suffered him to press her fingers a trifle more meaningfully than she considered appropriate. "Good evening, sir. I take it Lady Hardesty's company is gracing Caterham House tonight?"

Courtland blinked; unsure if there was a barb in the comment, he replied rather carefully, "Lady Caterham was kind enough to invite Lady Hardesty and extended the invitation to her guests."

"Lady Caterham always invites everyone who is anyone around about, and naturally she includes any guests they have staying." Of course. "However, my comment was occasioned by surprise that the invitation was accepted. This"— with a wave Madeline indicated the crowded room—"can hardly compare with London events."

More certain now that she was censoriously inclined, Courtland paused, then said, "We found ourselves growing rather dull, so . . ." He shrugged.

So they'd come to see what excitement they could stir up among the locals. Madeline inwardly sniffed, then remembered Lady Hardesty, and her view of Madeline herself, one of said locals.

Sheer devilment prompted her to smile on Mr. Courtland, making him blink. "Perhaps we might join her ladyship? I haven't had much chance to speak with her."

Although still wary, Courtland readily offered his arm. She took it and let him guide her through the throng to where Lady Hardesty was holding court in one corner of the room.

She was, Madeline inwardly admitted, a handsome woman, her sleek dark hair piled in artful curls on her head, her gown of blue satin in the very latest style. She was about Madeline's age, perhaps a year or so older, yet when Madeline joined their circle and Lady Hardesty smiled in polite welcome, Madeline saw that her face was a trifle hard, as if despite the creams and potions doubtless employed to keep her skin supple, despite the fine sapphires about her throat, life had treated her harshly.

But she greeted Madeline sincerely, and reacquainted her with the rest of the circle; all were Londoners, all Lady Hardesty's guests. Robert Hardesty was nowhere to be seen.

At the end of the greetings, Lady Hardesty bent a rueful look on Madeline. "I confess I'm grateful to you, Miss Gascoigne, for breaking the ice, as it were." She gave a little laugh. "I'm starting to think I'll have to live here for years before the locals thaw toward me."

Madeline refrained from suggesting that surrounding herself with her London friends was hardly conducive to encouraging locals to approach her. "Not so long. They'll come around." She met Lady Hardesty's eyes. "Once they take your measure." She paused, holding her ladyship's blue gaze, then added, "And once you've taken ours."

Correctly hung in the air.

Lady Hardesty blinked, then Mr. Courtland made a comment and Madeline turned to listen—and was immediately distracted by the sight of a curly dark head across the room. Tall enough to see over the crowd, she saw Gervase spot her and start the long process of winning through to her side.

Chatting politely, she waited. Very aware of his approach,

she knew when he realized who she was with—and hesitated. She nearly looked his way, but he'd tacked to come up beside her and she didn't want to appear so conscious of his presence. So on tenterhooks, so eager.

But then he was there, taking her hand, smoothly insinuating himself beside her, greeting the others with a chilly, aloof civility so unlike his customary ease that she nearly turned to stare at him.

"I'm so glad you joined us, my lord." Her welcoming smile far brighter than it had been for Madeline, Lady Hardesty spoke across her. "As I was saying to Miss Gascoigne, I'm eager to get to know those who live in the area a *great* deal better."

"Indeed?" Gervase read the open invitation in Lady Hardesty's eyes, and felt nothing but irritation. Why in such a crowded room had Madeline paused there?

"I understand you live in a real castle, my lord." Miss Bildwell leaned across the circle, all but batting her lashes. "It must be *utterly* romantic."

"Many suppose so but the reality is regrettably mundane." His tone was designed to depress all inclination to ask to visit said castle, and more, to make it plain he'd joined their circle for one reason only; he turned to Madeline. "My dear, Sybil wishes to speak with you, if you can spare her a moment."

Madeline blinked at him, but what she saw in his eyes must have made his underlying temper clear. "Of course." Allowing him to tuck her hand—which he hadn't relinquished—into the crook of his arm, she turned to Lady Hardesty and inclined her head gracefully. "If you'll excuse us?"

To Gervase's surprise, Lady Hardesty stared at Madeline as if she'd only just noticed her—all close to six feet of delectable curves sheathed in jewel-hued silk. How anyone could overlook his Valkyrie he had no idea, but after that stunned minute, Lady Hardesty managed a smile and nodded, sufficiently graciously, in return.

With a general glance at the others, the barest minimum to be polite, he drew Madeline away.

As he steered her diagonally across the room, she glanced at him. "I assume Sybil has no idea she wishes to speak with me?"

"None whatever." Over the sea of heads, he surveyed the room. "I simply saw no reason to waste my time or yours in that company."

Entirely in accord, Madeline smiled and looked ahead. "Where are you taking me?"

He glanced at her, slowed. "Where would you like to go?"

She met his eyes, then succinctly replied, "Somewhere private."

He studied her eyes, confirming she was serious, then looked ahead. "An excellent notion."

The note of intent rippling through his deep voice sent a quiver of anticipation sliding through her.

"The terrace, I think."

"There's lots of others out there."

"Not where I'm thinking of."

Convinced he'd be proved wrong, with an inward sigh she acquiesced and let him guide her toward the open doors giving onto the long terrace.

Their progress was interrupted, numerous acquaintances hailing them to exchange greetings and the latest local gossip. It took half an hour to gain the terrace flags, and another fifteen minutes before they won free of the knot of guests congregated just outside the doors, enjoying the balmy night.

At last Gervase drew her away; tucking her hand in his arm again, he strolled down the terrace away from the drawing room. The terrace ran the length of one side of the house; while she'd attended any number of Lady Caterham's events, Madeline had never walked to the far end—let alone around it.

When, after one swift glance back, Gervase whisked her around the corner, she halted in surprise. The terrace appeared to terminate in a curve at the end of its long length, but in reality the curve extended around the corner to form a landing above another set of steps leading down.

They now stood on the landing out of sight of those gathered near the drawing room, and were also screened from those guests who'd ventured down onto the lawns.

She smiled. "Perfect."

Turning to Gervase, she walked into his arms.

They were waiting, very ready to receive her, just as his lips were waiting to meet hers. Surrendering her mouth, she stepped into him, into the kiss, and was instantly swept into the now-familiar landscape, increasingly turbulent, fraught with suppressed hunger, with simmering passion barely restrained. She gave herself up to it, to the heat, to the moment, to what would come.

To what she wanted.

Like a searing wind, desire rose and took her. Caught her, engulfed her, overwhelmed her. Tossed on a sea of uncomprehending need, she gave in to the urgency, speared her hands through his hair, clung to him and kissed him back.

With all the fire she suddenly discovered she had in her.

Gervase mentally staggered under the onslaught, abruptly finding himself awash in a sea of heat, of flames that licked greedily over his body—following her hands.

He inwardly cursed; he wanted to catch them, end the torture before it had begun—but that would mean releasing her, dragging his arms from about her, his hands from her lush curves, from the avid, heated exploration that had suddenly, unexpectedly, turned mutual.

He couldn't do it.

Couldn't not respond to her flagrant invitation. To the blatant enticement she pressed upon him, with her lips, her tongue, with her fabulous body. She shifted, pressed into him, and his control—what was left of it—quaked.

He'd expected to have to persuade, to exert his talents to convince her, that she would still be wary, hesitant at best, that he'd have to cajole . . . instead, he was left reeling in her wake.

He hadn't expected her to surrender so easily, to give way . . . but as her tongue boldly tangled with his, as he felt her hands beneath his coat spread over his chest, he realized that wasn't the case. She hadn't given in—she'd changed her mind. She wasn't going along with his tack—she was pursuing her own.

She'd decided she wanted him.

Something akin to the angel's chorus rang triumphantly in his head. But he had no time to savor the triumph, not yet.

Because having decided what she wanted, she was intent on getting it.

Which would normally pose no problem whatsoever, except . . .

Thoughts whirled in his head, fragmented, disjointed, but clear enough for him to see the danger. She wasn't destined to be—hadn't been created to be—a woman lightly taken.

Unfortunately, as her present actions were most effectively demonstrating, she didn't know that. Every wanton movement only underscored her direction; she was hell-bent on having him take her.

Trying to battle his reaction to that realization as well as battle her was all but impossible.

He broke the kiss, dragged in a desperate breath—only to hear her hum in her throat, a purring, determined warning, then she bore him back until his shoulders hit the wall.

She was on him, using her weight to pin him; he could easily have thrown her off, resisted her, if he'd been able to summon the slightest will. Instead, he merely gasped, then inwardly groaned as she framed his face and kissed him.

Wild, unrestrained—as abandoned as he'd known she would be.

And she called to him. He could feel the rising beat in his blood; he was already hard, and that insistent beat was only going to grow more compulsive, more difficult to deny. Especially in the face of her urging, her clear and effectively communicated desire.

It took an exercise of will he hadn't known he possessed to force his hands from her, to seek and catch hers—and then abruptly, before she could think to demur, shift and turn, so he was pinning her.

Her kiss only grew more hungry; he had to pull back and lift his head before she, the sultry siren he hadn't until then fully appreciated she had in her, caught him again and pulled him under.

For a long moment, he stood gasping, panting, waiting for his head to stop spinning. He had her plastered to the wall, pressed to it, her hands anchored to the bricks on either side of her head. Her lips, her eyes, were only inches from his; she licked the former, slowly, then opened the latter and looked into his.

"Why . . . Oh." Her eyes searched his. "I suppose I should tell you. I've changed my mind."

If he hadn't been aching so badly, he would have made some clever quip; instead, he merely growled, "So I gathered."

She tilted her head. "So why have you stopped?"

"Because we can't go further—not here, not now."

She looked puzzled. "There are quite a few rooms in this house. I'm sure we could find one suitable for our purpose."

Lips setting grimly, he shook his head.

Her eyes narrowed. "Why?"

There was an edge to her tone that told him he better have an excellent answer. Luckily, he did. Leaning into her again, letting her feel his weight, he took her lips—gently, oh-so-tantalizingly, the contact not enough to satisfy either of them.

Ending the torture, he opened his eyes, waited for her lids to rise, caught her gaze. "Because I want you naked beneath me, and I want time—in the order of several hours—to savor your conquest."

Her eyes started to narrow again. Her lips parted—on a protest, he had not a doubt. Swallowing a groan, he covered them, pressed them wide and laid claim to her mouth; he wasn't up to defending something he knew had to be, not when every muscle in his body was in open revolt against his self-imposed edict.

Madeline boldly met his heat, his fire, with her own; she had no real argument with his vision, only his timing. They could take hours . . . next time. This time . . .

She'd come to Caterham House determined to learn all—at least the basics—of what she wanted to know, and she wasn't about to retreat without in some measure, to some degree, succeeding.

So she pushed against him, tried to lean into him and wriggle a hand free; that accomplished nothing—his grip was unbreakable—but sensing his reaction to the pressure of her body, she shifted against him, sinuously weaving a fraction side to side, rubbing her silk bodice against his coat. Twisting at the waist, she managed to slide her hip into and across the solid length of his erection.

He groaned into her mouth. Pulled back enough to growl, "Do you have *any* idea . . .?" then abruptly sealed her lips again.

Of course she didn't; that was what she was there to learn.

Before she could do anything further, he dragged her hands up, over her head, then changed his grip so he could trap both her hands in one of his.

His free hand lowered to her breast, covered it, squeezed. She gasped, and pressed the firm mound into his palm. He obliged and kneaded, then through the silk sought and found her nipple, circled it, then rolled the distended tip between finger and thumb.

Delicious shards of sensation streaked through her, sliding like fire through her veins to pool low in her belly. He continued ministering to her breasts until the heat flared into outright fire, the conflagration swelling, growing—until she rocked her hips against him.

He hesitated, still sunk in her mouth, his tongue sliding slowly along hers, then he released her breast, slid his hand down her ribs to her waist, then lower, over the curve of her hip to skim down her thigh as far as he could reach, then he caught her skirt, gathered the fine material until he could slide his hand beneath and touch her bare skin.

She gasped, quivered.

Gervase reached higher, palm and fingers tracing up her thigh, above her garter where the silken skin was hot to his touch. Despite his experience, he hadn't expected such tactile delight; she rode daily—her thighs were firm, resilient, promising a wild ride of a different sort, the satiny texture of her skin made only more fascinating by the feminine strength beneath.

The feel of that skin beneath his hand, his to caress at will, subtly seduced, weakened his resolve, had instinct overriding intellect. He wasn't thinking when his hand drifted higher, lost touch with rational thought when his fingers found the crisp curls at the apex of her thighs.

He brushed, caressed, slid his fingertips past, seeking the soft flesh those curls concealed.

Found it.

He stroked, caressed, urged on by her flaring response, by the fiery need that gripped her, that she sent pouring through him as she kissed him voraciously, urgent, hungry and greedy.

Impatient. That last was very clear as she shifted siren-like against him, evocatively pressing against his hand. The scalding slickness he'd drawn forth was hot enough, shocking enough, to shake some fraction of his wits into place, enough for him to read her desire clearly.

His lips still on hers, his fingers artfully circling, stroking, promising yet not delivering, he forced himself to focus, to consider as well as he could.

He might have drawn a line, knew vaguely that he had, and where it was, but he couldn't think of any reason to deny her this—the satiation of her immediate need. She was growing desperate; he responded, pressed his fingers further into the slick haven, into her. With one finger he breached her entrance, then pushed steadily deeper, penetrated her to his full reach—even muffled by their lips, he heard her evocative gasp, felt the bite of her nails as her fingers curled and gripped his restraining hand tightly, felt her body arch, bowing against his.

He held still for an instant, letting her feel, grow accustomed to the sensation of his finger within her.

Then he stroked. Deliberately, deeply, repetitively.

Although she tried valiantly, she never caught her breath; in less than a minute she shuddered, and shattered, fractured.

He released her from their kiss. Breathing raggedly, eyes closed, she sagged back against the wall. He watched her face while, his finger buried in her tight sheath, he savored the rhythmic contractions, tracked her release; courtesy of the diffuse moonlight her features were visible, but any expression in her eyes would be impossible to discern.

For the moment, her eyes remained closed; he knew he had to act, to withdraw his hand from between her thighs, to flick her skirts down, before she regained sufficient self-possession to press him further.

But . . .

Ironically, the very fact that he had to fight, had to battle his baser instincts, to not just withdraw his hand but let her skirt fall and ease back from her until there was air between them—rather than comply with the primitive imperatives of the beast within, roaring and raring to push her skirts higher, lift her and have her—shocked him to full awareness.

Since when had he ever been driven by desire?

Being subject to desire, being ruled by it, was a weakness, one to which he'd never succumbed. Cool rationality had always been his watchword, even in—especially in—all sexual affairs. Yet never in his considerable experience had desire, sexual need—the beast within she seemed to directly connect with—wielded such excruciating spurs; never had he had to battle the impulse to simply let the reins fall and take. To ravish and devour.

The realization of how close he'd come to that, still stood in danger of that, shook him to the core.

She opened her eyes, and looked straight at him.

He eased his grip on her hands, then let them go, but as she lowered her arms, he couldn't resist twining the fingers of one hand with one of hers, retaining possession that far.

Even in the poor light, he saw the frown that formed, marring the pure arch of her brows. She moistened her lips, and with remarkable imperiousness demanded, "Well?"

Holding her gaze, sensing the smoldering heat that still remained behind the word, sensing how strongly it drew him, he forced himself to raise his brows back. "Well what?"

If he didn't cling to cool superiority, she would have him yet.

Madeline frowned harder. "Aren't you going to . . .?" With her free hand she gestured weakly between them. She was operating on instinct, had been all along, yet while her experience in this field was all but nonexistent, she knew he'd retreated from—reneged on—the main event.

Given her determination to know, and know tonight, she was less than thrilled.

He shifted back, increasing the space between them. His brows remained high, his expression otherwise impassive. "I told you—not now, not here. If you want to know more, to experience more, then I have a price, one you need to be willing to pay."

Detecting, clearly, the challenge in his tone, she narrowed her eyes. "I thought your stated aim was to seduce me."

His lips curved tightly. "It is."

"Well then, what's wrong with here and now? Surely that qualifies, given I'm clearly willing?"

He studied her for a long moment, then shook his head. "No—not with you. With you, seduction equates to two hours and more of dedicated engagement in a venue conducive to the task."

Her eyes couldn't get any narrower. For one brief instant she considered throwing herself at him, literally, but he continued to hold one of her hands; through his grip she could sense his resistance, the tension, the determination to deny her any further engagement, and he was undeniably stronger and more experienced than she. Losing a wrestling match with him wouldn't improve her temper.

She lifted her chin. "Where?" Her tone was as cool, as definite, as his. "And when?"

He didn't smile; she saw not a single sign of gloating. "Tomorrow afternoon at two o'clock. I'll wait for you where the ride along the cliffs meets the path down to Castle Cove."

She thought, then nodded. "Very well." Pushing away

from the wall, relieved to discover her limbs once more hers to command, she retrieved her hand, then turned and walked to the corner.

He followed, keeping pace alongside.

As she rounded the corner, she haughtily confirmed, "Tomorrow on the cliffs above Castle Cove."

She'd intended to have the last word.

Instead, as they strolled toward the clutch of guests outside the drawing room, he murmured, his voice low, deep, steeped in sinful promise, "I'll be waiting."

Battling the sensual shiver his tone let alone his words evoked, she accepted defeat, and kept her lips shut.

Chapter 8

At two o'clock the next day, Gervase sat on a flat rock at the top of the path that led down to Castle Cove. He held Crusader's reins loosely in one fist while the big gray cropped the short grass nearby.

He stared out at the sea, at the long waves rolling in to gently wash the sands, their roar today muted to a soft *swoosh*, and tried hard not to think—not of the anticipation that knotted his gut, nor of the unexpected fear that, once away from him and with time to think, she would have changed her mind.

The sound of hoofbeats, regular and repetitive, reached him; even as he turned to see who approached, he was reminding himself how many people rode the cliff path on any day.

But it was her. Her hair, uncovered, marked her unmistakably as female; the fact she was astride a large and powerful chestnut confirmed her identity.

Nearing, she slowed, reining in to a walk. He rose.

When she halted, he was waiting to grasp the bit and hold the chestnut steady as she slid down from the high back.

She came around the horse's head. She was wearing a long full riding skirt over trousers, a matching jacket over a crisp linen blouse; it being high summer, jacket, skirt and trousers were of lightweight twill, dyed a regal blue. As usual, tendrils of her fine coppery-brown hair had worked loose to frame her face.

His eyes traced her features. "I wasn't sure you'd come." The confession was on his lips before he'd thought.

She raised her brows. "I asked for this . . . appointment." She studied him in return. "Did you think I'd balk?"

"I thought you might think again." Drawing Crusader around to flank her chestnut, he waved down the path, and started walking.

She gave a soft snort, and kept pace alongside. "Well, here I am. Where are we going?"

He didn't meet her gaze but pointed ahead, down the steep path.

Madeline looked, and only then remembered the castle's boathouse. It was almost as old as the castle itself, built of the same rough-hewn stone and set on a ledge, a natural rock platform that extended out from the cliff just above the high-tide line. Unlike most boathouses, this one had two stories. The ground floor had double doors like barn doors facing the sea, with heavy beams and tackle jutting out above to lift and swing boats out over the water, then lower them. The upper level sported a balcony built above the beams from which the tackle hung. There was no outer stair leading up, but unlike the windowless ground floor, the upper story possessed many wood-framed windows opening to the balcony and to either side. The back of the boathouse faced the cliff.

It wasn't far; they stepped off the path onto the ledge, and tied the horses up in the sheltered space between the building and the cliff. As she turned from securing Artur's reins, Gervase grasped her hand and led her to a door in the side wall. It was locked, but he had the key on his chain; setting the door swinging wide, he led her through, then closed the door.

The ground floor was dim and deeply shadowed; with all doors shut, the only light came from above via the stairwell. Madeline glanced around, noting four different-sized boats housed on blocks, with various pulleys and ropes dangling from above. Nearest to the sea doors sat two rowing boats.

Gervase saw her studying them. "When I took your brothers out, we used the sailboat—the one with the blue hull."

She glanced at one of the bigger boats; it carried a mast, currently lowered, and sails.

Gervase tugged her hand and headed for the stairs. "Up here." He glanced briefly at her, then started up. "This room's always been a retreat of sorts. My father had it refurbished for my mother—it was hers, her place, for years."

Ascending the stairs behind him, Madeline stepped up onto well-polished boards and looked around with no little surprise. The room wasn't what she'd expected. The stairs came up in one rear corner; slipping her fingers free of Gervase's, she walked slowly up the room, drawn to the wide windows facing the sea.

As if sensing her unvoiced question, he continued, "My mother was an artist—a watercolorist. She loved painting the sea."

There were expensive jewel-toned rugs on the floor, and the furniture, while not ornate, was of excellent quality, all dark wood chosen to complement the setting. There were chairs, both comfortable armchairs and straightbacked chairs with thick cushions, and a sideboard against one wall with three books haphazardly stacked upon it as if someone had brought them to the retreat to read. In one corner by the seaward windows a folded wooden easel draped in a paint-spotted cloth stood propped against the wall. Yet all that was incidental. Dominating the room, its central focus, set in pride of place with its foot angled to the balcony windows, stood a wide daybed with a thick mattress and many cushions. On a side table stood a bowl of fruit and a stoppered decanter filled with honey-colored wine.

The place was clean and smelled fresh; not a speck of dust lay on the lovingly polished wooden surfaces.

Reaching the windows, Madeline looked out over the waves, then turned and surveyed the room. It was easy to see why an artist would have loved this place; the light was both strong and dramatic, varying with the many moods of the sea.

She let her gaze return to Gervase, let it travel up his length from his boots to his face; he'd paused by the side of the daybed. "Your father must have understood your mother well."

"He adored her." His eyes on hers, he continued, "I was fourteen when she died, so I remember them well, seeing them together, especially here . . . my father loved Sybil, too, but it wasn't the same. My mother was his sun, moon and stars, and she loved him in the same way."

She studied him. When he held out one hand and beckoned, she hesitated, then slowly walked back to join him. "It must be . . . reassuring to have such memories."

He took her hand as she neared. "You can't remember your mother?"

She shook her head. "She died when I was three. I've a vague recollection of her, but none of my father and her together." As he drew her to him, she glanced around one last time. "So . . ." The breathlessness that had hovered, threatening to afflict her since she'd joined him on the cliffs, closed in. "Whose place is this now?"

His arms closed around her; she met his eyes. His lips curved. "Mine." He drew her against him and lowered his head. "No one comes here but me."

And now her. Even as his lips brushed hers, then confidently covered them, Madeline noted that—that he'd chosen here, his special place, one in which his parents' love still lingered, at least for him, as the scene for her seduction.

It was her last coherent thought before the pressure of his lips, the impact of his nearness—of his arms holding her, his hands controlling her, his lips and tongue tempting her—suborned her wits. Lured them, caught them, trapped them in a web of sensation, of kisses that promised, of caresses that hinted, gently yet definitely, of what was to come.

Oddly, she felt no trepidation; contrary to what he'd imagined, she'd had no second thoughts. She'd slept well last night, and woken calm and focused, content to know that this moment, and those to follow, would come.

That she would be with him here and now, that she would lie with him through the golden afternoon and learn what he would show her, teach her, and so experience what she'd thought she never would, all the forbidden glory that with him she could.

The kiss whirled her into a familiar landscape; she readily followed where he led. For long moments as their mouths melded and their tongues boldly caressed, she sensed that he needed to reassure not her but himself—to confirm that she truly was not just there, physically in his arms, but that she remained committed to their mutual plan.

If she could have, she would have smiled; instead, she reached up, speared her fingers slowly through his hair, letting her senses revel in the silky texture of the short curls, then she gripped his head and kissed him back.

A simple, unadorned demand he understood perfectly well.

She felt his breath hitch as her meaning washed over him, felt the change in him—the hardening of muscles, the tension that flowed into them—as he responded, reacted, as helpless as she, it seemed, in the face of the heat that flared between them.

He drew back from the kiss, lifted his head. His eyes caught hers; between them his clever fingers swiftly undid the buttons closing her jacket. The instant the last was undone, she shrugged the jacket off, letting it fall where it would.

His lips, set in a line she now recognized, curved just a fraction up at the ends, then his eyes dipped; he worked at slipping the smaller buttons of her blouse free.

She said nothing, just watched his face, sensed how the moment held him; he opened the blouse, paused, his eyes on what he'd revealed, then he drew a breath, tighter than she'd expected, and eased the blouse from her shoulders, his palms shaping her upper arms, then tracing down to her wrists. While she dealt with the tiny buttons at her cuffs, his hands roved her breasts, screened but in no way shielded by the fine silk of her chemise; his hands warmed her, lightly cupping, each caress tantalizing, too light to satisfy.

Her lungs were locked when, both cuffs undone, she drew her arms free. The blouse fell behind her. Lifting her arms, she reached for him; his lips curved as he gathered her in, and kissed her—took her mouth in a long, slow kiss that made her shudder.

With rising need.

She felt the tug at her waist as he undid the laces of her skirt; he held her to the kiss, immersing her in a cauldron of heating desire that swirled and swelled and steadily grew as he eased the laces free. Then she felt them release and he pushed the skirt down over her hips; it sank to the floor, crumpling in a pool about her feet.

His fingers immediately searched for and found the laces anchoring her riding trousers, equally expertly dealt with them. Then he drew back from the kiss. Eased half a step back, then he dipped his head and placed a kiss on one silk-clad nipple before going to his knees before her.

He drew her trousers down, revealing . . . His lips curved. "You do wear drawers. I'd wondered."

The unexpected comment surprised a small laugh from her, but she was more intent on him, on watching him as he undressed—no, *unwrapped* her. There was a suggestion of long-anticipated discovery in his usually impassive face, his features no longer quite so unreadable when invested with desire and its concordant emotions.

He stripped her trousers to her ankles, then rolled down her garters and stockings and held her boots as she, needing no direction, lifted first one foot, then the other, free. He swept her clothing aside, so she stood barefoot on the polished boards. Then he sat back and looked up—all the way to her face.

Despite her height, he was so tall himself that his face was level with her midriff. She looked down at him and arched a brow, wondering what he intended next.

His gaze lowered, slowly, to her breasts, then descended further to her waist.

Then he smiled.

And reached for the silk ties anchoring her drawers.

She would, she thought, remember that smile always. Raising one hand, she threaded her fingers through his hair—and watched, waited. Breath bated. Nerves tightening, flickering, skin flushing, heating. Her heart beating just a little faster, just a little harder.

Gervase felt her fingers lightly riffling his hair, understood the unspoken encouragement. She was with him, unquestioningly, unconditionally, even though he was perfectly certain she was following him blind. She didn't know what he would do; no matter how great her theoretical knowledge, he doubted she could guess. Quite aside from all else, he hadn't scripted this encounter; he'd thought of it often enough, but had been unable to see her and how she would affect him, unable to predict his responses let alone hers well enough to make planning at any level worthwhile.

So he was operating on instinct, pure and unfettered, following some inner guide he wasn't sure he fully understood.

The knot he was coaxing at last came undone; letting out the breath trapped in his lungs, replacing it with one even more shallow, he hooked his fingers in the waistband, releasing the gathers, then drew the soft garment down.

And simultaneously rose to his feet, one palm cupping the back of her knee, then sliding upward as he stood and stepped toward her—a long, evocative caress that swept with deliberation up the back of her thigh, sliding beneath the edge of her chemise and rising further until he closed his hand over one globe of her derriere, skin to bare skin, and held her to him as with his other hand he framed her face, and kissed her.

As he'd been wanting to kiss her—waiting to kiss her—for days.

Possessively.

There was no longer any need to disguise what he felt—what she evoked in him; she was here and she would be his—of that he no longer had the slightest doubt.

So he kissed her ravenously, let his beast have its fill, then, when she trembled and gasped, he drew back. Lifting his head, he released his grip on her bottom only to band his arm about her waist; his gaze locking on her heaving breasts, he eased back enough to jerk the ribbon tie of her chemise undone, hook his fingers beneath the gathered band and draw it wide, then he lifted it free of the ruched peaks of her breasts and drew the fine silk down.

To her waist, then he shifted his arm and drew it past, further, until it slipped from his fingers and floated to the floor, the sound a whisper of surrender.

One she heard. She shivered, inwardly quivered; her eyes on his face, her hands tangled in his hair, she searched his eyes, then licked her swollen lips. "You now."

He heard, but his gaze lowered and fastened on her breasts. He'd touched them, tasted them, but he hadn't before fully appreciated the reality. He felt her draw in another breath. "In a minute." He lifted his hand to lightly touch, to watch her nipple tighten even more. "In a moment."

Her breath tangled in her throat.

Easing his arm from about her, he gripped her waist for an instant, ensuring she was steady, then let his hands fall. "Just let me look."

He took one step back, then another, would have closed his eyes at the painful throb of his erection but . . . his entire awareness, his eyes, mind and senses, were too fascinated. Captured and held by the sight of her.

From the moment he'd first focused on her, he'd known she would be statuesque, that, naked, she would resemble a goddess—one of the Roman dieties, full-figured and proud.

But her clothes had disguised her charms to a greater extent than he'd guessed.

She was more, much more, than he'd expected.

Enough to turn his head, to steal his breath, to lock every last iota of awareness he had—on her. In that moment, he lived for nothing else—nothing beyond appreciating, worshiping, drinking in her beauty.

Her breasts were full, perfectly formed, high and proud, their skin creamy, with nipples a soft rose. Below, her ribcage narrowed to a surprisingly slender waist, one he could nearly span with his hands. The flare of her hips, the subtle swell of her taut belly, were the epitome of womanly perfection, entirely proportionate to her height, to the long, gracefully curved lines of her legs.

She stood before him, not exactly relaxed yet without any false modesty, much less shame; head tilting, a question forming in her eyes, she started to raise one hand.

"Just wait, please. . . ." He licked his dry lips. "Stand there and let me look."

She arched her brows, but let her hand fall.

He drew in a tight breath and circled her, his gaze lovingly roving every inch, every curve. Letting each facet, each perspective sink into his mind, and enrich his imagination. His passion, his desire.

His need.

He'd inherited his mother's artist's eye well enough to appreciate the play of light on her fine skin, the curves kissed by a radiance that seemed almost unearthly. Pearlescent. Precious.

Halting behind her, he set his fingers to her chignon, already halfway undone. Pins pattered on the floor as he released the heavy mass, felt the silky slide of the tresses over his hands. Stepping closer, he lifted the burnished mass to his face and inhaled, deeply, let the essence of her wreath through his brain.

Leaning forward, careful not to touch her skin with his hands, not yet, he brushed his lips to her temple, then ran his hands out, letting the bright strands fall over her shoulders.

"You are . . . unutterably beautiful." He breathed the words by her ear, then drew back. Forced himself to step back—and look. Study. This time, this innocence—him of her and her of him—would never come again.

Slowly, he continued around her.

He thanked every angel he knew that she wasn't

missish; although she watched him as he circled her, she stood calmly and made no move to cover her curves, her tantalizing hollows. The golden brown curls that adorned her mons fractured the light, shimmering like gold.

Shielding a treasure he ached to see, to touch, caress. To possess.

Madeline watched as he returned to stand before her. With her eyes she'd tracked his face; what she'd seen there, stamped in his features and blazoned in his amber eyes, had held her mesmerized. She'd felt the heated brush of his gaze wash over her bare skin; if anyone had told her, even an hour ago, that she would willingly stand naked while he examined her, she would have laughed. But that look in his eyes . . . for that, she would have walked naked over hot coals.

She'd known she—her body—could fix his attention and arouse him; she hadn't known that she—her body—could affect him to this extent, could command this degree of sincere, wordless reverence. Especially not from him. From a man as experienced as he.

Even less had she expected him to so openly let her see and know how enthralled he truly was.

In doing so he'd given her a gift, a precious pleasure.

When he halted before her, she reached for the lapels of his hacking jacket. "Your turn."

My turn.

He met her eyes, read her determination, and acquiesced. He was no more visited by modesty than she, not in this, not now, not between them. More, impatience, that telltale tension, gripped him; he didn't wait passively while she peeled his clothes from him but threw them off himself, sitting bare-chested to haul off his boots and stockings, then standing and unbuckling his belt, stripping off his breeches, flinging them aside.

Then he was naked, but not about to stand and let her

peruse. The instant he was upright, he reached for her and pulled her to him.

She gasped. Every bone in her body melted at the contact; she clung to his shoulders, the shocking heat of his naked skin searing hers. Her breasts pressed into the hard hot wall of his chest, nipples furled to tight points, excruciatingly sensitive as the crinkly hair adorning his tensed muscles abraded them. Her hips were firmly wedged against his rock-hard thighs, his hard hands cupping her bottom, holding her there so his erection burned against the taut cushion of her belly.

Then his head swooped, he found her lips, covered them, and took possession.

Of her mouth, of her body, of her.

She hadn't known what to expect, but never would she have imagined this—the heat, the sheer wildness that infected them both, that raced unfettered through them, igniting fires that consumed, that cindered any reservation she might have had, that vaporized hesitation and replaced it with ravenous need.

The conflagration affected him in the same way. His hands were everywhere, demanding and driven. His patent need evoked hers, built and sent it raging, surging like a wave to sweep her into a roiling sea. Of hot passion, of frantic desire, of that unrestrained, greedy need.

She clung to him, kissed him wildly, pressed to him and let her body speak for her, let the way she responsed to his increasingly driven touch, to every possessive caress, scream her willingness, her urgent desperation.

Hers only fueled his.

He half lifted, half tumbled her onto the daybed, following her down so closely their lips barely parted enough for her to gasp. She reveled in the sensation of his hard body beside hers; she twisted, pressing close, hooking one knee over his the better to hold him to her. The better to savor the hard muscled strength of him down her long length, to feel the wall of his chest against her breasts as he shifted over her, pinning her to the bed.

Their mouths had fused again, neither willing to forgo that contact, the slick heated pleasure of their mating tongues.

Then his hands found her breasts, and her focus shifted. To his touch, the quality of it, to this, a culminating possession. He kneaded, flagrantly demanding, then his wicked fingers found her nipples and she gasped through their kiss.

He played briefly, expertly winding the tension building within her, until, driven by the excruciating delight, she arched beneath him, consumed by their fire and begging for release.

His hands left her breasts and ranged lower, spanning her ribs, her waist, as they swept down to her hips, then pressed around and beneath. One hard thigh pressed hers wide, anchoring them, leaving her open and vulnerable—desperate, urgent and aching for his touch.

When his hand cupped her she cried out; when his fingers parted her folds and found her slickness, she nearly sobbed.

Her lungs were so tight, she couldn't breathe but through him. Fingers clenched in his hair, she held him to her, and with her lips and tongue urged him on.

Gervase needed no encouragement; he was already sunk deep in passion's thrall, closer to overwhelmed than he'd ever been. He'd imagined this first encounter would be slow, a gentle initiation during which he led her along the path to intimacy, to sensual fulfillment.

Instead there was heat and searing flame, a passion beyond his experience, and a need so profound that if she hadn't been so blatantly willing, controlling it would have brought him to his knees.

He had to have her, had to be inside her, had to make her

his—that was all the direction his mind let alone his body seemed able to accommodate.

Hot, urgent, it had to be this way.

As he pressed a finger deep into her sheath, and felt her tremble—not with shock or even surprise but with unalloyed anticipation—he made a mental vow to make it up to her next time, that their next engagement would have all the gentleness, the tenderness, that this one did not. Would not.

She arched, breaking their kiss, losing what little breath she had in a gasp so evocative—so provocative, so sensually desperate—that it rocked him.

He withdrew his finger, then pressed another in alongside, stretching her . . . but she was in no mood to be denied, even in such a cause. She shifted against him, her body arching against his in wordless entreaty. She rode every day and was stronger than any female he'd previously had under him; he couldn't easily control her, couldn't stop her from sensually wrestling—given his state, his already strained and tenuous control, and her aim, the outcome was a foregone conclusion.

Muttering a curse, he found her lips with his and pressed her back into the cushions, subduing her—appeasing her—with a kiss so demanding she had all she could do to meet him, match him . . . while he withdrew his fingers from the scalding haven of her sheath, settled his hips between her thighs, and entered her.

He slid in a little way easily enough, but then the untried tightness of her sheath slowed him. He pressed on, steady and sure as she quieted beneath him, as her whole awareness focused on his invasion.

Giving thanks she was so tall that he could easily kiss her while burying himself inside her, he used his lips and tongue to draw her back to the kiss, but this time she wouldn't be distracted; her inner tension returned, her fingers tightening on his upper arms, nails sinking in as he forged deeper into her—and swept past her maidenhead, barely any barrier.

She rode astride and had for a decade, another blessing.

Madeline felt the slight give, the faint sting, but the momentary discomfort was immediately swamped by a wholly different sensation. He didn't withdraw but thrust deeper still, seating himself fully, heavily, within her, and she was suddenly mentally, sensually gasping, trying to absorb, to take it in, to accustom her senses to his weight above her, pinning her to the daybed, to the hardness of his thighs pressing hers wide, his hair-dusted muscles rasping her smooth skin, but more than anything else to the hard, hot masculine reality buried deep within her.

It felt like hot steel encased in velvet; no wonder men so often referred to it as a weapon—a sword, a lance.

She inwardly shuddered, still caught in passion's flames but for an instant able to know, to clearly sense—and feel—physical vulnerability, a sensation she'd rarely experienced, to understand why he'd termed this a conquest.

His lips were still on hers, his tongue stroking hers, but although joined fully with her, he'd stilled, as if he were waiting. . . .

She realized she'd tensed; she wasn't sure why. On the thought, her muscles eased, the tension flowing away. Revealing the fire still burning, poised, waiting, flames hungry and eager.

Swelling again, growing, demanding.

As if he knew, before she could even think to move, he did; he withdrew, then thrust deep again, forging even further than before.

And the flames flared, roared as he repeated the movement. She gasped and clung to the kiss, eager again, desperate again.

Burning again.

Again and again he withdrew and thrust in; she found his rhythm and matched him. Clutched as the flames built, then raced down her veins; heat poured from them as he rode her hard, then harder, and she absorbed each thrust, each deep penetration, welcomed the passion, embraced the fire, drew it and him into her.

Until her core ignited, until bright tension gripped her so fiercely she thought she might die.

She pulled away from the kiss, desperately arching beneath him, head back, reaching for she knew not what.

Then ecstasy speared through her. She cried out, breathless, helpless.

And shattered.

Infinitely more powerfully than before. As if she'd been flung off some sensual cliff and every sense had fragmented.

Eyes closed, sightless, she drifted in the void, but then tactile sensation returned, and she felt him within her, hard, hot and unyielding; beneath her hands, in her arms, hard and heavy above her, she felt him holding still, heard his harsh, ragged breaths beside her ear, his chest laboring, his muscles locked as he fought to give her that moment . . . then his control gave way.

His lips found hers, covered them; with no longer even a vestige of sophistication he ravaged her mouth—unutterably glad, she appeased him, let him. Gave him what he had given her.

Her body unstinting.

Driven, his body rocked compulsively into hers, powerful and unrelentingly; she wrapped her arms about him and clung, tight, then he abruptly tensed, shuddered, and spent himself deep inside her.

She felt the warmth within, felt his weight as, his trembling muscles giving way, he groaned and slumped upon her.

Holding him in her arms, she felt her lips curve, satisfaction mingling with glorious satiation; the feelings burgeoned and rose through her, buoyed her, then swept her free, onto a calm and blissful sea.

Gervase stirred, then glanced at the woman sleeping in his arms. Warm, trusting, utterly relaxed, she remained asleep.

He stared at her, at her features relaxed in sated slumber, at her tumbling mass of hair now in wild disarray, at the magnificent creamy slopes of her breasts mouth-wateringly visible above the silk shawl he'd draped over her to shield her cooling skin.

The sight held him, transfixed him, then, carefully disengaging, he eased from her side. He sat on the edge of the daybed for a moment, head hanging, then he rose, stretched.

He glanced at her again; when she didn't stir, he padded soft-footed to the windows.

The sea, the sky, the expanse of cliff, the distant mound of Black Head—nothing beyond the window had changed.

Within the boathouse something had, but even now he had no idea what. What it was, what power had connived to sweep him so far beyond his customary control. Looking back, it felt as if some fate had intervened and handed the reins to his beast, denying his rational mind any say in how he took her.

Not that she'd helped, let alone seemed to mind. She'd given no sign that gentleness and tenderness were what she'd come to the boathouse, and him, to find; she'd had her own agenda, and that agenda had had more in common with his beast's wishes than his more calm and logical side.

Although he hadn't planned it, he'd had a definite vision of how this engagement would go, that he, calm and in control, would teach her, show her, introduce her to her own sensual nature . . . instead, she'd shown him something he hadn't known about himself, regardless of whether she'd intended to or not.

She couldn't have intended it; how would she, an innocent, have known?

Regardless, despite his vow of how their next encounter would go, having once indulged without restraint, screens or shields, he wasn't sure it was possible to retreat and come together in any mild and gentle, distant and controlled way, without igniting that raging heat.

Without succumbing to passion's relentless beat.

For the first time in his life, with a woman, he was unsure. Uncertain of where he stood sexually with her. He stared out at the surging waves. He would have to wait and see what she wanted, how she reacted; he would have to play by her wishes, be reactive and responsive to them, rather than make and follow any plan of his own.

That was an utterly alien concept—to have a woman calling his tune. So alien that he stood at the windows, staring unseeing at the waves, and tried to find some way, some path, around it.

Madeline watched him, let her gaze play over him. She'd woken the instant his weight had left the daybed, but had lain still and watched from beneath her lashes. He'd seemed distracted, mentally elsewhere; she saw no reason to refocus his attention—not until she'd looked her fill.

Like all the males of her acquaintance, he was totally at ease naked. She wasn't all that bothered over being nude herself; it was more perceptions of modesty that ruled her actions, but with him, there had seemed little point.

With the remnants of golden pleasure still coursing her veins, she lay back on the daybed and studied him—noted the proud set of his head, the broad shoulders tapering to a narrow waist and hips, the tight buttocks above his long, strong legs. Rider's legs, she'd once heard them called, long thighs heavily but sleekly muscled.

He was like that all over; she could appreciate anew the light she'd earlier noted as it played over him, over the dimples and hollows, the muscle bands that shifted and contracted under taut, lightly bronzed skin . . . as he turned his head and caught her staring.

Somewhat to her surprise, no blush rose to her cheeks. Instead, she watched as he turned from the windows and walked toward her. Mouth drying, she stared some more— still not blushing, instead battling to keep a cat-eyeing-the-unguarded-cream smile from her face.

She just hoped she didn't look too hungry.

The thought stirred her to action; sitting up, ignoring the silk shawl that had materialized over her as it slithered down to her waist, she reached across to the side table. Selecting a small bunch of grapes, she sat back, plucked one, and lifted it to her lips—and let her gaze travel once more to him. Noting with interest that despite their recent engagement he was again aroused, she reluctantly raised her gaze to his face.

And with becoming confidence, arched her brows.

Her question was transparent: What next?

He halted by the daybed; hands rising to his hips, he looked down at her—as if unsure what to make of her.

Indeed, she wasn't entirely sure what to make of herself; she felt . . . not new but different. As if during the last hour he'd freed the sensual woman who had always dwelt inside her, and somehow integrated that hidden self into her whole so that she could now without a blink, with calm assurance and a better certainty of who and what she was, sit there, naked, and watch him, naked too, and calmly wait to see what he would do.

When he didn't do anything but stare, a frown forming in his amber eyes, she leaned back against the raised head of the daybed, looked him in the eye—then plucked a grape and held it up to him.

He held her gaze for a fraught moment, then knelt on the

daybed and with his lips took the grape from her fingers, then slumped beside her. He chewed, swallowed, then reached across and took the stem and remaining two grapes from her hand, plucked one and held it for her to take.

She met his eyes briefly, then did.

He popped the last grape into his mouth, tossed the stem back into the dish, then sighed and settled back. Lifting one arm, he slid it around her; drawing her in, he placed a kiss on her temple.

Settling against his chest, her hand splayed over his heart, she waited.

After a moment he said, "You . . . I didn't think it would be . . . like it was."

"In what way?" Looking up, she met his eyes. "You have to remember I haven't done this before." Regardless, she wasn't such a ninny that she didn't know he'd been, at the last, utterly sated.

The look on his face was one to treasure; it wasn't often he was lost for words. Or rather, that he encountered so much difficulty over choosing which of the many replies that had plainly leapt to his tongue to give voice to.

Eventually, he said, "It wasn't supposed to be so fast and furious."

She studied him, raised her brows. "I rather like the fast and furious."

"Obviously." He hesitated, then asked, "Are you sore?"

She looked across the room, inwardly assessing, then shrugged. "Not especially." Not more than if she'd ridden hard astride for several hours. There was a small degree of chafing, a little heat, but . . . She met his eyes. "Nothing that would prevent me from doing it all again."

He searched her eyes, then shifted around to face her. "In that case . . ." Lifting one hand, he brushed back her way-ward hair, feathered his fingers over her jaw. "Let's try it again. Only this time we'll aim for the slow and gentle."

He tipped her face to his and kissed her—so gently, so tantalizingly she nearly growled with impatience. She drew back enough to say, "I'm rather *fond* of the fast and furious."

"Nevertheless, in the interests of your education, let's try it with less heat."

Inwardly wondering why he would want to, she mentally shrugged, kissed him back, and let matters take their course.

Chapter 9

The following afternoon, Gervase paced the clifftop path where it joined the track down to the boathouse. His face was set; despite his triumph—his victory in seducing Madeline—nothing had gone as he'd planned.

Not the first time—nor the second.

With *less* heat had been his dictate. Instead, going slowly had only intensified the firestorm that had raged between them, fueled by passions far more primitive, more urgent and powerful than any he'd previously felt. Why that was so, where such passions came from, why she and no other evoked them in him he didn't know, but again instead of him teaching her, it had been he who had had to grapple with stunning and startling revelations.

Not that she was teaching him; it was lying with her—joining with her—that opened a door to some novel and disconcerting landscape. She was as new to it as he, but that didn't seem to bother her—not in the least. She'd embraced every aspect—the fast as well as the furious in their heated-beyond-imagining couplings—with a wholehearted eagerness, an open delight, that had only dragged him deeper.

Further under the thrall of . . . whatever it was.

Until yesterday he hadn't known he—not even his beast—harbored such powerful and primal cravings.

He'd needed her, needed to be inside her, needed to see her, feel her writhing in abandon beneath him—and in that moment, he'd needed that more than he'd needed to breathe. Even to live.

In that ultimate moment of madness that she and only she could reduce him to, his entire existence seemed to hinge . . . on her. On having her, on proving incontrovertibly, in the most explicit way, that she was his.

Raking one hand through his hair, he paced, stalked, inwardly more uncertain than he could recall ever being in his adult life. He'd never been dependent on another person, not for anything; he'd been an excellent operative because he worked alone, entirely self-sufficiently.

Now . . .

He drew in a breath and looked out over the sea. He needed a wife desperately, but did he need Madeline?

Did he need her and what she did to him?

Hoofbeats reached him; he turned, looked. They hadn't made any plans to meet again, yet some part of him wasn't surprised to see her.

At least one part of him leapt at the sight of her.

He'd ridden down to the boathouse and left Crusader there, then walked up to pace the clifftop where the breeze was fresh. She halted beside him; he caught her chestnut's bridle as she slid from the saddle.

"I was coming to find you. I wanted to speak with you." She came around the chestnut's head, tugging off her gloves.

Speak with him? Her features were tight, her expression serious. "About what?"

She glanced up at him, pure Valkyrie, shield up, fully

armored. "About yesterday." Looking down, she tugged her glove free.

"Yesterday." A chill inched down his spine. "What about yesterday?"

"Well . . ." Lips tight, she brushed back a lock of hair the wind had blown across her face. "I came to acknowledge your victory, and to tell you that while I enjoyed the interlude, I believe it would be unwise—seriously unwise—for us to indulge again."

He opened his mouth—

She silenced him with an upraised hand. "No—hear me out." She paused as if recalling a rehearsed speech, then went on, "I realize that you . . . that your interest in seducing me stemmed from boredom, as we originally discussed. You clearly saw me as a challenge, in your words 'a conquest.' However, now you've succeeded, no matter how . . . exciting and instructive the result, given who we are, given we're so prominent in the neighborhood, given my brothers and your sisters, let alone Sybil and Muriel, given all those things I believe we should call a halt." Drawing in a deep breath, she met his gaze. "Neither you nor I should court the sort of scandal that would ensue should a liaison between us become common knowledge."

Gervase stared at her, struck dumb, not by her words but by his reaction, by the storm of emotions her intention had unleashed; they clawed and raged, threatening to swamp his mind and spill from his throat.

When he said nothing, she frowned. "I take it you agree?"

No! He scowled. "We can't talk here." Catching her hand, he changed his hold on her horse's bridle. "Come to the boathouse."

She tried to hang back. "Why can't we talk here? There's no one about and we can see for miles."

"And someone miles away can see us." Thank Heaven. He tugged until she stepped forward, then towed her along.

With an irritated humph, Madeline acquiesced. Reluctantly. She'd imagined having this discussion in the castle library; after all that had transpired in the boathouse yesterday, it was the very last place she would have chosen in which to bring their liaison to an end. But . . . he'd thrown her off-balance. After yesterday, she'd thought he'd be crowing, at least obviously smug. Instead . . . he looked grim, unhappy, dissatisfied. Why?

This was not a good time for her curiosity to raise its head. It should have had enough to keep it occupied after the events—and the consequent revelations—of yesterday. But no. So she allowed him to lead her to the boathouse, tie Artur up next to his big gray, then usher her inside.

He shut the door. She turned and faced him. "Now—"

"Not here." He gestured to the stairs. "Upstairs."

But at that even her curiosity balked. She frowned. "There's no reason we can't talk here."

"Don't be daft. I can barely make out your face."

She couldn't see his clearly either, but . . . she lifted her chin. "This won't take long."

Through the dimness, he met her gaze. A moment ticked by during which he plainly weighed his response; unbidden, an image of him tossing her over his shoulder and carting her upstairs popped into her mind. She blinked, instinctively tensed.

He growled and swung away. "I won't discuss anything while I can't see your face." He made for the stairs and went up them two at a time.

Slack-jawed, she stared after him. Then she set her lips. "Damn it!" Going to the stairs, she climbed them—gracefully. It would be childish to stamp.

But she was determined not to go beyond the post at the stairhead. Luckily he'd stopped just along from the newel post, leaning back against the railings above the stairs. His arms were crossed, as were his ankles; he regarded her through narrowed eyes as she halted beside him.

"Let me see if I have this right." He pinned her with a cuttingly sharp gaze. "After yesterday, your first foray into lovemaking, you've decided you've had enough and don't need to learn anything more—is that correct?"

She steeled herself to utter the necessary lie. "Precisely."

His gaze grew even sharper. "Didn't you like it? What we did on the daybed?"

Eyes narrowing, she studied him; his face gave little away, but his eyes seemed unusually stormy. She remembered he'd been strangely bothered by the, as he'd labeled it, "fast and furious" tenor of their joining. Surely he couldn't be worried over his performance, couldn't be feeling guilty? She might have snorted, but she knew boys—men—well. "If I said I hadn't enjoyed it, I'd be lying—as you're perfectly well aware. However"—looking down, she tucked her gloves into the waistband of her riding skirt—"whether I enjoyed the interlude or not has nothing to do with my decision."

Not a complete lie; it wasn't her enjoyment per se but what she'd finally realized that enjoyment and the quality of it meant. Falling in love with Gervase Tregarth when she knew perfectly well he wasn't in love with her was the very definition of unwise.

"I wanted to tell you—and have you agree"—she glanced at him but he was looking down, gaze fixed on a point in front of his boots; his jaw was set; he looked decidedly mulish—"that yesterday would be a solitary incident, never to be repeated. We—I—cannot afford to undermine my position in the district, not while I remain Harry's surrogate."

"No." He lowered his arms, lifted his head.

She stared into hard hazel eyes. "What do you mean, no?"

Gervase drew in a breath, and recklessly embarked on

the biggest gamble of his life. "I mean: No—that's not why you're running away."

Her lips set; her eyes narrowed to slits. "I am not running away."

"Yes, you are. You found yesterday exciting, fascinating, enthralling—and you're frightened."

"Frightened?" Eyes widening, she spread her hands. "Of what?"

"Of yourself. Of your own passionate nature. Of your own desires." He held her gaze relentlessly and spoke clearly, dispassionately—with just a lick of contempt. And watched her spine stiffen, watched her temper spark.

With total deliberation, he uncrossed his legs, straightened away from the railing to face her—and poured oil on her fire. "You're afraid of what you might learn if you continue to meet with me. You're afraid of the woman you become in my arms, a woman whole, complete—all she could be."

Her face blanked; she seemed shocked by the words that spilled from his lips, essentially without thought. Naturally. Although he was attributing the panic and fear to her, it was his own fears he was describing.

"You're afraid of learning more, of what you might feel once you learn it all—experience it all. All that might be between us."

With one hand he brushed back the hair haloing her face. She tensed, but allowed him to move nearer. Surprise and incipient anger warred in her eyes; had he been in control, his usual persuasive self, he would have capitalized on her temper, prodding it until she did as he wished, but having given voice to what was swirling inside him, having drawn this close to her, the focus of his roused and abraded emotions, he was no longer thinking clearly. Could only respond to the wariness in her eyes. "Don't be afraid." He leaned closer, brushed his lips to her temple. "There are times in life when one has to take a chance—make a leap of faith. When we simply have to . . ."

When he eased back, searching, she offered, "Step off the edge of a cliff?"

His lips twisted. "Nothing quite so fatal. More like setting sail and letting the winds take us where they will."

In convincing her, he was convincing himself.

Her eyes remained on his, searching them, searching his face. He'd drawn close enough to trap her if he wished, but with an effort he kept his arms relaxed; she had to come to him willingly for him to win her.

Again her eyes narrowed. "You're very good with words."

He let his lips curve. "I'm even better with actions." He held her gaze from a distance of mere inches. "Trust me."

Moving slowly, he fastened his hands about her waist, let his gaze lower to her lips. "Just try it and see. There's so much more you've yet to learn, yet to experience—and why not with me?"

A heartbeat passed, then two. He held his breath, not daring to look into her eyes in case she saw how important her answer was to him. How much she already meant to him.

Unexpectedly she sighed, long and resigned, then moved into his arms. "All right." She tilted her face, lifted her lips. "But this is very definitely not wise."

He accepted her offering with alacrity, covered her lips with his; the wave of relief that flooded him nearly brought him to his knees.

She was right; this wasn't wise. It wasn't even merely dangerous. It was unmitigated madness, on his part certainly—possibly on hers, too; Heaven knew he would never be an easy husband, but he couldn't draw back, couldn't deny this madness its due.

No more than he could deny the heat that rose between them, that welled and grew and flared into flame once she was in his arms. Once she was pressed against him, her lips beneath his, her mouth surrendered, his to plunder at will, once her body, sleek and supple, was locked against his, all he could think of was appeasing that heat, feeding the madness.

Letting it take him, rule him, drive him, conquer him.

Their clothes fell like autumn leaves, a scattered trail in their wake as inch by inch they made their way to the daybed.

Then they were there, naked on the thick cushions, the summer air whispering over heated skin as they touched, caressed, sighed.

Caught their breaths. Gasped. The evocative sound of her strangled moan shook him to the core.

This time, thank Heaven, it was slower, even if the heat was not one whit decreased, the intensity of each long-drawn moment only brighter, sharper. Regardless, he felt, if not in control then at least more aware—of her, of how she responded to each touch, of himself, and how she made him feel.

Time stretched as his hands and fingers played over the smooth curves and hollows, then his lips followed the same path, delighting, setting small fires to burn in their wake.

Madeline embraced every last sensation.

Closing her eyes, she opened her senses, with reckless abandon gave herself up to the moment—to him. She couldn't think, couldn't hear, could barely see—her world had shrunk to him and her, and the pleasure he evoked, and lavished on her.

A generous lover. The phrase swam through her head, then out.

A devilish lover; his lips trailed a path over her stomach, over the curls below, then he spread her thighs and kissed her there and she screamed. Breathlessly, helplessly, clung.

As he pleasured her to oblivion and beyond.

The afternoon spun about them as she fought against the drugging tide, pressed him back on the cushions and explored. He'd been right; she had so much to learn, and these moments with him, limited as they were certain to be, might be her only chance to satisfy the cravings of the woman he called forth, the sensual being she became in his arms.

But he seemed to have his limits, too, his own defined needs. Bare moments after she closed her hand about his turgid length, he muttered something, caught her wrist and removed her hand, flipped her onto her back and followed, spreading her thighs wide, his hips between, then joining them in one smooth motion.

She could only gasp and cling, hold tight as he drove them into a wall of flames. Straight through and on, into a landscape of scalding heat and demanding desire, of passion so hot it seared.

He bent his head and their lips met; together they rode on. Up.

Straight off the edge of the world into that void where nothing existed beyond the timeless moment, beyond searing sensation. He groaned, battled to hold them there for one last instant, then the power fractured, fell away, and they plummeted into earthly bliss.

She woke to find herself sprawled on her back on the daybed, with him sprawled, boneless and heavy, apparently non compos mentis, over her. Her lips curved spontaneously; she suppressed a silly, pointless giggle, trying not to shake and wake him.

In truth, there was nothing humorous about the situation; she made a valiant effort to sober, and failed. She couldn't understand why her heart insisted on singing . . . then she remembered, in the same instant scornfully told herself it simply couldn't be. Not yet. Fate, having sent him to her expressly with seduction in mind, would surely give her a little time to enjoy him before tampering with her heart.

No. She wasn't the sort to fall in love in a day, not even two. She wasn't a soft-hearted person; she wasn't all that trusting. She wasn't especially gullible, either; as long as she kept it firmly in mind that this—their liaison—was an exercise embarked upon solely to educate her, to extend her horizons beyond the boundaries that would otherwise have been, as long as she viewed this engagement of theirs with the cool detachment of a business arrangement, her heart would remain safely hers.

Unbidden, her hand drifted to his hair, to play in the soft curls. She thought again of his argument—that she was afraid of what might come. He'd been right about the fear, but not about *what* she feared. If he knew that she feared falling in love with him, he might well, out of honor, step back. But while that remained her secret she had nothing to fear, from him or from prolonging their liaison, as long as she kept her heart locked away.

She hadn't intended to court any risk at all—had seen no reason to, not last night—but now he'd demonstrated that there indeed was more to learn, then her reckless, curious Gascoigne self wouldn't rest, not until she'd learned it all. At least glimpsed it all.

He stirred, sighed; with a muffled grunt he lifted from her and slumped on his side beside her. Curled his arm around her, held her to him and nuzzled her ear. "You don't have to go anywhere, do you?"

Spreading her hand over his chest, she looked down the long muscled body displayed for her delectation. Hers to explore. "No. Not yet."

Gervase remained slumped on the daybed after Madeline had risen, dressed and gone. She'd insisted they shouldn't risk being seen leaving together; he'd acquiesced, not least because he needed time to digest all that had happened, and all that that meant.

At least he had the answer to the question he'd posed just before she'd ridden up. Yes, he needed her, Madeline Gascoigne. No one else would do; the instant she'd tried to cut and run, he'd known.

Incontrovertibly, beyond a shadow of doubt.

Worse, the primitive response that had gripped him had left no room for pretense. He wasn't giving her up—not now, not ever. Not even though he was going to marry her.

That last was no contradiction, not to his mind. Being in thrall to his wife—a Valkyrie, what was more—was not the way he'd imagined things would be.

He grimaced, then shifted to reach for the decanter and pour a little amontillado into a glass. Fortification.

Sipping, he relaxed on the cushions and took stock. Not that he could set any name, let alone any meaningful measure to the maelstrom of emotions her attempt to escape him had unleashed. That was how he'd in that instant seen it—as her escaping him—and he'd reacted, at least inwardly, accordingly.

He'd scrambled to find some way to draw her back; he'd succeeded, but only by mining his own vulnerability, a desperate act. Just voicing his fears had shaken him, even if he'd disguised them as hers.

Before he'd let her up from the daybed he'd extracted an agreement that they would meet again, that she wouldn't try to retreat from their now-established intimacy. Well and good; his immediate need was met. Yet now he'd got that much from her . . . where to from here?

Marry the damn woman as soon as humanly possible was the answer backed by every instinct he possessed.

He imagined proposing . . . .

Eyes closing, he dropped his head back and groaned. "If I tell her I want to marry her now, she'll think someone has seen us and I'm doing the honorable thing." He thought, then added, "Or worse, that I've simply come to my senses, realized I've seduced a gently bred virgin, and feel compelled to offer for her hand."

He grimaced horrendously. He didn't need even a second to realize what sort of argument proposing would land him in—one he'd never win. Opening his eyes, he sipped, felt the crisp wine slide down his throat. "This can't be happening."

If he proposed now, he'd risk losing all he'd thus far gained. Worse, he'd put her on her guard against him.

Frowning, his wits now fully re-engaged, he reviewed his campaign—as if winning her were a war with her and her hand the prize. While seducing her had seemed an excellent idea at the time, having won that battle and taken that hill, he'd now discovered that the position made his push to take his primary target harder, not easier.

He had to take another approach. A flanking maneuver.

Replaying her reasons for believing he couldn't possibly be interested in marrying her, while he'd undermined one—that he wasn't honestly attracted to her—the other three still stood firm, at least in her mind. Her age, society's expectations of the type of lady who would be his wife, and their compatibility in day-to-day dealings.

Given where they now were—given she'd already tried to step back—if he wanted to convince her he truly wanted to marry her, he would need to attack and weaken, preferably vanquish and quash, those other three reasons before he risked asking her to be his.

In light of the feats he'd routinely accomplished over his years as a spy, that shouldn't be beyond him. He drained his glass, eyes narrowing as he planned. Persuasion was his strong suit, but sweet words didn't work well with her—she was too wary, too cynical. Sweet *actions*, however . . .

By the time he sat up and set aside the empty glass, his new plan of campaign was clear in his mind.

"Sybil?" The following morning, summoned by Milsom to the drawing room, Madeline discovered that not only Sybil but Belinda, Annabel and Jane had come to call. Touching fingers with Sybil, acknowledging the girls' curtseys with a smile, she waved them to chairs, then sat beside Sybil on the chaise. "Is anything wrong?"

"Not *wrong*." Sybil fixed her with a sober gaze. "But I have to confess, Madeline dear, that this is a social call with a purpose."

"Oh?" Glancing from Sybil's unusually serious expression to those of her daughters, equally intent, for one dizzying moment Madeline wondered if someone had seen Gervase and her at the boathouse, on the path . . . but Sybil wouldn't have brought the girls if that were the case.

Turning back to Sybil, she raised her brows. "What purpose?"

Sybil leaned nearer. "It's the festival, you see. With the best will in the world . . . well, Gervase is a *man*, my dear, and desperately needs female assistance."

Madeline studied Sybil's blue eyes, then glanced at the girls. "I thought you . . .?"

"Oh, no, dear." Sybil sat back with a light laugh. "Not that we wouldn't be glad to help—and indeed we will as far as he'll allow. But you see, he thinks of us as . . . well, *dependents*. As ladies to be cosseted, not taken notice of."

"He's been our guardian for years, of course," Belinda put in, "so he views us as veritable babes—never to be taken seriously."

"The notion that on some issues we might know more than he, especially as he's been away for so long, never enters his head." Annabel looked disgusted.

"Yes, well"—Sybil bent a reproving glance on Annabel—"it's not that we don't value his protection and his care of us. No." She turned to Madeline and laid a hand on her sleeve. "Indeed, it's because we understand why he's unlikely to listen to advice from us that we've come to appeal to you."

Madeline suddenly found herself the object of four pleading looks not even her brothers could have bettered.

Sybil patted her hand. "We know how busy you are, dear, but if you *could* find the time, just to hint him in the right direction. Oversee things, as it were. I know I can rely on you to know just how to word advice so he'll follow it, and he'll listen to you." Sybil smiled. "The truth is, he's such a strong character that it needs an equally strong character to make any impression on him, and sadly none of us is up to his weight."

Madeline blinked, but as a good neighbor and friend she couldn't fail to agree. "I'll do what I can, of course. The festival is for the entire district, after all—only fair that a few of us share the organizational burden."

"Exactly!" Sybil beamed. "I knew you would know just how to put it. Now, I hope you're free to dine with us tonight? Just us"—with a wave she included the girls—"and Gervase. I thought perhaps you could bring your brothers, as well as Muriel, of course. It might be useful to learn if the boys have any suggestions for activities that might keep the younger males amused."

Madeline found herself agreeing, then Sybil rose, collected her shawl and her daughters, and with her usual sweet smile, departed.

Standing on the front porch waving the carriage away, Madeline considered, then sighed. Turning inside, she headed back to the office and the work still remaining from the previous afternoon.

There was absolutely no point in cultivating moss. Gervase had lived by that maxim for most of his thirty-four years; he saw no reason to eschew it now. So while Sybil and his sisters drove to Treleaver Park to cultivate Madeline, he bobbed on the waves, and cultivated her brothers.

He'd set out to find them after an early breakfast; fate had smiled and he'd intercepted them riding across his lands. He suspected they'd been on their way to search the caves tucked in the various coves that scalloped the western shore of the peninsula, but they'd been readily distracted by his suggestion of taking out his favorite sailing boat and tacking around Black Head to beat up the coast toward the Helford estuary to a fishing spot they all knew.

They'd dropped anchor in the inlet near the village of St. Anthony; they'd each flipped a line into the sea, and now sat slumped against the sides, watching the breeze ruffle the furled sail.

Although his gaze was on the pennant rippling from the top of the mast, Gervase was aware of the glance the three boys exchanged.

"I suppose," Harry said, "that when you were younger, you must have done runs with the smugglers."

Gervase hid a grin. He nodded. "Quite a few." Still lazily gazing up at the pennant, he went on, "In those days, there were runs every few weeks—at least one a month, often more. The wars, and the excise levied because of them, made smuggling a lucrative trade. Now, however . . ."

Appreciating how devoted Madeline was to his three eager listeners, and when he married her, then regardless of any legal obligation certain natural and moral responsibilities regarding them would fall to him, given all that he had no wish to inflame their already engaged enthusiasms regarding the smugglers, and joining their runs.

"Now the wars have ended, there's a rather large question over what smugglers will run—what goods will make smuggling worthwhile, whether there'll be reason enough to continue doing runs at all. At present, there's not much that would be worth the risk"—he lowered his gaze to sweep the three attentive faces—"which is why the gangs have gone quiet."

He let that fact, and the implied prediction, sink in, then smiled. "Have you heard how the smugglers helped His Majesty's services during the wars?"

Edmond's eyes went wide. "They helped our forces?"

"Often." Gervase settled his shoulders against the boat's side. "For instance, when I was in Brittany, at a little fishing port called Roscoff, near St. Pol-de-Léon, I had to get back to England, fast, and . . ."

For the rest of the hour that they bobbed in the inlet, he held them enthralled with stories of wartime adventures, some his, some of other operatives like Charles St. Austell and Jack Hendon, whose exploits had passed into legend.

Noticing the wind rising, he capped his last tale with, "So those are some of the adventures my generation had, but while your generation will doubtless have adventures, too, as the times have changed, those wanting adventures will need to look in other arenas. The exciting new challenges will assuredly come from some different, unexpected direction—that, my lads, is the nature of adventure."

Edmond and Ben grinned, then scrambled to help as he moved to ready the sail. Although Harry also smiled, Gervase noted his more pensive expression, and was satisfied. He hadn't had a chance to probe the cause of Harry's underlying restlessness; he hoped Madeline had acted on his advice and taken steps to include Harry in the work of the estate.

With their anchor raised and sail unfurled, the canvas filled, billowed, then snapped taut. The hull lifted and sliced southward through the choppy waves. Once they were under way, Gervase located Ben crouching before the mast. "Ben—why don't you come and take the tiller?"

Ben's eyes lit. He glanced at his older brothers, but both

only nodded him back toward Gervase and shifted forward to sit on either side of the prow, enjoying the bounce and spray as the boat beat swiftly down the coast.

Scrambling to join Gervase at the stern, Ben sat on the bench Gervase vacated and wrapped both hands around the wooden handle. "I haven't done this much before."

Gervase smiled at the breathless confession. Once Ben had a good grip, he switched to sit on the other side of the tiller, resting his hand along the upper edge—for Ben's re-assurance more than his. The seas weren't high, and they weren't so close to the shore or the outlying reefs that he wouldn't have plenty of time to seize the tiller and get her back on course should they go astray.

"You're doing well." He relaxed against the stern. "Just keep her nose in line with the cliffs—the wind's sitting just right for us to beat straight down to Black Head. I'll tell you how to manage when we get there."

Ben didn't reply, just nodded.

Gervase glanced at his face, saw the light shining in his eyes. Smiling, he sat back, entirely content.

Knowing one sure way to Madeline's heart, after lunch he set out on Crusader to visit his smuggling contacts. Not to ask about smuggling, but about whether there'd been any-thing to suggest that the wreckers had plied their trade dur-ing the squall that had struck during Lady Porthleven's ball.

This morning he'd distracted the Gascoigne trio, but to-morrow would be another day, and from their direction when he'd come upon them, and the few references they'd let fall during the morning's sailing, they were plainly still intent on searching for wreckers' treasure, not a safe pas-time if there had been recent wrecks.

He stopped in Coverack to speak with the innkeeper there, then rode north to Porthoustock, then on to Helford and Gweek, eventually reaching Helston itself, and Abel Griggs.

"Nah." Abel hefted the foaming pint pot Gervase set before him and took a deep draft. Lowering the pot, he wiped foam from his upper lip, then settled to chat. "Ain't been no action—not for us, nor for them. That squall was a bad one, right enough, but it didn't sit right for them. Far as we've been able to make out from the whispers and the remains of false beacons on the cliffs, they've only been using the reefs to the west, mostly laying in for the coves from Kynance to Mullion."

"Not to the east?"

Abel shook his head. "There's just the Manacles that side, and while they might be right jagged teeth lying there ready to rip out a ship's hull, they're difficult for the wreckers, leastways with the currents 'round that way." Abel studied his beer. "Besides, with the wind as it was in that squall, it'd only be a ship beating north for the Helford estuary that'd be at risk, and no captain on this coast would do that in a blow."

Gervase nodded. "True enough."

Reassured that there was—still—nothing for Madeline's brothers to find in the caves that dotted the western coves, he chatted with Abel about this and that, after his reminiscences of the morning reliving and recounting certain shared adventures from decades before.

He left Abel in the tavern on the old docks that had always been his "office" and headed back to Coinagehall Street and the Scales & Anchor where he'd left Crusader. He turned in under the arch of the inn's stableyard—to find Madeline striding toward him.

She checked at the sight of him, but then she smiled and came on, joining him where he'd halted under the arch. "I'm glad I found you."

He smiled back. "Good afternoon to you, too."

She pulled a face at him. "Indeed—good afternoon, and I hope it will be one. I'm on my way to the Stannary Court."

He raised his brows. "Do tell."

Her lips quirked, but she immediately sobered. "I had a visit this morning from one of our tenant farmers. He and his brother were approached with an offer to buy their tin mining leases by the same agent as before. Both Kendrick and his brother have heard rumors—fresh rumors—that the mines are in financial trouble, but Kendrick had the nous to come and see me before they accepted."

Eyes narrowing, she shook her head. "This can't go on. Some farmers will sell simply because they've been frightened into thinking they should."

"But why hie to the Stannary Court?"

Madeline met his eyes. "Because it occurred to me that whoever's behind this might have succeeded in buying a few leases—ones from holders we don't know or who haven't asked around. If that's so, then the clerk of the court would know of it, for he would have had to register the transfer of ownership."

Gervase stared at her for a long moment, then he took her arm. "Brilliant." Turning, he started along the pavement toward the court building beyond the inn; she fell into step beside him. "You're absolutely right—excellent deduction."

They walked a little way, then he looked ahead to where stone steps led up to the double doors of the Stannary Court. "Of course, the clerk isn't supposed to happily volunteer information regarding a new owner."

"No, he isn't." Glancing at him, she met his amber eyes. "That's why I was so glad I found you."

His lips curved. "You think, between us, that we'll be able to convince the clerk of where his true loyalties lie?"

Reaching the steps, she drew her arm free to raise her skirts. "I'd be very much surprised if, between us, we couldn't."

She climbed the steps and marched into the foyer, entirely confident with him at her back.

On the other side of the road, Malcolm Sinclair remained facing the bow window of the apothecary's shop. Via the reflection in the glass, he followed the progress of the couple into the building opposite—the Stannary Court.

He was rarely shocked by anything, but seeing that particular gentleman there—that, very definitely, wasn't something he'd expected. He didn't appreciate the sudden clenching in his chest, but innate caution warned against not paying attention, not properly assessing this unlooked-for, and undesirable, development.

He didn't know the lady, but she was unimportant. It was the man . . . the last time he'd seen him had been in London, and under circumstances that might well prove inimical to his current plans. But before he acted—reacted—he needed to know more.

Glancing sideways, he saw two old men, retired sailors by the look of them, sitting at one of the rough tables outside the tavern two doors along the street. Summoning his most amiable expression—he could charm birds from trees if he wished—he strolled along the pavement, pausing before the men's table to tip his head, smile and exchange comments on the fine day. They were a gregarious pair, making it easy for him to ask, "That building over there." He nodded across the street to the court. "What is it?"

They grinned and happily told him.

He raised his brows. "I see. I have to admit I know little about tin mining."

"Well," said one old tar, an evil grin creasing his face, "after smuggling, it's the main source of employment around here."

Malcolm looked suitably impressed. "I hadn't realized." He glanced at the court building. "Actually, there was a gentleman who just went in with a lady. I thought I recognized him, but I can't recall his name. Do you know if he's a local?"

The pair glanced at the steps. "His lordship, the earl, you mean?"

It required no effort to appear surprised. "Tall, well set up, well dressed. The lady was tall, too."

The second sailor nodded. "Aye, that was Miss Gascoigne—her as holds the reins for her young brother, Harry, him being Viscount Gascoigne of Treleaver Park. That's to the east on the peninsula."

"And the earl?"

"Tregarth, Earl of Crowhurst. He was a major in the guards, they say." The sailors exchanged a knowing glance. "Course, that's not all he was, as those hereabouts have good cause to know. One of our own, and in the thick of things with old Boney, he was. But now he's home, and with his uncle and cousin passed on, he's lord of Crowhurst Castle—that's down on the peninsula, too."

Malcolm smiled and thanked them. "He wasn't who I thought he was—just as well I asked."

"Aye, well, you do hail from London, and no doubt there's gentleman upon gentleman there—easy enough to get confused."

With a nod and a smiling salute, Malcolm moved on.

Inwardly cursing. His eyes hadn't lied; Tregarth was the gentleman Christian Allardyce, Marquess of Dearne, had joined after informing Malcolm of his guardian's suicide. Malcolm had seen the pair speak; they were, had been, colleagues, of that there was no doubt whatever in his mind.

So Tregarth was now Crowhurst, a major landowner, consorting with another major landowner, or the equivalent in the tall Miss Gascoigne, both almost certainly controlling multiple mining leases as was the general case in the area, and they'd been going into the Stannary Court . . . possibly to make inquiries over who had recently acquired mining leases, poaching on their turf.

Malcolm didn't like that notion, not at all, but most worrying was that Tregarth knew him as Malcolm Sinclair—while everyone else in the area, with the sole exception of Jennings, knew him as Thomas Glendower.

Dinner that evening at Crowhurst Castle was a relaxed and entertaining affair. Sybil, Muriel, Gervase and Madeline were outnumbered by the younger crew, who, after their initial wary reticence had been broken by Edmond asking Annabel how they'd managed to break the mill, proceeded to get along famously.

Regardless, Madeline was pleased to note that as the evening progressed her brothers remained on their best behavior, treating the three girls with a deference the girls seemed to take as their due. When the company rose from the dinner table, the boys leapt up, each drawing back one of the girls' chairs, then attentively falling into step beside them as they followed Sybil and Muriel from the room.

The sight made her smile.

"I apologize in advance should my dear sisters lead your brothers astray."

She turned as Gervase came up beside her. "What a strange thing to say." She placed her hand on his proffered arm. "And here I was thinking what a civilizing influence they seem to be exerting over my barbarians."

"Oh, they're civil enough at the moment." Together they ambled in their siblings' wake. "But when they don't get their way, they transform into hoydenish harridans."

She laughed. "Hoydenish I might believe, given the recent incidents, but I sincerely doubt they have it in them to be harridans."

"Trust me, they do."

They'd reached the drawing room; entering, they discovered their juniors had decided on a game of loo. Belinda was directing Harry and Edmond in fetching and setting up the table, while Annabel, Ben and Jane were on their knees fishing in the sideboard for the cards and counters.

Sybil and Muriel were already ensconced on one chaise, heads together chatting. With Gervase, Madeline repaired to its mate, from where they could observe the card table and, if necessary, intervene in the activities around it, but could otherwise converse in reasonable privacy.

"I think we should pay a visit to Mr. Glendower tomorrow morning—before he has a chance to ride out." She glanced at Gervase, brows rising.

He nodded. "It seems too coincidental that he recently bought the manor at Breage, with two mining leases, and then also bought two more."

They'd discovered that a Mr. Thomas Glendower was the only person to recently purchase any mining leases in the area. Further investigation had yielded the information that he'd also bought the small manor near Breage, and was now living there. It had been late afternoon before they'd learned his direction; they'd decided not to try for an interview so late, but wait for tomorrow to approach him.

"He must be our man," Madeline said, her tone determined. "The one behind the agent and the rumors."

"You've found him?"

Madeline turned. Gervase looked up to find that Harry had slipped away from the action about the card table; he stood at the end of the chaise beside Madeline. With their attention on him, he colored faintly, but persisted, "The man behind all these rumors? If you're going to see him, can I come?"

Gervase noted the clenching of Harry's fists at his sides, and hoped Madeline understood.

She turned to him, brows arching.

He returned her look, not quite impassively.

Her eyes searched his, then she turned to Harry. "If you want to."

Harry smiled; his hands unclenched. His eyes shone as he answered the question he'd correctly divined in Madeline's tone. "If he's the one creating all these problems in the district, well . . ."—he glanced at Gervase as if seeking the correct way to explain, then he looked again at Madeline—"it's the sort of thing Viscount Gascoigne should help with, and I'm old enough to start learning the ropes."

Madeline smiled, openly approving; reaching out, she grasped his hand and lightly squeezed. "Indeed. We'll be only too happy to have you along."

Gervase nodded his own, rather more masculine approval. "As your sister suggests, we should catch him before he has a chance to ride out for the day. If it is him, we don't want him luring more unsuspecting leaseholders into his net, so we'll need to make an early start." He glanced at Madeline. "Best if I meet you two at the junction at Tregoose—let's say at nine. We can ride on together from there."

Madeline and Harry agreed. Then Harry was imperiously summoned to the card table. He quickly went to take his place.

Madeline turned to Gervase. She searched his eyes, then arched a brow. "Was that your doing, or truly his own initiative?"

"Mostly his own initiative—I just nudged him into acting on it."

She tilted her head. "How?"

He smiled and sat back, his gaze going to the game; their conversation was drowned out by the already eager exclamations of their siblings. "By explaining how the smugglers' days are, if not quite over, then numbered, and that for adventures they—their generation—will need to look elsewhere."

Madeline studied him; his more relaxed demeanor in this company made him easier to read. Then she laid a hand on his sleeve, lightly gripped. "Thank you." She, too, turned to watch the game. "They'll accept that from you."

He didn't say anything for some minutes, then murmured, "I checked again to make sure the wreckers hadn't taken advantage of that bad blow a week ago. Apparently the wind was in the wrong quarter, and so regardless of your brothers' devotion to searching, they're not going to find anything that will bring them into contact with the wreckers."

"Thank you again." She touched his hand lightly.

They both grew absorbed with the card game, although not for the same reasons that held their siblings engrossed. Again and again they shared a look, a private laugh at the interaction, the antics, and all they revealed. Belinda might be sixteen, and Harry fifteen, but under the influence of excitement both shed their superiority and became the children they'd only recently left behind, happily and noisily engaging with the others in what degenerated into an uproarious engagement.

Madeline watched, and appreciated the moment, appreciated that Gervase saw it, understood it, too. Earlier in the evening, she and Sybil had drawn him into a discussion of various aspects of the festival; she had to admit she could now see Sybil and his sisters' point. He was so accustomed to command that he tended to ride over any but the most trenchant opposition—or, in her case, an opposing view put by someone of equally strong character unwilling to simply get out of his way.

She was also someone he had reason to wish to please, but, when she'd noted the way his sisters had been avidly watching them and had arched a brow at him, he'd reassured her with a murmur that neither the girls nor Sybil had any inkling whatever of their affair.

Which was a relief in one sense, yet it left open the question of why his sisters, and Sybil, too, were viewing her in quite such a way. Viewing her success in influencing him with something akin to smugness.

More, of approval.

She couldn't put her finger on what it was she sensed from them. In the end, she inwardly shook her head and told herself they were simply the four people most likely to applaud any lady who could deal with Gervase.

Late that night, with the rising wind howling about the eaves of the manor, Malcolm Sinclair was quickly and efficiently packing the last of his belongings when a tap at the library French doors had him glancing sharply that way.

Recognizing the shadowy figure beyond the doors, he strode over and unlocked them, leaving Jennings to enter and follow him back to the desk.

The implication of the box into which Malcolm was loading papers was transparent.

"You're leaving?" In the light of the lamp, Jennings's eyes grew round.

"Yes. And so are you." Grim-faced, Malcolm dropped in the last file, then reached for a piece of string. "Here—help me secure this."

Jennings obediently held the box closed; while he wrapped the string around and tied it tight, Malcolm explained, briefly and succinctly, whom he had seen in Helston that afternoon, where they'd been going, and what that meant. "While everything we've been doing here is perfectly legal, I have absolutely no wish to meet Tregarth and be asked to explain."

More specifically he didn't want to explain why everyone locally knew him as Thomas Glendower, rather than Malcolm Sinclair. He definitely didn't need Tregarth thinking back, and deciding to check for a connection between

Thomas Glendower and Malcolm's late guardian's nefarious scheme. The connection couldn't easily be proved, but to a man with the resources Malcolm feared Tregarth might possess, his secret might yield.

The authorities had been lenient over Malcolm's role in his guardian's illegal and immoral scheme, but if they knew of Thomas Glendower and his investment accounts, they might not be inclined to be quite so forgiving.

That was a chance Malcolm wasn't prepared to take. Aside from all else, he'd come to enjoy being Thomas, being the owner of this place. He resented having to leave so abruptly, to decamp and flee, but he was barely twenty-one; there would be time, eventually, for him to return to Cornwall, the manor and Thomas Glendower.

But he shared none of that with Jennings, who had no idea his alter ego existed. He cared not a whit if Jennings thought he was running like a scared rabbit; ego, he'd learned, was a weakness, a failing.

"We're going tonight." He met Jennings's gaze. "I'm leaving most of my things here. I'll be packed, saddled and ready to ride in an hour. How long will it take you to get ready?"

Jennings was staying at a tiny cottage in the hamlet of Carleen, a mile or so north. He narrowed his eyes in thought. "Shouldn't take more than an hour to get back to the cottage, pack and clear up, then get back here."

Curtly, Malcolm nodded. "Good. I'll meet you on the London road."

Chapter 10

$\mathcal{M}$idnight arrived; Madeline stood at her open bed-room window and listened as clocks throughout the house whirred, chimed and bonged. Everyone else was sound asleep; they'd got back from the castle more than an hour ago. Happy and tired, her brothers had trailed up to their rooms without her even having to hint; she and Muriel had exchanged fond glances and followed.

The household had settled. Unfortunately, she couldn't.

Restless, as unsettled as the weather, she'd drifted to the window to stare out at the clouds scudding over the sky, concealing, then revealing the waning moon as they streamed past, driven by a strong offshore wind.

Her room faced inland, overlooking the gardens at the front of the house. From their earliest years, her brothers had claimed the rooms facing the sea; as when younger they'd been noisy and clamoring, she'd moved to this room at the far end of the opposite wing.

When Muriel had joined them, she'd reclaimed her childhood room in the central block of the house; Madeline had grown used to her isolation, to her privacy.

She leaned against the window frame; warm air wafted in, lifting her hair, setting it floating about her face and shoulders. She was smiling to herself, imaging how she must look, when a shifting shadow in the gardens caught her eye.

A deliberately moving shadow. She'd already doused her candle; her eyes had adjusted to the night. She watched long enough to be certain that a man was approaching the house, but he was walking surely and purposefully, albeit carefully, rather than skulking.

Once she was sure he was making for the morning room French doors—a route she knew her brothers occasionally used on nocturnal forays—she left the window, paused, considering, by her dressing table, then hefted the heavy silver candlestick she'd left there, and on silent feet went to the door.

Her slippers made no sound on the corridor runner. She knew the house literally better than the back of her hand; hugging the shadows, she made her way to the head of the stairs.

She knew the male she'd glimpsed hadn't been Edmond or Ben, but in the poor light she hadn't been able to tell whether he was Harry or not.

The thought of Harry, of the evidence of his evolving maturity she'd witnessed that evening—and Gervase's earlier allusion to what might constitute the emerging Harry's idea of adventure—made her wonder just how much he'd truly grown.

Was the man she'd glimpsed Harry returning from some tryst?

Given the time since they'd returned, it was possible.

If it was he, he'd never forgive her if she roused the household; he'd be embarrassed beyond measure.

But if it wasn't Harry . . . they had an intruder in the house.

Straining her ears, she could just detect not footsteps but the faint creak of boards. From the familiar sounds, she tracked the man as he crossed the morning room; standing at the gallery rail, she looked down into the shadowy pit of the front hall, and saw the morning room door open.

Just in time she remembered her nightgown was white; she jerked back into the shadows, then inwardly swore. She didn't want the intruder, if he wasn't Harry, to glance up and see her at the top of the stairs. The candlestick was all very well, but surprise—as in her surprising him—would greatly help. But if she'd hesitated for just a second she might have been able to see if the man was Harry or not, but she hadn't, so she didn't know, and so now she had to retreat into the gloom behind the old suit of armor facing the stairhead.

And wonder if the intruder would climb the stairs.

As if in answer, a tread creaked. Raising the candlestick, she waited.

Straining through the shadows, she watched as a head slowly came into view.

Immediately she knew who it was. Stunned amazement held her motionless, long enough for him to reach the gallery. He glanced around; lowering the candlestick, she stepped around the armor to where the faint moonlight would reach her, and hissed, "What are you doing here?"

Gervase turned, studied her, then reached out and took the candlestick from her. "I couldn't sleep."

His gaze ran over her, from her head to her toes, paused at her bare feet, then, slowly, reversed direction. Blindly, he reached to the side and set the candlestick on a nearby sideboard. "As I was saying, I couldn't sleep, and as you haven't yet agreed to share my bed, I thought I'd join you in yours."

He'd spoken in a rumbling murmur throughout, but his tone had subtly altered, sending delicious anticipation skittering down her spine. However . . . "You can't be seri—"

She broke off as his lips covered hers. He'd moved so quickly, pulling her into his arms, she hadn't even had time to squeak, and then he was kissing her, answering her question in a highly explicit manner—and she suddenly knew why she hadn't been able to sleep.

Reaching up, spearing her fingers through his hair, she kissed him back. Voraciously.

For long moments they communed in the dark, then he broke off and darkly, nearly breathlessly demanded, "Your room?"

"End of the corridor." She waltzed him in the right direction. He steered her toward her door.

How they ever reached it, let alone got inside the room with the door shut upon the world, she never knew. But once they were inside, clothes flew, not that she had many to lose, but that left her with more to strip from him, more to goad her impatience to fresh and frantic heights.

Then they were naked, skin to hot skin, hands feverishly reaching, touching, stroking, caressing, stoking the fires that burned from within, making them blaze.

And then they were tumbling into her bed, onto the crisp sheets. She gasped, clung, clutched as he spread her thighs wide, wedged his hips between and with one powerful surging thrust joined them.

They wrestled and rode, laughed, gasped and battled for supremacy even while the conflagration within built, then roared, and came racing through them.

Until it took them, consumed them, seared them and fused them, until she clung, weak and close to weeping with pleasure. Suspended over the void, senses sharp and bright, tense and tight. Waiting. . . .

With one last thrust he sent her spinning, every nerve

alight, every sense fracturing into a million shards of glittering, earthly delight.

Warmth welled as he joined her; bone-deep pleasure swelled and spilled through her, golden glory filling her veins as, on a groan, he lost himself in her.

Smiling deliriously, she wrapped her arms about him and, without hesitation or intention, surrendered to the night.

Several hours later, she stirred, then woke to the unexpected sensation of a hard, still-hot, naked male body beside her.

Instantly she knew who it was—her senses didn't even jump, just purred. Turning onto her side, she looked at him, at the sliver of face she could see given he was slumped facedown on the pillow beside hers.

She looked, let her gaze caress; unable to resist the temptation, she let her feelings creep from within and stretch. Tentative and strange. What she felt . . . wasn't something she'd felt before.

Admitting as much was tantamount to acknowledging that this bordered on the dangerous, that fate's time—her boon—might already be running out. That if she wanted her heart to remain safe, untouched, untrammeled, then she should think of pulling back, of bringing this liaison to a close.

She shifted her gaze, looking past his shoulder to the open window beyond. To the night sky, still dark and heavy with cloud.

"I'll leave before it's light." At his mumbled words, she glanced at him. He continued, his voice muffled by the pillow, "No one will see or know."

She hesitated, then lifted one hand, set her palm to his shoulder, savored the width of the muscle, the latent strength, then slowly, following her hand with her gaze, she ran it down the long line of his back to his hip. "So . . . you'll stay for a while?"

Her soft whisper hung in the night.

He shifted, rolled onto his side, caught her hand and lifted it to his lips to place a heated kiss in her palm. Through the shadows he met her eyes. "I'll stay . . . for as long as there's night."

It was she who stretched and closed the distance to bring her lips to his; she who kissed him, then pushed him onto his back.

When she rose above him in the dark and impaled herself on his hard length, she sighed.

Dangerous it might be, but she knew she wouldn't be giving up this pleasure, giving him up, anytime soon.

Not because she would have to battle to deny him, fight him for every inch of separation, not because avoiding him would be a social and logistical nightmare. Regardless of all else, as she rode him slowly, savoring the heat, the sweet build of passion, knowing the firestorm that would eventually come, feeling his hands close strongly about her waist, feeling the delicious tension rise . . . no matter the distraction, or perhaps because of it, one truth shone clearly in her mind.

She wouldn't be curtailing their liaison because she didn't want to.

Because she didn't want to deny herself this pleasure.

Because she didn't want to give up the feelings that along with the glory of satiation filled and swamped her heart.

The next morning they met as arranged near Tregoose, where the road from Coverack joined the road from Lizard Point. Madeline rode between Gervase and Harry as they continued past Helston and out onto the road to Penzance.

Breage was a small village north of the road about two

miles west of Helston. The manor house they sought, however, lay to the south, between the road and the cliffs; they followed a narrow lane, then turned up a drive that ultimately led them to the front door.

No groom appeared to take their horses; looking around, they tied their reins to the low branches of a nearby tree. Then, with Gervase at her shoulder and Harry just behind, Madeline walked to the door.

Gervase's sharp knock was eventually answered by an older middle-aged man, his neat clothes concealed behind a worn apron.

He looked from one to the other, then settled his gaze on Gervase. "How can I help you, sir?"

"Lord Crowhurst, Miss Gascoigne and Viscount Gascoigne to see Mr. Glendower."

The man's eyes widened; he recognized the names. He bobbed a bow. "I'm sure the master would be happy to see you, m'lords, ma'am, but he's been called away. Urgent-like. He left early this morning."

"Did he, indeed?"

Madeline glanced at Gervase; his eyes had narrowed. Summoning a smile, she took charge. "And you would be?"

The man responded to her smile with a grateful nod. "Gatting, ma'am. Me and the missus do for Mr. Glendower."

"I confess we hadn't realized until recently that he'd come to live in the district. How long has he been here?"

"Only a month or so, ma'am. He stayed at Helston at first, but then he said he fell in love with the manor and bought it, and got us in—we were living with my Elsie's sister in Porthleven, but looking for a post just like this."

Madeline smiled understandingly. "Hard to come by in the country."

Gatting visibly thawed. "Indeed, ma'am. Is there anything I can do for you? Take a message for the master, perhaps?"

Brows rising, she exchanged a glance with Gervase, then shook her head. "Do you have any idea how long he'll be away?"

A cloud passed over Gatting's face. "No, ma'am. In his note he said he couldn't say, but that we'd be kept on indefinitely. His London solicitor will send our wages."

"Well, that's good news then, at least on your account. How did you find Mr. Glendower to work for?"

Gatting waggled his head. "Gentry can be difficult, begging y'r pardon m'lords, ma'am, but Mr. Glendower was a pleasant gentleman—young, not much past his majority, I'd venture, but he was nice, unassuming, easy to do for. Never any fuss or bother. My Elsie was relieved we didn't have to move on."

Harry leaned around Madeline. "Did he say where he was going?" When Gatting looked at him, Harry tipped his head toward Gervase and her. "We might be going up to town, and if he's there, we might look him up if you could give us his direction."

"Indeed." She nodded. "That would be the neighborly thing to do." She looked inquiringly at Gatting.

Who grimaced. "Aye, he did say it was to London he was going, but he left no word of where. Said just to keep any letters that might come for him, although he didn't expect any."

"Did he have another man with him?" Gervase asked. "An agent, or a servant or groom?"

Gatting shook his head. "It was only him. Said he didn't need any man's help to get himself dressed or saddle his horse."

"Did he have many callers?"

"No, m'lord, not a one as far as we know." Gatting paused, then amended, "Well, Elsie did say he'd had a caller one day, while we were off down to Porthleven. Said there were two chairs in the parlor with cushions squashed.

Course, he could have just sat in both himself, but she seemed to think it wasn't so and someone had called. But howsoever, we didn't ask."

"Naturally not." Madeline smiled benedictorially on Gatting. "Thank you, Gatting, you've been most helpful."

Gatting bowed. "I'm only sorry the master wasn't here to greet you, ma'am."

With nods, they turned away.

They didn't speak until they were back on the track; Gervase reined in just before the main road. "So, we're left wondering whether our conjecture is correct, and Glendower, having bought two mining leases recently, is in truth our 'London gentleman.'"

She grimaced. "No agent, or at least none sighted. And the Gattings don't think Glendower is a wrong 'un." She met Gervase's eyes. "One thing I've learned is that staff generally know."

He nodded.

"But," Harry said, "if Glendower is our man, then if he's left the area and returned to London the rumors and the offers for leases should cease."

"True." Gervase gathered his reins. "If they do, then he's almost certainly the one behind them, but if he remains absent . . ."

"Then the problem he's been causing in the district will simply go away." Madeline glanced at him. "If he stays away and all our problems evaporate, there's no reason we need to pursue him, is there?"

Gervase nodded, his expression a touch grim. "That would be my conclusion—and unless I miss my guess, that was his conclusion, too."

She widened her eyes. "You think he realized we were about to descend on him?"

"Don't ask me how, but his sudden departure at the crack of dawn seems a little too coincidental for my money."

Madeline considered, then shrugged. "As long as he remains out of our hair, I'm content to leave him be." Shaking her reins, she urged her chestnut forward.

As he held Crusader back to let her pass, Gervase's gaze fell on the bright corona haloing her head; he remembered how it had felt when last night he'd run his hands through it, and decided she was right.

He and she had other fish to fry.

Flicking Crusader's reins, he followed her onto the road.

At noon that day, eight men, all hailing from the London stews, gathered in the small parlor of a ricketty cottage outside Gweek. They knew each other at least by repute; a motley collecton of bruisers, thieves and cutthroats, they found themselves joined in what would in the general way of their lives have been an unlikely alliance.

As ordered, they'd traveled down to Cornwall singly or in pairs. They'd arrived at the cottage over the previous day.

The cottage, they'd just learned, was to be their home while they performed the duties required by their new master. For all of them the accommodation, cramped and rundown though it was, was a significant improvement over their London holes; when their master, taking up a stance before the cold hearth, asked if they had any complaints, all eight shook their heads.

Even had they had complaints, none would have voiced them; quite aside from the fact the gentleman paid well, there was something about him that discouraged even the most hardened from even contemplating crossing him.

"Good." The gentleman—he was obviously and unquestionably that, even though he wore a black cloak, a hat low over his brow and a black silk scarf loosely wound around his chin—spoke with the bored accents of one born to rule. "As I informed you in London, I need you to locate and seize a cargo of mine that was due to arrive here, delivered to the banks of the Helford River, nine nights ago. The ship . . ."

He paused, dispassionately surveying their faces, then imperturbably went on, "Sailed from France, from a port in Brittany, by way of the Isles of Scilly. It was crewed by Frenchmen, not locals, although I was assured the French captain was one of the sort who knew these waters well."

The largest of the men, a hulking brute with small, surprisingly intelligent eyes, shifted his weight. "Smugglers?"

The gentleman looked at him. "Is that a problem?"

The bruiser shook his head. "No, sir—just wanted to make sure we knew who we might be rubbing up against."

The gentleman inclined his head. "A wise question, and in that regard I can tell you that the crew of this French ship was not connected with any of the local arms of the fraternity. This run was one executed without their knowledge."

He hesitated, then went on, his tone growing chillier, "However, after leaving the Isles, the French ship appears to have disappeared without trace. It's possible the local smugglers intercepted the run. They might have seized my cargo, or know where it is. In addition, my sources tell me that there are wreckers active on the Lizard Peninsula. And the night the ship was due to arrive, there was indeed a storm. So it's also possible the wreckers are now in possession of . . . what's rightfully mine."

He paused, mastering the anger that welled at the thought. Fate, a fickle female he'd long thought to be irrevocably on his side, had, it seemed, suddenly turned against him and handed his treasure—his prize—to others, denying him his due, his rightful triumph.

How could he gloat over outwitting his nemesis without his prize?

With an effort of will, he blocked off the thought; he would find his treasure, then he would gloat. "The wreckers are secretive, violently so, as one might expect. Your task is to investigate the local groups—smugglers and wreckers alike—and discover what they know of any recent cargo."

Shaking back the enveloping cloak, he tossed a heavy purse on the small table in the room's center; the purse landed with a dull clinking, immediately transfixing all eight pairs of eyes. "That's for your expenses." He looked at the bruiser who'd spoken earlier. "Gibbons, you're in charge of the purse. See that the money's used well. If you need more, more will be forthcoming, but only as long as it's spent in the right cause."

Gibbons nodded and reached for the leather pouch. "Aye, sir."

The gentleman glanced around. "You're all experienced— you know how to ingratiate yourselves, and how to cover your backs, and your tracks. That's why I hired you. Operate in pairs, drink the locals under the table, buy them a woman, loosen their tongues by whatever means come to hand."

Coldly, he ran his gaze around the circle of speculative expressions. "I want that cargo, and I don't care what you do as long as you locate it." He smiled in chilly promise. "Once you have, we'll decide how to seize it."

All eight men grinned, avarice gleaming in their eyes.

Satisfied, with a curt nod he turned to the door. "I suggest you get to it."

The eight waited until the door closed behind him, then waited some more, until they heard the retreating clop of horse's hooves. Then and only then did they relax.

Gibbons hefted the pouch, weighing it. "I'll say this much for him, he doesn't stint." He glanced around at his companions, then grinned. "Well, lads, no time like the present. We'd better do as he said and get drinking."

With laughs and cackles, all eight headed for the door.

Three hours later, Madeline sat in the drawing room at Crowhurst Castle inwardly smiling in pleased approval as Gervase presided over the final meeting of the festival committee. With only two days to go, all the myriad details were coming together nicely, but her satisfaction was occasioned more by Gervase's ready acceptance of his rightful role.

She was really very pleased she'd suggested that the festival return to the castle.

Mrs. Entwhistle, beside her on the chaise, consulted her copious lists. "And the barrels for the apple-bobbing will be brought in by Jones, the innkeeper from Coverack, so that's one thing your people won't need to deal with, my lord."

"Excellent." Sitting negligently at ease in an armchair, Gervase crossed that item off his own list, the one Mrs. Entwhistle had handed him when she'd arrived. "And the horseshoes?" He looked at Gerald Ridley.

"Oh, indeed! We—my stablelads and I—will take care of that. The area by the stable arch, you said?" Brows knit, Gerald scribbled on his own list.

"That's right." Gervase amended that item, then scanned the page. "Have we covered everything?"

"It seems so," Mrs. Juliard said, consulting her copy.

Everyone looked up—at Madeline.

She smiled. She didn't need to consult her copy. "I can't think of anything we've missed, or any arrangements we've failed to discuss. Indeed, we've added a good few amusements which should help in keeping the whole running smoothly."

Glancing around the faces, she ended smiling at Mrs.

Entwhistle. "I think we're all to be congratulated. We've done an excellent job of planning—now it's time for the execution, which is in many more hands than just our own."

"Indeed." On Mrs. Entwhistle's other side, Sybil beamed at the company. "And on that note, I suggest we ring for tea. Would you mind, Madeline dear?"

Madeline rose and tugged the bellpull. When Sitwell appeared, Sybil ordered tea while the rest of them settled to chat.

In due course, the trolley arrived, and tea and cakes were dispensed. Madeline assisted Sybil, then turned to tell Squire Ridley about Mr. Thomas Glendower.

"Well, well." Gerald beetled his thick brows. "Time will no doubt tell. I'll keep my ears open and let you and"—he nodded to Gervase as he joined them—"his lordship here know if I hear anything more about mining leases."

"Indeed, please do." Gervase exchanged a glance with Madeline. "If fresh rumors circulate, or more offers eventuate, then Glendower isn't our man. It would be useful to know one way or the other."

"Absolutely." Gerald nodded. "I'll pass the word."

Gervase touched Madeline's arm. "Mrs. Juliard has a question about the trestles we'll be using for the embroidery displays. Could you . . .?"

She smiled. "Yes, of course."

Together they crossed to Mrs. Juliard; the question about the trestles was easily resolved. Gervase stayed by Madeline's side—or rather kept her by his—deferring to or drawing on her experience as various committee members verified minor details and asked last-minute questions.

It wasn't until, all such questions answered and with all theoretically ready for the morrow when the physical arrangements would be set in place, the company drifted into the front hall, making ready to depart, and the vicar turned to them, Gervase with Madeline beside him, and took his leave of them with a jovial, "I have to say that this year seems specially blessed and the festival looks set to exceed all our previous efforts," all the while smiling at her and shaking her hand before, with smile undimmed, shaking Gervase's, that Madeline realized just how far into the background Sybil had faded.

Looking around, she located Sybil by the drawing room door with Mrs. Caterham.

"Good-bye, Madeline dear."

Recalled to her place—by Gervase's side—by Mrs. Entwhistle, Madeline squeezed her fingers lightly. "Until tomorrow, Claudia. And don't fret. All will go swimmingly."

"Oh, I'm sure it will." With a twinkle in her eye, Mrs. Entwhistle turned to shake Gervase's hand. "Now we have you and his lordship both overseeing the whole, I'm sure nothing will dare go wrong."

Madeline's smile felt a trifle distracted. She glanced again at Sybil, but she seemed to feel no burning need to take her rightful place beside Gervase. More, like the vicar, all the others seemed to take it for granted that Madeline should be the one standing beside him.

She felt a little odd—an unwitting usurper—but as Sybil merely smiled sweetly, uncomprehendingly, when she succeeded in catching her eye, and did nothing about coming to replace her, she inwardly shrugged. It was doubtless just habit formed over the previous years when the festival had been held at the Park and she had, in fact, been the hostess. Everyone was used to her in that role, including Sybil, and with Sybil hanging back, without any real thought everyone recast her in the position. Perfectly understandable.

There was no reason whatever to make anything more of it, to read anything more into it.

She hoped they understood that.

His hand at her elbow, Gervase steered her onto the porch

at the top of the front steps; she'd earlier agreed to stay behind and go over the castle forecourt and ramparts with him,
with chalk marking out the booths and various spaces for
tents and other activities.

So she stood beside him before the castle front doors and
waved while the others rode or drove away—and tried not
to think of what image they were projecting, and what in-
correct ideas might consequently stir.

Chapter 11

"*A*h—good morning, Jones." Madeline smiled at the innkeeper from Coverack as he stood beside his cart, eyes wide and startled as he scanned the frenetic activity already overflowing the castle forecourt. She pointed. "If you'll take those barrels over there, to that spot beyond the steps, and then speak with Sitwell—he's at the top of the steps—about filling them."

"Thank you, ma'am." Jones tipped his cap. "Right circus, this is."

Madeline only smiled in reply, then moved smartly to dodge a donkey hauling in a cart. "Hello, Masters." She nodded to the old wandering merchant; he'd been a goldsmith in his prime, and now traveled the country visiting festivals and fairs. "Back with us this year?"

"Always, Miss Gascoigne." Masters bowed and doffed his hat. "One of my favorites, the Peninsula Summer Fesitval."

"Well, we're always glad to have you. We've kept one of the prime spots for your booth." She pointed out Gervase, a tall figure standing by the edge of the lawn directing the peddlers and merchants to their alloted places, and dealing with the inevitable grumbling. "Just speak with his lord-ship, Lord Crowhurst, and he'll show you where to set up."

"Thank you kindly, miss." Masters led his donkey on.

Madeline glanced around; with every minute that passed—with every additional person who came in through the gates to deliver this or that, or to lend a hand with as-sembling the various stalls, booths, tents and trestles—the bustle in the forecourt increasingly resembled a swelling melee.

She'd lived through the event many times, but the area they'd used at the Park had been more open. Although un-der the open sky, the forecourt was bounded by the castle's tall inner bailey walls on the east, north and northwest, the castle itself on the south, and beyond the lawns, the ram-parts to the southwest, overlooking the sea. The area was more protected from the wind and the weather, all to the good. However, the prevalence of stone walls hemming most of it in meant the noise level was significantly greater. She could barely hear herself think.

"Tomorrow will be better," she assured Mrs. Entwhistle when she came upon that harassed lady in the shifting throng and she commented on the cacophany. "Today ev-eryone is shouting instructions, not talking."

"Indeed!" Mrs. Entwhistle shouted back. "One has to positively scream to be heard."

They parted. Madeline moved through the crowd, keep-ing her eyes peeled for potential problems; she'd always had this role, even before the festival had moved to the Park. She knew the locals better than anyone else, and they lis-tened to her, even the men. And it was mostly the men and youths who were there that day, the sound of hammers and saws and oaths filling the air as they labored, all good-naturedly giving their time so their families could enjoy the festival tomorrow.

A few women had come bearing cloths and bunting to decorate some of the stalls; reaching the ramparts, Madeline looked out over the sea, then up and around at the sky, and decided the women's efforts would be safe enough. The weather looked set to remain fine.

Turning, she surveyed the seething mass of people, each and every one absorbed and intent on some task, and inwardly smiled. She was about to plunge into the crowd again when she glimpsed Harry, then located Edmond and the shorter Ben in the same knot of youths all helping with one stall.

The boys had ridden over with her that morning; there was no way they'd miss the day. Curious as to who they'd elected to spend it with, she circled closer.

Her halfbrothers were helping erect one of the larger tents used by the tavern owners from Helston to sell their ale. Lips thinning, Madeline saw which tavern it was, and immediately understood the attraction for her brothers. "Noah Griggs." She inwardly sighed, remembering Gervase saying that the man's older brother, Abel, was the leader of the Helston smuggling gang. "I suppose I might have known."

She'd spoken under her breath, so was surprised to hear, "Indeed you might," whispered in her ear.

She managed not to jump; it was harder not to shiver. Turning her head, she met Gervase's eyes. "I suppose it was naïve of me to think they might have forgotten their interest in the smugglers."

"In such a situation?" He met her eyes and smiled. "Undoubtedly naïve."

Drawing her arm though his, he stood close, his large frame protecting her from the buffeting of the crowd. "Just think—today they can with impunity, indeed, in complete, albeit feigned, innocence, spend time under Abel's eye, listening to the stories he's no doubt entertaining the lads with, and perhaps do enough to have Abel and his brother—he's the tavern owner, did I mention?—look upon them kindly."

She humphed. "Abel might look upon them kindly, but I won't."

"Ah, but you can't really say anything, can you?"

She sighed. "I suppose not." Turning, drawing her arm from his, she looked around.

"I'm on my way to check the booths along the east wall." He caught her eye. "Why don't you come with me?"

She was tempted, but . . . remembering yesterday and the circumstances that had placed them in misleading propinquity, she shook her head. "I should check on the spinners and weavers, and see if the cloth merchants have arrived. They're over by the northwest gate."

He looked into her eyes, then smiled, lifted her hand to his lips and lightly kissed. "Join me when you break for lunch. By then I'll need my sanity restored."

She laughed, nodded and they parted.

Tacking through the crowd, she found the spinners and weavers setting up their wheels and looms, and facing them, cloth merchants, milliners and haberdashers from Helston and even as far as Falmouth. A lacemaker from Truro had made the trip; she found her being helped to set up her traveling booth by Gervase's sisters.

Smiling, she stopped by the trio and welcomed the lacemaker. She'd bought lace from the woman before and knew she produced excellent work. "I'll be sure to drop by tomorrow to see what you have."

The lacemaker blushed and bobbed a curtsy. "Of course, Miss Gascoigne, but"—she glanced at the three girls—"I'm thinking you might need to be early."

"Ah!" Laughing, Madeline met Belinda's eyes. "Buying trim for your come-out gowns?"

"Well," Belinda said, "she gave us a glimpse and it seemed very fine."

"Oh, it is." With a smiling nod to the lacemaker, Madeline turned to move on.

With quick nods to the woman, the three girls went with her.

"Is it nearly lunchtime?" Jane stretched up on her toes, bobbing to look past the milling heads to the clock set in the wall above the stable arch.

Madeline checked. "No, not just yet, but if we head that way, by the time we reach the steps it should be time to go in."

The girls happily ranged around her, Belinda on one side, Jane on the other, with Annabel beyond.

Belinda drew breath, rather portentously. As Madeline glanced her way, she said, "*About* our come-outs . . ."

When she went no further, Madeline prompted, "What about them?"

"Well, you see"—Belinda frowned, twisting her fingers—"given what happened to Melissa and Katherine, we wondered . . . well"—she glanced at Madeline—"is it *usual* for a just-married lady to send her husband's sisters off that way? Just not want to have them around?" Belinda's hazel eyes searched Madeline's face. "We thought you might know."

Madeline studied those hazel eyes, very like Gervase's, then glanced at Annabel, met her blue eyes, then dropped her gaze to Jane's eyes, recalling what Gervase had earlier told her. In that instant, she more fully appreciated what had been behind the girls' disruptive actions.

Looking up, she drew in a slow breath, then glanced at Belinda. "I honestly don't think you have anything to worry about. Your brother would never send you away—and if you imagine any lady he married might see you as rivals for his affection . . . quite aside from that being unlikely in any lady he would choose to wed, any lady who attempted to get between him and you three would quickly find she'd misjudged."

They continued to tack slowly through the crowd. When Belinda frowned, clearly unconvinced, Madeline smiled wryly and added, "Your brother is a very strong man, not just in a physical sense but in all ways. No lady I've ever met would be strong enough to bend him to her purpose if that purpose was one he was set against."

"*No* lady?" Jane queried. When Madeline looked down at her, she opened her eyes wide. "Not even you?"

Madeline laughed and laid a hand on Jane's shoulder. "Not even me." Looking across the heads to the steps, she added absentmindedly, "Not that I'd wish to do anything so silly as send you three away."

Glancing back at Belinda, she saw a small swift smile cross her face.

"No." Belinda looked down as they neared the steps. "But that's you—we were worried about someone else. You know us, so you're different. Other ladies might not react to us in the same way."

Smiling fondly, Madeline lifted her other hand to Belinda's shoulder and squeezed lightly, reassuringly. "Any lady your brother chooses will think the same. Now hush, for there he is."

Gervase was standing at the top of the steps. He'd seen them approaching. He scanned his sisters' features, then his eyes narrowed and fixed on Belinda's face.

He looked rather grim as they reached him, but to Madeline's surprise all three girls beamed delightedly at him as they went past, lured by the promise of sandwiches.

Narrow-eyed, he turned to watch them go; slipping her arm through his, she urged him in their wake. "The spinners and weavers look to have settled without drama, thank Heaven." As they passed into the cool of the hall, she glanced back at the mass outside. "Have my brothers come in, do you know?"

"They're already inside."

Castle staff balancing platters of sandwiches passed them, ferrying the fare to the trestles set up to one side of the steps, sustenance for all those who had come to help and set up for tomorrow's big day.

Turning back, Madeline found Gervase's grim expression had eased. He laid his hand over hers on his sleeve. "Come—the committee are lunching in the dining room."

She let him lead her in and seat her beside him. A cold collation was laid out on the sideboard; she consented to allow him to fill her plate while she listened to the latest words from each of the committee, and added her own observations.

Despite various hiccups, everything was going well. Everything looked set for a wonderful festival.

While they ate swiftly, knowing they had to return to the chaos outside soon, she thought of his sisters and their underlying fear. She was usually so consumed keeping abreast of her brothers' lives, she rarely had emotional attention to spare for others in the district, even Gervase's family, her closest neighbors and nearest in station.

The three girls were seated at the end of the table in earnest conversation with her brothers. Surreptitiously she glanced at Gervase. He was helping her with her brothers; he'd certainly made her more aware of Harry's impending maturity. Perhaps, in this, given their new closeness—their liaison—she might return the favor and make sure he properly understood the basis for his sisters' fears.

Yet once they returned to the forecourt they were surrounded by the crowd, then separated by the demands of various helpers for direction or clarification. More peddlers and merchants were arriving with their booths and tents; the afternoon winged by in organized and happily good-natured chaos.

The sun was in the west, slowly sinking behind the wall, before the cacophany started to abate. The locals who'd helped with the stalls and trestles called good-bye and drifted home; satisfied with their arrangements, the peddlers retreated to their camp outside the castle walls, while the traveling merchants ambled off to their temporary lodgings in nearby barns and stables. One by one the committee members found Gervase and took their leave. Madeline, however, stayed to the end.

He found her with Sybil on the ramparts; as he neared, he heard Sybil say, "They were convinced they risked being bundled off to live with their Great-Aunt Agatha in Yorkshire—one can understand their horror, of course."

Coming up with both ladies, Gervase pretended he hadn't heard, that the whipping wind had blown the words away before he'd caught them. He smiled as they swung to face him. "All, I'm surprised to be able to report, has sorted itself out." He met Madeline's eyes. "You were right about the peddlers and merchants and their booths, but actual fisticuffs were avoided."

She returned his smile, holding back her whipping hair.

The wind gusted, plastering Sybil's light gown to her frame. She shivered. "If I'm not needed any longer, I'm going inside." She patted Madeline's arm. "I'll see you tomorrow, dear."

"Muriel and I will come as early as we can."

Gervase grimaced. "How early is early? When does this affair start?"

Madeline grinned. "Officially, as you must remember, you and Mr. Maple open the festival at ten, but people start arriving from seven o'clock."

Offering his arm, he groaned. "And I suppose I'll need to be visible from then, to keep order by my mere presence?"

She chuckled, took his arm; they started strolling along the rampart. "It would help, but from eight o'clock, perhaps.

Most of the earlier souls will be stall keepers or those wanting to lay out displays. The idly interested won't appear until after they've breakfasted. However, you will need to have your men on the gates from first light. Just to be certain."

He nodded. "I've already got that arranged."

They walked on, enjoying the freshening wind that blew in their faces, looking out over the sea, at the long breakers rolling in to crash in froth and foam on the shore below.

"Your sisters spoke to me," she eventually said. She glanced at him, trying to read his face; defeated, she grimaced and looked ahead. "Sybil said you know what was behind their strange behavior. I must admit, although you'd mentioned it before, I hadn't really thought how they might extrapolate from Lady Hardesty's behavior, how very threatened they would feel."

She glanced at him again. "They asked me if such a thing—a newly married lady sending her sisters-in-law away—was normal. I assured them it wasn't, but . . ." Pausing, she drew breath. "Regardless of what you might think, their fear is a reasonable one. It's something I often forget, that many ladies are not as in charge of their own destinies as I always have been."

His lips twisted; he caught her eye. "The truth is—and I admit I haven't been in any great rush to assure them of this—they'll have as much say in their lives as you've had in yours. For obvious reasons at present that's not a wise point to stress, however . . . you really don't need to worry about them."

She smiled and faced forward. "I know—I did tell them you'd never allow them to be sent away like the Hardesty girls. Still, it'll be in their minds until you choose your countess and they can convince themselves they've no cause for worry."

When he didn't say anything, she looked at him. "I have

known them all their lives, and while I haven't spent much time with them to date, that will change when Belinda and then Annabel make their come-outs. I'm quite fond of them, you know."

He smiled, entirely genuinely; lifting her hand from his sleeve, he kissed her fingers. "They're lucky to have your friendship, and your support, especially over their come-outs."

She blinked. He was perfectly aware that wasn't what she'd meant. A moment passed, then she shrugged lightly. "I'll be happy to assist in any way I can, but of course their primary sponsor will be your countess."

He fought to keep all intentness from his smile. "Indeed."

They'd reached the far end of the ramparts; as they went down the steps to the forecourt, she said, "I must find my brothers and head home."

"I saw them over by the horseshoe area." He led her in that direction.

They found the boys engaged in an impromptu game, trialing the layout with the castle stablelads. Edmond and Ben were ready to leave, but Harry begged off, saying there was something he'd meant to check but had only just remembered. "I'll follow once I've learned the answer."

Madeline looked at Harry—Gervase could see the question blazoned in her mind—but then she caught his eye, then inclined her head to Harry. "Very well. But don't stay too late."

She, Edmond and Ben saddled up; Gervase waved them off, then headed for the castle, leaving Harry helping the stablelads to gather the horseshoes and level the earth around the peg.

Climbing the steps, he wondered what Harry needed to check; on the porch, he glanced back—and saw his sisters, a colorful trio, hurrying, chattering, toward the castle. He turned and walked into the front hall before they saw him. He waited in the shadows inside the door until, their feet pattering, their voices light, they rushed in.

"You three." His quiet words brought them up short, had them swinging his way. He caught the fleeting guilt before their expressions hardened and, as one, they tilted their chins at him.

"Yes?" Belinda inquired.

He fought to subdue a grin. "A word, if you please, before you rush off to change."

Belinda frowned; she'd been about to use changing for dinner as an excuse. He gestured to the drawing room, currently empty. With a light shrug, she surrendered and led the way.

Annabel and Jane followed her. Strolling in behind them, he wasn't surprised when they halted and faced him as he shut the door.

"What is it?" Belinda asked.

He met her gaze, then Annabel's, and lastly Jane's. "While I appreciate your sentiments and would hope to have your support should I require it, I would infinitely prefer that you do not try to use your undoubted wiles on Madeline."

As one, they frowned at him.

"Why not?" Annabel asked. "We did perfectly well this afternoon."

Belinda nodded. "Jane was particularly good."

Jane smiled beatifically. "She wants to take care of me now."

He was suddenly unsure just what they had done. Let alone achieved. "Just what did you say?"

"It wasn't what we said, " Belinda informed him, "but how we said it. Madeline now knows the *threat* we face should you marry some lady who doesn't take to us, and she's wise enough to know that our *belief* in that threat isn't totally without foundation."

"*Not* just a figment of our imaginations," Annabel put in.

"So, of course, being the sort of person she is, and acting in her usual capacity as de facto protector of the weak in this neighborhood, she now feels protective of us." Belinda beamed at him. "Which is precisely how we want her to feel, and if you have any nous at all you'll see that that's to your advantage."

Once again he was getting that feeling of slowly sliding out of his depth. He had a nasty suspicion that with his half-sisters, he was going to be feeling that increasingly. He took a moment to regroup, then said, "I agree that today you succeeded in your aim without causing any problem, but what concerns me is . . ." How to put it? "If you press too hard and open her eyes too early, you're liable to scupper *my* efforts. For various reasons, I have to bring her around to the notion of marriage, convince her of the benefits *before* I even hint at such a thing. If you jerk her to awareness too soon, then *my* row is going to be much harder to hoe, and—if you'll recall—Madeline marrying me is the outcome we all desire, you three included."

"Well, of course," Belinda said.

"Indeed," Annabel stated.

Jane just nodded emphatically.

He searched their bright eyes. "So you won't make any further attempts to manipulate Madeline or tamper with her emotions?"

Belinda flashed him a brilliant smile. "Don't worry. We won't do anything that might make it harder for you to win her hand."

The other two smiled and nodded.

Gervase studied their expressions, and knew that was the best he was going to do. "Very well."

Still smiling, they bustled to the door.

"Just remember," he reiterated as they reached it. "No more manipulating Madeline."

They each cast him a smiling, sisterly glance as they went out, leaving him anything but reassured.

He returned to the forecourt to find Harry waiting to speak with him.

"If you have a moment, there's, ah . . . something I'd like to discuss."

"Of course." Gervase waved to the ramparts and they headed that way.

Reaching the steps, they went up, and strolled along, faces to the wind, much as he had earlier with Madeline. Harry remained silent, clearly nervous. More used to interrogating than waiting for confidences, Gervase was wondering if there was something he should say to ease the lad's way when Harry slowed, halted, and turned to look out to sea.

Halting a pace away, Gervase studied his profile, then looked out over the waves, too.

"It's . . . about Madeline." Harry drew in a tight breath and rushed on, "You see, we've—Edmond, Ben and me—well, we've noticed you seem quite taken with her and we wondered . . . well, she's our sister and there's no one else who might ask, so as I'm her brother . . ." Harry hauled in a huge breath and swung to face him. "We thought I should ask—"

"What my intentions are." Gervase nodded, serious and quite sober. He kept his gaze on the sea, giving Harry time to recover his equilibrium. "Indeed. That's entirely appropriate."

He hesitated, then forced himself to go on; he might have skirted the edges of his dilemma in warning off his sisters, but given the right Harry had claimed, a right he unquestionably possessed, age or no, then he had to answer with the truth—which meant he had to articulate a problem he'd been doing his best to ignore. "The crux of the matter is I am interested in offering for Madeline's hand, but she has yet to agree even to consider such an offer." He paused, then went on, "As you're aware, she is, quite literally, her own master—and I use that term advisedly. When I first . . . drew close to her, she noticed, of course. Through our subsequent discussions it was made abundantly plain that she absolutely refuses to credit any vision of herself as my countess."

"But . . . *why*?"

Gervase turned to see Harry blinking at him.

"I mean, there's no reason she couldn't be your countess, is there?" Harry frowned. "I know we're not that old or experienced, but it seemed as if everyone else"—with a gesture he encompassed the surrounding neighborhood—"sees her in that light, or near to it, already."

"Indeed. There's no impediment whatever—other than in your sister's mind. I fully intend to change her mind, but you've no doubt had experience of how easy that is to accomplish, especially when she believes she's right."

"Ah." Harry's expression blanked.

"Just so. However, I am endeavoring, and"—Gervase started to stroll once more—"am determined to prevail. That, however, is going to take time and . . . a certain degree of persuasion."

He was silent for a full minute, searching for words with which to convey what he knew he must. "So now you and your brothers know of my intentions, my sisters know, Sybil knows—"

"I think Muriel knows, too," Harry said.

Gervase inclined his head. "All those who need to know, know or have guessed. The only relevant person who doesn't know my intentions is . . . Madeline herself." He held up a hand to stay Harry's surprised query. "The reason for that is simple—she told me her entrenched views regarding the notion of herself as my wife *before* I could broach the subject.

So to have any real chance of her accepting my offer—this being Madeline—I have to convince her to change her mind about her filling the position of my countess before I speak, indeed before she gets any inkling that making an offer is my intention, and indeed was from the first."

Harry was silent for several minutes, working through the emotional logic, then he grimaced. "If you make an offer first, before she thinks the notion is reasonable, she'll refuse—and avoid you like the plague thereafter, so you can never get near enough to convince her she's wrong."

Gervase's reply was dry. "I thought you'd understand."

They'd reached the end of the ramparts. Halting at the top of the steps, they surveyed the forecourt, a field of trestles and booths and awnings.

After a moment, Gervase murmured, "I'd appreciate it if you and your brothers kept your knowledge of my intentions a close secret until I succeed in changing your sister's mind."

"Oh, we will—never fear." Harry flashed him a grin. "We wouldn't want to queer your pitch."

Gervase smiled easily back. They started down the steps.

As they reached the cobbles, Harry sighed. "Females are so damned difficult, aren't they?"

"Indeed," Gervase returned, jaw firming. "That, and more."

Unfortunately, as he'd realized some time ago, females were also beings it was impossible to live without.

He kept repeating that truism to himself throughout the following day while endeavoring to keep an easy smile on his lips while about him females of every degree ran amok. Those closely related to him were the worst.

The day of the festival dawned bright and clear; by seven o'clock, as Madeline had prophesied, stall holders were filing into the forecourt, opening up their booths, laying out their wares. By eight o'clock, when after a rushed breakfast he came out to stand at the top of the castle steps, many locals with produce or handicrafts to display or enter into the various competitions were flowing through the main gate.

Burnham, his stablemaster, came to the bottom of the steps. "When do you want us to open the other gates, m'lord?"

Gervase considered the stream of people being greeted by two burly grooms as they passed through the main gate. "As soon as there's any queue at the main gate, open the other two. Just remember to keep two men at each gate."

Burnham touched his cap. "I'll make sure. There's enough of us to spell each other, so we all get a look at what's about."

Gervase nodded. Then, squaring his shoulders and summoning an easy smile, he went down the steps and plunged into the already swelling melee.

The unexpected talk with Harry, combined with his sisters' helpful efforts, had brought home to him that in pursuing Madeline, his intentions were transparent to most around them and would only become increasingly so. He wasn't hiding his interest in her from others; there was, therefore, no reason not to use others—their attitudes, their expectations—to further his aim.

Consequently, he'd made suitable arrangements for the day.

When Madeline arrived at the castle with Muriel and her brothers it was nearly nine o'clock. Gervase met her by the castle steps. Sybil came out onto the porch, Belinda, Annabel and Jane in her wake.

Greetings exchanged, Sybil, surprisingly, took charge. "Now," she said, "I've insisted that as he's been away for so long—indeed, has never been the host of the festival before—Gervase should spend the day circulating among our visitors. I'll remain here and act as coordinator for any problems—the girls will run any errands or messages that need to be delivered."

Madeline smiled. "I'll help." The role of overseer was usually hers.

"No, that's not sensible," Sybil declared. "You know everyone better than anyone—you're the logical person to assist Gervase. The other committee members will soon be here to help me."

Madeline blinked. She glanced at the girls. "But surely the girls would rather enjoy the stalls?"

"Oh, we've been around already," Belinda assured her. "And there'll be time to go around later, once everything settles down."

"We've already bought yards of lace," Annabel said. "And the glovemaker is keeping three pairs aside for us."

"I see." Madeline didn't, not really.

As she glanced at Gervase, Muriel said, "You'd best get going, the pair of you. Madeline, you can keep an eye out for your brothers while you're wandering—they've already disappeared."

Gervase took her arm. "Don't try to argue. I ceded to Sybil hours ago."

With an inward shrug, Madeline allowed herself to be led down the steps and into the crowd.

The next hour went in smiling and greeting people— farmers, their wives, laborers and workers from the nearby towns. The Summer Festival was always well attended and drew visitors from as far afield as Falmouth as well as the majority of people from Helston. But it was first and foremost a local festival.

On Gervase's arm, she scanned the milling throng. "Literally everyone who lives on the Lizard Peninsula will be here today."

He covered her hand where it rested on his sleeve. "That's why your presence by my side is so crucial. While I know my own workers, and can even name most of their wives, I've yet to place the majority of others. I might have stayed here every summer through my youth, and attended numerous festivals, but as I never imagined I'd inherit the title I put little effort into fixing other people in my mind."

She glanced at him. "You're doing well enough."

"With your brain to pick, I'm sure I'll manage."

She meant to humph at his presumption, but laughed instead. The truth was she was enjoying herself more than at previous festivals; on his arm, with no more onerous responsibility than to whisper identities to him, she was largely free to drink in the gay atmosphere, listen to the laughter, the excited chatter of children, the occasional shrieks punctuating the never-ceasing babble of conversations.

There were few true strangers present; even the peddlers and traveling merchants were regulars, familiar faces. She introduced Gervase to them, too. They circled the forecourt; as they neared the base of the steps once more, they saw the vicar, Mr. Maple, beaming and chatting with Sybil and Mrs. Entwhistle on the porch.

Gervase glanced at the clock on the stable arch. "Nearly time to do the honors."

Together they ascended the steps. The other members of the committee gathered around, all pleased that everything had thus far gone as planned, then Mr. Maple, in stentorian tones polished by years of speaking from his pulpit, exhorted all those in the forecourt to gather around.

"My friends!" He beamed down upon them. "I'm delighted to welcome you to our annual Summer Festival. As is customary, I'm here to give thanks to all who contribute to our day, and to render the thanks of the parish and our church for the bounty that will flow from your activities this day. And so . . ."

Gervase had moved to stand beside and a little behind the vicar; he would speak next. Realizing, Madeline inched her arm from his, intending to step back to stand with the other committee members, but Gervase lowered his arm and caught her hand.

She glanced at him, but he was looking at Mr. Maple as that worthy intoned a prayer, invoking God's blessing on their day. Gervase's hold was too firm for her to slip her fingers free, but if she tugged, it might seem as if he were forcing her . . .

"And now I'll pass the stage to our new earl, Lord Crowhurst." Beaming, Mr. Maple turned to Gervase, stepping back so Gervase stood front and center of their little group—with Madeline by his side.

She could do nothing but smile amiably, her attention shifting to Gervase as he smoothly and with transparent sincerity welcomed the crowd to the castle, then briefly outlined the schedule of events, remembering to note the numerous new additions. He named the members of the committee to grateful applause, then concluded with his own wishes that everyone enjoy their day and the efforts of their fellows displayed on the trestles, booths and tents filling the forecourt.

He then declared the festival officially open, to which the crowd responded with a rousing cheer.

The crowd dispersed, fanning out to fill the aisles between the booths and stalls. Turning to her and the other committee members, Gervase smiled, clearly pleased and at ease. He complimented Mrs. Entwhistle, who looked thoroughly relieved now her planning had come to fruition; Mrs. Juliard and Mrs. Caterham exchanged quick encouraging words, then hurried off to supervise the judging of the first competitions.

"Don't forget, my lord," Mrs. Juliard called from halfway down the steps. "We'll need you to present the knitting and embroidery prizes in half an hour."

Gervase acknowledged the appointment with a nod.

When, preparing to descend once more to the forecourt, he tucked her hand firmly back in the crook of his arm, Madeline told herself she was being overly sensitive—no one else seemed to see anything remotely noteworthy in him keeping her so blatantly by his side.

Just as well; he seemed determined not to let her go. Whether he viewed her in part as a crutch or a shield, she didn't know, but he plainly believed her rightful position was beside him. She felt a touch wary; it should have been his countess on his arm—would people imagine she had designs on the title?

She watched the reactions of all, gentry and countrymen alike, yet when they joined Mrs. Juliard beside the displays of local knitting and embroidery, despite the many they'd encountered not one seemed to view her presence by Gervase's side as in any way remarkable.

Passing along the display, watching Gervase pretend an interest no one imagined he truly had, she leaned closer and murmured, "You don't have the first notion of the difference between petit point and gros point."

"Not the first, second or any notion whatever." He met her eyes. "Does it matter?"

She grinned and patted his arm. "Just take your cue from Mrs. Juliard." She'd intended delivering him to that worthy and stepping back, but again, the instant she drew her hand from his sleeve, he captured it.

He kept her beside him—trapped between him and Mrs. Juliard—while he smiled, presented the prizes to the beaming ladies and shook their hands.

When they eventually moved on, her hand once more on his sleeve, she looked at him. "I can't remain forever by your side."

He raised his brows. "Why not?"

"Because . . ." Looking into his amber eyes, she realized there wasn't any good answer—any answer he might accept.

Understanding her dilemma, he grinned. "This time, the organization isn't your responsibility—indeed, the only responsibility you can lay claim to is to guide me through the local social shoals, and otherwise to enjoy yourself."

She humphed. Muttered, "Enjoying myself can hardly be classed a responsibility."

Yet as they circled the forecourt again, she found herself noticing and taking in—enjoying—a great deal more of the festival's delights and its atmosphere than she ever had. The wares displayed in the booths and on the long trestles were fascinating and tempting, the produce arrayed on the various stalls impressive. She bought lace, two pairs of gloves and a long roll of ribbon. The lace and ribbon she tucked into the pockets of her apple-green walking dress; Gervase helpfully volunteered his coat pocket for her gloves.

The hours flew. Every so often they were summoned by one or other of the committee members so Gervase could announce the winners and award prizes for the various competitions. The one for the best local ale was clearly his favorite; having weathered the knitting and embroidery competitions, none of the other crafts presented any real challenge.

Everyone lunched on traditional local fare—pies, pasties and sandwiches—provided by the local bakers and pie-makers in conjunction with the taverns who had set up tents and benches to serve the hungry festivalgoers. Madeline sat on a bench in the sunshine beside Gervase, and neatly consumed a pastie while he devoured three pies. When he asked, she had to admit that she was indeed enjoying herself; she'd never felt so relaxed, not during a festival.

Whether it was the effect of the warm sunshine, or the relief that everything was running so smoothly, or the inevitable effect of being surrounded by so many people all enjoying such simple pleasures, as the afternoon wore on she started to feel she was viewing the world—a familiar yet different world—through rose-tinted spectacles.

Nothing seemed able or likely to dim her mood.

Not even sighting the Helston Grange party amid the crowd. They'd arrived in the early afternoon; one group of fashionable ladies gowned more appropriately for a stroll in Hyde Park were progressing down one aisle, eyeing the country wares with a disdainful air.

Noting the sniffs and dark looks aimed at their backs, Madeline hid a smile; if the ladies had glimpsed those reactions, they wouldn't be feeling quite so superior.

"And that, I assume," Gervase murmured from beside her, "is Robert Hardesty."

Madeline followed his nod to where Lady Hardesty was strolling down another aisle on the arm of a handsome dark-haired gentleman Madeline hadn't set eyes on before. The pair was closely attended by Mr. Courtland and two others she'd seen at the vicarage—with Robert Hardesty trailing in their wake.

"Yes, that's Robert." Madeline watched for a moment; it was almost as if a small cloud had appeared to mar the otherwise glorious day, and was hanging over Robert Hardesty's head. His expression was not blank but undecided, as if he were unsure what feelings to express, yet . . . "He doesn't look happy." He looked like a dejected, rejected puppy.

"Certainly not an advertisement for the joys of matrimony," Gervase dryly remarked.

Madeline grimaced. "No, indeed."

Although neat and well dressed by country standards, set against his wife's sophistication and the transparently polished appearance and address of her court, Robert looked like the youthful country-bred baronet he was; he couldn't, and likely never would, hold a candle to his wife's admirers.

More importantly, Lady Hardesty was making not the

smallest effort to suggest she had even the most perfunctory interest in him.

Lips thinning, Madeline eyed the spectacle for a moment longer, then looked around, noting numerous others—Mr. Maple and his sister, the Juliards, the Caterhams—who were likewise viewing the small scene. A vignette among many, yet it spoke so clearly—and, did she but know it, would assure Lady Hardesty of no fond welcome in local social circles.

"From which performance I deduce"—Gervase turned her away, steering her toward the east wall—"that her ladyship harbors no ambition to be accepted into local drawing rooms other than on sufferance."

Madeline raised her brows. "So it would appear."

They didn't speak again of Robert Hardesty, but that vision of him, of the demonstrated unequalness of his marriage and the unhappiness that flowed from that, hovered at the back of her mind—the small dark cloud in her otherwise glorious firmament.

"Your brothers seem uncommonly interested in what my father would have termed 'female geegaws.'" Gervase nodded to where Harry and Edmond, with Ben darting ahead or pushing between, seemed absorbed in ribbons and lace doilies.

Madeline grinned; tugging on Gervase's arm, she drew him away.

He would have led her to them; arching a brow, he fell in with her wishes.

Smiling, she looked ahead. "It's my birthday in a few days. I invariably receive trinkets and furbelows chosen from the festival stalls."

"Ah." After a moment, he said, "I suppose, down here, there aren't all that many alternative sources of inspiration."

"Actually"—leaning close, she confessed—"I always find myself examining the items displayed and cataloguing any that I might find myself unwrapping in a few days. It's become something of a game to see if I can identify what will catch their eye when they think of me."

He glanced at her. "And do you guess correctly?"

"Occasionally. Strangely it's Ben who seems to most accurately guess what I'll like best."

"Perception untainted by rational thought," Gervase declared. "Unfortunately, as soon as a male grows old enough to grasp the essential difference between male and female, the ability is lost."

He sounded perfectly matter-of-fact; Madeline laughed and they strolled on.

Chapter 12

$\mathcal{T}$he Peninsula Summer Festival of 1816 was a resounding success. Later that evening, in the carriage with Muriel and her brothers on their way back to the castle for the celebratory dinner Sybil was hosting for the committee and their families, Madeline reflected on the day.

Unbeknown to any but the castle staff, Gervase had arranged a stunningly unique end to the event—a three-cannon salute by the big guns that had throughout the long years of the wars stood at emplacements along the castle's seaward wall, keeping watch over the cove. Gathering Mr. Maple, towing Madeline in his wake as he had all the day, he'd climbed the castle steps, collected the attention of the crowd still milling in the forecourt, thanked them, then given the order for the salute to be fired in honor of them all.

The first boom had shaken the crowd, but even before the echoes had died people were exclaiming, cheering and clapping, children rushing to the ramparts to watch the next firing.

Madeline remembered the moment with a smile. A golden end to a glorious day.

Their carriage was the last to rock to a halt before the castle steps. The castle staff and many local volunteers had worked swiftly and efficiently to restore the forecourt to its normal spacious state; the fading light hid the depredations visited on the lawns and ramparts. A sense of relief and satisfied accomplishment had enveloped both place and people; the members of the committee were all smiles, with gratified congratulations passed all around.

The dinner went well. Madeline was unsurprised to find herself seated beside Gervase. In reality there was no one else who could more appropriately be seated there; her position didn't mean, and wouldn't be seen as indicating, anything more.

After a relaxed meal during which formality was dispensed with in favor of the less rigid rules usually applied to family gatherings, the gentlemen elected to rise with the ladies and accompany them to the drawing room, there to continue sharing the various tales and anecdotes gleaned from the day.

Lady Hardesty and her guests had been observed by many; listening to the comments, Madeline noted that none referred directly to her ladyship, focusing instead on the manners of her friends. It was a subtle, polite, yet pointed rebuke, no less real for being unspoken. Lady Hardesty was on notice; everyone seemed agreed on that.

They'd only been back in the drawing room for ten minutes when Muriel touched Madeline's arm.

"No—don't get up." Muriel leaned down to speak quietly to her where she sat relaxed in a large armchair. "You were on your feet all day. As were the boys." She nodded to where the trio were gathered on a bench, all but nodding, valiantly trying to stay awake, as were Gervase's sisters, the Caterham girls and the Juliards' younger son. "I'll take our lot home—I'm ready to leave myself—but you should stay awhile."

Before Madeline could react, Muriel looked beyond her to where Gervase sat in the chair alongside. "I'm sure his lordship will be happy to drive you home later. No need for you to cut short your evening. You deserve to have some fun."

"Oh, but—" Caught totally off-guard, Madeline glanced at Gervase.

To find him smiling—entirely too sweetly—at Muriel. He rose and bowed. "His lordship will be only too delighted. I'll drive Madeline back to Treleaver Park after the party breaks up."

Muriel beamed at him. "Excellent."

Madeline stared at her aunt. Muriel wasn't exactly a man-hater—she was a widow after all—but she had little time for personable gentlemen, deeming most not worth her time.

Gervase, clearly, fell into a different category.

"I . . ." She glanced up at Gervase.

He arched a polite brow. "We've only just started recounting all those little things that might have gone better—it would be useful if you would stay."

But it was no longer her responsibility to run the festival; after today, certainly once he married, that role would fall to his countess.

He studied her face, then simply said, "Please."

Her eyes on his, she drew in a breath, held it, then surrendered. "Very well." She looked at Muriel. "If you're sure . . . ?"

"Of course I am." With a dismissive wave, Muriel headed off to extract the boys.

They came to make their farewells, bowing politely to the company before exiting quietly in Muriel's wake.

"They look asleep on their feet." Mrs. Caterham leaned closer to speak to Madeline. "As do our two, but now your boys are gone I daresay they'll curl up there with Sybil's girls." So saying, she turned back to listen to Squire Ridley expound on the comeuppance of two knaves who'd tried to make off with some horse brasses.

"Never saw such brass in my life, heh?" Gerald chortled and slapped his thigh. "But we fixed them. Burnham set them to mucking out the stableyard—with so many horses in the lines there was plenty to do."

Several hours sped by in companionable sharing. Mrs. Entwhistle took notes, although there'd been no serious difficulties to record. Eventually, with a pervasive sense of satisfaction enfolding them, the guests rose and took their leave of a tired but delighted Sybil.

In the front hall, Madeline hung back beside Sybil while Gervase walked out to the porch, chatting with Mr. Maple.

Sybil delicately stifled a yawn, then grinned at Madeline and put a hand on her sleeve. "Thank you. I know you don't think you did very much, but indeed, having you beside him made Gervase's day a great deal easier."

Sybil glanced at the door, confirming Gervase was still occupied. "It's easier for you, having grown up here knowing your place. It's not as difficult even for me, because I've had time to grow accustomed. But I've worried how he will cope—not because he won't but because he hasn't had much time to gather all the background knowledge he needs." Again she smiled at Madeline. "That's what you give him, dear—solid ground on which to stand."

Gently squeezing Madeline's arm, Sybil released her. "I know he appreciates your help—I just wanted you to know I do, too."

Madeline smiled; she would have disclaimed, but doing so would have made light of Sybil's thanks, and she was too fond of Sybil to hurt her feelings.

Then Gervase reappeared, striding toward them. He met Madeline's eye. "Burnham's bringing my curricle around."

"In that case," Sybil said to Madeline, "I'll leave you to Gervase's care, dear. Good night."

"Good night."

Gervase nodded to Sybil. "I'll see you in the morning."

"Indeed, dear." With a benedictory wave, she drifted toward the stairs.

"Come." Gervase offered his arm.

Madeline took it and let him lead her out to his curricle.

Within minutes they were bowling through the castle gates, then east on the lane along the cliffs. The light was poor, but Madeline felt completely relaxed, completely confident of Gervase's ability to manage the powerful blacks he had harnessed between the shafts.

The moon shone fitfully, weak and waning, screened by high clouds, yet there remained sufficient light for her, leaning back against the curricle's seat, to study his profile. To consider what she saw there, cast like a Roman coin against the dark backdrop of the sea.

The events of the day scrolled through her mind. He needed a wife, a fact no one could question. But what sort of wife? Until today, she hadn't dwelled on the point; no cogitations had been required to know that whatever the specifications she wouldn't fit. But after today, especially after viewing Lady Hardesty with poor Robert in tow, the question had grown more important, more insistent.

Like Sybil, she wished Gervase nothing but happiness. More than most she knew what he'd sacrificed during the war; to her mind society owed him some reward, specifically a contented life. It would be a travesty of justice and fairness if he didn't have that.

Which meant he needed the right wife.

But what, in that context, constituted "right?"

Before seeing the evidence of Lady Hardesty, she would have suggested a London beauty, a daughter of some peer of suitable rank with a solid background in the glittering world of the capital.

But of what use was knowing the order of diplomatic precedence, or the most fashionable type of tea to serve a duchess in the afternoon, if one's husband's most urgent question was whom among numerous local functionaries gathered together it was politic to recognize first?

She'd answered that question, in one form or another, on several occasions that day, and while any lady might learn the answer, learning presupposed an interest in doing so, and that—as not just Lady Hardesty but also her female guests had demonstrated—was not a quality London ladies necessarily possessed.

The curricle's wheels rhythmically rattled along the well-beaten track.

She'd stood in Gervase's countess's shoes for the day; she shouldn't find it impossible to imagine the lady capable of filling the position, yet her mind remained blank, unhelpfully vacant, no matter how she tried to focus, to conjure . . . no more could she think of any local lady of the right age, the right background, let alone one capable of holding his interest.

He checked the blacks, jerking her attention back to the moment. Slowing to a crawl, he turned his pair; she glanced around and realized he was taking the track to the boathouse.

It took a second to question her own impulses, then to inwardly shrug.

With the horses at the top of the steep path, he drew them to a halt, then climbed down and handed the reins to her. "Stay there and mind the brake."

She'd started to swing her legs out, but stopped, considered, then swung them back. He went to the leader's head; grasping the harness close by the bit, he started leading the pair down.

Having someone on the brake was necessary in case the horses tried to go too fast or the curricle's wheels slipped; the path was too steep, his horses too valuable to risk. Keeping the reins loose in one hand, her other hand on the brake, she let him guide them down.

The curricle fitted neatly into the space behind the boat-house. It felt normal to let him take her hand and help her down, then steer her inside and up the stairs. It was the third time she'd been there with him, in his private place; she was a little surprised by how comfortable and confident she felt—serene and assured—as he led her to the daybed, then turned her into his arms.

He kissed her, the exchange long and sweet, drawn out as she returned the pleasure. When he drew back, her fingers were tangled in his hair, his already busy with her laces. He looked down at her face, his own a medley of sharply delineated planes and shadows. "I wanted to thank you."

She smiled. "Everyone already has. Multiple times. But what I didn't tell Sybil, I'll tell you—I need no thanks. I enjoyed my day thoroughly."

His lips curved, she thought rather wickedly, but in the poor light she couldn't be sure. "But I wanted to thank you in my own way."

Her gown slithered to the floor; she struggled to quell a too-hungry shiver invoked by the sensation of his hands, hard and knowing, and their heat, closing about her waist.

She licked her lips, stretched up to murmur against his, "Your way?"

"Mmm." His gaze had lowered to her breasts. His hands rose, then reverently closed. "You said you thoroughly enjoyed your day. In return for your help, it seems only right that I ensure you also . . . thoroughly enjoy your night."

His fingers flexed; she caught her breath. They played and her lids fell, lips parting on a soft, impossibly evocative—undeniably erotic—gasp.

He dipped his head, covered her lips, and with consummate mastery swept her into the dance.

The one he'd taught her.

One where their bodies spoke more clearly than words ever could, where each touch carried meaning as well as pleasure. Where lips and tongues and hands orchestrated and communicated with a degree of eloquence unimagined, where bodies, minds and even souls could speak with a directness unfettered by any of the intrinsic limitations of verbal speech.

As, all hot naked skin and long tangling limbs, they tumbled onto the daybed, she realized she could say so much more this way. As he drew her beneath him and with one powerful thrust joined them, as she embraced and clung, then encouraged and exhorted, then unshackled her wilder self, letting it free to ride with his, as the heat and the passion rose and consumed them, here, like this, she could open her heart and let the truth come tumbling out . . . and no one would hear.

Only she knew as she crested and clung, as throwing her head back, she let the glory claim her, just how deep, how strong, how irrevocable and powerful that glory now was. What depths of her heart and soul it had plumbed.

Just how irretrievably and ineradicably it had become a part of her.

Only she knew.

The storm washed past, the frenzy died, subsiding into blissful aftermath. Lying on her back with him slumped, boneless and heavy, over her, eyes closed, her fingers idly stroking through his hair, she smiled, and told herself it didn't matter. That no matter the cost, only she would know, and no matter what the cost, she would readily meet it—just to know she could feel like this.

To know what it was like to be all she as a woman could be.

He'd given her that, and for that gift, she'd be forever grateful.

Lifting her head, she pressed a gentle kiss to his temple, then lay back, relaxed, and let satiation claim her.

An hour later, Gervase lay propped against the daybed's raised back, watching while Madeline delicately sipped a glass of amontillado, then bit into a ripe plum. The dark purple juice stained her lips, threatened to overflow at one corner, but then her tongue darted out and lapped.

He forced himself to look away. Reaching for the hand that held the glass, he raised it so he could brush a kiss across her knuckles. "Thank you for staying by my side today—your insights were invaluable."

Still chewing, she smiled.

Before he could think too much he went on, "No one else could have done it. Having you there, by my side, felt right. The others thought the same."

She swallowed, then lightly shrugged. "Your role used to be mine, so I suppose in a way it was a trial run for you." She looked down, inspecting her fingers. "Next year, you'll have your new countess to assist you."

He managed to keep the frown from his face; she hadn't made the connection he'd intended.

Before he could think of something to jog her mind in the right direction, she looked up and met his eyes, searched them. "You needn't worry anyone will read too much into my being by your side today. Everyone will realize I was merely helping you find your feet."

Setting aside the glass, plum finished, she slid around onto her belly, her bare rump distracting him, and proceeded to lick her fingers clean—further distracting him.

"That's not what I'm worried about." Disgruntled irritation colored his tone. "I'm perfectly sure everyone else read the situation correctly."

She glanced at him, tried to read his mood; expression quizzical, she tilted her head. "So what is bothering you?"

You. He wondered what it was going to take to open her eyes—to make her see that no one else viewed her as in any way ineligible to be his wife. More, that everyone else was starting to assume that she would fill the position. Looking into her eyes, he felt frustration well. He wanted their engagement settled, wanted her hand acknowledged as his—by her most of all. His sisters' artful manipulation and Harry's direct question had only exacerbated his natural irritation at having to play such a roundabout game.

His natural inclination was to take the Valkyrie by the horns and insist on submission, on total surrender, but with this particular Valkyrie . . .

He'd kept his expression impassive; he knew she wouldn't read anything in his eyes. Reaching out, he set one hand in the indentation of her waist, then stroked slowly down, over the lush curve of her hip and derriere. "I'm in two minds over whether I've thanked you enough."

Her eyes had widened slightly at the caress; now they widened even more. With undisguised interest.

"Hmm." On that sultry murmur she shifted, turning to him as he turned to her. "Perhaps . . . maybe . . . I deserve a second helping?"

He bent his head and set his lips to hers, and set about confirming, reaffirming, his hold on her, on her body, and at least for those moments, on her mind.

But as for her heart, let alone her soul . . . when it came to those, he had no assurances. When it came to those, he was operating blind.

Some hours later under the cloak of the same night, Helen Hardesty again made her way to the gardener's cottage on the banks of the Helford to meet with her sometime lover.

She found him pacing in the dark like a caged tiger. "I take it you've had no good news?"

"No, damn it! The cargo seems to have disappeared into thin air, which is nonsensical. It can't have. It must be here somewhere—and someone must know where."

She'd never seen him so intensely aggravated. Her impulse was to go to him, to spread her hands over his chest and distract him, but she knew well enough to wait until he calmed. "Nothing from the peddlers at the festival?"

"No. I asked at the stalls and booths selling curios and antiques—no one had, or had seen or heard of, even the most minor piece of the cargo." He glanced sharply at her through the gloom. "I have men in the area, scouring the peninsula, and in Falmouth. There's been no word of a wreck, and nothing—neither information nor the goods themselves—has reached London."

"You would know?" She was surprised.

"Oh, yes." His tone sounded vicious. "Believe me, I'd know."

He paced some more; she watched him, waited.

"I want you to start nosing around—*quietly.* I want to know if anyone has heard of anything that might in any way relate to the missing cargo. Whether anyone's been approached by someone wishing to sell items of that nature—museum-quality jewelry, timepieces, snuffboxes, lamps, silverware." He shot her another hard glance. "Concentrate on the gentry. I already have men covering the rest."

She studied him, then, judging him settled enough to approach, she closed the distance, laid a hand on his chest, looked into his face. "Why are you so obsessed with this cargo? I know it's a fee—a payment due to you—but it's not as if you need the money. Your family's one of the wealthiest in the land."

For a moment, looking into his still, contained face, she wondered if she'd gone too far.

But when he spoke, his voice was even, his tone flat. "You don't need to understand why I want it, only that I do."

She grimaced. Lifting her arms, she wound them about his neck. "Very well. I'll do as you ask and with all due caution see what I can learn."

"Do." He looked down at her, then accepted her blatant invitation and kissed her.

When he lifted his head, she murmured, "For my usual payment, of course."

He laughed briefly. "Of course."

Raising his hands, he closed them about her breasts; bending his head, he recaptured her lips, then steered her back until her spine met the closed shed door.

"Come on." The next morning, Harry led Edmond and Ben down from the cliff path north of Lowland Point. "We can walk along the sands and look into each cave we pass."

Leaping down to the beach, Harry waited until the other two joined him, then walked down to the strip of hard-packed sand above the retreating waves and started to trudge north along the shore.

He didn't expect to find anything in the caves, but the exercise kept Edmond and Ben happy; both were certain that if they just looked hard enough—if they searched every cave honeycombing the peninsula's cliffs—they'd be sure to find hidden treasure.

Whose hidden treasure was a moot point.

But for Harry the time spent tramping along the beaches, watching the ever-changing sea, gave him time to think, to wonder, to imagine. To examine his options and what he wanted of life. And how to achieve that.

He'd started by looking in on Madeline in the office; he'd half expected her to smile and wave him away—tell him he didn't need to bother his head with the accounts and ledgers, with the various questions she, in his name, dealt with every day. Instead, she'd taken his offer to learn and help seriously. He now spent part of every day with her, learning of his patrimony and how to manage it.

He'd made the offer to help because he'd felt he should; he'd never imagined he would find fields and crops and yields so intriguing. But he had; now his biggest worry was to keep his enthusiasm for "work" within bounds—and contrarily pretend to some interest in his brothers' hunt.

"Watch out!" Edmond yelled.

Harry glanced back to see Ben, who had chased after a retreating wave, come scampering, laughing and whooping, back up the sand—only to trip, stumble and fall, and have the wave catch him, and froth and surge around him.

As the wave receded, Ben sat up spluttering. He was drenched.

Harry and Edmond exchanged a glance, then burst out laughing.

Ben sat in the sand, picking feathery strands of seaweed from his hair and flinging them off.

Harry and Edmond staggered up, clutching their sides.

"Your face . . ." Edmond gasped.

"Fumblefoot," Harry said.

Ben looked mulish. "I didn't trip. Well, not over my own toes, anyway."

He didn't wait to hear his brothers' opinions on that, but instead scrambled down to a spot below his feet and started sticking his fingers in the sand. "Here." He stopped poking and started digging.

Harry frowned and shifted closer. "What?"

"It's here." Ben worked his hand into the sand. "What I tripped over. The wet sand keeps filling in the hole. . . ."

Edmond glanced at Ben's face, then crouched down and used his hands to pull the sand back from the spot where Ben was digging. Harry did the same on the other side; between them, they eased aside the surrounding sand enough to stop it sliding back immediately Ben dug down.

"Got it!" With a wriggle and a wrench, Ben pulled a sand-encrusted object free. A thick strand of seaweed dangled from it; wrapped around it, the seaweed had anchored the object in the sand.

"Look out!" Edmond pointed down the beach to where another, larger wave was rolling in.

Leaping up, they ran back to where the sand was dry.

Ben stopped and brushed at the damp, compacted sand clumped all over his find. Metal winked; the object was shaped like a long oval big enough to cross Harry's palm. But the wet sand stuck.

"Here—let me." Pulling his shirt from his breeches, Harry lifted the oval from Ben's hand and, using his shirt-tails, carefully dried it, then poked, flicked and blew the sand free . . . a clump covering the center finally fell away.

"Oh, my God." Harry stopped and stared.

Edmond's and Ben's eyes grew round. Their mouths fell open.

Ben recovered first. "We did it!" he shrieked. He danced around. "We found buried treasure!"

"Sshhh!" Edmond said. He grabbed Ben and held him still.

"Shut up!" Harry glanced around.

So did Edmond and a contrite Ben. But there was no one on the beach but them, no one on the cliffs that they could see.

"Sorry," Ben mumbled. He looked back at their find.

Then, simultaneously, the three looked down the beach to where they'd made their discovery, the sand now smoothed by the wave. They walked back, searching the surface, kicked, prodded, poked, but there was no sign of any other buried items. Finally retreating from the incoming waves, they glanced at the cliffs again.

"Lucky it's so early. No one's about." Halting, Harry studied the oval; the other two gathered close, staring as he cradled it in his palms. "It's a brooch, isn't it?"

Edmond picked it up and turned it over, exposing a long pin running the length of the oval. "It looks like a brooch." He set it back on Harry's palms right side up.

Reaching out a wondering finger, Ben traced one delicate metal curve. "That's gold, isn't it? And are those diamonds?" The awe in his voice touched them all. "And what's that?" He pointed to the large rectangular stone in the brooch's center.

Harry swallowed. "We'll need to take it home and clean and polish it, then we'll be better able to see . . . but I think that's an emerald."

They stared in stunned silence, then Edmond, the most practical, said, "What should we do with it?"

Harry raised his brows. "Is it even ours to decide?"

"Of *course* it's ours," Ben hotly declared. "You saw me find it—it's treasure trove. We asked about the laws and that's what they say—anything found below the tide line is treasure trove and belongs to the finder."

"True." Edmond nodded at the brooch. "So what—"

"I know what we should do with it," Ben said. "We should clean it and give it to Madeline for her birthday. Much better than that scrappy scarf thing we got at the festival."

"It's not a scarf," Harry said. "It's a fichu, and she'll like it and use it, but most ladies use a brooch to hold their fichus in place." He held their find up between thumb and forefinger. "A brooch like this."

He looked at Edmond, then at Ben, and the decision was made.

"Right, then." Edmond turned and headed toward the path they'd scrambled down. "Let's take it home and wrap it."

Chapter 13

$\mathscr{M}$adeline's birthday fell two days later. She awoke to sunshine, and stretched luxuriously in the comfort of her bed, a smile curving her lips as she wondered what the day would hold.

Her brothers had been so busy over the last two days, she'd had to be careful not to stumble into any of their whispered conferences—with each other, with Muriel, and even with Milsom and other members of the staff. They had something planned, that much was obvious, but as to what . . . they'd succeeded in hiding that from her, no mean feat.

Rising to wash and dress, she was conscious of welling anticipation.

Family tradition decreed that gifts were presented at the breakfast table; she reached the parlor to discover two packages, one on either side of her plate.

"Happy birthday!" her brothers chorused.

Muriel's gentler "Happy birthday, dear" followed.

Smiling and thanking them, Madeline sat in the chair

Milsom held for her. He bowed. "The very best wishes of the staff on your birthday, miss."

"Thank you, Milsom." Settling, Madeline looked from one package to the other. The larger and flatter showed evidence of multiple attempts to get the tissue paper to lie straight; its bow was lopsided. The smaller but thicker one was much neater—Muriel's. She picked that one up first, and stripped away the wrappings.

"New riding gloves." In butter-soft black leather, beautifully stitched, the gloves hadn't come from the festival. She smiled at Muriel. "Thank you. My current pair is driving me crazy—the buttons keep catching."

"I've noticed." Muriel nodded to her gift. "Those ones are cut to be more fitting about the wrist—they don't have buttons."

"Excellent." Trying them on, Madeline confirmed they fitted perfectly. She held out both hands, admiring the new gloves—pretending not to notice her brothers' fidgeting, the impatient glances they threw each other.

Not bothering to hide her fond smile, she looked down at the other package. "Now what, I wonder, could this be?"

A scarf was her first thought as she felt its softness, but as she lifted the package to rest it across her plate, she felt the weight of some heavier object in its center. "Hmm . . . a mystery gift." She stripped off the gloves and laid them aside, then untied the bow and ceremoniously unwrapped the gift, playing to the boys' anticipation.

She lifted the last leaf of tissue free. . . . Peering at what she'd uncovered, she blinked. Twice. "Good heavens." She heard the awe in her voice, was distantly aware of the swift, satisfied glances the boys shared.

Slowly, a trifle stunned, she lifted the large oval brooch—a cloak brooch from the days when cloaks were the norm. Holding it up, she let her senses drink it in— from its weight and color, it had to be gold, by the way the light fractured and blazed in the stones, the smaller surrounding ones had to be diamonds, while the large rectangular stone in the center, a little paler than forest green, had to be an emerald.

The piece was formed to represent a knot of oak leaves surrounding and supporting the central stone, with tiny acorns formed from the diamonds and a smattering of beautiful pale gold pearls.

Where did you get this? were the words that leapt to her tongue. But she glanced at her brothers, at their eager, expectant faces, and substituted, "It's beautiful." Her reverent tone underscored her sincerity.

They relaxed and grinned widely.

Then she could draw in a breath and inquire, "Where did you get it?"

"We found it," Ben said. "At the festival."

"On one of the antiquities stalls," Edmond offered. "The old peddler who sells bits of metal he's dug up from all around—nails, stirrups, all sorts of bits and pieces."

"It didn't look like that when we bought it," Harry said. "We've spent the past two days cleaning and polishing it. It had hard-packed earth stuck all over and was grimy and dirty. You can see where the surface of the pearls got pitted—we rubbed and rubbed to bring back the sheen."

Madeline peered more closely. "Yes, I see." She glanced down the table at Harry, at the other end, then at Edmond and Ben—at their happy, pleased, open faces. "Well—what an amazing find!"

"Of course we had to give it to you," Ben said.

She smiled. "Thank you—all three of you."

Laying the brooch aside, she finally turned to what else their package contained. Using both hands, she lifted out a delicate gossamer and lace fichu. Again it was no effort to smile delightedly; she'd seen it on one of the festival stalls. "This is perfect, too—I'll wear it tonight with my new gown." She glanced at the brooch. "And as my new gown is green, I can anchor the fichu with the brooch."

The boys looked doubly pleased, exchanging yet more of their triumphant glances. Madeline wondered what else they'd organized; she expected to spend her day much as usual, capped by a quiet celebratory dinner with the family and their closest neighbors and friends. Assuming the boys were anticipating their neighbors admiring their gifts shown off against her new gown, she gave her attention to her breakfast, recommending they do the same if they wanted to ride out with her to check on their furthest-flung fields.

Her day progressed more or less as she'd planned. All three boys remained with her, as they usually did on her birthday, sharing her day. This year, however, their interaction had altered, with Harry asking many more questions, and being much more involved with the duties that heretofore had been solely hers. That required an adjustment on her part, but she found it easier than she'd thought; Harry was sincerely interested now, not simply asking because he felt he ought.

They returned to the house rather later than she'd planned. After luncheon, they spent the afternoon in the office, she and Harry going over accounts and orders, then discussing projections and plans for the harvest.

She was surprised to hear the clocks strike five. "Already?" She glanced at the sunshine outside, then shrugged. Pushing back from the desk, she rose. "Come along. I have to bathe and dress, and so do you."

Herding the boys upstairs, she sent them down the corridor to their rooms. "The guests will be arriving at half past six—I'll expect to see you clean and neat in the drawing room by then."

They mock-grumbled, but she saw the excited glances

they darted at each other. Confident they'd be ready in time, she left them to their ablutions, and went to tend to hers.

A nice soak in a relaxing bath left her feeling pampered. Tying her silk wrapper over her chemise, she sat before her dressing table and applied herself to brushing out, then restraining her flyaway mane, twisting it into a tight knot she anchored on top of her head.

Adding extra inches to her already exceptional height, but it was *her* birthday, and the only gentleman whose opinion she might court would still be taller than she.

Rising from the stool, she took extra care donning her new silk gown, then arranging the delicate fichu about her throat and tucking the ends in the deep valley between her breasts. She'd been right; the fichu set off the plain neckline of the deep green gown to perfection. Standing before her cheval glass, she contemplated the irony that by screening her ample breasts, the translucent fichu drew attention to them, rather than deflecting it.

Picking up the brooch, she turned it over in her hands, admiring the play of light on the gems, then releasing the pin, she fiddled until she had it positioned perfectly just below her décolletage, fixing the ends of the fichu beneath the fabric of her gown. Clipping it in place, she studied the effect. She rarely wore much jewelry, primarily because very few pieces were designed for a woman of her stature. But the cloak brooch was the perfect size—indeed, the perfect piece—to complement her charms, large enough not to look lost yet not so large as to overpower.

Unusually pleased with her appearance—unusually aware of it, if truth be told—she picked up her Norwich silk shawl, draped it loosely over her elbows, then headed for the door and the stairs.

It wanted but a few minutes to half past six o'clock, yet somewhat to her surprise she reached the front hall without seeing anyone—neither staff nor Muriel, who usually came down early. Walking into the drawing room, she discovered her brothers, too, had yet to make an appearance.

Gervase, however, was waiting for her.

Standing before the hearth, he looked devastatingly handsome in a dark evening coat and trousers. Yet. . . . She glanced around. "Where is everyone?"

"They'll be here shortly." Strolling to meet her, he took her hand, kissed her fingers, smiled into her eyes. "I came early."

"But it's nearly—" She glanced at the mantelpiece clock and broke off. Frowned. "I could have sworn it was nearly time." The clock, which she'd never known to be wrong, said it was not yet six o'clock.

Gervase glanced at it. "That seems right."

Frowns weren't good for the complexion; she willed hers away. "Well . . ." She glanced around, intending to invite him to sit.

"It's a lovely evening. Let's stroll in the garden." He'd retained his hold on her hand; twining her arm with his, he turned to the French doors left open to the terrace. "Perhaps we can find a suitable place in which I can give you my gift."

She laughed and allowed him to sweep her out into the fresh air. As it was early, there was nothing she needed to do, not until more guests arrived.

They strolled across the lawns, taking unvoiced pleasure in each other's company, in each other's nearness. Then he asked, "How's Harry's interest in the estate developing?"

"Astonishingly well." They spent some minutes chatting about her brothers. "They gave me this brooch."

They'd reached the arbor under which, weeks before, she'd boldly kissed him. The roses rambling over the structure were now in full and heavy bloom, scenting the evening air with their heady perfume. Remembering her reasons for kissing him then, thinking of all that had passed between them since, she smiled; swinging her skirts about, she sat on one of the benches lining the two closed sides of the arbor, and tapped her finger to the brooch.

Gervase sat beside her, tilting his head the better to study it. He frowned. "That appears to be a very fine piece."

She grimaced. "At first I thought the stones must be paste, but paste doesn't catch the light like that."

"Nor does it have inclusions"—he, too, tapped the central stone—"but real emeralds almost always do. Just like that."

"The pearls look real, too." She sighed. "They told me they'd found it on one of the peddlers' stalls at the festival. There's one old man who comes every year—he's known as Old Joe, but no one knows much about him. But he does have old, dirt-encrusted oddities, things he's dug up at some of the old Iron Age or Roman sites, so it's possible they did find it among the lumps on his stall, or one of the similar stalls. There were three."

He waited until she looked up, caught her eyes, searched them. "Are you worried that they finally stumbled on some wreckers' treasure?"

She wrinkled her nose. "That's possible, I suppose, but rational thought suggests that if they didn't find it at the festival—and other than an instinct that they weren't *precisely* telling me the truth, there's no reason to suppose they didn't—then they might have found it buried among our grandmother's things. There are boxes and boxes in the attics, with all sorts of bits and pieces, and they often go fossicking up there. While I would hope there was nothing of this value still up there, it's entirely possible our grandmother misplaced this piece. She had a huge wardrobe and a jewel collection to match."

He smiled. "Unlike you."

She shrugged. "I'm not really one for jewelry. So little seems to suit."

Reaching into his coat pocket, he returned, "That's because you're unique, and so it needs to be made specially for you." He laid a tissue-wrapped package in her lap. "Like these."

Madeline frowned at the package. "However did you get time to have anything made?"

"I have my ways, my contacts."

"Hmm." She unraveled the ribbon and unwrapped the contents—spilling an ivory fan with rose-gold filigree sticks, beautifully wrought, and what she took to be a rather strange wide bangle in two pieces into her lap.

She picked up the fan, flicked it open, marveled. "I've never owned anything half so beautiful." She met his eyes. "Thank you."

He smiled and she looked down, set aside the fan and picked up the odd bangle, trying to figure out how. . . .

"Here—let me."

She surrendered the two pieces, linked by some sort of mechanism. He fiddled for a moment, then turned to her, and lifted his arms above her head. . . . Her eyes widened. "They're hair ornaments!"

"Indeed. Specially designed to aid in controlling your wayward locks." Gervase slipped the two halves over and around her still-reasonably-neat knot, then wound the little screws to tighten the vise. "There."

He sat back, studied the effect, and smiled, well pleased. He'd had the piece made in the same rose-gold filigree as the fan; the warm sheen of the gold only emphasized the rich luster of her hair, the vibrant brown shot through with copper and red. He met her eyes. "Perfect."

She studied his eyes, then lifting one hand, framed his jaw and leaned in to press a gentle, slow kiss on his lips. "Thank you," she murmured when she eventually drew back. She looked again at the fan, then flicked it open; they rose and started back to the house. "Everyone has given me such useful, thoughtful gifts."

"What did Muriel give you?"

"Riding gloves without buttons."

He laughed.

She was defending her ability to manage buttoned gloves when they strolled back onto the terrace and into the drawing room—

"Oh! Here she is!"

"Happy birthday, Madeline, dear!"

Halting, Madeline blinked as the chorus rang in her ears.

"And many more to come, heh?"

She stared in surprise at an entire roomful of guests. She'd had a moment's warning as they'd approached the French doors and the level of conversation—surely too great for the few guests they'd invited—had registered. But Gervase had had a firm hold on her elbow; he'd swept her over the threshold—into this.

She was instantly surrounded, immediately immersed in the business of accepting everyone's good wishes and thanking them. Eventually she came upon Muriel, smiling smugly, in the crowd. She spread her hands in amazement. "How did this come about?"

Muriel grinned. "Your brothers decided it was high time you had a *proper* party for your birthday. It was their idea. The rest of us"—Muriel's gaze rested on Gervase, still beside Madeline but currently distracted by Mr. Caterham—"just helped them make it happen."

Madeline glanced at Gervase, remembered . . . "How did they manage to get me down early . . .?" She glanced across the room at Harry, chatting with Belinda and Annabel. "The clocks?"

"Indeed. Quite ingenious of them. They had Milsom and the maids set every clock in the house forward half an hour while you were out riding, then they changed them all back again—all except the one in your bedchamber—while you were bathing."

Madeline shook her head, but she was smiling.

What her brothers had decided constituted a "proper party" began with a banquet for sixty. Madeline couldn't recall the last time the long dining table had had every leaf added, and every chair in use.

Harry, seated opposite her at the head of the table, proposed a toast to which everyone responded with a cheer. And then the food arrived, served on the huge silver platters that so rarely saw service, with crystal glasses and gleaming cutlery. The noise of conversations enveloped the table. Bemused and deeply touched, she smiled and chatted, then simply relaxed and enjoyed herself.

But there was more enjoyment to come. Somewhat to her surprise, the question of the gentlemen passing the decanters never even arose; at her signal, intended for the ladies, the company rose as one, and followed her and Gervase— not back to the drawing room but into the ballroom.

Which had been opened up for the event.

Looking around, twirling to take it all in, she let her amazement show. "How on earth did they manage all this without my noticing?"

Gervase grinned. "It seems they planned well."

She thought—remembered how all three of her brothers had remained in the office, how all had asked questions, kept her occupied through the afternoon. "The office is on the other side of the house, in the other wing. They kept me there all afternoon."

"They held you prisoner?"

She smiled affectionately. "After a fashion."

Their plans had included musicans and dancing. The next hours winged by in untrammeled pleasure; she waltzed with Gervase twice, then later gave in, to herself as well as him, and danced the last waltz with him as well.

The French doors to the terrace stood open throughout the evening, letting the balmy night air wash over the gath-

ering. The room was more than large enough to accommodate their number without crowding, allowing everyone to
move freely, talking with this one, then that. The musicians
seemed inspired by the gay atmosphere and happily kept
playing into the night.

Everyone had an excellent time, as they assured Madeline when, hours later, one by one, they took their leave.
Gervase had remained by her side throughout the evening;
that everyone in the neighborhood was expecting to hear an
announcement of their engagement any day he no longer
had the slightest doubt. But, of course, with him standing
by her side, no one had been so gauche as to mention it, or
even hint at it, for which he was grateful.

He'd accompanied her into the front hall. He stood a little
behind and to her side as with Muriel she farewelled the
guests; when he wished he could fade into the background,
at least to some degree.

But then he saw Harry hanging back by the wall nearby,
his eyes locked on him. Harry caught his eye, then tipped
his head down the hall to where the shadows hung more
heavily.

Turning to Madeline, Gervase chose his moment to touch
her arm and whisper, "I'll be back." Then he drifted to
where Harry was waiting.

Harry nodded in thanks, his gaze passing beyond Gervase
to rest on Madeline. "It's about that brooch. We just wanted
to check." He met Gervase's eyes. "We found it on the beach
below the tide line. That makes it ours, doesn't it?"

Gervase nodded. "Which beach?"

"The one north of Lowland Point, immediately beyond
the headland."

Gervase let a moment go by while he considered the possibilities. "The brooch is yours in law, and you're entitled to
gift it to Madeline. It's not wreckers' treasure—there's been
no wrecks listed so far this summer and I have it on good

authority that the wreckers aren't working the Manacles."

"So there's no reason we shouldn't look for more?"

He paused, then met Harry's eyes. "Hold your brothers back from searching further for the moment. Let me check again in Falmouth if any registered ship has been listed as overdue. If none has, then it's possible there *has* been a recent wreck on the Manacles, but of a smuggler's vessel."

"So the brooch might have been . . . whose?"

"If it was coming in on a smuggler's ship, there's no way to tell, but frankly I can't imagine why smugglers would be dealing in such goods."

They both looked at Madeline, thinking of the brooch.

Harry frowned. "It doesn't seem likely, does it?"

Gervase shook his head. "The other possibility is that it's an item from some long-ago wreck that for some reason happened to wash up now. I've heard that the Manacles can hold wrecks for decades, if not centuries."

"I've heard that if a ship gets wrecked out there, there's often nothing ever found—no debris or even bodies."

Gervase nodded. "So just because there's no evidence of any wreck doesn't mean there wasn't one."

The last guests were chatting with Madeline; Sybil and his sisters had left long ago. He shifted. "I'll check in Falmouth and let you know. Until then, stay away from the cliffs and coves."

Harry nodded. "We'll wait to hear from you."

They parted and Gervase returned to Madeline's side. He was the last to bow over her hand. "I hope your day was memorable."

She smiled. "It was, and the evening even more so." Suddenly reminded, she put up a hand to her hair, feeling for the wispy strands that usually slipped loose—and finding none. "It worked!" Her smile turned radiant.

He smiled in return. "Indeed. I thought it might."

He bowed again, then to Muriel, standing beside Madeline. At the last he met her eyes. "I'll see you anon, no doubt."

With that he left her, and strolled out into the night to where the grooms had his curricle waiting.

He didn't drive home.

Madeline had wondered about his "anon"—then had wondered if her unvoiced wish that he would come to her that night, making a magical end to what had been a perfect day, was too wanton. Yet when she glimpsed him crossing the lawn heading for the morning room doors, her heart leapt.

Earlier she'd removed her new brooch and fichu, laid them carefully aside, then climbed out of her gown, but rather than don her nightgown, she'd wrapped a silk robe over her chemise and sat before her dressing table mirror so nimble-fingered Ada could unclasp the golden circlet locked about her topknot.

"Absolutely beautiful," Ada had breathed, setting the circlet next to the fan. "Fancy him thinking of such a thing."

"Hmm." Picking up her brush, Madeline had dismissed Ada, then had sat brushing out her hair.

And wondering . . . which activity had made her rise and, still brushing, go to stand by the window and look out.

She watched Gervase until he disappeared from sight. She stood for a moment, imagining him opening the French doors and coming inside, then crossing the morning room to the hall. Pushing away from the window, she went to the dressing table, laid down her brush, and headed for the door.

The instant he turned down the long corridor to her room, Gervase saw her, limned in golden candlelight, framed in the open doorway at the end, waiting for him to join her. A soft, subtle smile played about her lips; she'd never looked more like a seductive Valkyrie.

He couldn't stop a smile curving his lips in response, was aware of anticipation rising. Didn't think to stop it coloring his expression.

Her smile deepening as he approached, she stepped back, aside, to let him enter. He halted just inside the room and waited while she shut the door.

Then she turned. Before she could speak, he stepped closer. Raising both hands, he framed her face. Felt the delicate bones, the silken skin beneath his palms. Gloried again that with her, he didn't have to tip her face far to meet her eyes, to study the peridot depths, a more intense, mysterious green in the candlelight. To read in them her expectation of pleasure and delight . . . at his hands, with him.

He closed the distance and covered her lips with his, gently, without any sense of rush, without any of the reined hunger that between them usually ruled. He kissed her slowly, savored the sweet taste of her as she met him . . . with the same sense of unhurried ease, as if she, too, recognized that this was a time to follow a different drum, to indulge their passions in a different way.

A way that spun them out, that stretched and extended each moment until it felt as fine as crystal, as fragile as spun glass, until sensation was stripped raw, left naked and exposed for them both to see, to know and appreciate every tiny touch, every scintilla of delight, to feel each as clearly, as acutely, as ice on heated skin.

As usual, he'd come to her with no detailed plan, no plotted approach, yet with one definite, absolute aim—to give her this night, and make it something special. Something better, magical, a night in which passion, desire, and intimacy reached new heights, breached new horizons.

And so they lingered, immersed in the kiss, sharing breaths, and each caress . . . letting the simple communion stretch until the thrum of passion was a third, more urgent heartbeat.

One they shared, one both acknowledged.

Yet when he drew back, glanced down and reached for her robe's sash, she placed her hands over his, stopping him.

"No." She waited until he looked up and met her eyes. "My birthday—I get to choose the games."

There was a light in her eyes, soft, glowing, one he hadn't seen before; more powerful than any cage, it held him immobile as, her lips lifting in a madonnalike smile—one of secret knowing—she pressed his hands back, down, then reached for his coat.

The candle on her dressing table bathed them in golden light as, slowly, she undressed him, and he let her. The slow steady beat they'd set with the kiss had become a tattoo, one they continued to move to, one that orchestrated each movement as with infinite patience she divested him of waistcoat, cravat, shirt. As she circled him, small hands trailing, leaving fires flickering under his skin.

She took his hand and led him to her bed, had him stand beside it so she could kneel at his feet and remove his shoes, his stockings, then his trousers, letting the discarded garment fall from her fingers to one side.

Naked, he stood before her, watched her sit back on her heels and slowly, studying—savoring—every inch, lift her gaze from his thighs to his groin, to his waist, to his chest, to his shoulders, ultimately to his face.

Her eyes locked with his. She placed one hand on his thigh, steadying herself as she slowly wrapped her other hand about his erection.

His lungs locked. He felt his jaw set, clench, sensed the heat rise within him as she tightened her grip, then looked down. And swept her thumb *slowly* over, then around the sensitive head.

He closed his eyes on a smothered groan, let his head fall back, felt his chest seize as she boldly caressed. Clenching his fists, he felt his senses reel, reminded himself that this was her choice—her wish, her want, the gift she'd chosen to claim.

The thought made his head swim, fragmented what little rational thought remained.

He sensed her lean nearer, felt the sweep of her silken hair against his naked skin, over his thighs, his groin. The wash of her breath over the head of his erection made his lungs tighten, the touch of her lips made him shudder.

Then she took him into her mouth, into slick heat, into scalding wetness, and he lost touch with the world, was swept into some other where time was suspended and sensation ruled, and there was no reality to which to cling.

Only this—the slow, long-drawn torture. Only her and her wishes, her caresses, her ministrations.

His head reeled; he felt giddy, enough to sink his hands in her rippling mane and anchor . . . himself and her. Holding her to him, reveling in the slow, steady suction of her mouth, the different pressure of her lips as she experimented. The lighter touch of her fingers on his sack as she played.

And searched for the ways to pleasure him.

Found them, used them. Lavished pleasure and more upon him.

That last slowly penetrated the fog of sensation wreathing his mind. She was pleasuring him . . . but he'd intended this night to be for her.

The inexorable rise of the tide she was increasingly expertly evoking, the inevitable that loomed nearer with every harsh breath, shook him to panicked awareness. "Enough." His voice was weak, hoarse; he had no idea if she understood.

Forcing his hands from her skull, he reached for her chin, easing her mouth open, getting her to release him.

She did, then rocked back on her heels. Both hands on his thighs, she looked up into his face. "Didn't you like it?"

Her voice was a sultry siren's, reaching through the night.

He stared down at her face, confirmed she was in earnest. "Too much."

The growled words seemed to satisfy; her madonna's smile reappeared.

"Come here." He reached for her shoulders. "It's your birthday—it's you—your senses—I should be delighting."

She allowed him to draw her up, but her smile had deepened. Her chuckle as she let him draw her into his arms was beyond erotic. "Oh, you are."

He wasn't up to deciphering what she meant; taking a firm hold on his will, he wrapped her in his arms and kissed her. Took her mouth in a long-drawn engagement, a claiming undisguised, a campaign of conquest that had only one possible end.

She allowed it—more, she encouraged him, her hands gripping, urgency building, yet still held at bay.

He waltzed her, still adhering to that slow, compulsive beat, into the familiar landscape of their passions, heightened, made broader, more intense, more vivid by their mutual refusal to rush, their determination to dally until every possible sensation had been wrung from each stage.

She let him tug the sash of her robe free, let him slide the garment from her shoulders and strip away her chemise, on a gasp rode out the keen edge of sensual shock when their bodies finally met, heated skin to skin, long limbs pressing, hands seeking, gripping, arms banding. Her surrender still hovered on her lips when he covered them anew, when he drank in the passion surging through her.

He gorged on it, on the feel of her naked in his arms, so responsive, so ardent—and all his.

His to pleasure, now and forever; his to lavish all his

expertise upon. She was the reason for his past; she was his future.

His hands spread, caressed, boldly possessed; trapped within his embrace, she fed him her delight, the elixir of the pleasure he gave her, and flagrantly urged him on.

Until he lifted her and tumbled them both onto her bed, where the pillows lay plumped and waiting, where the covers were drawn down the better for them to give passion and pleasure free rein.

They jostled, and she laughed, the sound one of sheer delight. He heard it, felt it kick beneath his heart. A shaft of pleasure finding its mark.

He rolled to put her beneath him, but she attacked him; his lips curved under hers as she tried to bear him back. For long moments they wrestled, no quarter yielded, no thought given to the inevitable effects of their bodies tangling, pressing, sliding, nudging . . . until abruptly they reached that fraught point where passion and desire were honed to an edge, and culmination could no longer be denied.

They both knew it, felt it, sensed it; both stilled.

Then he pressed her back, reached for her leg, lifting to curl it over his hip.

"No—*wait*." Head pressed back into the pillows, Madeline got the words out, breathless, weak, but he heard. Her hand splayed on his chest, she never would have been able to hold him back, but he halted, stopped.

Met her eyes.

The undisguised desire she saw burning in his made her smile, made her determination to have her own way stronger, more acute. More necessary.

Lifting her hand, she framed his jaw—sensed them both battling to hold back the welling tide. Their breaths mingled, ragged, harsh, close to desperate. Their lips, separated by mere inches, throbbed. "Let me."

She said the words, saw them register, saw confusion cloud his eyes.

"But tonight—"

"Is my night." She held his gaze. "And this"—with her body she pushed against him to roll him back—"is what I want."

For an instant he didn't move, didn't budge despite her weight, but then he gave way, surrendered, and rolled onto his back.

She smiled and followed.

He met her eyes as he settled back, head on the pillows, large heavy body stretched out on her white sheets half beneath her.

She held his gaze, and knew he understood.

What followed was the gift she chose, that above all others she had wanted. It was she who was in charge, she who set the pace, he who consigned the reins into her keeping and let her do as she willed. As she wished.

Let her caress him, let her fill her senses, her mind, her soul with him.

Let her hands roam his chest, his ridged abdomen, his hips, spreading fire beneath skin already scorching.

Let her move upon and around and over him, hands, fingers, mouth, tongue, silken limbs, her silky hair, all part of her symphony of sensation.

All part of her devotion, her claiming.

In this, she had no measure—no yardstick, no plan. She moved to the beat of that different drum, her heart, her senses, her soul in tune. She gave herself over to it, gave herself up to him, and stinted nothing in the giving.

She gave him all, surrendered all, until she held them, his awareness and hers, in the palm of her hand.

They caught their breath. Held it.

Then together forged on, let her stretch the moments out

until they were both frantic, until desperation gripped him as powerfully as it seized her. Until passion was a sharp-clawed beast howling through them both—until she rose up and took him in.

Until she straddled him and sheathed his hard length in her scalding softness, sinking down *slowly*, lids falling, breath bated, taking him inside her deep, then deeper, until she had him all.

Until she possessed him all.

Then she rode him.

Through the night slowly, through the moonlit shadows, clinging, both of them, to the very edge of control.

Walking a knife edge.

Riding a path at the very edge of their cliff, so close to oblivion each moment was dizzying, lungs locked so tight they could barely breathe. Pausing, when it all became too fraught, too intense, too much, to kiss, to, fingers linked, tightly clasping, catch their breath . . . until they could ride on.

Higher.

And higher.

Thought had been eradicated long ago; for both there was only sensation. That, and a oneness, a sharing, bone-deep.

A connection that flowered, fully and completely, as their breathing grew more labored, as at the last their lids fell as they took the final teetering steps up to the peak. . . .

Glory burst upon them, taking her, then him. A bright sun of sensation imploding within, sending shards of delight lancing through their veins, sending pleasure beyond reckoning coursing through them, swamping and sweeping all consciousness away.

Sundering them from the world, whirling them beyond the stars, a single brilliant moment of unutterable bliss, stretching, holding . . . until the void, that place beyond feeling, gently closed around them, hiding them away, enfolding them in peace.

They drifted back to earth.

Slowly.

Like water dripping into a bowl, consciousness returned, the ability to think only gradually restored.

Gervase lay on his back, eyes closed. Nothing—no previous encounter—in his life had prepared him for this.

For complete and utter satiation.

It lay heavy in his veins, had sunk deep into his muscles.

Had touched something within him, some element inside him, that had never before been involved.

Frightening, exciting, thrilling . . . addictive. All that, and more.

Madeline lay slumped, beyond boneless, over him. His arms lay protectively across her back; he didn't intend to ever let her go.

But she'd surprised him.

The strength she possessed, the determination, too, but it was her Valkyrie will—a feminine strength—that had held and fascinated and conquered him.

He smiled ironically, inside; his facial muscles were still too relaxed to manage any expression.

The strength she'd wielded to conquer him hadn't been hers alone. At least half had come from him, from his willingness to cede to her, to surrender . . . not to her, herself, but to the power that between them, together naked in the night, rose up and bound them. Controlled them. Drove them.

Ruled them.

The power that, through her, commanded him.

A scarifying notion in some ways.

Before he could think further, she stirred. She lifted from

him, then sank back into his arms, leaving their legs entwined. Her hair was a gilded mass hiding her face, but he felt her press her cheek to his chest, then touch her lips to his skin.

"Thank you." Madeline let the words whisper past her lips, an intimate confession in the dark. "That, more than anything else, was what I wanted for my birthday. I wanted you. Just you."

For me. For my own. For one night out of time.

Chapter 14

"I cannot tell you, my lord, how pleased I am to see you back in the district, in your rightful place." Lady Felgate fixed her protuberant eyes on Gervase as he made his bow to her. "Absentee earls—indeed, gallivanting senior noblemen of any sort—are to be deplored. It is not what the country needs."

Straightening, Gervase knew better than to argue. "Indeed. I plan to remain at the castle for the foreseeable future."

Lady Felgate brightened. "Excellent! We must see what we can do about finding you a local gel to take to wife." Her ladyship waved at her ballroom. "Plenty here—go and look."

Gervase promptly complied, at least as far as following Sybil into her ladyship's ballroom. His looking, however, consisted of scanning the heads, searching for a bright one taller than most. Not finding her, he inwardly sighed and consigned himself to escorting Sybil to a nearby chaise, then attempting to cling to his own company until Madeline arrived.

Lady Felgate was a character, one of those ancient bel-dames whose eccentricities everyone put up with simply because doing so was easier than resisting. The ball she held every summer at Felgate Priory was a local institution, one everyone attended—again because it was easier than attempting to avoid it.

That did, however, mean that everyone—literally every lady and gentleman in the district older than eighteen—would appear in her ladyship's ballroom that night.

"Thank you, dear." Sybil drew her hand from his arm and sank onto a chaise by one wall. She glanced around. "I can't see Muriel or Madeline, can you?"

"No, but they'll be here soon, no doubt."

"If you see them, do direct Muriel this way."

With a nod, Gervase moved away, inclining his head to Mrs. Entwhistle as she bustled up to speak with Sybil.

In some respects, the crowd was a boon; there were suf-ficient tall gentlemen present to give him cover. Gervase kept moving, slowly tacking through the crowd, acknowl-edging greetings, exchanging the usual pleasantries, yet maintaining the fiction that he was on his way to join some-one. That, he'd long ago learned, was the best way to wait for someone in an arena such as this; he always had a reason to move on.

Smiling, nodding, even chatting, required little mental effort to sustain, leaving the better part of his mind wres-tling with a subject he rarely addressed—his feelings. On the one hand he felt buoyed and encouraged by Madeline's bold actions of the previous night, even more by her admis-sion that she'd wanted to make love with him as her most special birthday treat. Contrarily, an odd uneasiness rippled beneath his usual confidence, undermining it in a way he neither liked nor understood.

The source of that uneasiness was that unsettling power

that had grown between them, that he'd sensed and known was there from the first, but that he'd tolerated, allowed to be, accepted on the grounds that anything that drew her to him, that held the promise of tying her to him, was in his best interests.

He still felt it was—knew it was—that it wasn't something he wished to lose, at least in the sense of it linking them, and tying her to him.

What he wasn't so sure about—what was making him increasingly edgy—was the way it now tied him to her.

"My lord!" Just ahead, Mrs. Juliard waved to him.

He paused by her side, greeting her—and a young lady he learned was her niece.

"Harriet's come to spend some time with us. I was just telling her what a pity it was that she missed the festival at the castle. She was quite intrigued to hear about the cannons."

Gervase smiled into Miss Juliard's youthful countenance—and wondered how on earth any sane person could imagine, as Mrs. Juliard clearly hoped, that his interest might fix on such a young, naïve lady.

But he liked the Juliards, so he made the appropriate noises; he was preparing to part from them, to utter a polite lie, when he suddenly knew—simply knew—that Madeline had arrived. Lifting his head, he looked across the room—straight at her where she'd paused just inside the main doors.

She looked delicious in apple-green silk, with both her brothers' gifts on display—and his gifts, too, in her hair, and dangling from her wrist.

Turning back to the Juliards, he smiled; he had no more need for lies. "If you'll excuse me, ladies, there's someone I must speak with."

They parted with smiles and nods; Mrs. Juliard hadn't truly harbored any high hopes.

He had to cross the better part of the ballroom to reach Madeline; within a few feet he was reining in his impatience—he couldn't actually *push* through the crowd. It took a good ten minutes to cover the distance without drawing attention to his fell intent . . . and when he neared her, he discovered someone else—several someone elses—had reached her before him.

Slowing, then halting, he inwardly swore.

She was surrounded by a coterie of Lady Hardesty's guests. The sight made him pause—to reconnoiter before he rushed in. Courtland was there, by Madeline's elbow, the cad, along with four other tonnish gentlemen. He wouldn't have trusted any of them with his sisters.

He certainly didn't trust them with Madeline but . . . even from ten feet away he sensed she was holding her own. Her Valkyrie shield was fully deployed. However, the fact that, despite there being five outwardly attractive ladies, friends of Lady Hardesty, in the party, all five gentlemen, including the handsome man on whose arm Lady Hardesty herself leaned, had their predatory gazes firmly fixed on Madeline told Gervase all he needed to know.

Lady Hardesty and her friends were no longer especially desirable prey, at least not to those five gentlemen. That was why all five were looking at Madeline as if she were a lamb. A frolicking, innocent, delectable lamb.

Resuming his stroll forward, he made for her side. He kept his gaze on her face. As he'd hoped, she sensed his presence before the others did, glanced his way, then stepped back, creating space for him by her side.

Space he smoothly filled. "Madeline, my dear." With a confident smile, he took the hand she offered and bowed, inwardly gloating at the smile she'd turned on him; it still held a vestige of social veneer, but no one with the slightest experience could, on seeing it, doubt that he and she were lovers.

"Gervase." She, too, used his given name, made it soft and private. "I wondered where you were."

Straightening, he met her eyes, read in them that she'd reached much the same conclusion he had and was eager to make clear to the five other gentlemen that she had no interest whatever in them.

He squeezed her fingers, then laid her hand on his sleeve, covering it with his—and only then looked at the others, letting his gaze travel the circle of faces to come to rest on Lady Hardesty.

"Lord Crowhurst. How delightful!"

He very nearly blinked. Lady Hardesty had clearly missed his and Madeline's blatant message.

With a smile that promised lascivious delight, Lady Hardesty offered her hand. "Well met, my lord."

Reluctantly lifting his hand from Madeline's, he grasped her ladyship's fingers, half bowed, and released her. "Lady Hardesty. Ladies." He nodded, distantly aloof, to the other females.

Smiling, Lady Hardesty introduced him to the two he hadn't previously met.

One, a Mrs. Hardingale, a patently dashing matron, fixed him with an arch look. "Tell me, my lord—is this truly the most major ball in the area?" She glanced around, then brought her gaze, eyes laughing, back to his face, clearly inviting him to denigrate the company of his neighbors.

He regarded her impassively. "I believe it is one of the more major events, certainly a long-established one." He paused, then added, "It's usually a very pleasant affair."

Madeline lightly gripped Gervase's arm, whether in support or warning she wasn't sure, but she needn't have bothered; Mrs. Hardingale simply looked nonplussed, unsure whether the comment had been a jibe and if so, whether she should take umbrage.

Two of the other ladies tittered—actually tittered. Madeline managed not to stare.

Lady Hardesty moved forward; releasing the arm of the gentleman beside her, she crossed the circle to place a hand on Gervase's other arm. "My lord." She looked up into his face, ignoring Madeline entirely. "I'm especially glad to see you. I've been wanting to have a word with you." Her voice was low, sultry; her brows arched lightly. "If I may?"

Say no. Madeline subdued her glare with an effort, held down the unexpected and alarmingly violent reaction that erupted from somewhere within her. Gervase shifted, drawing her if anything closer—a blatant attempt to make Lady Hardesty notice that she was on his arm.

Lady Hardesty did notice, but she merely glanced at Madeline, smiled lightly, then turned back to Gervase—as if Madeline had been an animated potted palm. A horse would have warranted more attention. Madeline's temper, a force of nature rarely engaged, started to spiral. Upward.

"I was wondering, my lord"—Lady Hardesty edged closer, looking down, hoping to make Gervase lean toward her to hear her words—"whether I could prevail upon you to give me a few minutes of your time . . . in private?"

Lady Hardesty looked up—combined with her nearness, endeavoring to trap Gervase with her dark eyes.

Madeline could barely believe the woman's hide. She glanced at Gervase—what she saw eased her temper, allowed her to press it back.

He was looking down his nose at her ladyship—from a very distant, exceedingly superior height. "I fear not. Miss Gascoigne has promised me the first waltz, which I believe will be commencing soon."

As set-downs went, that was as direct as a gentleman could acceptably be.

But Lady Hardesty merely smiled—at Gervase, then,

again with a mild, oblivious air, at Madeline. "I'm sure one of these gentlemen would be only too happy to take your place, my lord." She brought her fine eyes to bear once again on Gervase's face. "I greatly fear that my need for your company far exceeds Miss Gascoigne's."

No one could willingly be so obtuse, and Lady Hardesty was no fool, not socially. Madeline suddenly understood; for the first time in over a decade, she blushed. Lady Hardesty and her friends—as a quick glance at both the gentlemen and the other ladies confirmed—saw her as too tall, too countrified, too old, too much a spinster left on the shelf to ever have any real chance with Gervase.

They thought he was merely being polite to a neighbor, that his attentions to her were inspired by protective friendship, nothing more . . . for what more could a gentleman of his ilk feel for a lady like her?

The realization was a slap, one she absorbed, but . . . her temper roared to full life and snapped its leash.

But she—it—got no chance to act, to react.

Gervase spoke. Coldly, collectedly, his diction so precise each quiet word cut like a saber. "I fear I failed to make myself clear. Miss Gascoigne promised me the first waltz because I not just asked, but made a heartfelt plea for the honor." Locked on Lady Hardesty's face, his eyes had turned agate-hard, his gaze chilly. "And there is nothing—I repeat, *nothing*—on this earth that would persuade me to forgo that pleasure."

He paused; despite the babel surrounding them, not a single sound seemed to penetrate the now-silent circle. No one shifted; Madeline suspected most were holding their breath.

"I trust," Gervase finally said when the silence had grown taut, "that you now understand?"

Lady Hardesty had paled; frozen beside him, a tiger with teeth she'd presumed to tease, she didn't know what to say.

Gervase shifted, removing his arm from under her hand, then he curtly nodded—a clear dismissal—and turned to Madeline. "Come, my dear." As if he'd snapped his fingers, the opening bars of the first waltz floated over the heads. He smiled, intently. "I believe we have a waltz to enjoy."

She returned his smile with perfect grace, nodded regally to the now-silent ladies and gentlemen, then allowed him to lead her away.

He took her straight to the dance floor, and swept her into the dance.

For long minutes, she let herself flow with the music, let the sweeping revolutions soothe her, let her temper—satisfied and all but purring—settle once more.

They were precessing back up the long room when she sighed with pleasure, and focused on his face. "Thank you for rescuing me." She knew that was why he'd joined Lady Hardesty's circle. She studied his eyes, his still-stony expression. "I'm only sorry doing so forced you to make such an extravagant comment."

He blinked; his features eased. Openly puzzled, he arched a brow at her.

She smiled. "About your heartfelt plea for the honor of waltzing with me, and of nothing on earth being enough to make you forgo the pleasure."

He frowned at her. After a moment during which he searched her eyes, he asked, "What in all that did you find 'extravagant'?"

She sent him a wry but smiling look. "You know perfectly well that you're the only partner I'll willingly waltz with. If you ask me to waltz, I'm not going to refuse—no 'heartfelt plea' likely ever to be required."

"Good." He drew her closer, spinning them effortlessly through a tight turn. "However," he continued, as they fell into the long revolutions once more, "should you ever refuse,

I would indeed plead, even go down on my knees, to secure your hand for a waltz." He met her eyes. "I like waltzing with you." After a moment, he added, "I *appreciate* waltzing with you. I *adore* waltzing with you—and not even that is stating it too highly."

She looked into his eyes, and pleasure, warm and seductive, filled her. She smiled. "I like waltzing with you, too."

"I know. And I like that, too." He had to look up to steer them through the other whirling couples. When he looked down again he trapped her eyes. "So you see, there wasn't anything the least extravagant in what I said. It was the truth as I know it."

He was utterly serious; Madeline felt her heart stutter, felt the glow within spread. But . . .

"They're from London, and rather maliciously inclined. You'll be returning there in autumn to look for your bride—they could—"

"You needn't concern yourself with that." The sudden edge in his voice, almost a snap, was a reminder that that subject—his bride—was not one any gentleman would discuss with his . . . lover.

Despite the sudden lurch of her heart, she kept her expression mild and inclined her head. "Very well."

She looked over his shoulder, and tried to recapture the magic of the waltz, but even though she was revolving in his arms, the soothing pleasure now eluded her.

Her mention of his bride had doused it. Had created a gulf between them, one that remained for the rest of the evening even though he stayed by her side throughout. They chatted with their neigbors and others from the district, outwardly so assured that no one would have guessed that inside, they were both mentally elsewhere, both thinking.

About the same thing.

They didn't speak or even allude to it again, but when the

ball was drawing to a close, and ahead of the rush Gervase escorted her and Muriel to their carriage, after helping Muriel up, he turned to her. Her hand in his, he studied her face, her shadowed eyes, then bent his head and whispered, "Come to the boathouse. Meet me there tonight."

He straightened and looked at her—waited for her response.

She nodded. "Yes. All right."

Relief seemed to wash through him, but it was so faint, so fleeting, she couldn't convince herself she'd truly seen it.

He helped her into the carriage, then shut the door and stood back. He raised a hand as it rocked forward.

She stared out of the window—stared at him as long as she could—then, with a sigh, she sat back. Closed her eyes. And started to plan how she would get to the boathouse.

On the terrace flanking Felgate Priory's ballroom, Lady Hardesty strolled on the arm of her occasional lover—who had finally deigned to be seen socially with her. She'd noticed him in the crowd, chatting amiably with numerous locals, from which she'd deduced that his tale of an elderly relative might just be true. He had to be staying with some recognized family in the district to have received one of Lady Felgate's summonses.

He'd stopped by her side earlier, cutting her out so they'd been alone amid the throng, but only to give her his latest instructions. Although she knew why she obeyed him, the necessity still irked. Unfortunately, he wasn't the slightest bit susceptible to her wiles. Even more unfortunately, that was part of his allure.

"So what did you learn?" he demanded, the instant they were sufficiently distant from the other couples taking the air. The night was unusually hot; the suggestion of a storm hung in the air.

She sighed. "I had to send Gertrude to ask—she wasn't

with us earlier, when Crowhurst was so vicious. Whoever would have imagined he'd defend Miss Gascoigne so fiercely? Amazing though it seems, he must be bedding her—it's the only possibility that makes sense."

"I don't care about Crowhurst or which woman he elects to tumble. I want to know about that brooch."

Menace and violence ran beneath the precisely enunciated words. His fingers bit into her arm. She spoke quickly, "Indeed, and for that you have both me and Gertrude to thank. She had to hide the fact she was one of us and pretend she was some lady visiting the district—she did an excellent job following my directions."

"And?"

"Miss Gascoigne said she received the brooch for her birthday."

"From whom?"

"Her brothers. And yes, Gertrude asked—according to Miss Gascoigne they bought it from one of the traveling traders at the festival." She paused, glanced at his face. "You must have missed it when you looked."

His eyes had narrowed. "I didn't miss it."

He sounded beyond certain. She frowned. Eventually she ventured, "So the boys lied?"

"Oh, yes. They lied—a perfectly believable lie in the circumstances. And the only reason they would lie is . . ."

She waited. When his gaze remained distant, locked on the dark gardens, and he said nothing more, she prompted, "What? Why did they lie?"

His lips curled in a snarl. "Because the buggers have found my treasure, and they don't want anyone else—even their sister—to know."

Madeline left her room half an hour after returning to it. She'd let Ada help her remove her new hair ornament and gown, then had sent the sleepy maid to her bed.

Ignoring her own, she'd dressed in her riding skirt and drawers, opting in the circumstances to dispense with her trousers; who, after all, would see? Aside from all else, the night was unusually warm, heat lying like a blanket over the land, still and unmoving. Slipping through the dark house, silent as a ghost, she made her way to the side door, let herself out, then headed for the stables.

Artur was happy to see her, and even happier when she placed the saddle on his back. A ride, be it by moonlight or sunlight, was all the same to the big chestnut. Any opportunity to stretch his powerful legs was his idea of Heaven.

He carried her swiftly along the cliff path. The castle loomed on the horizon before her, the battlements and towers silhouetted against the starry sky. There was little moon but the sky was clear; the radiance of the stars washed silver over the fields, over the waves, and glowed brightly phosphorescent in the surf gently rolling in to bathe the sands below.

Madeline saw the beauty, absorbed it, but tonight it failed to distract her from her thoughts. The same thoughts that had haunted her since that moment on the Priory's dance floor.

The unexpected, unprecedented clash with Lady Hardesty and her guests had forced to the forefront of her mind a number of facts she'd been ignoring. She wasn't a glamorous London lady, the sort the ton would see as a suitable consort for Gervase; it had been easy to ignore that point and its ramifications while they'd had only locals around them.

Lady Hardesty and her friends had brought home the fact that she could never compete with them and their peers—their unmarried sisters from whom Gervase would choose his bride. But she'd always known that, had accepted it from the first.

What she'd allowed herself to forget—had willfully let slip from her mind—was that he would, indeed, at some point, return to London to choose his bride. Accepting that, acknowledging that, *keeping* it in mind made her own position crystal clear.

She was his temporary lover, nothing more. A lover for this summer; when autumn came, he would leave, and she would again be alone.

She'd thought she'd accepted that, understood it, but now . . . now she'd unwisely allowed her heart to become involved, it ached at the thought. It hurt to think their time would soon be over.

Bad enough. It ached even more to think of him with another.

Lying with another. Kissing another. Joining with another.

That was the other thing the clash had brought to light—not, as she'd first imagined, her Gascoigne temper, but something rather more explicit.

She'd been jealous, and not just mildly so. When Lady Hardesty had moved to engage Gervase, her fingers had curled into claws. At least in her mind. But what had shocked her even more than her reaction—one she had no real right to feel—was the violence behind it.

Given her Gascoigne temperament, that didn't bode well. While in the main her family were even-tempered, good-natured, that streak of recklessness that affected them all made indulging emotions such as real anger and violent jealousy a very bad idea. People who could, and would, in the heat of a moment risk just about anything had to be careful.

Which raised a question she'd never thought to ask: How on earth would she, could she, interact with the lady Gervase would ultimately make his wife?

She couldn't imagine the answer. No matter how much she lectured herself, she'd always be that poor lady's worst enemy.

She would have to . . . what? Go into a nunnery? How could she possibly live at Treleaver Park and not stumble constantly across the poor unsuspecting woman?

The thought, the possibilities, and the scenarios her imagination, now awakened to the notion, supplied were simply too horrendous to contemplate. When she reached the top of the path to Castle Cove, she had the beginnings of a headache, but no clue how best to proceed. She reined Artur in, then started him slowly down, letting him pick his way in the poor light.

She knew why she was there—because Gervase had asked her. Because he'd held out the prospect of another night in his arms—and if she was going to have him, be able to be with him and indulge her feelings—those it would have been wiser not to allow to bloom and grow, let alone blossom—only until he left to find his bride, then she would take all he offered, every last interlude.

She hadn't asked for this, hadn't been searching for it, but fate had sent him to her, and she, a Gascoigne to her soul, had recklessly fallen in love. So she'd embrace it, let the bud bloom for as long as possible before what had grown between them was forced to die.

Time enough to face that horror when it came.

Her emotions felt raw, too close to her surface, when she turned onto the ledge and saw Gervase waiting by the side of the boathouse. He caught Artur's head; when she slid down from the high back he led the gelding behind the building and tied him alongside his big gray.

Returning to her side, he took her hand. She felt his fingers close, firm and strong, about hers, felt them shift, stroking, as he paused and through the shadows searched her face; his was, as usual, unreadable. Then he glanced at the sea. "Let's walk on the beach."

Surprised, she turned, let him lead her down the stone steps cut into the edge of the ledge and onto the soft sand. Her hand in his, he started toward the waves.

She pulled back. "Wait."

He stopped, turned back as she drew her hand from his and sat on the steps. Rucking up her skirts, she pulled off her riding boots and stockings, and set them aside. Seeing, he followed suit, toeing off his shoes, pulling off his stockings, leaving them beside hers on the steps.

Retaking her hand, he set off; she kept pace beside him as they trudged down to where the retreating tide had left a section of compacted sand on which they could more easily walk. Reaching it, he turned east, away from the castle. They set out at a pace that quickly slowed to ambling. Neither spoke, but their thoughts—mutual, she had not a doubt—lay heavy between them.

They strolled a little way, slowing even more as they both watched the waves roll in, small and gentle, their edges laced with phosphorescence. When he said nothing, she drew in a tight breath. "About what I said this evening—"

"On the dance floor—"

They'd spoken over each other; both stopped, and faced the other.

Their eyes met. He nodded. "You first."

"I wanted to say . . . to assure you that I understand." When he searched her eyes, waited, she went on, "About your bride. I know that you'll need to return to London, to choose a bride, then bring her back here. I wanted to say that when the time comes for you to do those things—" She broke off and gestured with her free hand. "I won't make a fuss."

She met his eyes, held his gaze. Drew in a breath and, lungs tight, lied. "I don't want you to imagine I've changed my mind and expect more from you just because . . ." Again words failed her; a gesture had to suffice.

"Because we've become lovers?"

His voice sounded harsh, but that might have been the sea. She nodded, put up a hand to hold back her wafting hair. "Because we've drawn close."

His eyes had remained locked on hers; his expression wasn't as rigidly impassive as usual, but she couldn't identify the emotion behind it.

Then he sighed through his teeth, a hiss of frustration. "You *don't* understand."

She blinked. He sounded exasperated.

Releasing her hand, he gripped her shoulders, drawing her closer, his eyes locked on her face. "You haven't understood anything at all."

She frowned. "I just told you I understand perfectly."

"What you've just told me is that you've missed . . ." He broke off, his eyes narrowing on hers. "Or is it ignored?"

She narrowed her eyes back. "What? What in all this am I ignoring?"

His jaw set. "*This*."

He pulled her to him and kissed her.

She had one moment of lucid thought: That she knew all about *this*. All about the heat, the yearning, the need. All about the passions that would flare, rage and swallow them.

A second later, the heat, the yearning, the need, the passion and the desire that swam in its wake, caught her, and ripped every scintilla of thought away. Replaced it with sensation.

And behind the sensation, as she was learning to expect, came emotion.

Stronger; every time she was with him it grew and swelled. More powerful; she couldn't any longer deny it, let alone ignore it.

It drew her, captured her, drove her—to sink against him

and yield, to surrender and take, to set aside all restraint and simply love him. Physically, yes—she now understood why the act was termed lovemaking—but the more precious, more costly gift she had to give dwelled in what powered the physical—her intention, her commitment, her devotion to him.

They'd come together too often for his kiss to be anything but incendiary; he'd meant it that way, so it was. His lips were hard, commanding, ruthlessly demanding, and she readily complied.

Readily surrendered her mouth, gasped when his hand closed over her breast. She barely registered him opening the front placket of her riding dress, then stripping it away—because by then the only thought in her head was to be naked in his arms.

Her dress fell to the sand, followed by his jacket, neckerchief and shirt, her chemise and his trousers . . . only when her drawers whispered down her legs and the sea air caressed skin rarely exposed did she realize . . .

She drew her lips from his, gasped, "We're on the beach."

"So?" His hands spread, he held her to him, her hips molded to his. "There's no one else within miles. Just you and me, the stars and the sea."

"Yes, but . . ." She blinked; pushing back her hair, she stared at him, then glanced at the beach, wet sand and dry sand, couldn't imagine . . .

He laughed briefly. "In the surf. Come on."

"What?" But he was already striding down the beach, towing her with him. She followed, still stunned. "In the waves?"

He glanced back at her. "Surely, as a Gascoigne, you're not going to balk?"

"Being a Gascoigne has nothing to do with it," she muttered under her breath. They reached the waves; she braced for their icy touch—and experienced an altogether different sensation. The summer had been warm, the days long and hot; the sea, at least in the shallows, had heated. The water purled around her feet and legs as he drew her relentlessly on; it felt cool against her already heated skin, but not cold.

The sensation was pleasant, a tempting, distracting sensual contrast.

It became even more so when he finally stopped, beyond the breaking waves where the water reached to his waist, planted his feet and pulled her around and to him, into his arms—and kissed her again.

Ravenously, voraciously—a kiss and a claiming deliberately calculated to set their fires raging again.

The resulting conflagration took less than a minute to reduce her once more to a state of heated, urgent, hungry and greedy, desperate need.

He knew—he lifted her, hoisted her against him; needing no direction, she locked her arms about his neck, wrapped her legs about his waist and kissed him back, all fire and determination, willing him, needing him, to take her.

The glide of his blunt fingertips over the slick, swollen flesh between her thighs had her gasping. She clung to their kiss, urged him on, demanded—then sighed, a near sob, as his fingers pressed in, thrust deep . . . but it wasn't enough. Not nearly enough.

Gervase read her spiraling need through their kiss, through the desperation that reached him so clearly, that so powerfully joined with his own. He didn't truly know what had possessed him, only that he had to have her now, here, had to make her see . . .

He savaged her mouth, driven by that pounding primal need to make her his—and have her acknowledge it. Have her know it, comprehend it, understand it.

The waves were retreating, their repetitive surge a caress in itself. His fingers buried in her sheath, he stroked, and felt her sob. But the water was level with his hand, the to and fro motion distracting, both water and air cooling what didn't need to cool. Holding her against him, supporting her weight, he walked deeper into the sea.

She knew, clung, waited until he stopped again with the water at mid-back, below her shoulders, leaving the waves flirting with her breasts, with her tightly furled nipples.

The sensation evoked a strangled gasp, then she tightened her legs around him and shifted, restlessly seeking, wanting.

Inwardly smiling—his beast intent and slavering—he drew his fingers from her sheath, positioned his erection, then thrust up as he pulled her down.

They both lost their breaths.

Lips parted, they gasped; from under their lashes, mere inches apart, their eyes locked. Slowly he lifted her, then brought her down again, thrusting even deeper, filling her to the hilt.

She exhaled, her breath washing over his lips, breathing with him as he moved her upon him, her breasts rising and falling as his chest did the same.

Her gaze lowered to his lips; he shut his eyes, concentrated on all he could feel. . . . She closed the last inch between them and pressed her lips to his.

Gave him her mouth, welcomed his tongue, wrapped him in her arms and let their own tide take them.

Slow, forceful, repetitive; a drawn-out excruciatingly intense loving.

They'd learned not to rush, and the surge of the waves about them helped. The steady, measured, inexorable rise and fall gave them another rhythm to cling to when their own grew too fraught. The coolness of the water helped keep the heat from cindering their wills too soon, let them stretch the moments out, and out, and *out* . . . let them commune in the dark sea, in the depths of the night, with the wild cliffs behind them and the stars above, the surf a constant whisper in their ears, alone but for nature all around them.

He gave himself up to it, completely, utterly, and prayed she would know, that she would see. That she might, tonight, finally understand.

The end was spectacular, even for them. It came upon them in a rush and caught them, shattered them. Wrung every last iota of passion from them, then flung them high, beyond the world, where every sense vaporized and glory filled the void—and filled them, glowing in their veins as they slowly spiraled back to earth, to the sea, the waves and the darkness of the night, to the comfort and inexpressible joy they found in each other's arms.

Chapter 15

When at last she lifted her head from his shoulder, Madeline stared into Gervase's face, and tried to fathom what the last moments had meant, what they'd revealed.

The power between them—fueled on her part by what she recognized as love—had only grown stronger, but . . . did he feel it, too?

If he did . . . what was it he felt?

A suddenly very vital question, but one his expression, more stoic than impassive, did little to answer.

"Can you stand?" He sounded resigned.

Realizing her legs were still locked around him, she straightened them and tried; she was stable enough.

She drew her arms from his shoulders; he took her hand.

"Let's get back to the boathouse."

She let him steady her through the waves. In the boathouse she would be able to see his eyes, and perhaps get some idea of what was going on, what it was that seemed to be shifting and resettling in the landscape between them.

She'd thought she'd got it right, but he seemed to want to tell her she'd got something important wrong.

They reached their clothes; he handed her his handkerchief. "Just dry your hands—there are towels inside."

She did, then they collected their clothes and walked up the beach, the breeze cool but not cold on their damp skin; picking up their footwear, they climbed the steps to the boathouse door.

They went up to his retreat; leaving his clothes on the table, he lighted several candles, then went to a cupboard against one wall and pulled out towels. Turning from placing her clothes on a chair, she accepted one, and set about rubbing the last of the sea and its salt from her skin.

That done, she patted the wet ends of her hair, which predictably had escaped. Long, wet strands hung to her shoulders; squeezing them in the towel, noting he had much more to rub dry, she drifted to the long bank of windows overlooking the sea.

And thought of what she felt, wondered what he might be feeling.

Eventually she turned, and saw him sitting on the edge of the daybed, watching her. He searched her face, then held out a hand, beckoning. "Come here."

She considered, then did. They had to talk; she had to learn . . . whatever it was he wanted to tell her.

He took her hand, with his other hand plucked the towel from her slack grasp and tossed it to lie with his. Then he drew her to him, reached for her waist, turned her, swiveled and shifted back, drawing her down to the daybed, settling her between his thighs while he lay with his shoulders propped against the raised back.

Her back to his chest, she couldn't see his face; he was a hot, solid, muscular cushion behind her, his legs lying alongside hers.

She relaxed against him, into his embrace as his arms

closed around her; he nuzzled her temple, brushing her hair aside with his chin to place a gentle kiss there.

Closing her eyes, she savored the closeness for one long moment, then asked, "Until when are you planning to remain in the country?" The most important, vital question, one she could no longer not ask.

He didn't immediately reply, but then said, his voice even, "Forever."

She frowned. She knew him well enough to gauge the nuance in his voice. He meant forever, literally. Opening her eyes, she started to turn, to look into his face.

His arms tightened, keeping her still. Then he sighed. "There's something I have to tell you." A moment passed, then he went on, "It would help, a lot, if you remain as you are and listen, and say nothing—do nothing—until I tell you the whole."

She stayed silent and still within his arms. Wondering . . . suddenly worried.

He drew breath, then said, "I already know who I want for my wife."

Her heart constricted, a sharp pain. She moved, unable to stay still.

He tightened his hold. "Just listen."

There was an urgency in his voice, a taut tension that surprised her, made her listen even though she didn't want to hear.

"I didn't know who she was when I returned to fix the mill. But my sisters, and Sybil, too, forced me to look at her— really look. And when I did, I saw . . ." He paused, then went on, his words falling by her ear, earnest and intent; he wanted her to understand. "I already knew my criteria—the things I wanted in my bride. Age, birth and station, temperament, compatibility and beauty—that was my list. The lady in question obviously satisfied all those criteria except that I didn't know her well, so couldn't tell if we'd be compatible."

He drew breath. "So I set out to discover if we were." He paused; she suddenly felt cold, suddenly felt an inner quiver. She couldn't think. Then more softly he asked, "Do you remember when I told you what our first kiss was about— what I said? But before we got to that, you'd already told me in no uncertain terms that you would never believe, *refused* to believe, that I would want you for my wife."

A shiver materialized. She ignored it, frowned. "*Me?*" He shifted, and she wriggled and turned. Stared at his face as he flicked out the silk shawl that had been lying on the daybed's back and spread it around her shoulders. She gripped it, clutched it, staring, stunned, at him. "You want to marry *me?*"

He met her eyes and quietly stated, "All along I wanted to marry you."

He paused, then went on, "If you remember, I told you I wanted you warming my bed." He pointed toward the castle. "My bed—the one in the earl's chambers, the one only my countess will ever grace. That's where I wanted you— that's what I meant."

She still couldn't take it in. "You meant to marry me— virtually from the first."

"After that first kiss, yes."

"But . . ." Confused, she gestured around them, pushed back her hair. "What was all this about, then? The game we've been playing? My seduction?"

His lips twisted, a wry grimace. "You told me why you didn't believe—no, why you *knew* I would never seriously consider marrying you, why you believed I never would. You listed your reasons, remember. You had four—that I wasn't honestly attracted to you, not physically, that you were too old, that you weren't the sort of lady society would accept as my countess and that we would never get along, the two of us, not in the sense of living together, because we're too alike."

She stared at him, her eyes slowly narrowing as she connected actions with his words . . . she suddenly understood why he was being so careful, why he was tense. "You've been attacking my reasons. One by one."

His lips thinned. "Undermining them. You didn't give me much choice. I came home from London frustrated beyond bearing—and then I found you, and realized you were the one I wanted, the one I'd been going to London to search for. You were here, under my nose all along, and all I'd had to do was open my eyes. Once I had . . . I wasn't about to accept your dismissal and meekly go away."

She snorted. "You don't know the meaning of the word 'meek.'"

"True." The tight smile he flashed her was more warning than reassurance. "So I set out to prove to you that I honestly desire you—you can't possibly question that anymore. And you must by now realize that no one else sees either your age or your nature as in any way disqualifying you for the position of my countess. All our neighbors, all of local society would see a marriage between us as an excellent match."

"Oh, my God!" Her eyes widened, her lips parted in shock. Then she glared at him. "Who else knows? You said your sisters and Sybil—who else?"

He wasn't surprised by her reaction, that much was clear from his grimace and ready answer. "*Not* the whole neighborhood—it's not exactly something I would shout from the steeple."

"Thank Heaven for that. So who?"

He sighed. "My sisters and Sybil—as I said, they pointed me in your direction and insisted I look, so they were aware from the outset of my interest."

She remembered his sisters at the festival, all they'd said. "Dear Heaven! Your sisters are worse than you."

"Very likely—a point you might want to bear in mind."

She narrowed her eyes at him. "No others?"

He pressed his lips together, then said, "Muriel's guessed, I think. And your brothers."

"My *brothers*?"

He nodded. "Harry spoke to me—entirely correctly. They'd noticed my interest, even if you hadn't."

She stared at him, stunned again. "Good God." She couldn't think of anything else to say.

For a long moment, she simply sat there, naked on the daybed, clutching the shawl about her shoulders, facing him, completely naked, her hips and legs wedged in the space between his knees, and tried, frantically, to get her mind to take in all he'd said, and readjust her world.

In the end, she blinked, focused on his eyes, and asked, "What now?"

"Now?" His jaw set. "Now we go on until you're convinced we can get along on a daily basis, and then you agree to marry me and we arrange a wedding—and *then* I get to have you warming my bed." Taking her free hand, he urged her up. "And if we're to get you home before dawn, we'll need to get dressed."

She glanced at the windows, at the faint lightening of the sky; he was right. Standing, she found her head whirling. "Wait." Letting the shawl fall to the daybed, she clutched his arm. "You're rushing ahead too fast."

Releasing him, she went to the chair and tugged her chemise from the jumbled pile of her clothes. She struggled into it, then turned to see him looking down, buttoning his trousers. "Just because we've been lovers I'm not going to meekly say yes and marry you."

He looked up at her. "You don't know the meaning of the word 'meek.'"

She grimaced, and reached for her drawers. "As I said, we're much alike. And that doesn't necessarily augur well for domestic peace."

"It does, however, mean we'll usually understand each other."

Stepping into her silk drawers and pulling them up, she gave her attention to settling and tying the drawstring at her waist. If she'd stood on painful ground before, at least she'd been confident she knew the landscape. Now he'd shifted everything, and she no longer felt confident of anything at all.

She shot him a dark glance. "I notice you haven't said that because we've been intimate I have to marry you to preserve my reputation."

"Indeed—do, please, notice that." He cast her an equally sharp glance, then started tying his neckerchief. "If I thought such a ploy had a hope in hell of succeeding, I'd be pushing the argument for all it's worth. Explaining the facts of life to Harry—"

When she gasped, he shot her an irritated look. "But as I know you'll only dig in your heels harder if I take that tack, I didn't even consider it."

"Good—because it won't work."

"I know—see? Understanding at work."

She humphed, and wrestled her riding dress into place. "You'll have to help me with these laces."

Shrugging on his jacket, he came over and did so, swiftly redoing what he'd earlier undone. She felt him tie off the knot, but then he paused. Then he turned her to face him.

His hands on her shoulders, he looked into her face, into her eyes. For once let her see into his, past his guard—see clearly and without equivocation the possessiveness he was reining back.

"I want you as my wife—and I don't like having to wait. But I know you're not yet ready to agree. However, as I told you at the outset, I want you warming my bed—for the rest of my life. Whatever you want, whatever you need to get you to agree, I'll do it, I'll give it. Whatever it takes, I want you as mine."

She held his gaze steadily, let a moment tick past, then simply said, "I need to think."

He nodded and released her. As he moved away, heading for where he'd left his boots, he murmured, "If you feel anything for me, don't take too long."

Gervase insisted on riding all the way back to the Park with her. Which did nothing to clear her head, or stop her whirling thoughts.

When she woke the next morning—late—she felt muddleheaded, but found she couldn't think about, couldn't concentrate on, anything else. Not until she'd decided on this, on them, on him and how she should deal with him.

What she wanted from him in order to agree to be his. What else she needed to know. Whether she dared.

Marriage between people like them was not something to be embarked on lightly, not a link to be recklessly forged.

Leaving Harry to face the ledgers alone, she pleaded a headache and went to walk in the rose garden. To pace.

She'd seen falling in love with Gervase as a risk, a danger, but had embarked on their liaison, their affair, anyway, then, when love had sneaked up on her and blossomed so easily, she'd blithely—recklessly—surrendered to it. She'd meant to stay on guard and be wise, but it—he—had somehow slipped under her shield and lodged in her heart.

That was one thing. Unrequited love when she was merely his temporary lover was a scenario she'd been willing to face and cope with . . . at least she had been until she'd realized just how strongly she felt about him, how possessive of him she'd grown.

Regardless, she'd accepted the risk and couldn't now retreat. So she loved him, and knew it. But did he love her?

When they'd been no more than lovers, that hadn't truly mattered. Now he'd asked for marriage, it did. A liaison lasted for a finite time; marriage was forever. If she agreed to marry him and he didn't love her . . . what then?

Could she bear it if, years from now, he found another, a lady whom he did love, and turned from her?

She honestly didn't think she could.

Head down, hands clasped behind her back, she paced unseeing along the paved path between the burgeoning bushes.

How could she learn if he did, or could, or would, love her? She was too well acquainted with the male of the species to place any reliance on words, especially those uttered in the heat of the moment, under duress—especially, for them, emotional duress. No matter what he swore, or how sincerely he spoke, she wouldn't accept mere words as proof of his affection.

Where else to look for such proof? That was the first of the questions facing her—the first she had to answer.

The scent of roses wreathed about her. She paced, and thought, and wrestled with her feelings, and tried to imagine his. After a largely futile half hour, she headed inside, her way forward unresolved but her goal at least clear.

To avoid a potentially soul-destroying marriage, or alternatively to grasp a shining prize, she had to find some way to discover whether Gervase Tregarth truly loved her or not.

Somewhat to her surprise—to her unease—the one question she hadn't even needed to ask was whether she wanted to marry him. That, she'd discovered, not entirely happily, was a want already engraved on her heart.

A little before noon, Gervase called in at Tregarth Manor, the manor house outside Falmouth where he'd been born. He spent an easy half hour chatting with his cousin, who now lived there with his wife, confirmed that he no longer felt any strong connection to the place—it was no longer "home"—then headed on to his destination, Falmouth itself.

He paused on the last hill above the town, studied the roofs sprawled about the harbor, then shook Crusader's reins and headed down, the steady clop of the big gray's hooves following his thoughts around and around.

As they circled one female—one frustrating, stubborn, when it came to herself blind Valkyrie he was one step away from forcibly seizing and carrying off to his bed. And keeping her there until she agreed to marry him forthwith.

Even now, hours after the fact, he was still grappling with the frustration that had gripped him when he'd realized the direction of her thoughts. Lady Hardesty's blindness—which would have made Madeline's more understandable except that they lived in deepest Cornwall, not London—and the insult the group had, albeit unintentionally, handed her, had made him see red. Literally. He was still amazed he'd handled the moment with passable civility. "Civil" wasn't how he'd been feeling.

But then to discover that she had *still* not grasped the notion that she was the lady best suited to be his wife, that she *still* saw herself as a passing fancy, a local lady he'd seduced to be his mistress for the summer, had all but shredded his control.

He'd felt distinctly violent in that moment on the dance floor, then even more so when on the beach she'd confirmed her complete lack of comprehension of all he'd spent the last weeks trying to show her. To demonstrate to her, because actions spoke so much louder than words.

In her case, not even actions had sufficed; she'd thought her way around them, rationalized them—had made them fit her entrenched view that she was *not* the lady who would be his countess.

But she was. His jaw clenched; he tried not to let his grim

determination seep into his expression—no need to scare the other travelers on the road.

Regardless of her willful stance, she was the one, the lady who would, as he'd informed her, warm his big bed at the castle for the rest of his life.

In the face of her determined refusal to see, he'd jettisoned his careful approach and told her the blunt truth—not solely so he could more openly forge ahead with his campaign to win her, but equally in response to her question of how long he would remain in the country—how long he would remain with her—and the vulnerability he'd sensed behind it.

He didn't *know* if she loved him as yet, but he suspected she was at least close to it. That realization had been the only bright moment, one moment of blessed relief among the other, less happy revelations of the night.

So now she was at least thinking of him and her in the appropriate way, and considering agreeing to marry him. He hadn't exactly proposed; he inwardly winced as he recalled what he'd said, how he'd put it. But at least she now knew how he felt, how he saw her.

Of that, at least, she could no longer harbor any doubt.

Unbidden, his mind ranged ahead, to their wedding—he assumed it would be at the church at Ruan Minor. That seemed likely; both their families were part of that congregation. He knew the church well, could imagine himself standing before the ancient altar, could imagine turning and seeing her, walking up the aisle to his side . . .

Crusader jerked his head, jerking Gervase from his dream. He realized; frustrated irritation swamped him. "Good God! Now I'm fantasizing." His sisters would laugh themselves into fits. It hadn't even been the wedding night he'd been fantasizing about.

"First things first," he muttered beneath his breath. How to get her to agree.

Slowing Crusader to a walk as the first cottages neared, he considered what he could do, what ammunition he had. He could bring in the heavy artillery and recruit her brothers . . . or unleash his sisters, Sybil and even Muriel; he was sure they'd all be happy to fight for his cause.

If she proved obdurate, and he got seriously desperate, such actions were an option. However . . . he grimaced; trying to understand women in general was hard enough, but trying to understand her . . .

Instinct was all he had to guide him, and that urged him to give her at least a little time—time enough to see and accept his constancy, that he was determined, had been from the first and wasn't about to lose interest and change his mind, much less draw back. For someone of her character, her particular traits, convincing her of that would be half his battle—and something he would need to achieve on his own.

How?

Visions of stocking the boathouse with flowers, of arranging to have a rose on her pillow every night, of learning what she most craved—new novels, the latest music sheets, what else?—and getting those things for her, all the usual things a gentleman might do to assure a lady of his affection, danced through his mind, but none of those actions would work, not with her.

They might even make her suspicious of him and his motives.

In the battlefield terms with which he was most familiar, he needed to make his point more forcefully, not simply nip at her cavalry's heels. He needed some more powerful and definite way to make a statement.

Cobbles rang beneath Crusader's hooves as the town closed around them. Setting aside his mental quest for some suitably dramatic action, Gervase straightened in the saddle and refocused his mind on his immediate objective.

He knew the town well, and many there knew him. Passing the town hall, he turned down Market Street and headed for Custom Quay. His first port of call would be the harbormaster's office.

The early afternoon found Madeline in the arbor, sitting on one side bench studying the daisy she held in her fingers. She was tempted to try the "he loves me, he loves me not" test—it seemed as likely to yield an answer as any of the other approaches she'd thought of; despite her earlier efforts to clear her mind, she'd accomplished very little that day.

Sighing, she sat back and surrendered—gave her mind up to the topic that despite her best efforts had dominated her thoughts. Perhaps examining the pros and cons of marrying Gervase might shed some light.

The benefits were easy to enumerate—being the countess of a wealthy earl was nothing to sneeze at, being the mistress of his castle, the social position, the local status, even being closer to his family—his sisters and Sybil—all those elements spoke to her, attracted her.

And when it came to her brothers, he was the only man she'd ever met whom she trusted—had instinctively trusted from the first—to guide and steer them in the ways she couldn't. To understand them as she did, and join with her in protecting them as needed.

Lots of benefits. But she could see the difficulties, too. They were harder to put into words, but were nonetheless real. Most derived from the fact she'd initially identified, one he hadn't attempted to deny. They were very alike. Both were accustomed to being in control of their world, and largely in command of it.

If, for each of them, the other became a major part of their world . . . what then? Both of them had managed largely alone for all their adult lives. Finding the ways to share command at their respective ages—to accommodate another as strong as they themselves were—would not be an easy task.

That was one point where they might stumble. She knew herself too well to imagine she would ever be the sort of female to retreat from a path she was sincerely convinced was right. Regardless of any potential danger to herself . . . and therein lay the seed for serious discord. Because she knew how he would react. Just as she would if their places were reversed.

He was a warrior, a being raised to protect and defend— but so was she.

That brand of strength, of commitment, ran in his blood, and in hers. It was what had had him risking his life in France for over a decade, what had had her without a blink sacrificing the life most young ladies yearned for to care for and protect her brothers.

He was what he was, and she was who she was, and neither of them could change those fundamental traits. Which raised the vital question: Could they, somehow, find a way to rub along side by side, to live together without constantly abrading each other's instincts, each other's pride?

Heaving a long sigh, she gazed at the house, peacefully basking in the sun. Rather than finding answers, the more she thought about marrying Gervase, she only threw up more questions.

Worse, crucial but close-to-impossible-to-answer questions.

Inwardly shaking her head, she rose; still entirely planless and clueless, she started back to the house.

The sun was well past its zenith when Gervase led Crusader off the Helford ferry, swung up to the gray's back, and set him cantering out of the village south along the road to Coverack and Treleaver Park beyond.

He'd left Falmouth an hour ago having satisfactorily fulfilled his reasons for going there. After the harbormaster's office, he'd talked to a number of the officers from the revenue cutters bobbing in the harbor, then had ridden on to Pendennis Castle to check with his naval contacts there.

No official had heard so much as a whisper of any ship lost in the last month. No records, no complaints, nothing.

Quitting the castle, he'd ridden back into the town to the dockside taverns to seek the unofficial version. But that, too, had been the same. So if the brooch Madeline's brothers had found did hail from a recent wreck—one for which someone around might harbor an interest in the cargo— then that wreck had to be some smugglers' vessel, moreover, one not local.

He was inclining to the belief that the brooch must have come from some wreck of long ago.

That belief had been reinforced by a chance meeting and subsequent discussion with Charles St. Austell, Earl of Lostwithiel, and his wife, Penny; Gervase had stumbled upon Charles in one of the less reputable taverns. His erstwhile comrade-in-arms had been doing much the same as he, keeping up acquaintance with the local sailors he'd developed as contacts over the years.

Charles had been delighted to lay eyes on him. Gervase had found his own mood lifting as they'd shaken hands and clapped each other's backs. They'd sat down to share a pint, then Charles had hauled him off to the best inn in Falmouth, there to meet Penny.

And Charles's two hounds. The wolfhounds had inspected him closely before uttering doggy humphs and retreating to slump beside the hearth, allowing him to approach their master's wife.

Gervase had been impressed; he was seriously considering getting Madeline a similar pair of guardians. Despite Charles's excuse that he'd brought the hounds to be company for Penny, it was plain—at least to Gervase, and he suspected Penny—that Charles felt much more comfortable having the hounds to guard his wife while he went trawling through the dockside taps.

Thinking of how his and Madeline's life would be once she moved to the castle—especially if and when any children came along—although he had no intention of leaving her side for any length of time, having two such large and loyal beasts to guard her while he rode out around the estate . . . he could appreciate Charles's thinking.

He clattered through Coverack and turned for Treleaver Park. The mystery of the brooch still nagged at him, but when he'd told them the story, Charles and Penny, both of whom, like him, had long experience with local smuggling gangs, had inclined to the same conclusion as he. The brooch was most likely from some ancient wreck.

Indeed, as Penny had pointed out, echoing his own thoughts, it was hard to imagine why smugglers would have been ferrying such a cargo.

Yet that nagging itch between his shoulders persisted. He'd decided to get Harry, Edmond and Ben to show him where they'd uncovered their find, just in case the precise location suggested anything else—any other possibility.

The Treleaver Park gates were perennially set wide; he trotted through and up the drive. The westering sun was lowering over the peninsula when he drew rein in the forecourt.

Dismounting, he waited, then running footsteps heralded a stablelad, who came pelting around the corner to take his reins.

"Sorry, m'lord." The youth bobbed his head and grasped the reins. "But there's a right to-do indoors. We was distracted."

"Oh?" Premonition touched Gervase's nape, slid coolly down his spine. Unwilling to gossip with the stablelad, he nodded and strode swiftly up the shallow steps and through the open front door.

There was nothing odd about the open front door; most country houses, especially those with younger inhabitants, especially in summer, left their doors wide. What was odd was the absence of Milsom.

Gervase halted in the middle of the hall; voices—including Madeline's—reached him.

He was too far away to make out the words; he followed the sound down the corridor to the office.

Milsom was standing just inside the door, his countenance a medley of shock, concern and helplessness.

Madeline was perched on the front edge of her desk, leaning toward her brothers—Harry and Edmond—both bolt upright in chairs facing her.

One look at her face—at the bleak fear therein—had Gervase striding into the room. "What's happened?"

She looked up; for one instant he glimpsed relief, then her face, her expression, tightened. "Ben's . . ." She gestured helplessly, plainly torn over what word to use. "*Gone.*"

The tremor, the underlying panic in her voice, shook him.

Harry had swung around; he met Gervase's eyes as Gervase halted beside Madeline, taking her hand, holding it, not releasing it. "We don't *know* what's happened. Ben's disappeared, and we don't know where he is." Anguish colored Harry's eyes and voice.

Years of experience took over. Gervase dropped his other hand onto Harry's shoulder, gripped. "Take a deep breath, then start at the beginning."

Edmond's eyes, too, were wide, his expression stricken.

Drawing in a huge breath, Harry held it for an instant, then said, "We rode to Helston midmorning. We thought we should check whether there'd been any more rumors about the tin mines. We went down to the Pig & Whistle— it's the best place to learn things like that, and we knew we'd meet some of the other lads there, the ones who tell us things."

Gervase nodded. "It's a rough but useful place." The Pig & Whistle was one of the taverns along the old Helston docks.

Relief washed through Harry's eyes. "Exactly. But, of course, because it's so rough we didn't want to take Ben into the tap with us—and anyway, Old Henry, the inn-keeper, doesn't like 'nippers' brought in."

"Perfectly understandable." Madeline leaned forward, meeting first Harry's, then Edmond's eyes. "I don't blame either of you in the least for leaving Ben outside."

She'd had a moment—a moment Gervase's arrival had granted her, his stalwart presence had allowed her—to as-similate what she'd learned. A minute to grasp the implica-tions as well as the horror, and focus on what had to be done. Having Harry and Edmond sinking under unneces-sary guilt was the last thing she needed.

"So you left Ben outside," Gervase said. "Where, ex-actly?"

"He was sitting on the bench along the front of the tavern when we went in," Edmond said. "He was happy as a grig, swinging his legs and watching the boats on the river. He didn't want to come inside—he doesn't like the smoke and the smells." Edmond's voice quavered. "That was the last we saw of him."

Harry swallowed, nodded. "When we came out, he was nowhere in sight."

"How long were you in the tavern?" Gervase asked.

Harry and Edmond exchanged glances. "Half an hour?" Harry looked up at Gervase. "Forty minutes at most. We came out with Tom Pachel and Johnny Griggs, and Ben was gone."

"We searched—all four of us," Edmond said. "The oth-ers helped when they realized we were worried."

"The more we searched, still others joined in." Harry

took up the tale. "We covered the entire docks, but there was no sign of Ben anywhere. That's when Abel—Johnny had fetched him—said we should ride home while the rest of them kept looking." Harry glanced at Madeline. "Abel said we should find you and tell you."

She gave mute thanks for Abel Griggs. She glanced at Gervase. "They arrived only a few minutes before you."

He nodded.

She tensed to rise from the desk, but through his hold on her hand Gervase halted her. He met her gaze briefly, then turned again to the boys. "Through all the searching, did anyone say anything at all about seeing Ben wander off, or seeing someone approach him, speak with him—anything like that?"

Harry glanced at Edmond, then looked at Gervase. "Old Eddie was the only one who said he saw Ben, but, well"—Harry grimaced—"you know Old Eddie. You can't trust anything he says after midday, and he was well away by the time we talked to him."

Old Eddie was one of the town drunks.

"Never mind his state," Gervase said. "Tell me what he said."

"He said a flash cove came up to the bench and spoke with Ben, not just a hello—they had a conversation. Eddie said it was all sunny and happy as you please. And then Ben upped and went off with the man."

Gervase frowned. "A flash cove? Eddie used those words?"

Harry nodded. "I suppose he meant a flashily dressed gentleman."

Gervase didn't reply; Madeline glanced at him in time to see the muscle in his jaw clench. Glancing sideways, he met her eyes, hesitated as if he wanted to explain, then he shook his head infinitesimally and turned back to Harry and Edmond. "No other sighting, nothing at all?"

Harry shook his head.

Edmond wriggled. "Mrs. Heggarty said she saw a man and a boy walking up her street—the one past Coinagehall Street—but she couldn't say if it was Ben or not. She's blind as a bat, so it could have been anyone. She couldn't say anything about the man."

Madeline had heard enough. She looked at Milsom, waiting by the door, opened her mouth to ask for Artur to be saddled—only to hear Gervase say, "Before we go haring back to Helston there's things we should do—arrangements which will make finding Ben easier, quicker and more certain."

She glanced at him, saw the seriousness in his eyes. "What arrangements?"

Gervase drew breath, swiftly reviewing the list that had formed in his head. He didn't want to tell Madeline, let alone Harry and Edmond, what a 'flash cove' was. Old Eddie had been a London gentleman's gentleman until he'd become too fond of the bottle; to Eddie, as to Gervase and anyone with knowledge of London's underworld, a 'flash cove' meant a swindler or trickster usually based in London who made a living by leading others astray—usually into the clutches of some more powerful and nasty villain.

No matter how inebriated Old Eddie had been, if he'd said a flash cove, that was what he'd meant. But what such a person was doing in Helston, let alone why he'd approached Ben . . . despite all the possibilities, instinct screamed that Ben's disappearance had something to do with the other inexplicable thing that had recently come into his young life. The brooch.

Gervase met Madeline's eyes. "We need to assemble a search party, one big enough to scour the town more or less in one fell swoop. You need to gather the men on the estate, all those you can mount. Also send a note in my name to Sitwell at the castle asking him to do the same with my

people and send them to Helston to wait for us there." He
paused, thinking, then nodded. "That should give us enough
men."

Madeline blinked, then nodded; rising from the desk,
she moved around it to her chair. She frowned. "Should
we—"

He held up a hand. "While you write those notes, I'll
send one of your grooms to Falmouth. I was there earlier
today and ran into a friend—another member of my club—
Charles St. Austell, Earl of Lostwithiel. I'll ask Charles to
do two things. First, to talk to the mayor and the governor
of Pendennis Castle and get a roadblock set up on the London road." When alarm crossed her face, he forced a reassuring smile. "A precaution. Let's hope there's no need
for it, but it won't hurt to have that in place just in case."

That he was considering "just in case" seemed to calm
her; she nodded and sank into her chair.

He held her gaze. "The other thing I'm going to ask is for
Charles to meet us in Helston. He has his dogs, two wolfhounds, with him, and I recall him mentioning that they're
excellent trackers."

And Penny would accompany Charles; nothing was more
likely. Gervase hoped the arrival of another lady of similar
standing would help distract Madeline, and stop her from
imagining the worst.

He was able to imagine far worse scenarios than she, but
he knew it was pointless and likely self-defeating. Neither
he nor she could afford to allow panic to deflect them, not if
they wanted Ben back, safe.

To her, he said, "I'll leave you to write those notes." Then
he looked at Harry and Edmond. "I'll need a groom to take
my message to Falmouth—you two can help me with that."

He glanced back at Madeline.

She was reaching for paper and pen. "Send Fanning—
he's reliable under pressure." She looked at Harry. "Send all

the other grooms to me—I'll have notes ready for them soon."

"Milsom can stay and assist you." Gervase locked his gaze on the boys. "Come on—let's get my message off."

With last glances at Madeline—who already had her head bowed over a note—Harry and Edmond rose and followed Gervase into the corridor.

They found Fanning in the stables; Gervase recited his message to Charles, had Fanning repeat it, then sent him off. Leaving the other grooms saddling up to take Madeline's notes to the castle and surrounding farms, Gervase beckoned the two boys to accompany him and headed back to the house.

Pausing outside the side door, he turned to them. "Where's a safe place to talk?"

Harry exchanged a look with Edmond, then volunteered, "The library."

Gervase waved them ahead of him; he followed them along a corridor and into the library.

Closing the doors behind him, he faced them. They'd turned and fixed big eyes on him.

"What is it?" Harry asked.

"Does Ben know where you found the brooch? Was he with you when you found it?"

Both nodded. "It was he who tripped over it in the sand," Edmond said.

Harry's eyes had widened. "Do you think he's been kidnapped over the brooch? By the wreckers?"

"No." Gervase spoke quickly to dispel the looming horror. "*Not* the wreckers, that much seems certain. However, I told you I'd check again in Falmouth to see if there was any missing ship listed—that's why I was there today. I learned there definitely isn't any legitimate ship missing."

He caught Harry's gaze. "As we discussed before, that leaves only two reasonable explanations for that brooch.

Either it's from a long-ago wreck—or from a smugglers' vessel that went down on the Manacles in that bad blow two weeks ago." He felt his lips thin. "As there have been no local smugglers' vessels lost, until half an hour ago I was tending to the ancient wreck as explanation. Now . . ." He paused, then looked at them. "I can't imagine any other reason for someone to grab Ben—can you?"

Both boys' eyes had grown round. Both thought, then shook their heads.

"You think—" Harry's voice squeaked; he cleared his throat and tried again. "You think someone wants the brooch and . . ." He frowned. "That doesn't make sense."

"No—not if they're after the brooch. But . . ." He'd never used two schoolboys to test his reasoning before, but he had enough respect for their mental acuity, and their involvement, to try. He moved to sit on the arm of a nearby chair, bringing his face down to Edmond's level.

"Consider this. If a ship did go down in that gale, then if it wasn't one of our smugglers' ships, it had to be one from the Isles of Scilly or from France. French captains especially wouldn't necessarily know that it's impossible to beat up the coast to the Helford estuary in a wind like that—that it would blow them onto the Manacles. Let's say that's what happened— a French smuggling vessel was wrecked two weeks ago."

He caught the boys' eyes, first Harry's, then Edmond's. "If a French vessel was heading for the Helford estuary, then someone had arranged that—the ship had to have been carrying a cargo some person here, in England, didn't want the authorities to know about. A cargo that had to be kept secret. But that person waited, and no ship arrived. Let's say he knew—as most do—that these coasts are haunted by local smugglers and wreckers. So when his ship didn't come in, he starts searching—"

"For any evidence of his *cargo*," Harry said.

"And he saw the brooch . . . when?" Edmond frowned. ·

"It's not as if Madeline was wearing it at the festival where anyone could have seen it. How would some blackguard have sighted it—especially enough to recognize it?" He focused on Gervase's face. "That's what you mean, isn't it? That someone saw it and knew it was from his lost cargo." Edmond looked at Harry. "But we didn't show it to anyone— not even Aunt Muriel—before we gave it to Madeline. And she only wore it at her party—"

"And then at Lady Felgate's ball." Solemn and somber, Gervase nodded. "You're right. We know everyone who was at Madeline's party—we've known them for years. It wasn't anyone there. But Lady Felgate's ball was attended by almost everyone on the peninsula—"

"Including people who aren't from around here," Harry put in. "People who are visiting for the summer with local families."

"Exactly. There's no saying who might have noticed the brooch, and the person involved might not even have attended the ball—someone might have mentioned the brooch to them later." Gervase grimaced. "It's such a unique piece, even a vague description would be enough for someone who was familiar with it to recognize it."

"But we told Madeline we bought it from that peddler," Edmond said. "No one but you knew we'd found it on the beach."

"And I didn't tell anyone." Gervase frowned, then pulled a face. "The person looking for the lost cargo was at the festival, of course. He would have checked with all the peddlers—the most obvious source for recently washed-up items. When asked where she got the brooch—and untold ladies at the ball did ask—Madeline said you'd given it to her for her birthday and that you'd found it at one of the peddlers' stalls at the festival. But our man knew that wasn't true, ergo you three were lying—which to his mind would mean you had found his lost cargo."

"So . . ." Harry's voice died; he stared at Gervase. "Is it someone from London who's kidnapped Ben?"

Pure instinct had prompted him to suggest the barrier on the London road; Gervase wryly noted his instincts were still sound. "Most likely, but we can't assume they'll take him to London. I just wanted to ensure they don't take him out of the area—at least not easily. The London road was the obvious one to block. The authorities will search all carriages and conveyances of any sort, so if they do try to take him away . . . hopefully, we'll prevent that." Given the time lapse between when Ben was seized and when the roadblock would go up, if the villains had started for London immediately, they might slip past before the barriers were in place.

Gervase pushed the thought aside; he had to concentrate on what he could do, what he could achieve. And Ben being taken to London was a long shot.

"Let's try to think like our villain. He's lost his cargo, sees—or learns of—the brooch, realizes you three found it somewhere. He wants to know where, so he grabs Ben—or arranges to have him seized—reasoning that being the youngest, he's the most likely to tell him what he wants to know without fuss."

Harry snorted. "He'd have been better off grabbing me. Ben's the most stubborn of us all."

Edmond nodded. "He'll probably lie—send the man off to some other beach."

Gervase blinked. If Edmond had so immediately thought of that, there was a good chance Ben would, too. "All right. Let's say Ben tells the man he found the brooch somewhere—either the right beach, or another."

"What will they do with Ben?" Harry rushed to ask.

Gervase hid his reaction, but then he thought further. . . . "Actually, it's most likely they'll set Ben free. They won't consider him any real threat. They'll leave him somewhere out of the way, far enough so he can't raise any dust until they've recovered the cargo and are long gone. There's no reason they should harm him—easy enough to make sure he doesn't know anything that might identify them, not once they get away from here."

The easing of Edmond's and Harry's tension was obvious. They breathed more easily.

"How is our villain going to recover his lost cargo?" Gervase posed the question. One flash cove, most likely from London, was in the neighborhood, most likely in the pay of their villain. How many more of his ilk might be around? Regardless . . . "Once Ben tells him a location, he's going to go searching, digging in the sand."

Gervase rose, glanced around. "Are there any maps in here?"

"Yes." Edmond hurried to a low shelf, pulled a large folio free, then lugged it to the desk.

Gervase and Harry gathered around as Edmond opened it and spread out a large map of the peninsula. "Show me which beach it was," Gervase demanded. "How close to Lowland Point?"

"Right there." Harry put his finger on a spot immediately north of the headland.

Gervase glanced at the Manacles, marked as a line of jagged teeth to the right of the beach in question. "All right. If Ben tells them the truth, our man will go to that spot. He might well bring others with him to do the digging and any carting, but he will come himself—he'll want to see his cargo retrieved."

For a moment, he stared at the map, then he glanced at Harry, caught his eye. "We need to keep a watch on that beach. If Ben does send them there, we need to catch whoever comes to dig up the lost cargo. I'm going to put you in charge of a group of your men—all from here so they'll look to you for command. I want you to take the men to the right stretch of beach and keep a watch over it—you know how to hide in the caves, and along the cliffs. Stay out of sight unless our villain or his henchmen arrive—they'll almost certainly not be locals. Then . . . you'll have enough men to capture them."

Harry swallowed. He held Gervase's gaze, then nodded. "Yes. Of course."

"Don't worry." Gervase clapped him on the shoulder. "You'll have your head stableman and others you know with you." He turned to Edmond. "You'll need to ride with Madeline and the rest of us to show us exactly where Ben was when last you saw him."

Gervase glanced one last time at the map, then turned to the door. "Right—let's get going."

The boys fell in on his heels. They returned to the front hall; swiftly, Gervase made arrangements with Milsom, with the older man's help selecting experienced men as well as a few eager young stalwarts for Harry's "troop."

Milsom retreated to dispatch a footman to ferry his orders to the stables. As Gervase turned back to the boys, Edmond asked, "Ben is going to be all right, isn't he?"

Madeline hurried down the stairs in time to hear the question. After dispatching her last note—the one to the castle—she'd rushed upstairs to pull her riding trousers on under her walking dress—no time to change gowns—then she'd stopped in Muriel's room to explain. Her aunt napped in the afternoons when she could; she'd been horrified, but had borne up under the strain, relieved—as Madeline was— to know that Gervase was there and helping.

Now, hearing Edmond voice her own fearful question, she felt her heart contract, felt herself wait, breath bated, for Gervase's answer.

He'd heard her footsteps; he turned, met her eyes, then smiled gently, reassuringly. He turned back to Edmond, looking down into her brother's face. "The most likely thing to happen is that after Ben gives them a location for where you found the brooch, they'll leave him somewhere, trussed up so he can't raise the alarm while they come to search for the rest of the lost cargo. There's no reason for them to harm him. Once we catch them, we'll be able to learn where they've left him."

Madeline felt her eyes widen. "Brooch? *Lost cargo?*" Clearly she'd missed something major.

Gervase met her eyes. "I'll explain all on our way. We have to get moving." He glanced at Harry. "Harry's leading a band of your men to keep watch on the beach where they found your brooch." He caught her gaze, clearly willing her not to slow them with more questions, to trust him. "Can you fetch a shirt of Ben's, or a neckerchief? Not something washed but something he's recently worn next to his skin. It'll give the dogs his scent. Two pieces would help— Charles has two dogs and we might want to send them in different directions."

Drawing in a huge breath through the vise clamped about her lungs, lips thin, she nodded. "I'll get them." Turning, she hurried back up the stairs.

Behind her she heard Gervase repeating orders to Harry, calm and certain, reassuring in his clarity.

She swept into Ben's room; it took but a moment to sort through the pile of dirty linen flung in a corner. Selecting a shirt he'd worn the day before, and his nightshirt, she rushed back into the corridor, paused, then, bundling the linens up in one arm, she ran to her own room.

The brooch—how the devil was it linked with all this?— lay on her dressing table. She swiped it up, stared at it as it lay on her palm; she couldn't believe it was worth anyone's life, certainly not Ben's, but . . . if the men who had kidnapped Ben were after it, she'd trade it in a blink.

Stuffing it into the pocket of her dress, feeling it heavy

against her thigh, she raced out of the door and headed for the stairs.

She clattered down to find Gervase and Edmond waiting for her. Muriel had come down and was standing with them.

"Take care—all of you," Muriel said. "And bring Ben back."

Madeline swooped and kissed her cheek as she passed. "We will."

She met Gervase's eyes. He nodded. "Let's ride."

Outside they found a milling crowd, all mounted. She saw Harry conferring with Simpkins, their head stableman, then Harry called the group about him to order. He glanced back, once, at her, raised his hand in a salute, nodded to Gervase, then led his small band off.

Madeline stared at his back as he rode down the drive.

"Here. Mount up."

She turned to find Gervase holding Artur's head. "Oh— thank you." Shaking her wits into order, she stuffed Ben's clothes into the saddle pocket, then shoved her boot in the stirrup, grasped the saddle and swung up to Artur's back.

The instant she had her reins in hand, Gervase turned to his gray and mounted. He nudged the huge horse close, then lifted his head to address the others. "Straight to Helston by the best route. If we get separated, we'll meet outside the Scales & Anchor."

Murmurs of acknowledgment sounded all around.

Gervase nodded at her. "Lead off."

She swung Artur's head for the gate and loosened his reins.

They were galloping by the time they cleared the gates at the end of the long drive; glancing around, she noted Gervase keeping an eye on Edmond, but he soon saw there was no need and pushed forward to ride alongside her.

"They can ride as well as I do," she called.

He nodded. "So I see."

"So what's going on?"

He glanced back, then called to her, "You and I are going to outdistance everyone else. We'll be waiting for them in Helston—I'll explain everything then."

Regardless of all else, even her own understanding, she wanted Ben rescued as soon as possible. So she nodded, and looked ahead. And urged Artur on.

Chapter 16

hey gathered outside the Scales & Anchor, a crowd
large enough to fill the street. Abel Griggs and his
lads joined them, as did many of the local men and boys. It
was early evening when Gervase organized the assembled
multitude into groups and sent them out searching, quartering the town, spreading outward from the old docks where
Ben had last been seen.

Leaving Abel installed on the bench outside the Scales &
Anchor to receive any reports, Gervase took Madeline's
arm and together they walked swiftly to the mayor's house,
a short distance away.

"Good gracious!" Mr. Caldwell, the mayor, was shocked
by their news. "Of course you must search. Do you have
enough men? We could call out the militia—entirely appropriate in such a case."

Gervase inclined his head, acknowledging the offer. "No
need as it happens, not because we can't use the men, but
because most have already joined us."

"Good, good." Short and tending toward rotund, Mr.

Caldwell bobbed his head, looking stunned. "Shocking thing, to have a youngster kidnapped."

"Indeed." Taking Madeline's arm, Gervase eased her away—before Caldwell started speculating on Ben's plight, something Madeline didn't need to hear. "If you'll excuse us, we must get back to the search."

"Of course, of course!"

With a nod, her face expressionless, Madeline turned away and let Gervase lead her down the path and back into the street. Her features were set; she felt locked away inside herself, as if everything were happening at a distance, yet she knew that it was real, the here and now.

She knew Ben had been kidnapped and was in danger.

Gervase had explained all she hadn't known while they'd waited for the others outside the inn. In large measure the explanation was incidental; to her, the only thing that mattered was Ben—finding him, rescuing him, safe and unharmed.

Her detachment, she was beginning to realize, was a boon.

If she thought about the situation too much, let possibilities form and take shape, panic welled and threatened to overwhelm her, to sink her mind in a morass of emotions, but with Gervase beside her she could hold back the black tide and function as she needed to—as Ben needed her to.

Gervase's hand tightened over hers on his sleeve. "One thing at a time—that's how to approach this."

Her gaze on the pavement ahead of them, she nodded.

The sound of clattering hooves, deep woofs and a sudden hail had them both looking up. Two riders were walking their horses up the street, a gentleman and a lady, with two huge hounds ranging alongside, drifting from one side of the road to the other, scenting this, then that.

Drawing rein just ahead of them, the riders dismounted, the lady kicking her feet free of her stirrups and sliding down before the man could assist her. He glanced at her, then, his reins in one hand, came forward. Smiling. "The old tar outside the inn said you'd come this way."

Gervase's lips lifted; he shook hands with the gentleman, then turned to Madeline. "Charles St. Austell, Earl of Lostwithiel, and his wife, Lady Penelope. The Honorable Miss Madeline Gascoigne."

Madeline forced a weak smile and shook hands.

"Just Charles," the gentleman said, squeezing her hand in kindly fashion. He was as tall as Gervase, but black-haired, with large dark eyes; beyond that, they were of similar build, and shared the same elusive sense of intentness, of being very much alert and aware, even when relaxed.

"You must be quite frantic with worry." Lady Penelope, a willowy blonde with a look in her gray eyes that said she was not to be trifled with no matter what her husband might imply, took both Madeline's hands in hers and smiled understandingly. "And do call me Penny." She looked at Gervase. "So we're here—the dogs are here. I suggest we make a start so we can find this young lad."

Charles flashed Madeline a grin. "She's a bossy sort."

Madeline raised her brows. "In that case, she and I will get along famously."

Penny chuckled. "Indeed."

The dogs pressed close, one on either side of Charles and Penny, looking up at Gervase and Madeline with great canine grins, as if they, too, were eager to get on.

"I brought two pieces of Ben's clothing," Madeline said. "Things he's recently worn. I left them in my sadde pocket."

"Our horses are at the inn," Gervase said. "We can start from there."

They walked quickly back to the inn, dogs and horses in tow. Madeline noticed Penny glancing at her trousers, visible beneath her gown's hem given she was striding along.

Penny was striding, too; although a few inches shorter than Madeline, she was taller than most ladies. As they reached the archway leading into the inn yard, Penny caught Madeline's eye. "I confess I'm intrigued. I assume you ride astride? How do you find others take to the trousers?"

Madeline's smile was wry. "I've been wearing them— usually under a riding dress—for more than a decade, so everyone around here has grown used to the sight. But I have to ride a lot, and this is Artur"—she gestured as she led them to where the big chestnut stood tied to a rail—"so a sidesaddle isn't really an option."

"Oh, but he's a beauty." Penny stroked Artur's long nose, appreciatively cast her eye down his length. "Powerful, too."

Madeline nodded as she pulled Ben's clothes from her saddle pocket.

Beside them, Charles nudged Gervase. "We're redundant."

"Not for long." Madeline turned with the clothes. She offered them to Charles. "How do you want to do this?"

After consulting with Gervase, Charles elected to put both dogs on leashes. He pulled the long leather strips from his saddlebags. "We don't want them finding the scent and then racing too far ahead of us. If your brother's on his own, he might get a nasty shock to see these two charging toward him."

"They won't hurt him," Penny put in.

"But they won't be very friendly toward anyone who's with him, regardless of whether they're friend or foe." Charles finished fastening the leashes; he handed one to Penny. "Let's go to this bench he was last seen sitting on and start from there."

They did. Abel stayed on outside the inn, but those searchers who had returned—all with no news—followed Charles, Gervase, Penny and Madeline down to the old docks. The shadows were starting to lengthen. The tavern was deserted; all the patrons were helping with the search.

Charles had the dogs sit before the bench, gave each a piece of Ben's clothing to sniff, then he showed them the spot on the bench where Edmond said Ben had been sitting. Both dogs sniffed, milled, danced—looked up at Charles expectantly; this was clearly a game they knew. "Find," Charles said.

Instantly both dogs put their noses to the ground, turned, and headed back along the dock, then up a street that ran roughly parallel to Coinagehall Street.

Everyone followed, hurrying. Charles and Penny jogged, keeping the dogs from racing ahead. The wolfhounds tracked with confidence and ease, moving fluidly; it seemed Ben's trail was, to them at least, obvious.

The small procession tacked onto a side street, then swung around another corner. The turns continued, but it was apparent that their quarry had struck across the town in one definite direction.

Gervase felt his chest tighten as that direction became plain. He glanced at Madeline, saw from her set expression and the dawning horror in her eyes that she had worked it out, too.

As he'd feared, the dogs reached the High Road, ran a little way along, then stopped. And sat. And looked at Charles; even unfamiliar as he was with the beasts, Gervase could interpret their confident and satisfied demeanor.

They'd followed the trail to the end.

Charles glanced around, then cocked a brow at Gervase.

"The London road." Face impassive, he turned to Madeline. "The man brought Ben here, then he got into—or was put into—a carriage."

Madeline met his eyes; her face was nearly as expressionless as his. She nodded, then looked around. Then she turned to those who had followed them through the streets. The group had halted a few feet away, not liking the conclusion of their search any more than Gervase and Madeline.

Somewhat to Gervase's surprise, Madeline singled out

three of the men. "Harris, Cartwright—Miller. You all live in this area, don't you?"

All three nodded, pushing through to the front of the small crowd. "Yes, ma'am."

"Right—come with me. Ben was taken in broad daylight in the middle of the afternoon. This is one of the busiest parts of town at that hour—someone must have seen something."

Gervase joined them; he went with Miller down one side of the street, knocking on doors, speaking to the occupants. The shops along the street had closed for the day; all had their shutters up, but most of the shopkeepers lived above their premises; once they understood what had occurred, all were only too happy to answer their questions.

They soon found three different people who unequivocally confirmed than Ben had been steered by a man, not a local and not a gentleman, to a waiting carriage, then lifted into it. No one had noticed him struggling, but all agreed he'd been lifted quickly, and might not have had time to react. Then the man had climbed into the carriage, shut the door, and the carriage had rolled off—toward London.

"Four good horses." Charles repeated the words of one of the witnesses, an ostler from one of the inns who'd been passing.

Gervase met his eye, then looked at Madeline. "London. No reason to have four unless they're traveling that far."

Madeline looked into his amber eyes and tried to contain her fear. Whoever had abducted Ben, they were taking him to the capital.

They hurried back to the Scales & Anchor, mounted up, and took to the London road in the wake of the unknown carriage. There was an outside chance that the barriers outside Falmouth had been put in place in time . . . they rode furiously, the sun sinking at their backs.

The last red-gold rays were fading, the sky in the west

ablaze, when they came into sight of the improvised block-ade, a gate set across the highway manned by soldiers from the Pendennis garrison.

The lieutenant in charge came up as they drew rein. He recognized both Gervase and Charles, and snapped off a salute, with a nod for Madeline and Penny.

"No sign?" Gervase asked.

"No, sir. We halted every carriage and cart and searched them. No boy of any sort has gone through."

Gervase looked at Madeline, met her eyes. "We'll con-tinue on to London."

We. There hadn't been any question, of course, yet Mad-eline had been relieved not to have had to argue. Being left in Cornwall while Gervase chased the carriage to London was unthinkable; she couldn't *not* follow Ben, no matter that it was unlikely they could catch the carriage before it reached town, and that she had no notion of how to proceed once they got there.

Gervase would have; she clung to that and asked no questions—explanations would only slow them down and she could ask all she wished in the carriage once they were away—and let him organize all that needed organizing.

He was good at it, and thorough to boot. At his suggestion they rode to the main posting inn just outside Falmouth. By then, evening was drawing in, the long twilight taking hold; it deepened as the innkeeper, recognizing both Gervase and Charles, leapt to carry out Gervase's orders. Ostlers scur-ried, readying horses, a coach was selected and made ready, and the inn's best coachman summoned from his cottage.

The inn yard was lit by flickering flares by the time all was ready.

Charles and Penny, who'd declared themselves at Ger-vase's and Madeline's disposal, had agreed to go to Crow-hurst Castle, to explain and watch over things there and at the Park. Gervase concisely outlined the mission he'd delegated to Harry—to watch over the beach where the boys had found the brooch.

"I'll go to the beach myself, speak with Harry, and ensure the watch is kept up day and night. No telling what this blackguard or his henchmen might do." Charles met Madeline's eyes, took her hands in his, pressed reassuringly. "Don't worry. You two concentrate on getting young Ben back safe and sound—you can leave all here to us."

Sober and serious beside him, Penny nodded. She held Madeline's gaze. "We'll watch over your other brothers. We'll be here when you get back."

Madeline tried for a smile, but it was a weak effort. Having some other lady step in to watch over Harry and Edmond—she knew without asking that Penny understood; she'd mentioned she'd had a younger brother herself—was a huge relief. With that aspect taken care of, she could indeed focus her entire being on rescuing Ben.

Gervase turned aside as someone called to him.

Opening the door of the carriage, a sleek vehicle with four strong horses between the shafts, with the experienced driver who swore he knew every pothole on the London road and just how to manage his leaders to get the best pace now on the box, Charles handed Madeline up.

Then Gervase was back; with a last word to Penny, then Charles, he climbed into the carriage and sat beside her.

Charles leaned in through the door. "If you reach London without catching them, call on Dalziel."

Grim-faced, Gervase nodded. "I will."

Charles saluted, stepped back and shut the door. He called up to the coachman.

A whip cracked, and they were off.

Night had fallen, the darkness dense and complete beneath thick clouds before Madeline's mind cleared enough to appreciate the comfort of the coach, the warmth of the bricks Gervase had placed at her feet, the softness of the traveling rug beside her on the seat.

They were incidental comforts, but soothed nevertheless. The weather had turned; the night was cool.

Her blood seemed cold, too—too chilly to warm her.

Glancing out of the window at the variegated shadows flitting past, she wondered how far they'd come, how far ahead of them the carriage fleeing with Ben was.

Large and solid beside her, a source of steady warmth—steady reassurance and comfort—Gervase had closed his hand around hers as they'd left the inn yard in Falmouth, and hadn't once let go. Now he lifted that hand, brushed his lips to her knuckles. As if he could read her mind, he murmured, "We'll check at the major posting houses. It'll take a few minutes, but if they halt on the road, we don't want to overshoot them."

She looked at his face, his profile. "Do you think they will stop?" She hadn't allowed herself to imagine that.

He sighed. His lips twisted. "No. Whoever he is, he's not stupid. He knows a hue and cry will be raised and that we'll search for Ben. What he couldn't know is that we'd realize so soon that he's heading for London. He won't expect us to be so close on his heels."

She nodded and looked forward, letting her fingers lightly grip his, letting his hold on her hand, letting him, anchor her. One part of her mind was simply frantic; she'd never in her life felt this way—so at the mercy of a situation that was far beyond her control.

So helpless.

So vulnerable, not over her own well-being, but over the well-being and the life of one who, she knew, had been a surrogate child. Ben was the baby she'd reared; she held him closest of all to her heart.

If it had been herself at risk, she wouldn't have felt this

clawing panic, this fragility. An attack on her she would have met and weathered without emotional strain; an attack on Ben—on any of her brothers—was different. Such an attack held the power to devastate.

Gervase settled her hand on his thigh, his long fingers locked around hers. The steel beneath her hand, the sense of protectiveness the simple act conveyed . . . she noticed, appreciated, gave mute thanks, but could not, at that moment, find words to phrase her gratitude.

He hadn't bothered to waste so much as a minute trying to leave her behind; he'd understood, and accepted, and bowed to her right to go with him after Ben. Most men, especially gentlemen, would have argued, and been grumpy when they lost. Instead, he'd done everything possible to ease her way, to support her in her quest . . . no, their mutual quest. That felt odd in one way, but strangely right. He'd earned the right by his behavior, his understanding, to stand by her side.

Closing her eyes, she swallowed. Took a moment to savor that truth, one moment to acknowledge it. And what it meant, what it portended.

Loving him was one thing, accepting him into her life quite another. Had she already let him in, unconsciously, without, until now, being aware of it?

Regardless, now was not the time for thinking of such things. She breathed in, let the subject sink deeper into her mind, refocusing instead on Ben, and their chase.

Normally a fast, well-sprung carriage would take two full days of traveling to reach London; even with good horses, the journey meant well over twenty-four hours on the road, even in summer. But most carriages didn't drive through the night; they, however, were. It was risky, more because of the state of the roads than due to any corporeal threat, but that was why Gervase had insisted on Falmouth's best coachman, and he'd hired his mate as well, so they could spell each other through the night, and then on through the following day.

The rhythmic rocking of the carriage, the swift, regular thud of the horses' hooves, reassured her; they were doing all they could. Gervase's hand remained locked about hers, his shoulder beside hers, there for her to lean on—something she'd never imagined she would ever do—his hard thigh solid and warm alongside hers. Every touch, every nuance of his presence calmed and steadied her.

They were on the villain's heels and traveling as hard and as fast as it was possible to go. All that remained was to wait, to exist in a sort of limbo of heightened but restrained expectation, until the other carriage slowed and they caught it—or, better yet, it stopped.

The carriage they were chasing didn't halt for the night. They didn't, either.

They got confirmation of its passing at numerous post-houses. They would stop and Gervase would get out to make inquiries; usually within minutes he would be back and they'd be on the road once more.

The night waned; dawn came and the sun rose, and they continued on at their near breakneck pace. The day wore on; Madeline felt cramped, limbs and muscles protesting the unaccustomed inactivity, but she wasn't about to quibble, let alone complain.

Despite their unrelenting pace, Gervase was assiduous in insisting she, and the coachmen, too, got down to stretch their legs at regular intervals, usually while they were changing horses. While the coachmen oversaw the ostlers, he'd escort her into whichever inn they'd stopped at, order something light and quick for them both, sending ale and sandwiches out to the coachmen.

Breakfast and lunch were taken in that fashion.

Although the breaks were kept to a minimum, they were another example of Gervase's protectiveness, an all-but-instinctive habit of ensuring the welfare of those in his care. Even if those people tried to argue, as, on the first occasion, Madeline had. She'd been overruled in a tone one degree away from dictatorial . . . she'd noted it, but, subsequently, when she'd realized the wisdom behind his actions, she'd inwardly shrugged and the next time complied without caviling. There was, it seemed, a time and place for authoritative men.

They rattled into Amesbury in midafternoon. The coachman's mate blew on the yard of tin; when they swung under the arch of the Blue Gun & Pistols, the ostlers were already leading out fresh horses, others waiting ready to unbuckle the harness and lead their current four animals away.

Madeline got down, but remained in the yard watching the activity while Gervase circulated, questioning the head ostler, then, at his direction, climbing onto the inn's front porch to speak with an old man in a rocking chair.

He returned as the final buckles on the harness were being tightened; the coachmen were already on the box, reins in hand.

His face grim and set, Gervase nodded curtly to them. "On to London." Gripping Madeline's arm, he helped her up the steps into the carriage, then followed.

She waited until they were bowling along again before asking, "What is it? What did you learn?"

He looked at her for a moment, then said, "Nothing new. It's just that . . ." Frowning, he paused, staring, she suspected unseeing, across the carriage.

She waited. Eventually he went on, "They passed this way a few hours ago. The old man on the porch used to be the head ostler here—his eyesight's excellent, and he knows carriages and horses. He saw the carriage we're after go past."

Black, relatively new, with a green blaze on the door; they'd got the description from the first posting inn beyond Falmouth.

"He recognized the carriage's marking—he said it's from one of the major London posting inns. But it was the horses that caught his eye. Prime 'uns, he said, hired nags but the best to be had, which explains why we haven't caught up with them. They're using the same quality of post-horses we are, which means there's money behind this. The plan and its execution are the work of someone other than a London flash cove."

Madeline studied his face. "You thought some gentleman, some man of our class, was involved—someone who could have seen the brooch at Lady Felgate's ball, or known someone who had."

He sighed and sat back. "Indeed. That's what's worrying me. If he—the man behind this—was in Cornwall, where his wrecked cargo also presumably is, and I do think we're on sound ground assuming only he would have recognized the brooch, then why is he taking Ben to London? Why not question him in Cornwall, and then go straight after the lost cargo?"

She didn't even try to think it through. "Why do you think?"

He drew a long breath, let it out with, "I think he's leading us away." He paused, then went on, "I think *all* this is part of his plan—not just the flight to London but us following as well. That's the reason he's spending money so freely to keep his carriage ahead of ours—he intended all along for us to follow. He can't know we are, but he's assumed we are."

She grimaced. "He's right."

"Indeed. He chose to kidnap Ben—or at least one of your brothers—not solely to learn where they found the brooch, but also because any of them would be the perfect pawn to draw us—you and me—away from the peninsula. He doesn't know Charles is there in our stead. With us gone, he'll assume the peninsula itself will be largely rudderless, at least in terms of dealing with the likes of him."

Cold fear had welled; it clutched her heart. "What will he do with Ben when he reaches London?"

Gervase glanced at her, met her eyes. "We've been assuming he's with Ben in the carriage, but on reflection I don't think he is. He's too canny, too clever. He'll have had his henchmen seize Ben. He's probably already in London, waiting for them to deliver him there." He paused, imagining it—imagining what he would do were he in the villain's shoes.

"He'll speak with Ben and ask about the brooch—he may try to disguise his purpose but he will, eventually, ask. The circumstances of that meeting will make it impossible for Ben to identify him later—he's too clever to take that risk."

He drew in a long breath. "And for the same reason, I think, once Ben gives him an answer, that he'll order his henchmen to release Ben somewhere in London. He knows we'll be searching, and he has no reason to be party to murder—as long as Ben can't identify him, he has nothing to fear."

Madeline had been following his reasoning; she nodded. "And leaving us quartering London, of all places, trying to locate one ten-year-old boy . . . that will keep us fixed there for the foreseeable future."

"Leaving the peninsula, as far as he knows, open territory, undefended." Gervase studied her face; the afternoon sunshine lit the hollows and planes, showed the strain of the past twenty-four hours, but he could see nothing in her features or her eyes, when they met his, to suggest she'd followed where his mind had ultimately led.

Summoning a smile, he raised her hand to his lips, kissed, then lowered his arm and faced forward. "We're doing all we can to catch that carriage—at the moment, that's all we can do."

He felt reasonably certain the villain would order Ben's release somewhere in London—most likely in the stews. What he wasn't anywhere near as confident over was whether the man's unsavory henchmen would follow his orders to the letter, or instead decide to make what they could off a gentry-bred ten-year-old boy.

That was the stuff of nightmares, but every bit as bad was the thought of what might transpire should the henchmen obey—and leave Ben wandering the slums of London. With no protector, alone—helpless.

Evening was closing in when they reached the outskirts of Basingstoke. The nearer they'd drawn to the capital, the more other carriages, carts, mail coaches and drays had thronged the road; their pace had fallen significantly.

Madeline bore the frustration by silently repeating Gervase's observation that the traffic would slow their quarry just as much.

Neither of them had slept the night before, just short naps, unsettled, no real rest; tiredness was now a real burden, dragging at her mind.

The horn blared; a minute later they turned under the arch of the Five Bells, one of the town's major posting inns. The instant the carriage rocked to a halt, Gervase opened the door and got down, shutting it behind him. Madeline leaned across the carriage and watched as he spoke with the head ostler, whose team was wrestling the big post-horses out of their harness.

Gervase asked questions, the head ostler answered, then

Gervase nodded curtly; he paused for a second, then turned and strode back to the carriage. Face grim, he opened the door, and held out his hand, beckoning for her to take it and descend.

Grasping his fingers, she did; looking into his face, she asked, "What is it?"

He met her eyes. "They stopped here to change horses. The head ostler got a chance to glance into the carriage. He saw a young lad—Ben—asleep on the seat, wrapped up tight in a blanket. Ben might have been tied up, restrained in some fashion, but the ostler didn't see any bonds. However, from his description of the two men in the carriage, we were right in thinking they're just henchmen—the reason the ostler glanced in was because he couldn't imagine where such men got the coin to travel in such style."

"So . . ." Madeline glanced at the front of the carriage, at the shafts propped on blocks as the horses were led away. Not seeing fresh horses being led out, she frowned. "I assume we'll be off as soon as possible . . .?"

Brows rising, she glanced at Gervase; he met her eyes.

"Their carriage is more than an hour ahead of us. We've caught up significantly, but we're four to five hours from the capital—even racing as we are, we can't catch them in that time, over that distance."

The fear she'd held at bay throughout the day clutched at her heart. She kept her eyes on his, held to the contact as she prompted, "So . . .?"

He didn't look away. "So we're going to have to accept that they'll reach London ahead of us and disappear into its streets—and we're going to have to search for Ben there, when they let him ago. The one point in all that in our favor is that it won't be immediately. The villain will need to meet him first, so the earliest they'll release Ben will be tomorrow afternoon."

She searched his amber eyes, read in them a steadfast,

rock-solid promise that they would find Ben. She eased out the breath tangled in her throat. "So what now? What do you suggest?"

"We'll continue to London, but there's no longer any sense in pushing ourselves or the horses." He glanced around. "We'll take a break here—have dinner, a short rest—before taking to the road again. This is an excellent inn—their table is highly regarded."

She didn't think she could eat, or if she did, all food would be tasteless, but she'd lectured her brothers often enough over recklessly taking unnecessary risks.

Gervase's lips eased as if he read her mind. "You'll be little use to Ben when we find him if you're fainting with hunger."

She humphed. "I never faint. But perhaps dinner would be wise." Now she thought of it, she hadn't eaten anything substantial since a light lunch the day before.

Gervase took charge, leading her into the inn, sending the coachman and his mate into the main taproom to eat and refresh themselves, then commanding rooms in which he and she could wash away the dust of the road and the day, before retreating to a private parlor where a substantial dinner would be served as soon as they were ready. While it felt odd to have someone else organizing things for her, giving orders for her comfort, he was efficient and effective, and seemed to know precisely how not to step on her toes, how to make it feel perfectly natural for her to metaphorically lean on him, to allow him to care for her. Seductive support—that's what it was—but in this instance she let it wrap about her.

Shown to a pretty bedchamber, she glanced into the mirror, sighed, and set to work to repair the depredations of the journey. A quick wash revived her; the maid shook out her gown, frankly scandalized at the trousers she still wore beneath.

Redonning her gown, she removed the trousers; arriving in London in such attire definitely qualified as another unnecessary risk. Letting down her hair, she combed her fingers through it, subduing it as best she could, then she twisted the mass back into a knot and secured it, more or less, with her remaining pins.

Returning downstairs to the private parlor, she found Gervase, similarly refreshed, waiting. They sat down at the table and the food was brought in; contrary to her expectations she could taste the game pie well enough, and she was indeed famished.

Between them they accounted for most of what the beaming innwife set before them. Nevertheless she felt a spurt of relief when, as the innkeeper cleared away their plates, Gervase gave the order for their coachman to make ready and the fresh horses to be put to.

As the door shut behind the retreating innkeeper, Gervase turned to see her wiping her fingers on her napkin. "No need to rush—we'll be on our way soon enough."

Laying the napkin aside, she frowned. "How will we proceed when we reach London?" Her head felt clearer—clear enough to ask a question she hadn't, until then, spared much thought for; she'd been focused on catching up with the carriage and Ben before town.

Gervase had given the matter long and considerable thought. "We'll go to the Bastion Club."

She frowned. "I thought it was a gentlemen's club."

"It is—or was. But of our seven members, five are now wed, and other than me, no one actually stays there anymore. Christian Allardyce, the other yet to marry, has his own house in town. He only uses the club as a bolt-hole—a place to hide from his female relatives and others who want to hound him."

"Oh." Her expression suggested she was intrigued—

intrigued enough to fall in with his plan. "So we can go there, and . . .?"

"Using the club as a base, I'll organize a search for Ben. I'll call on whoever's in London—Christian's there, I know. I'm not sure about Trentham—or Dalziel."

"Your ex-commander?"

He nodded. "He has . . . abilities, facilities, minions we can only guess at that he can mobilize." Pushing back his chair, he rose.

She frowned; giving him her hand, she let him draw her to her feet. "But will he? Dalziel, I mean. After all, he doesn't know me or Ben from Adam."

"That won't matter to him. It's the need he'll respond to—a young boy abducted in these circumstances, then abandoned in London." He felt his jaw, his face, start to set in stony lines; he tried for impassive instead. "He'll help— he won't need to be asked twice."

She seemed to accept that. He led her to the door. Pausing before it, he met her eyes. "Ready to go on?"

Lifting her chin, she nodded, every inch his Valkyrie. "Let's get back on the road."

They rolled into London in the predawn. The sky had barely lightened from the night's black velvet, the eastern horizon a pale stripe of dark gray pearl. They hadn't pressed the horses but had made good time; it was between three and four o'clock, the hour in which no one stirred, honest man or villain. The streets were silent as their horses, tired but still game, plodded on.

Madeline sat forward looking out at the sky. Gervase studied her profile, knew she was thinking of Ben, wondering where he was, how he was, whether he was well. Finding Ben; his entire personal focus had drawn in to just that—nothing else rated, not until he had Ben back in Madeline's arms.

He'd given the coachman directions several times. When the carriage turned into Montrose Place, he leaned out and called softly, "Number twelve—the green gate ahead on the left."

The coachman drew rein; the carriage slowed, then rocked to a halt immediately before the gate.

Opening the carriage door, Gervase stepped down to the pavement. The house, like all the other houses in the street, stood in darkness. He turned back to Madeline, leaning forward to peer through the door at the shadowy outline beyond the stone wall. "Wait here. I'll go and rouse them."

He'd arrived at the club in the dead of night on a number of occasions, so it was no surprise to find his confident knock answered within minutes by a sleep-rumpled Gasthorpe dragging on his coat. What always amused Gervase was that the portly ex-sergeant-major, now majordomo, seemed able to scramble into his clothes and look passably neat in just those few minutes.

"My lord!" A smile lighting his face, Gasthorpe beamed and swung the door wide. "It's a pleasure to welcome you back."

"Thank you, Gasthorpe, but I'm not alone. I have a lady with me—the Honorable Miss Madeline Gascoigne—and we'll need to use the club as our base." Gervase met Gasthorpe's widening eyes. "Miss Gascoigne's young brother has been kidnapped. We chased the blackguard's carriage to London, but couldn't catch it—we'll need to organize a search come first light."

At the first sign of trouble, Gasthorpe's eyes had lit. "Naturally, my lord." Glancing out into the night, noting the carriage at the curb, he drew himself up. "If you'll conduct the lady indoors, I'll have a chamber—the larger one to the left of the stairs—ready momentarily."

Gervase nodded, relieved he could rely on Gasthorpe's abilities and his discretion. He turned to the street, then recalled . . . and turned back to Gasthorpe. "We had to set out on our chase unexpectedly from Helston. We've no luggage, no clothes bar those on our backs." He grimaced. "And we've been on the road more or less continuously since the evening of the day before yesterday. We'll also need to house the coachmen—there's two of them—for as long as we stay. I suspect we'll need to race back to Cornwall at some point, and they're excellent whips."

Gasthorpe drew himself up. "Leave everything to me, my lord. We've been rather quiet of late—it's a pleasure to see action again."

In spite of the hour, despite the situation, Gervase grinned; he knew what Gasthorpe meant. Stepping off the porch, he said, "Incidentally, Lostwithiel sends his regards. I've left him and his lady holding the fort at Crowhurst."

"Very kind of the earl—I hope we'll see him, and his lady, here one day soon."

Gervase's grin grew wider. "I'll tell him." They truly would have to rethink their use of the club, or Gasthorpe and his helpers would run mad. None were the usual sort of staff; inactivity didn't suit them.

Returning to the carriage, he helped Madeline to the pavement; she glanced around while he gave the tired coachmen directions to the mews behind the house, then she let him twine her arm in his and lead her up the path to the door.

"Your butler's going to be shocked to his back teeth."

He chuckled. "We don't have a regular staff. Gasthorpe acts as majordomo. He was a sergeant-major during the wars, and you may believe me when I say that I've yet to see him at a loss regardless of the many and varied—and sometimes quite startling—demands we've all at one time or another made of him." He looked ahead to where the hall was now aglow with warm candlelight; beyond he could hear the rapid-fire thump of feet as footmen ran up the stairs, rushing to do Gasthorpe's bidding. "If you doubt me, just watch how he handles this."

Madeline did have doubts, severe doubts that any male-oriented household could cope with their wholly unexpected and unprecedented demands, but by the time Gasthorpe showed her into a simply furnished but exceptionally neat and comfortable room, indicated his arrangements with a decorous nod and begged her to ask for anything he'd failed to provide, every last one had been swept away.

"No, indeed." Tired eyes taking in the fine linen night-shirt laid upon the bed—a man's but perfectly serviceable in her present straits—and the towel and washbasin with its matching pitcher steaming, the single candle alight on the dresser, she could feel her muscles unknotting. "Thank you—you've done excellently. This is more than I expected."

"If I might suggest, ma'am, if you leave your gown outside the door, I'll have the maid from next door freshen it for you."

She felt silly tears prickle at the back of her eyes as she turned to the dapper little man who was so patently delighted to be of service. "Thank you, I will. You've been exceptionally kind."

He smiled and bowed his way out of the door, closing it gently behind him. Madeline sighed, then smothered a yawn.

Ten minutes later, washed and clean, with her hair a loose veil about her head and shoulders, she was sound asleep between the crisp sheets.

Gervase stood in the doorway and considered the sight. She'd blown out the candle but faint light washed the room; by its soft glow he could see that the tension of the day, the tightness about her eyes and lips, had faded.

The observation calmed some restless, primal part of him. He considered the bed—its less-than-adequate width—

then with an inward sigh turned away. Shutting the door silently, he made for the bedchamber across the landing.

Gasthorpe had served them tea and crumpets in the library while their rooms were being prepared. When Madeline had retired, Gervase had remained to write notes—calls to action—only two, so it hadn't taken long.

Gasthorpe had verified that of all the club's members, only Christian Allardyce was still in town—the others had retired to their country estates for the summer and weren't expected to reappear in London, at least not within the next few days.

Ben's fate would be sealed by then; they'd either find him within the first two days, or they likely never would.

Going into his room, closing the door, Gervase forcefully put that thought out of his mind, and concentrated, instead, on how to locate Ben.

Shrugging off his coat, unbuttoning his cuffs, he grimaced. Gasthorpe had his two notes; they'd be delivered with the dawn. The only thing left that he, Gervase, could presently do to improve their chances of finding Ben was to pray that the second gentleman he'd informed hadn't yet left London.

Chapter 17

$\mathcal{A}$s Gervase had expected, Christian was the first to answer his summons. Gasthorpe roused him at nine o'clock with the news that the marquess had arrived and was waiting for him at the breakfast table.

Rubbing sleep from his eyes, Gervase splashed water over his face, then swiftly shaved and dressed, giving thanks for the marvel that was Gasthorpe; aside from providing the razor, a newly purchased brush, cravat, and shirt, the major-domo had worked wonders with his travel-worn coat and breeches and his boots shone. At least he no longer looked like he'd just ridden in from the Russian Steppes.

Exiting his room, he paused, considering the door across the landing. Crossing silently to it, he opened it and looked in; Madeline was still sound asleep, the covers over her shoulder, her hair a red-gold mane spread across the pillow. Contradictory impulses clashed; one part of him wanted to leave her there, recuperating in peace, yet she would expect to be included in any councils concerning Ben's fate, and had every right to be present.

Inwardly sighing, he crossed soft-footed to the bed. Brushing back her hair, he bent and placed a kiss on her cheek. As she roused, murmured, then turned to him, he trailed his lips across to meet hers. A gentle, undemanding kiss. Then he lifted his head, watched her blink awake.

She focused on him, then glanced around. "Oh." Shuffling onto one elbow, she looked at the window. "What's the time?"

"Nine o'clock. Christian Allardyce is downstairs at the breakfast table. Join us when you're ready."

"Yes, of course." She started struggling up.

He turned to the door, and discovered a little maid hovering, hand raised, frozen; she'd been about to knock, then had seen him.

He smiled, nodded the maid in, saying to Madeline as he continued to the door, "Assistance has arrived. She's even brought a fresh gown."

"What . . .?"

Reaching the door, he glanced back to find Madeline staring in disbelief at the maid, who was carrying not only a gown but linen, brushes and pins.

Shutting her open mouth, Madeline looked at him as if for explanation.

"The wonders of Gasthorpe." With a grin, he saluted her and left, closing the door.

He sobered as he went down the stairs.

Christian Allardyce, Marquess of Dearne, was sitting at one end of the breakfast table attending to a sizable serving of ham and eggs. He looked up as Gervase entered. "Excellent. I'm all agog. I was going to come up and demand instant explanations, but Gasthorpe warned me there was a lady on the premises." Christian raised his brows. "So what's afoot?"

The limpid innocence in Christian's gray eyes did nothing to hide his avid curiosity, or his suspicions. Gervase held his gaze for an instant, then grimaced and headed for the sideboard. "I'm going to marry her, but for God's sake don't mention it. She hasn't yet agreed."

"Ah—you're at that stage." Returning his attention to his plate, Christian said, "So what's brought you both here, in something of a lather, as I heard it—and what is it you want my assistance with?"

His plate piled high with ham, sausages and two eggs, Gervase sat in the chair next to Christian, and told him.

Simply, concisely, nothing of substance held back.

By the time he'd finished, Christian was frowning. Mopping up the last of his egg with a crust of toast, he popped it into his mouth, chewed; eyes narrowed, gaze distant, he said, "So you think this ploy—bringing the boy to London—is a ruse to get you both out of Cornwall?"

Gervase nodded. "Normally Madeline acts as her fifteen-year-old brother's surrogate—she's held the reins of the position for so long, and so well, she's the de facto Gascoigne and everyone in the neighborhood looks to her for leadership, even more so given I haven't been there."

Christian's brows rose. "She sounds like an unusual lady."

"She's a remarkable woman," Gervase said, "which is why this villain wanted us both here in London. With both of us gone, there's no one on the peninsula with the authority, the position or the experience to lead. There are only minor gentry on the peninsula itself, a few minor barons north of the estuary, but even if they were roused to action, by they time they came to investigate a stranger with a crowd of bully boys digging up a beach, it would all be over, the villain long gone."

He paused, then grinned, not humorously. "Of course, our villain didn't know Charles was lurking—I've left him and Penelope at the castle, keeping watch."

"So when our villain arrives . . ." Christian pulled a face, the equivalent of male pouting. "I don't know about you, but I have a deep-seated aversion to letting St. Austell have all the fun."

"Indeed. Which is another excellent reason for finding Ben with all possible speed—not that we need another reason, but still—so we can race down to Cornwall and be in at the end ourselves."

"Not another reason," Christian said. "A carrot. Dealing with the villain will be our reward for finding Ben quickly."

Senses pricking, Gervase looked up and saw Madeline framed in the doorway. He smiled and rose. "There you are—come and join us."

"Thank you." Madeline smiled warmly, her heart unexpectedly aglow. She'd come downstairs overwhelmed by concern and incipient panic, then she'd heard Gervase's words, his description of her, his and his colleague's clear confidence that they would find Ben and deal with the villain; she'd drawn breath, felt their implied assurance sink in, felt their confidence buoy and steady her. Walking into the room, she transferred her gaze to the other gentleman, who had smoothly risen to his feet.

"Dearne, Miss Gascoigne." He bowed, then smiled engagingly. "But I hope you'll call me Christian."

There was something in his manner—a gentle air, an invitation to laugh at all and everything—that had her smiling easily in return. She inclined her head. "Madeline, please." She sat in the chair Gervase held for her, glanced around to see him head for the sideboard—decided to let him feed her and turned her attention to his friend. "I understand you're another member of this rather strange club."

"Indeed. I won't bore you with the details of its founding, but it has, I would say, served its purpose well." He smiled at her in a way that made her wonder just what the true purpose of the club was.

Before she could think of how to ask, Gervase returned to the table. "I've rung for tea." He set a plate piled with kedgeree, ham and a fat juicy kipper before her.

She looked at it, and wondered when she'd mentioned she loved nice kippers; she couldn't recall ever doing so, so how had he guessed? Inwardly shrugging, she murmured her thanks, picked up her knife and fork, and sampled the kedgeree. It was delicious—and she realized she was starving.

Accustomed to the table habits of males, she barely noticed the silence that enveloped the table. Gervase was still absorbed with his sausages, while Christian sat back and sipped coffee with the air of a man satisfactorily replete.

From under her lashes, she studied him, curious to observe another of Gervase's cronies. Like Gervase and Charles, Christian had much the same build; she recalled Gervase had originally been in the guards, and suspected the same held true of the others—they all had the classic guardsmen build, that of tall, broad-shouldered, saber-swinging horsemen.

As for the rest . . . gray eyes, a certain self-deprecating streak, as if he were cynically amused with himself, but underneath she could readily see the same reliably ruthless strength she'd come to value in Gervase, that unswerving commitment to defending and protecting, be it the weak, the helpless, their friends, their family or their country.

It was all the same to them; it was simply who they were.

And nothing would ever change them.

Nothing would ever soften them.

To her mind, that was as it should be; the thought was more comfort than threat.

She forked up the last tiny piece of kipper just as Gervase pushed away his plate. She looked up and smiled as

Gasthorpe poured tea for her; she patted her lips with her napkin, picked up the delicate cup and sipped—and nearly closed her eyes and sighed.

She glanced around, but Gasthorpe had gone. She turned to Gervase and Christian. "I don't know where you found him, but Gasthorpe is a treasure. I don't know how he managed it, but he found this gown." She broke off to explain to Christian that they'd set out on their pursuit without baggage. She glanced again at the gown. "He said it belonged to the lady who used to live next door—he borrowed a maid from there for me, and to adjust the size and let down the hem."

"The lady would be Leonora," Christian said. "Now Countess of Trentham."

"Trentham." Madeline looked at Gervase. "He's another of your members, isn't he? He married the lady next door?"

Gervase nodded.

Finishing her tea, she set the cup down. She felt fully restored, ready to face the world and any villain in her quest to rescue Ben. She glanced at the men.

As usual Gervase, sipping his coffee, seemed to read her mind. "I've already told Christian the whole story." At his words, somberness settled about them, upon them. "We need to decide how best to search for Ben. Christian agrees he's unlikely to be released until the afternoon."

Christian leaned forward, hands clasped on the table. He met Madeline's gaze. "I've been thinking, evaluating the ways—the best ways—to locate Ben." He glanced at Gervase, then looked again at Madeline and went on. "It's likely that when they release Ben, they'll set him free in a slum, in the stews. They won't want him found too quickly—the villain wants you to stay in London for a few days at least. So we should assume that Ben will suddenly find himself alone on the street in a dangerous part of town."

Again Christian paused, then said, "I have contacts,

numerous acquaintances, in London's underworld. What I propose is that I contact those who are essentially the overlords of each of the slums, and alert them to the situation—send them a description of Ben, and tell them we want him back unharmed. They'll put the word out, and their people will all be on the lookout for Ben. The chances of them finding him quickly, and unharmed, are high."

Madeline studied the gray eyes fixed unwaveringly on hers. "What's the drawback? Obviously there is one."

Christian's lips quirked; he inclined his head. "Indeed. I won't send out that message unless you approve. The drawback is that, to be rescued by the overlords of London's underworld, Ben would, necessarily, come into contact with them and their minions—and I wouldn't be truthful if I didn't say that some of them are more than revolting enough to make any lady swoon."

She studied him for a moment, then said, "A delicate lady, perhaps. Even me, perhaps. But what of an innocent but insatiably curious, country-bred ten-year-old boy?" When Christian raised his brows, surprised by her tack, she glanced at Gervase. "You know what you're talking about, have experience of it—I don't. But you should be able to remember being a ten-year-old—would you at ten have been shocked and horrifed, or would you have thought it a grand lark to be consorting with villainous underworld figures?"

Gervase grimaced. He looked at Christian. "I don't know about you, but it would have been a lark to me."

Christian pulled a face. "Me, too."

"And what's the alternative?" Madeline asked. "Trust to chance that someone kind and honorable happens to find him first? I've never been in any slums or stews, but I don't think I'd be happy taking that approach." She pushed back from the table. "How do we go about sending these messages? Perhaps I can help write them?"

Christian glanced at Gervase. "So we do it?"

Rising, Gervase waved to the door. "So the lady decrees. Let's adjourn to the library."

They did. They spent some time drafting their message, then Christian and Madeline, seated on opposing sides of the desk, started copying it in neat, legible script.

Gervase paced and looked over their shoulders. There was no place for him to sit to help them, and his scrawl wasn't all that neat.

"We've plenty of time," Christian said without looking up. "Those areas don't stir until noon—as long as we send out these notes by then, they'll have plenty of time to spread the word before Ben is let loose in their domain."

Gervase humphed and kept pacing. He and Christian had agreed that it would most likely be later in the afternoon rather than earlier that Ben would be released. Which meant there would be hours yet to wait. . . .

The distant sound of the front door knocker had him turning expectantly to the door.

Christian glanced that way, too, then, as the sound of firm footsteps on the stairs reached them, he set down his pen.

Her concentration absolute, Madeline continued transcribing.

She heard the door open, heard Gasthorpe announce, "Mr. Dalziel, my lords."

Blinking, she glanced up as a deep, dark voice drawled, "Dearne. Crowhurst. I understand there's something you believe I should know about."

Primitive precognition sent a frisson arcing through her. Madeline stared at the tall gentleman who strolled with unutterable grace into the room. He was outwardly similar to Gervase and Christian, tall, broad-shouldered, dark-haired, the long, austere planes of his face a testimony to his heritage. Yet beneath the urbane, sophisticated veneer, there was an element of something else—something harder, sharper, altogether more subconsciously alarming. She felt unexpectedly glad that Gervase stood, at least metaphorically, between her and his ex-commander.

There were dangerous men, and then there were the impossibly dangerous; Dalziel belonged in the latter category.

Whoever he was; she could now see the evidence on which Gervase and his colleagues based their belief that Dalziel was no mere mister.

Gervase moved forward to shake his hand. "Glad we caught you—I was afraid you might have left town."

A faint smile flirted about Dalziel's mobile lips. "Not quite yet." He turned to shake hands with Christian, then glanced briefly at her before looking, inquiringly, at Gervase.

With a smile for her, Gervase turned to Dalziel. "Allow me to present the Honorable Miss Madeline Gascoigne." To Madeline he added, "Dalziel, who you've heard me mention."

Madeline remained seated; they were all towering over her but even if she stood they would still be taller, and there was a certain statement to be made by remaining where she was—queens remained seated—so she faced him, head high, smiled graciously and, consciously imperious, offered her hand. "Good day, sir."

She caught another upward twitch of his lips as Dalziel took her fingers and very correctly bowed over them.

"An honor, Miss Gascoigne, although I believe it's something less than pleasant that has brought you to town."

"Indeed. Some blackguard has kidnapped my youngest brother." Madeline looked at Gervase.

He waved Dalziel, whose gaze had grown sharper, to a

chair. "Sit down and I'll tell you the story." He glanced at Madeline. "I'd better begin at the start."

Sinking into a chair, elegantly crossing his long legs, Dalziel nodded. "You perceive me all ears."

While Gervase related the tale of how her brothers had found the brooch, and subsequently where she'd worn it, the information he'd gathered on where it might have come from, then Ben's disappearance and all they knew of that, Madeline turned back to the desk and continued penning Christian's notes. Christian, too, continued, but from time to time he'd look up, frown—and the ink would dry on his nib as he became distracted with the story.

Madeline didn't bother to recall him to his task; there were only a few more notes to write, and it was barely eleven o'clock. Christian had said it might be counter-productive to send the notes out before noon, and at least writing them gave her something to do to fill in the time, making her feel she was actively engaged in the task of rescuing Ben. Lips compressed, she wrote on, aware of Dalziel asking questions, of Gervase replying.

She could see, comprehend, that Dalziel could be intimidating, but he wasn't a threat, and as long as he could and would help them rescue Ben, that was all she cared about.

"So this brooch might well be the key." Dalziel frowned; Gervase had given him a brief description of the brooch. He grimaced. "I wish you'd brought it with you."

Madeline lifted her head. "I did." Reaching into the pocket of her borrrowed gown, she drew out the heavy brooch; she'd taken it from her own gown, wanting to keep it with her. Setting down her pen, she swiveled from the desk and held out the brooch to Dalziel; when he took it, lifting it from her palm, she looked at Gervase. "I thought if by chance we meet this blackguard face-to-face, he might be willing to exchange Ben for it."

Gervase met her eyes, but then glanced at Dalziel.

Madeline did, too, as did Christian.

Dalziel had made no sound, no movement to draw their attention; it was his stillness, the sheer focused intensity of it, that had seized their collective attention.

Cradling the brooch in his long fingers, he was staring at it as if it were the Holy Grail. "Good Lord," he breathed.

When he lapsed back into awestruck silence, Christian hesitantly prompted, "What?"

Dalziel drew in a long breath, then leaned back in the chair. He laid the brooch on the arm, his fingers tracing the curves, the pearls. "Our paths, it seems, cross again."

His tone was distant, detached. Madeline glanced at Gervase. He looked as puzzled as she.

His gaze on the brooch, Dalziel at last continued, "Let me tell you what's been keeping me in London—one of the things, at any rate. As we—the members of this club and I—know, there's some person, some Englishman, a member of the aristocracy, who was a French agent during the wars, but who escaped detection. He's continued to elude me, and all others, but we know he exists, that he is a flesh-and-blood man."

He paused, then looked up at Gervase, then Christian. "Flesh-and-blood men usually require payment for their services. We've had a net in place for years, identifying any payments that came via the usual channels of cash, drafts or any other of the customary monetary instruments. We've accounted for all such payments, leaving unresolved the question of how our elusive last traitor was paid."

Long fingers lightly tapped the brooch. "After Waterloo—indeed, even before that—we'd started getting reports from the new French authorities. They were perfectly willing to work with us to trace any payments made by Napoleon's spymasters. However, we still turned up nothing—nothing we hadn't already found—until some enterprising French clerk started an inventory of the palaces, and the artworks and artifacts contained therein, the jewelry collections amassed by the various princely families of the ancient regimes. He started reporting pieces missing. Not wholesale ransacking but one piece missing here, one there. At first he assumed it was simply mislaid items, the natural outcome of the disruption of war, but as he discovered more such missing items, he began to sense a pattern. That's when he approached his masters, and they sent his list to me."

Dark eyes narrowing, Dalziel lifted the brooch, slowly turning it between his fingers. "Would it surprise you to learn that on that list is an oval cloak-brooch dating from the age of Charlemagne, Celtic goldwork with diamonds and pearls surrounding a large rectangular emerald?"

His voice faded into absolute silence.

Madeline broke it. "Are you saying that the man after the brooch, the one searching for a cargo the brooch formed part of—the man who has Ben—is this unidentified traitor?"

Dalziel's eyes rose to meet hers. His jaw set. "I fear so." He paused, then added, "As it happens, that increases the likelihood that your brother will be released unharmed once he's identified the beach for our traitor. Our man is careful and clever—he's only killed once that we know of, and then he was forced to it, when a henchman who knew his identity was cornered. Murder attracts too much attention—he'll just want Ben to be lost for a while, more to keep you occupied than anything else. You're right about that." He looked down at the brooch. "Now we know it's him, things make more sense."

He stared at the brooch, then leaned forward and carefully handed it back to Madeline. "Regardless of what happens, please don't *offer* to give it back. If he demands it and there's no alternative . . . but don't volunteer it."

She considered the brooch, felt its weight in her palm. Understood why he'd given it back to her, into her keeping, appreciated his comprehension. She looked up and met his dark eyes. "Thank you. I won't."

He nodded, then looked at Gervase. "I think we can conclude that your blackguard is indeed our old foe, and he's after that cargo. No surprise he was wise enough not to agree to be paid in French sous, and careful enough to wait until now to bring his ill-gotten gains into England, and used French smugglers to do it. Far safer to cache his thirty pieces of silver in France while Napoleon was in power, and bring it over now, long after the wars are over and, so he would reason, no one's watching anymore."

Gervase nodded, his gaze locked on the brooch. "It all makes a certain sense."

"Indeed. We've already established what sort of man he is. He has no need of money, but items such as that"—Dalziel watched as Madeline slipped the brooch back into her pocket—"the treasures of kings and emperors, those would hold a real incentive for him—something only he was clever enough and powerful enough to gain, something no one else could ever have."

Christian snorted. "Symbols of his greatness."

Dalziel nodded, then came to his feet in a rush of nervy energy. "He'll want that cargo. After all this time, all his planning, waiting for his moment of triumph—he'll be fixated on regaining his treasure." He smiled chillingly. "And fixated men make mistakes."

He looked at Gervase. "Regardless of what happens here today, I'll be on my way to Cornwall this afternoon."

Gervase's face hardened. "Madeline and I won't leave here until we find Ben."

Dalziel nodded. "I'll help in whatever way I can, but this might be our last chance at catching this man and I can't let it pass."

"We'll have to find Ben first," Madeline said.

Dalziel nodded again, more curtly. "I'll put all the forces I can muster at your disposal before I leave—"

"No, you don't understand." Her voice held a hint of suppressed humor, enough to make Dalziel frown at her.

"What don't I understand?"

She knew she was supposed to be intimidated by that voice, by his chilly diction, but she now had his measure. She held his gaze calmly. "The Lizard Peninsula is large—you won't be able to watch all the beaches, nor will you be able to monitor access to the peninsula itself—there are too many ways to reach it, including by sea. To catch your last traitor, you'll need to know which beach he'll be heading for. And until we find Ben, you won't know that."

Dalziel's frown didn't lift. "But we know which beach the brooch came from."

She nodded. "Indeed. But as Edmond—another of my brothers—pointed out, it's more than likely Ben will lie."

The frown evaporated; frustration took its place. After a moment, Dalziel flung himself back into his chair. "Haven't you taught him not to lie?"

She inwardly grinned at the disgruntled grumble. "I have, but the lessons don't take well with Ben. Perhaps when he grows older. Regardless, at present, he lies quite beautifully—he's so . . ."—she gestured—"*fluent*, even when I know he's not telling the truth, he makes me think I might be wrong."

Dalziel stared at the floor, then grimaced. "All right." He lifted his head; his eyes pinned Christian, then moved to Gervase. "So how are we going to locate the whelp?"

Suppressing a smile, Madeline turned back to the desk. She completed the last of Christian's notes while around her a wide-ranging discussion of how to scour London, especially the slums, raged.

Dalziel was making plans to contact various commanders in the Guards as she laid the last note on the pile. She glanced at the clock. Twenty minutes to twelve. She turned to Christian, intending to suggest he send for the footmen they'd told her Gasthorpe would provide, when the knocker on the front door was plied—not just once or twice but with persistent, repetitive force.

The three men broke off, turning to the door. It was shut, muting sounds from the front hall below, but the knocking had stopped.

Ears straining, Madeline listened . . . heard a light, piping voice politely ask . . .

She was out of her chair, past Dalziel and flinging open the library door before any of the men could blink. Sweeping to the stairs, her heart in her mouth, she paused on the landing, looking down into the hall, to the group before the front door. Then she grabbed up her skirts and rushed headlong down.

"*Ben!*" She couldn't believe her eyes, but there he was; she saw the relief that washed over his face as he glanced up at her call, disbelieving her presence as much as she had his.

Reaching him, she swept him into her arms, hugging him wildly, only just remembering in time not to lift him from his feet, bending over him and clutching him to her instead, her hands patting over him.

"Are you all right?" His clothes were dusty and disarranged, rumpled and soiled, but not torn or filthy.

He nodded; he was clutching her quite as fiercely as she was clutching him. But then he pushed away; reluctantly she forced herself to ease her hold. He looked up into her face. "There was this man—"

He broke off as he noticed Gervase, who had come down the stairs, Dalziel and Christian at his back. Ben smiled, a trifle shy. He nodded to Gervase. "Hello, sir." His gaze traveled on to rest on Dalziel, then Christian; his eyes widened, then he looked up as Gervase neared.

Smiling, Gervase laid a hand on Ben's shoulder and lightly squeezed. "You've no idea how glad we are to see you. But how did you get free—and how did you know to come here?"

Ben looked into his face. "You told me, remember? When we were fishing, you told us about your club in London. You said it was in Montrose Place. When those horrid men pushed me out of the carriage in an awful street"—he glanced at Madeline—"it was smelly and dirty and the people looked mean, I found a hackney cab."

Turning, he pointed to the heavyset, frieze-coated individual watching the proceedings through the open front door. "Jeb's hackney. I told him I was a friend of yours—Lord Crowhurst of Crowhurst Castle—and if he brought me to your club in Montrose Place, then the people here would pay him twice his fee."

Looking up at Gervase, Ben made his eyes huge. "You will pay Jeb double for bringing me here, won't you?"

"Not double. Triple. With a tip." Dalziel moved past Gervase to the door, fishing in his coat pocket. "Indeed, quadruple the fare is not too much in the circumstances."

Jeb looked beyond awed. He took the coins Dalziel handed him, stared at them. "'Ere—this is way too much."

"No," Dalziel said. "Believe me, it's not. If I had my way you'd get a medal."

Jeb looked uncertain. "All I did was drive 'im here from Tothill. It ain't even that far."

"Nevertheless. You did your country a great service today. If I was you, I'd take the rest of the day off."

"Aye." Jeb shook his head, studying the largesse in his palm. "I might just do that." He bobbed his head, started to turn away, then looked back, weaving to look past Dalziel and Gasthorpe at Ben. "Anytime you come back to the capital, nipper, you keep an eye out for Jeb."

Ben beamed his huge, little-boy's smile. "I will. Good-bye. And thank you!"

"Seems it's me should be thanking you," Jeb mumbled as he headed off down the path to the street where his mare stood patiently waiting.

Dalziel turned back to the group in the front hall.

Ben looked up at him, curious and intrigued. "I don't know you."

Dalziel smiled at Ben; Gervase blinked. It wasn't the sort of smile he was accustomed to seeing on his ex-commander's face. Boyishly charming wasn't the half of it.

"You don't know me yet, but you will." His gaze on Ben's face, Dalziel waved to the stairs. "Let's go up to the library and you can tell us all—all the gory details of your kidnap, confinement and escape." Effortlessly, with no more than a look, he drew Ben to him and turned with him to the stairs. "Have you breakfasted yet?"

"No." The thought of food brought Ben up short; he started to turn to Madeline.

"No matter. Gasthorpe—you've met the redoubtable Gasthorpe, haven't you?"

Ben shot a shy grin at Gasthorpe, who had shut the door and was now waiting by the side of the hall for his orders.

"Gasthorpe," Dalziel continued, with just a touch on Ben's shoulder steering him up the stairs, "will bring sustenance suitable for your years. You can eat while you set your sister's mind at rest."

Ben glanced back at Madeline, but seeing her following in his wake with Gervase beside her, meeting her encouraging if misty-eyed smile, he grinned, looked ahead, and happily trooped up the stairs.

When they were all in the library, comfortable in armchairs set about the hearth, while Ben wolfed down the cheese and ham sandwich Gasthorpe had provided, Gervase caught Christian's eye and saw his own bemusement reflected there. It was patently clear who had elected himself Ben's interrogator.

For one moment, Gervase wondered if he should resent Dalziel's claim, but he wanted Ben to look upon him as an unthreatening, always trustworthy friend, and acting as an interrogator, even in relatively mild fashion, wasn't a good way to nurture such a connection. So he sat back and watched, quietly fascinated, as his ex-commander displayed a side of himself none of his ex-operatives had imagined he possessed.

Sitting opposite Ben, who was ensconced in the chair between Madeline's and Gervase's, Dalziel exuded the sort of blatant confidence guaranteed to fix a boy's attention; the command that confidence concealed was subtle, yet still there, giving his performance a near-irresistible edge.

He waited with feigned patience until Ben had finished the sandwich and drained his glass of milk before commencing, with an easy, encouraging smile. "Now—let's start from when you were sitting on the bench outside the inn in Helston. The man who approached you—what did he say?"

Wriggling forward in the chair, Ben dutifully replied, "He asked how to get to the London road. He said he had to meet a man with a carriage there, and was lost, and time was running out. He offered me a shilling to show him the quickest way."

Ben colored and shot a glance at Madeline. "I know I shouldn't have taken the money, but it wasn't far, and it was daylight and people were about."

Madeline reached out and touched his hand.

"Indeed," Dalziel said, his tone even. "So you'll know not to do it next time. So you showed this man to the London road, then he picked you up and slung you in the carriage."

Ben nodded. "It was a big black traveling carriage—it had four horses."

"And they tied you up and gagged you and whisked you off to London."

"Yes." Ben paused, then volunteered, "But they didn't hurt me or anything, not even when I kicked their shins."

Dalziel nodded. "They were under orders to keep you hale and whole." He paused, then went on, "So they brought you to London, to some place in the slums."

"Was that the slums?" Ben glanced at Gervase, who nodded. "It was awfully dirty."

"I expect it was," Dalziel allowed. "You reached there early this morning, and they kept you there, but not for very long."

"They'd told me in the carriage at the start that they were just fetching me for some gentleman who wanted to ask me something. I couldn't understand why I had to go to London, but they said they didn't know what he wanted to ask—they were just carrying out his orders and doing what he told them. They told me he wasn't one for explanations." Ben paused, then slid his hand across the chair's arm to grasp Madeline's. "They told me if I knew what was good for me I'd tell him what he wanted to know, and quickly." He looked at Dalziel. "They weren't joking—I think they were trying to warn me."

Dalziel raised his brows. "Sometimes one finds honor among thieves. So . . . they took you to meet the man this morning."

Ben nodded. "They stayed with me in a smelly room through the night, then after ten o'clock this morning—I could hear bells pealing the hours—they said it was time to go and meet him."

"Where did they take you?" The tension in Dalziel's voice was hard to detect, but there.

"It was only downstairs. To another room—I didn't see it because they blindfolded me, but it seemed cleaner."

Dalziel exchanged a quick glance with Gervase. It

sounded like a brothel—a cleaner room downstairs for meeting "guests," a room that would have been deserted in the morning. Dalziel looked at Ben, and repeated, Gervase suspected for Madeline's benefit, "You were blindfolded, so you didn't see the gentleman—the one who questioned you."

Throughout, Dalziel asked few questions. He made statements, told Ben's story, and left it to Ben to correct or expand.

Ben shook his head, brow furrowed as he recalled. "He *was* a gentleman—he spoke like us." Head on one side, he looked at Dalziel. "He sounded a lot like you."

Dalziel slowly nodded. "A gentleman of the ton, a member of the aristocracy—that's who we think he is. As you say, one of us. So he spoke with you—what did he say?"

"He told me that if I answered his question, he would order the men to take me into the streets a little way away and let me go. That I would be free to return to Cornwall and my family, as long as I answered his one question—he warned me he'd know if I was lying." Ben blushed.

Dalziel smiled. "So you answered his question, and told him that you and your brothers found the brooch you gave your sister for her birthday on . . . which beach?"

Ben frowned at him. "How did you know that was what he wanted to know?"

"Because he's a traitor I've been chasing for some time. And your sister and Crowhurst here realized it was something to do with the brooch." Dalziel paused as Ben mouthed an "Oh," then prompted, "So . . . which beach did you send him to?"

Ben shifted, then looked at Madeline. "I did lie—I didn't want him finding our treasure, if there's more of it buried in the sand, and I didn't think you'd mind if I lied to him." His jaw firmed. "He was a bad man, stealing me away like that."

Madeline smiled, and squeezed the hand she still held. "It was perfectly reasonable to lie to him."

Reassured, Ben looked at Dalziel. "I told him we found the brooch in Kynance Cove."

Gervase caught the look Dalziel sent him, the faint lift of one brow. "It's on the other side of the peninsula from Lowland Point—the beach where they found the brooch and where Charles and Harry are keeping watch."

"Will they notice if our quarry heads down to this other beach?" Dalziel shifted forward, preparing to rise.

Gervase shook his head, doing the same. "It's nowhere near. Our man could take a small army down to Kynance Cove and only a few farmers—"

"*Shush!* Wait."

He broke off; glancing around, he saw Madeline waving them to silence.

Her gaze was fixed on her brother. "Ben—why Kynance?"

Ben squirmed, shot a glance at Dalziel—who reacted not at all—then glanced at Gervase, before looking back at Madeline. "Because it's the cove the wreckers use. Not just to hide their stuff—there hasn't been any this season—but their boats are in some of the caves, and they meet there, too."

He drew in a breath, then looked at Dalziel. "I sent the man there because he was a bad man, and anyone with him will be bad, too, so if they're going to stumble across any of our people, it ought to be the wreckers—they're even worse."

Dalziel was still for a moment, then he looked at Gervase. "You really have wreckers down there?"

Gervase felt his face grow blank as he envisioned what might occur. "Oh, yes." He refocused on Dalziel. "It could be a bloodbath."

Dalziel considered, then raised his brows. He looked at

Ben; his lips curved. "A trifle bloodthirsty, perhaps, but overall that was very well done."

Ben looked relieved; he turned to Madeline and grinned.

Dalziel rose, as did Gervase and Christian; he smiled genuinely, with the air of a wolf in fond expectation of his next meal. "So all that's left is for us to fly down to Cornwall, and trap our fine traitor at Kynance Cove."

Chapter 18

*M*adeline had had more than enough of being jolted about in a flying carriage. The one aspect that made this second breakneck journey infinitely more bearable than the first was Ben; he was lying curled up on the seat, his head in her lap, dozing as they raced along.

It was now midmorning; as before, they'd traveled through the night, stopping only to have fresh horses put to. Gervase, Ben and she were traveling in the lead in their hired carriage, with the same two Cornish coachmen on the box. Christian and Dalziel were following close behind in a well-sprung carriage with the marquess's coat of arms blazoned on the side.

That, and the unvoiced rivalry between Christian's coachmen and their two coachmen had, more than anything else, contributed to their remarkable pace. They'd left London within an hour of Ben revealing all; now, not even twenty-four hours later, they were nearing their goal.

Madeline saw a familiar landmark flash past. "We're nearly into Helston." Looking across the rocking carriage, she met Gervase's eyes. "Where should we head first?"

His lips curved, more in reassurance than a smile. "I told the two maniacs up top to go straight to the Park. They know the way."

She nodded and looked out of the window again, conscious of a strange urgency building—to reach home, to confirm that Harry and Edmond were there, unharmed, that no action had taken place while they were away. An underlying itch to make sure all in her domain, all those she cared for and thought of as in her keeping, were safe, that everything was as it should be.

That the unknown traitor hadn't already made some move.

As usual, Gervase seemed to read her mind. "Our villain might arrive before us, but he won't escape us, not this time. He'll go down to Kynance Cove, and we'll trap him there."

She searched his eyes, darkly amber in the carriage. "Do you think the curricle ahead of us is him?"

Gervase nodded. "It seems likely." They'd questioned the ostlers at the posting inns they'd stopped at; once out of London, as they'd traveled through the night it became clear there was a curricle ahead of them, flying through the dark. Only one occupant, unfailingly described as a dark-haired tonnish gentleman, but not one anyone recognized enough to put a name to.

Not many people chanced the roads—even the highways—at night, not at the speed they were risking. Gervase continued, "He had at least two hours', possibly more, head start, and he's driving a curricle with four in hand—much lighter and faster than us. He would have reached the peninsula this morning, but even if he goes straight to Kynance and starts searching, as there's nothing there to find and it's a good-sized beach, he'll still be searching later today—when we get there to capture him."

Madeline frowned. "He's not going to be searching alone. One look at Kynance—Ben said he simply told him that beach—and he's going to realize he'll need help." She caught Gervase's eyes. "He'll have others there—who will he recruit?"

"I don't know, but it's possible he already has men in the area he can call on, like the two who lured Ben away. He usually plans carefully, and he's extremely cautious. He's had to be to keep out of Dalziel's clutches."

She humphed. "Your ex-commander called this traitor 'fixated'—I can think of one other who seems rather 'fixated.'"

"True, but Dalziel has been after this man for years, and for the last six months, in between tying up all the other loose ends left after the war, he's been almost exclusively trying to hunt him down. It won't sit well with Dalziel—or, indeed, with us, the seven of us—to have to let this last traitor slip through our fingers, not now we know he's real."

He paused, then added, "Even more so now that we know he was paid with a cargo of items such as your brooch. Dalziel mentioned there were over thirty similar items the French have so far identified as having gone missing in the same odd manner. With every piece ranking as priceless, their total value is rather more than a fortune. Given what he must have traded to be deemed worth such a price . . ." His face hardened. "It's not only Dalziel who wants to see him hang."

Hearing his tone, Gervase glanced at Ben, and was relieved to see he was still dozing. No need for him to become fearful in retrospect; he'd come through his ordeal without noticeable harm, the only indication that he'd been deeply afraid being the way he kept a tight grip on Madeline's hand.

The carriage slowed, then came the sudden clatter of the wheels on cobbles.

"Helston." Madeline looked out at the familiar facades slipping past.

Ben stirred, then pushed up, sat up. He yawned, rubbed his eyes, then looked about brightly. "Nearly home."

Madeline smiled. Reaching out, she tousled his hair, then with her fingers combed it into place. "Yes. Nearly there."

They cut straight through the town, then continued south on the road that ran down the peninsula to Lizard Point. Two miles out of Helston, the carriage veered east, onto the road to Coverack.

Half an hour later, the carriage swept through the open gates of the Park and bowled up the long drive.

They pulled up in the forecourt with much crunching of gravel and stamping of hooves. Ben was poised at the carriage door, ready to leap out; the instant the carriage rocked to a halt, he swung the door open and did.

Shifting along the seat to follow him, Madeline looked out.

Grooms had come running around the house; behind them, she saw Harry, followed by Charles, appear on the front porch.

Both paused, saw Ben chattering to the grooms and the coachmen. Madeline smiled, waiting to see the tension that held Harry and Charles ease. . . . It didn't. Faces grim, they stepped down from the porch and came striding to the carriages, Harry in the lead.

"Something's wrong." A species of dread clutched at her—but she could see Harry, hale and whole, and Ben was dancing with exuberance.

Gervase glanced out, then gently moved her back. He stepped out of the carriage, then handed her down.

She looked up as Harry reached them. "What is it?"

Harry looked tortured, but entirely unharmed. He shot a helpless glance at Gervase, then met her eyes. "They've taken Edmond."

What? She couldn't even get the word out; panic strangled her.

Dalziel and Christian had come to join them. "Who's Edmond?" Dalziel demanded.

Harry blinked, then replied, "My brother."

"A year younger than Harry." Madeline snapped out of her panic; Gervase's fingers had closed around hers, hard, firm, reminding her she had no time to panic. "How? He was supposed to be here, safe at home."

Charles grimaced; he looked unusually somber. "We've only just got the news ourselves. Come inside, and we can all hear the tale."

He drew Harry back, collected Ben with a gesture. "You must be Ben."

As ever curious, Ben fell in beside Harry, waiting to be introduced.

Madeline tried to draw in a breath past the vise clamped about her lungs. Her head was reeling.

Gervase wound her arm in his and leaned close. "It will be all right. We got Ben back—we'll get Edmond back, too."

Filling her lungs, she lifted her head. She glanced at Christian and Dalziel, both of whom stood waiting for her to precede them, sensed more than saw their nods of agreement, their commitment to that cause.

She was definitely not alone. Head rising a fraction more, she nodded. "Indeed. Let's go in."

In the front hall, they discovered a small crowd gathered about two men—Crimms, the boys' groom, and Abel Griggs—both propped on straightbacked chairs and being tended by a bevy of helpers; Milsom and Ada were there, with two maids and a footman.

Muriel, a shawl clutched about her thin shoulders, was overseeing. "Keep that compress on, Abel Griggs, or you won't be able to see out of that eye come sundown."

Abel grumbled, but did as he was bid. It was instantly apparent both men had been beaten; Abel had a huge knot on his forehead and a black eye, while Crimms looked faint, wan and bruised all over, his livery dusty and torn.

Appalled, Madeline stared. She couldn't imagine how Abel Griggs came to be in her front hall, much less in such a state. She looked at Harry, then at Charles, who was looking decidedly grim. "What happened?"

Charles replied, his accents clipped, "They were set upon and beaten—both were coshed and left unconsious on the road. However . . ." Pausing, he drew a deep breath. "To start at the beginning . . . Harry and I remained keeping watch at the beach." He looked at Gervase. "Penny's at the castle with the dogs—she was to send word if she heard anything that might be part of this."

Gervase nodded. Charles went on, "This morning Harry and Edmond pointed out that our position wasn't strong if the villain came in by sea—he'd have the beach before we could reach him, and at night we might not even see him. We also couldn't hold all our men permanently at the beach—we discussed reinforcements. The boys suggested— and I concurred—that it would be wise to notify the local smugglers, not only to ask if they'd be willing to swell our numbers, but also to make sure they didn't get drawn into the villain's game on the wrong side."

"Sound reasoning," Gervase said. "I assume that's why Abel's here?"

Charles nodded. "Edmond offered to ride to Helston and explain—he knew Griggs and where to find him. I sent Crimms with Edmond, of course." Charles eyed Abel Griggs. "All I've gathered so far is that they were set upon while riding back, and their attackers took Edmond."

Gervase glanced at Crimms; the groom was barely conscious. He transferred his gaze to Abel, who was squinting at him from under the compress. "So what happened, Abel? Edmond reached you?"

Abel nodded. "Aye—he did. He told me the story, that there might be some action around Lowland Point, and asked could we help. He told me you"—he nodded at Gervase—"and some friends of yours were in on it, and it weren't nothing rum but could be a bit of liveliness."

He shrugged. "Me and the boys have been quiet for some time—since the end of the war there ain't been much cause for us to launch the boats. Seemed like this lark young Edmond spoke of might be an excuse to get our keels wet again. So I sent word to the boys, and was riding back with young Edmond and Crimms here, when we was set on."

"Where?" Gervase asked.

"Just outside Helston." Abel's one good eye got a distant look. "A curricle went whizzing past—we pulled to the side to let it go through. A gentleman all muffled up and a lady in a cloak—didn't reckernize either of 'em, but they was both quality, sure as eggs. Left us in their dust, they did, then we rode on. 'Bout ten minutes later we reached the junction of the road down to Lizard and the road coming this way, and a group of men leapt out from the ditch and from behind the hedge there. Some had cudgels. They pulled us from our horses. We fought, but there were at least six of 'em—too many. Left me and Crimms for dead, they did. But it was Edmond they wanted."

Abel glanced at Madeline, standing between Muriel and Harry with Ben clutched before her. "Didn't hurt him or nothing—just dragged him off."

"Any idea where to?" Charles asked.

Abel turned his good eye to the men. "That's just it—stap me if that curricle, with the gentleman and lady in it, wasn't waiting further down the road to the Lizard. The bastards—beggin' your pardon, ladies—looked to be dragging Edmond to the curricle, then one of them saw me looking, and hit me again." He pressed the compress to the knot on his forehead. "That's the last I remember."

Madeline stirred. She looked at Milsom. "Milsom, please fetch some brandy for Mr. Griggs and Crimms."

Abel inclined his head. "Thank ye kindly, ma'am." He glanced at Gervase. "Once we came to our senses, Crimms and me, we managed to grab our horses, and thought it best we come on here to report what had happened."

Gervase nodded. "A good thing you did." He glanced at Crimms, who still looked exceedingly seedy, then at Madeline. "Perhaps we should go into the drawing room to confer."

She blinked, nodded. "Yes, of course."

"Abel—if you're up to it, I'd like you to join us." Gervase looked at the groom. "I suggest Crimms should lie down for a while."

"I'll see to it, my lord." Milsom took charge of Crimms, leaving the footman to help Abel into the drawing room.

Changing venue gave everyone a moment to regroup. Madeline sank onto the chaise, Muriel beside her, Ben pressed tight on her other side. Harry perched on the side of the chaise, close at hand.

Her wits were still reeling, trying to fit the events into some sensible, understandable picture, but panic, thank Heaven, was effectively held at bay—by Gervase, sitting in an armchair nearby, and his three friends, who pulled up chairs and settled in a large, intent group.

Entirely focused on getting Edmond back, safe and unharmed. They and their concentration were a reassuring sight.

Dalziel looked at Abel as he eased carefully onto a straightbacked chair. "The men who attacked you—were they locals?"

Abel shook his head. "Definitely not from anywheres 'round here. Not Falmouth, nor even Plymouth." He frowned. "If I had to guess, I'd say they was Londoners." He squinted at Dalziel. "Been some time since I've been there, but that's how they sounded. Rough-and-ready customers, a bit more dangerous than the usual tavern thugs."

The men all frowned. Gervase shifted, attracting Abel's attention. "You said you sent word to your boys—what did you tell them?"

Abel grinned. "Told them to get the boats and come in to Castle Cove. Figured if you was truly in on this, that's where we'd start from—easier to put in there than anywhere around here . . . and truth to tell, I wanted to check that it was as young Edmond said, and all was on the up and up with you. Youngsters sometimes get carried away, as well I know."

Despite her underlying antipathy to the old reprobate— she could hardly approve of the leader of the biggest band of smugglers in the area—Madeline found herself smiling understandingly, albeit weakly.

Dalziel caught Gervase's eye. "Your ground."

Gervase glanced at Madeline, met her eye for a reassuring instant, then glanced at the men—his three friends and Abel Griggs. To Abel he said, "We chased a gentleman we believe to be a traitor we've had in our sights before, the same man we believe kidnapped Ben, back here—he would have arrived this morning, driving a curricle."

Abel's lined face grew grim. "A traitor, you say?"

Gervase nodded. "He was headed for Kynance Cove—"

"Kynance!" Harry looked at Ben. "You told him Kynance?"

Ben nodded. "I didn't want him running into anyone— not you and Ed"—he looked at Abel—"or your men, either. So I sent him and his bad men to Kynance Cove."

Abel's eyes had grown round. "I thank you for the thought, young Ben, but . . ." He looked at Gervase. "Kynance ain't exactly deserted, you know."

Gervase nodded again, lips thin. "So our villain—it had to be he you saw in that curricle—pauses to pick up some lady. Why we don't know, who we don't know. Did you see anything of her—hair color, gown?"

Abel shook his head. "Had the hood of her cloak up. Couldn't even tell if she was tall or short."

Gervase grimaced. "Let's leave the lady for the moment. Our man reaches the peninsula—he must have alerted his followers, somehow sent them ahead so they were on the road to Kynance. He raced down to join them, and so passed you, Crimms and Edmond."

Gervase's eyes narrowed. "He recognized Edmond. He already knew—or thought he knew—that his cargo was buried somewhere on the beach at Kynance Cove, but he hadn't brought Ben back with him, because Ben was his pawn to keep us in London. But suddenly there was Edmond, who would also know where the brooch had been found."

He glanced at the others. "Remember, he doesn't know we're so close behind him. He'll imagine he has at least twenty-four if not more clear hours to find his cargo and leave the area without any real risk of being caught."

"Edmond won't tell him anything," Harry said. The worry in his voice rang clearly.

Gervase met his gaze, then glanced at Madeline. "I think, when Edmond realizes the man is heading to Kynance, and thinks the cargo is there—"

"Ed'll know I lied," Ben piped up. He glanced at Harry. "He'll guess—the man's heading in the wrong direction. The man'll take Ed to Kynance, and ask where we found the brooch."

Harry stared at Ben, then looked at Gervase. "Ed'll say we found it in the middle—that way they'll have to search up and down the whole cove."

Gervase raised his brows; he nodded slowly. "All right—let's say that's what happens. Our villain will keep Edmond while his men search—he'll keep him until his cargo's found. Edmond is now his hostage in a way—he won't harm him."

"No." Dalziel caught Madeline's eyes. "Harming the boy won't figure in his plans. Even if Edmond sees his face, from what we've learned from others there's nothing to distinguish him from countless other gentlemen, so that won't place Edmond at greater risk. Our man is too fly to unnecessarily commit murder. " He looked at Gervase. "So at this moment we have our villainous friend and Edmond at Kynance Cove, and he'll be busy searching there long enough for us to capture him. How do we accomplish that?"

Everyone was nodding in agreement.

"Maps?" Charles raised a brow at Harry.

"I'll get them." Harry rose and left.

Madeline hugged Ben closer. He looked up at her and grinned. "Ed'll be all right—you'll see. Gervase and the others will get him back."

The confidence shining in Ben's big eyes made Madeline smile, and surreptitiously blink.

Harry arrived with the maps. The men pulled a table to the center of the floor and stood around it, Gervase tracing the roads, pointing out the Park, the castle and Kynance Cove. "This is the place, but the cliffs are all but barren—totally devoid of cover. They'll be able to see us approaching from miles away, so that's not an option."

Dalziel frowned. "But they'll be down in the cove searching and they don't know we're coming—will they think to post lookouts?"

"No question of lookouts at the moment," Abel put in, "nor of them being down on the sands."

They all turned to stare at him. He blinked, then looked at Gervase. "Tide's in. Kynance beach will be under water for the rest of the day—no way to search until the waves draw back, and they won't until after sunset."

"So they'll be up on the cliffs, looking down, unable to search?" Christian asked.

Abel nodded.

Silence fell; the men exchanged glances, rejigging their ideas.

"He won't wait." Dalziel shook his head. "He'll search at night. Waiting even until first light will cut his time too short—he won't risk anyone catching up with him. And the longer he stays in the area, the greater the risk someone will notice, and he'll instantly see that being at the very tip of the Lizard Peninsula, in that cove, is a trap of sorts just waiting to be sprung."

"We can certainly seal the area off," Charles said, studying the map anew. "If we put men on the road up from Lizard Point, he'll drive right into their arms."

"Especially as he won't know they're there," Christian said.

Madeline noticed that Dalziel was not so much pacing as circling, a panther deciding when and how to spring. Gervase, on the other hand, had grown still, but it was an intense stillness she now recognized as ruthlessly contained tension. Like her, he was quivering to be off, to do, but he knew how to control the impulse to action, how to manage it.

Evenly she said, "If they can't go down to the cove, but will as soon as the tide retreats, then they'll be waiting on the cliffs—they'll be able to see us when we're literally miles away, and have plenty of time to . . . react." She drew in a shaky breath. "Edmond will be in too much danger, of being whisked away at the very least, if we try to surround them now, while it's daylight."

The men all looked at her, all considered. None argued.

"We need a plan." Dalziel flung himself into his chair. "Let's assume he waits with his little band on the cliffs until the tide turns and it's night, then he goes down, taking Edmond with him, and they start searching—that's when we close in. So"—he looked up at Gervase—"how do we do that?"

The others resumed their seats, all except Charles, studying the map. Muriel touched Madeline's sleeve, whispered she was going to check on Crimms, and left. Madeline listened as the men tossed around options—the men they could muster, how best to split them up, how best to converge on the cove—

Abel coughed, and caught Gervase's eye. "One problem you ain't taking into account." Gervase raised a brow; Abel continued, "It'll be a wreckers' moon tonight."

Gervase stared at him, then softly swore, surged to his feet and went to look out of the bow window, searching the western sky. "He's right. The wind's turned and there's a storm blowing in."

"Aye—the clouds will cover the moon, and the wind's in the right quarter to blow ships onto the reef off Kynance." Abel grimaced. "And as they've had no chance yet this season, no question but that that crew, whoever they be, will be out there tonight, setting false beacons on the headlands, doing their damnedest to lure some poor unsuspecting captain in. Which'll mean they'll be up on the cliffs themselves tonight." Abel looked at Dalziel. "I don't care how many London bully boys your man has with him, he'll not get anywhere near Kynance once the sun goes down."

Christian raised his brows. "Can we leave it to the wreckers to keep him from the cove?"

"No." Dalziel's voice was flat and cold. "He'll recruit them. He's never been slow to use others. He'll offer them sure cash, and all they'll have to do for it will be to join his men and search—not even chance their regular work."

Abel slowly nodded. "Not that I know any of 'em, mind, but I've heard it said that if you offer them hard coin, they'll kill their own mother."

Madeline felt chilled. All she could think of was that Edmond was in the thick of that. . . . Her eyes widened. Horror slid icy fingers down her spine. "Edmond will recognize the wreckers—he'll know who they are." She looked at Gervase. "They'll kill him."

Gervase held her gaze. "They won't get a chance to—we'll get there before the traitor leaves. Until he finds his cargo and departs the scene, Edmond is safe. Once he leaves, Edmond won't be, but as our villain's not going to find his cargo in Kynance Cove, Edmond will be there when we go in to rescue him."

The evenly voiced statement had her blinking, had her incipient panic subsiding like a pricked balloon. She swallowed, nodded—felt calmer. Enough to smile reassuringly at Ben and Harry when they looked to her for confirmation.

Thank God for Gervase.

She hugged Ben to her, and repeated the words in her head.

"How many of them are there—these wreckers?" Dalziel, narrow-eyed, looked at Abel.

He shrugged, glanced at Gervase. "Ten, maybe. No more." As if in explanation, he added, "They're landlubbers, you know—the lot of 'em—while smugglers are all sailors. There've never been that many wreckers, or the rest of us would know, but they've always been vicious about secrecy, so no one's ever been certain who is and who ain't, and no real way to tell, not in these parts. Only thing we do know is that their favorite cove these last years has been Kynance."

Dalziel nodded. "How many nonlocals has our villain gathered?"

They tossed around numbers, and settled on less than ten.

Dalziel looked at Gervase. "How many men can we muster?"

The answer was in the thirties. "Possibly more, depending on what I find when we reach the castle." Gervase caught

Dalziel's gaze. "I assume you're suggesting a little local housekeeping while we're dealing with our fine traitor?"

Dalziel shrugged. "If fate is steering us in that direction, then I for one say we shouldn't fight the current. There's more than one villain in our world."

The others murmured agreement.

Madeline sat, hands clasped around Ben's, with him leaning against her, and listened while they discussed and planned how they would put paid to the local wreckers, overcome the imported ruffians and capture the man who had kidnapped Ben, and now Edmond—at the same time keeping Edmond safe.

While she saw nothing to argue with in the plans that slowly took shape, there was one thing—one aspect—they'd overlooked.

"So"—Dalziel looked down at the map around which they'd all again gathered, Abel included; Gervase had just finished explaining the terrain of the clifftops, confirming that approaching undetected over land was impossible— "we'll have to walk into the cove around the shoreline."

"Can't." Gervase shook his head. "The way's impassable at several points."

Dalziel looked at him, then raised his brows. "How, then?"

Gervase looked across the table at Abel. "We go in by sea."

Abel grinned, a startlingly ferocious sight. "Aye—there'll be a small fleet putting into Castle Cove soon enough."

They transferred their headquarters to the castle. Gervase and Madeline went ahead on horseback, leaving the others to follow in a procession of carriages. They left Harry and Ben at the Park; Ben had had enough excitement for the moment, and Harry accepted that he had to remain in case the men left as a token force at Lowland Point needed further direction.

Side by side, Gervase and Madeline clattered into the castle forecourt and dismounted. Before they reached the top of the castle steps, Belinda, Annabel and Jane rushed out.

Eyes wide, they grabbed Gervase. "You have to come and see!" Jane tugged him forward.

"There's boats—lots of them—coming into the cove," Belinda informed him.

"The sailors look rough—are they smugglers?" Annabel demanded.

Gervase raised his hands, palms out. "Yes, I know." He looked at Annabel. "And yes, they're local smugglers."

"Really?" Belinda's eyes grew huge. She turned back into the house. "How exciting!"

Annabel said nothing, just followed, the same look of fascination on her face.

"Maybe if we ask nicely they'll take us for a sail." Releasing Gervase, Jane ran after her sisters.

Gervase stared at their retreating backs, then looked at Madeline.

She met his gaze, read the mute appeal therein. Lips lifting, she patted his arm. "I'll go and speak with Sybil, and your sisters as well. You'd best get down to the cove."

"Thank you." His relief was heartfelt; it rang in his tone.

Raising her hand, he brushed a kiss over her knuckles, then left her, striding back down the steps and heading for the ramparts. Madeline watched him go, then went into the house.

She found Sybil in the drawing room with Penny. The girls were ranged before their mother, seated on the chaise, asking permission to go down to the cove.

"Madeline!" Sybil turned to her with relief. "What is this about smugglers taking over the cove—do you know?"

"The biggest local smuggling gang have just brought

their boats into the cove, but girls?" She waited until all three girls looked her way. "I'm afraid we've a very serious situation on our hands."

She told them the story; Sybil, Penny and the three girls all listened with rapt attention, exclaiming here, horrified there, relieved at the last when she told them that the gentlemen were planning to rescue Edmond that evening.

When she finished, the girls, now sober and quiet, exchanged glances, then looked at her. "We'll behave, we promise—you and Gervase have enough to worry about without us teasing you."

She smiled, feeling the gesture go rather wobbly. "We'd both appreciate it—tonight is going to be difficult."

She rose, intending to go and find Gervase, to see what he was doing.

Penny rose, too. "I should find my husband—I'm certain I heard his voice some time ago, and the dogs have been too quiet, which means they're probably out with him."

They left the drawing room together; behind them, Sybil called Sitwell in to ask about their unexpected guests and give the necessary orders.

Madeline waved to the door at the back of the hall. "Let's go up to the east battlements—they give an excellent view out over the cove."

They climbed the stairs, then went out onto the windswept battlements. Giving up her hair as a lost cause, Madeline walked to the raised stone walls and looked out. "There." She pointed to where, far below, a small fleet of rowing boats bobbed on the waves. Then she noticed the doors of the castle boathouse were open. "They're lowering the castle's boats, too."

Penny and she watched as first one boat, then another was swung out on the boom and lowered into the water. Gervase and Charles were manning the winch; two of the men helping jumped down into each boat, sat, took up the oars and rowed the boats across the cove to join the others by the castle watersteps.

Madeline counted the seats. "They can carry . . . eighteen, not counting the oarsmen, who'll have to stay with the boats."

Penny leaned on the wall beside her. "How many villains will there be on the beach—Londoners plus wreckers?"

"They're not sure, but perhaps as many as twenty."

"But some of those will be on the cliffs."

"Two lookouts, at most." Madeline wrinkled her nose. "We can send more men by land, but the odds for the assault on the beach—as they're terming it—aren't that good. Those who go by land won't be able to reach the cove in time to be of any help there." She looked out for a moment more, then, lips setting, turned away. "It'll be hand-to-hand fighting on the beach."

Penny glanced at her, then followed her down the stairs. "I know it's easier to say than do, but don't worry. I've seen the Bastion Club members in action, and of one thing you may be certain—one way or another they'll win."

Madeline nodded. She hoped they would, but after nearly losing one brother to the murky underworld of London, she wasn't about to remain quietly at home while the members of the Bastion Club rode like white knights to the rescue. No matter what they thought—no matter what Gervase thought—she knew where her place should be.

She bided her time; she needed to catch Gervase alone, but not in a corridor or abovestairs—somewhere they could speak privately yet in a formal setting.

The men spent the next several hours getting their arrangements in place. Gervase's library-cum-study became the hub of all activity; she joined the group there, expecting her customary malelike status to allow her to be an unnoticed observer, but unfortunately Christian, Charles and Dalziel saw her clearly as a female—more, as a lady—and behaved accordingly.

They were very aware she was there, that she was listening.

As for Gervase, his view of her had radically altered; he certainly didn't view her as he once had. Although subsumed beneath the unexpected rush of action, their evolving link, the sexual and emotional connection between them, hadn't waned in the least; the curious hiatus—where he wanted to marry her while she simply didn't know—was still there, like a caught breath, as if they were poised on some emotional edge, waiting to see, to learn, which way they would fall.

Because of that she accepted she had to tread warily, carefully, with him.

The door opened and Charles strode back in; Penny slipped in on his heels. "None of our scouts sighted the curricle." Charles had gone out to the forecourt to confer with three grooms they'd sent across the fields and along the cliffs, as if they, local lads all, were simply enjoying a ride. "No sign of any unusual activity along the cliffs above Kynance Cove."

Gervase grimaced and looked down at the detailed map spread over his desk. "Lizard Village is small, but there are numerous scattered farmhouses, cottages and, even more useful, barns in that area—they could easily have taken over one or more."

"He's certainly clever enough to get out of sight while he's waiting for the tide to turn." Dalziel was once again circling. "I suggest we resist the temptation to search further. The last thing we want is to let him know we're here, preparing to pounce."

Pausing, he met Gervase's eye, then glanced at Charles and Christian. "This may well be our last and best chance to catch this blackguard—we know he'll be in that cove to-night. We should focus on taking him then. If he learns we're near, in the neighborhood, despite his desire for his cargo his instinct for self-preservation might yet be strong enough to make him bolt."

The others nodded.

Madeline opened her mouth, but before she could speak, Gervase added, "And he does have Edmond."

Dalziel nodded, reassuringly grim. "Indeed."

Penny joined Madeline by the side of the room; together, they listened—Madeline suspected both of them critically—while the final dispositions were made. As well as Gervase and this three friends, Abel was there, along with Gervase's head stableman, one of Abel's brothers, Gregson the bailiff, and a selection of others.

Christian wasn't especially at home on the waves; he was the obvious choice to command their land forces—the small band of grooms, farmers, gardeners and laborers they'd assembled.

"So we block the road here." Leaning over the map, Christian put his finger on a particular spot. Craning past the various shoulders, Madeline saw he'd indicated a place just south of Cross Lanes.

"There's a curve and a dip," Gervase said. "He'll be on the downward slope heading toward you by the time he sees you."

Christian nodded. "I'll station enough men there to stop a curricle as soon as we get there, just in case for some reason he gets the wind up and flees early, but assuming he'll be on the beach at least until you make your move, I'll take the rest of the men and scout around. It might be wise, given the area we're trying to secure, to make sure there are no horses available for him to commandeer, in case he gets away from us at the beach."

Dalziel nodded curtly. "We take all possible precautions."

He studied the map, then grimaced. "As you so rightly point out, the area is big—any net we fashion will necessarily have big holes. If he slips past us at the cove and doesn't take his curricle, it's not going to be easy to prevent him escaping."

"But this," Gervase said, "is the best we can do."

The others nodded.

"So"—Gervase looked at Charles—"to the action on the beach."

He and Charles had the most experience with smugglers and skirmishes, if not outright battles, on beaches, waged from the sea.

Charles wrinkled his nose. "I can't see any point in carrying pistols, can you?"

Gervase shook his head. "Too wet, not terribly useful at such close quarters given how confused it's bound to be, and not useful enough given the numbers we'll face."

"Unlikely any of them will be carrying pistols either." Charles grinned, a distinctly anticipatory wolfish expression. "So it's blades—swords, cutlasses, daggers."

Both Abel and his brother were nodding.

Gervase glanced at them. "There's a small armory here. I'm assuming your men will have their own weapons, but we can make sure everyone in the boats is well equipped."

"Aye," Abel said. "We might need a few extra blades, just to cover things."

"Right." Dalziel shifted. "Now for the timing."

Madeline noted the puzzled glances Christian, Charles and Gervase threw him—and the subsequent flick of their eyes to her and Penny—before they followed their ex-commander's lead.

She narrowed her eyes. They weren't going to discuss the details of the assault on the beach in front of her and Penny.

Beside her Penny humphed, obviously having come to

the same conclusion. Glancing at her, Madeline saw Penny's gaze boring into her husband; she intended getting the details from him later.

Madeline looked at Gervase, considered, then she arched a brow at Penny. "I think I'll go and organize with Sybil to have dinner brought forward. Coming?"

Bending a distinctly jaundiced look at the males gathered about the desk, Penny sniffed. "I may as well."

They left the room on their appropriately ladylike mission, but once the early dinner had been organized, Madeline slipped back into the library, this time alone. She drifted to the far end of the room and stood looking out, plainly not attempting to overhear the men's plans.

She didn't need to hear them; she was more than capable of planning herself.

Sitwell arrived to announce the cold collation laid out in the dining room for the gentry, and the kitchen for everyone else. The others drifted out. She waited, knowing Gervase wouldn't leave the room without her. . . . What she hadn't counted on was his ex-commander's irritating insight.

Dalziel didn't leave either. When all the others had gone, he stood by the desk with Gervase—both of them with their gazes trained on her.

Patiently waiting to escort her to the dining room.

Lips thinning, she walked back up the room toward them. If Dalziel thought to, by his presence, prevent her input into their plans, he would need to think again.

It was his dark gaze she held in the instant she halted before the desk, then she turned and met Gervase's amber eyes across the map. "I'll be in the boats going to the cove, too."

Gervase's eyes, his face, hardened. "No. You need to stay here."

She raised both brows, her gaze steady on his. "You don't rule me." She flicked a glance at Dalziel. "And neither do you." She looked again at Gervase. "If I ask Abel to take me, he will. He can't afford to antagonize me, and all in all, I don't think he'll think my request unreasonable—" Gervase opened his mouth to protest—she silenced him with an upraised hand and a tight smile. "Once he hears my reasons."

Lips compressed, Gervase studied her. He flicked a glance at Dalziel, standing silent and still a pace to her right, then looked back at her and asked, "What reasons?"

She inwardly smiled, knowing her battle won, but she allowed nothing beyond calm certainty to color her tone. "Let's consider your plan for rescuing Edmond. You'll have the boats ease close, but remain far enough back so they aren't sighted by those on the beach. One boat will slide in close to the point itself, where the water's shallower, and you and Dalziel will go over the side and wade to shore— unlikely any men at the center of the beach will see you at night. You'll be well out of the range of any flares. While Dalziel goes after the traitor, you"—with her head she indicated Gervase—"will find and release Edmond—we assume he's restrained in some way, but it will be too dangerous to leave him trussed up while a fight rages about him."

She paused, and cocked a brow at Gervase. "Have I guessed all that correctly?"

Grim-faced, he nodded.

"Very well. To continue, Charles, remaining with the boats, will give you two however many minutes to—what's the phrase?—achieve your objectives? Then he'll bring the boats in and a fight will erupt all along the beach. During that fight, your specific task will be to protect Edmond. You'll order him to stay behind you, and stand guard as it were over him." She held Gervase's eyes. "That's what you're planning to do, isn't it?"

His eyes cut to Dalziel before he met her gaze. "That's the gist of it."

Neither could see where she was leading them, what hole

in their plans she'd discovered and was about to point out. She could sense unease coming from both of them.

She smiled, not smugly but—she couldn't help it—a touch patronizingly. "While you're defending him, who will be restraining Edmond?"

Gervase frowned. "I'll order him to stay back. He'll—"

"*Listen?*" Incredulity oozed from the word. "Please remember you're talking about a fourteen-year-old boy—no, let me rephrase that more accurately—a fourteen-year-old male *Gascoigne*—who after being seized by a villain and his rough-and-ready henchmen finds himself in the thick of a pitched battle between the forces of good and evil, on a beach, with smugglers on his side, swords and knives flashing in the dead of night." Her voice had risen slightly, her diction hard and precise; she pinned Gervase, then turned to subject Dalziel to her gaze. "Do you seriously imagine he'll meekly stand back, watch, and not join in?"

They stared at her, speechless. Unable to answer, because she was right.

Satisfied, she drove home her point. "The instant he sees anyone he knows threatened, he'll dash in to help. Armed or not." She paused, then added, "Regardless of any injunction or prohibition you think to make, however forcefully."

Silence fell. Gervase's expression was stony, his eyes flat agate, impossible to read.

"Will he listen to you?" The quiet question came from Dalziel.

She met his eyes. And smiled thinly. "Oh, yes. You may be absolutely certain he'll listen to me. And obey me. He's been doing that for all of his life, and he knows there are instances when obedience is not negotiable. He'll do as I say."

From the corner of her eye she saw Gervase's lips twist, but when she faced him his expression was as unrelentingly impassive as ever. How, in light of that, she knew he was to the bone opposed to her going onto the beach she couldn't say, but she was. His opinion reached her clearly, without the need for words.

Dalziel turned; he walked a few paces away from her. "When you're on the beach, you'll need to be able to defend yourself—and Edmond, at least to some degree."

He turned back, and she saw he now held two light swords; she looked up and confirmed they were the pair usually crossed over the mantelpiece. Gervase must have taken them down—one for Dalziel, one for himself.

Both swords were unsheathed. Dalziel hefted them lightly in his hands—then tossed one, hilt first, to Madeline.

She reacted without thinking, deftly plucking it out of the air, her fingers and hand sliding with familiar ease into the hilt.

It was Dalziel who blinked.

But then he waved her away from the desk with the sword he held. "For instance, what are you going to do if . . ."

He swung at her, not with force but with the transparent intention of disarming her. Habit again came to her aid; she whipped her blade up and blocked.

And had the satisfaction of seeing his eyes widen.

He disengaged with a twist and came at her again, but this time she was prepared; grabbing up her skirts, she sidestepped, slammed her blade down across his, forcing it to the side, low. The unexpected move unbalanced him; before he could recover she stepped inside his guard, lifted one slippered foot and jabbed sharply at the outside of his knee.

His leg buckled.

Flailing wildly, he fought to right himself. Ducking his arm, twisting out of his reach, she kicked a small footstool behind him, then shoved hard at one shoulder.

The look on his face as he went down was pure magic.

Even better was the look in his eyes as, flat on his back,

he stared up the long length of her sword, from the tip she pressed into his neat cravat to her hand, steady on the hilt.

Eventually, eyes narrowing, he lifted his gaze to her face.

She smiled. Openly smug. "I have three brothers. I don't fight fair."

He didn't blink. "You've been trained."

She raised her brows. "Well, of course. Did you think only men could wield swords?"

He was clever enough to make no reply. She let her smile soften, lifted the sword's tip from his throat. "My father taught me, then had me taught, so I could later teach my brothers, then have them taught."

Raising the sword, she studied it, then looked at Gervase. He'd said nothing throughout—hadn't moved an inch—yet she'd been conscious of the explosive tension that had gripped him the instant Dalziel had "threatened" her.

She met his gaze, then tossed the sword to him. "I have my own weapons—I had them brought from the Park." She looked at Dalziel, but it was to Gervase she spoke. "You needn't worry about me on the beach—any locals there will recognize me, the others at the very least will know me for a woman, and just as you did, they'll underestimate me. They won't strike hard—they'll imagine I'll be easy to disarm. But underestimating women is never wise."

Stepping around Dalziel, she headed for the door.

Behind her Gervase shifted. "We'll have to wade through surf waist-high or deeper—"

"You needn't worry." At the door, she turned and met his eyes. "I won't be wearing skirts."

With that final decisive declaration, she opened the door and went out.

Gervase stared at the partly open door, remembered the early dinner waiting for them. He looked down at Dalziel. His erstwhile commander slowly sat up; draping his arms over his bent knees, he looked disgustedly at the footstool.

Despite all—the seriousness of the situation, the sheer horror he felt over Madeline having inserted herself into the thick of their planned action and in a way that left him with no viable arguments—he felt his lips twitch.

He rapidly straightened them as Dalziel lifted his gaze, eyes narrowed, to his face.

"If you ever breathe a word of this to anyone, I'll deny it."

Gervase couldn't help it; he grinned. "The memory will be its own reward."

he sun went down and night closed in. It was dark and stormy, but at least it wasn't raining. On the castle watersteps, Gervase stood by Madeline's side, his fingers about her elbow, waiting for the larger of the castle's rowboats, manned by a select crew of Abel's "boys," to draw alongside.

He'd made one—only one—attempt to dissuade Madeline. He'd followed her upstairs to change into garments more conducive to slogging through waves and then fighting on a beach; entering the bedchamber Sybil had assigned Madeline on her heels, he'd shut the door and faced her.

She'd glanced at him, then raised a brow.

He'd looked into her eyes. He understood all too well her motives in going. Admired them, and her, even though he, all he was, was in violent opposition. "I don't want you to go."

"I know. But I have to. I can't *not* go." She hesitated, then added, "It's not that I don't trust you to protect Edmond— it's because I know Edmond, and I trust *him* all too well to behave exactly as I said."

He'd paused; he hadn't thought she didn't trust him—that

hadn't entered his mind. He'd wondered for one second if there was any leverage there . . . then he'd leaned his shoulders back against the door.

Sinking his hands in his pockets, he'd watched her unbutton her jacket. "I honestly don't know how I'll react if you're there—if you're beside me in what might very well be close and dangerous fighting."

He hadn't meant to tell her that, but it was the simple truth.

She'd looked at him; head tilting, she'd studied him for a long moment, then she'd smiled—wry, in some indefinable way tender. "It looks like we're going to find out." She'd looked down, unlacing her riding skirt. "You know I have to go."

He had known; despite the railings of his more primitive masculine self, somewhere deep inside he understood and accepted that. She'd been her "brothers' keeper" for more than a decade; impossible to ask her to step aside—to change and become a different person, a different woman, a different lady—now, just because he couldn't bear even the idea of her being exposed to danger. And deep inside, he valued her as she was; he couldn't with any sincerity argue for a change.

He'd sighed, briefly closed his eyes. "Very well."

He'd turned to go; grasping the knob, he'd heard a similar sigh from her.

"It isn't only for Edmond that I'm going—he's not the only one I . . . feel compelled to protect. If not actively defend, then at least watch over."

He'd glanced back, but she hadn't raised her head, hadn't looked his way.

"I know you understand because you're like that, too. What you might not appreciate is that some women, some ladies, feel the same. We protect, we defend—it's what we do, who we are." Then she glanced at him. "It's what I am—and I can't change that, not even for you." She'd smiled, a swift, rather misty gesture, and looked down at her laces. "Especially not for you."

He'd hesitated, then he'd left the door, crossed the room, swung her into his arms and kissed her—swift, urgent. Sweet.

Raising his head, he'd looked into her eyes, amazed all over again at how dazed she—his Valkyrie—became, then he'd felt his face harden; setting her on her feet, he'd nodded and turned away. "I'll meet you at the back of the front hall."

He had, later, and escorted her here, to wait for the boat that would carry them—her, him and Dalziel—to the beach. The smugglers brought the boat cruising in alongside the steps; Gervase caught the rope one threw him, pulled the boat in tight, expertly steadied the prow. Dalziel stepped down into the boat. He turned to assist Madeline; with his free hand Gervase steadied her as she followed, clad in her trousers and a shirt and drab jacket borrowed from a groom. The instant she was safe aboard, Dalziel moved back and sat on the rear crossbench; Madeline stepped over the fore bench and sat in the middle of the boat.

As soon as she was seated, Gervase let the rope play through his hands. He made a quick half leap into the boat as the oarsmen, with perfect timing, pushed away from the steps.

He sat and they were away, the four oarsmen pulling strongly, smoothly, through the night, through the increasingly choppy waves.

The journey around Lizard Point in the dark, with a storm blowing up and the seas rising, wasn't one for faint hearts.

The boats pitched and dipped on the waves, but all those at helms and oars were seasoned sailors who knew these waters, knew where the currents ran, how best to use them. Spray washed over the prows, half drenching those crouched between the oarsmen. The wind strafed, knife-keen; no one had worn hats.

Had it been winter, the trip would have been impossible. As it was the summer seas, although cold, weren't freezing, and the wind, although biting, wasn't iced; as long as the boats steered clear of rocks, the long minutes were bearable.

They eased around Lizard Point, yard by yard making way through the surging waves.

How long the journey took, no one could guess; no one had risked carrying a timepiece. It was full dark, the sky above a roiling mass of charcoal and midnight blues, when through the spume and spray they glimpsed flares in Kynance Cove, the first cove north of Lizard Point.

"He's there." Dalziel leaned forward, staring across the tops of the waves; they were so big, those in the boats, bobbing up and down on the deep swell, only occasionally caught a clear view of the beach.

"No beacon." Gervase scanned the dark where he knew the clifftops were. He glanced at Dalziel. "The wreckers must be working with him, or they'd have their beacons lit by now."

Between them, Madeline shifted. "I've counted twenty-three men on the beach."

More than they'd expected, but not so many as to jeopardize their plan. "We'll deal with them." Gervase swayed with the roll of the boat. Gripping her shoulder, he lightly squeezed, then caught the helmsman's eye; with his head he indicated the rocks at the southernmost tip of the cove.

The helmsman nodded, and leaned on the rudder. As the boat swung, the oarsmen waited . . . then grasped their oars and bent to. Silently their boat cleaved through the waves, leaving the others in their small flotilla drifting, dipping their oars only to hold their position strung out in a line parallel to the beach.

In one, Madeline glimpsed Charles saluting them.

Gradually the rocky point drew near. On the beach proper,

the retreating tide had left a ten-yard strip of reasonably dry sand at the base of the towering cliffs. Her lungs tight, nerves taut, Madeline searched the cove, scanning furiously every time the swell raised them high enough for a clear view; finding the figure she sought, she groped blindly for Gervase, found his arm and gripped, pointing. "There. Edmond."

Her brother was a small figure made even smaller because he was sitting cross-legged close to the cliffs, between the point they were heading for and the center of the cove where, as Harry and Ben had predicted, the attention of all others on the beach was concentrated.

Flares—tall poles wrapped with oil-soaked rags—were planted in the sand in a large ring, creating a circle of light that made the shadows immediately beyond even darker. Edmond sat at the edge of the flickering glow. The awkward angle of his arms suggested his hands were tied behind him.

In the heavily lighted area ringed by the flares, many men were digging, sifting through the heavy sand. Other than one man guarding Edmond, no lookouts had been posted on the beach. All activity, all attention, was focused on the excavation; they didn't expect to be interrupted, certainly not via the sea.

Madeline recognized some of the men digging, and her heart sank. Leaning into Gervase, she whispered, "The Miller boys." John Miller's two sons.

Gervase followed her gaze, grimly nodded. "And the Kidsons from Predannack."

The night would have repercussions beyond those they'd anticipated. Earlier Madeline had glimpsed a man in a greatcoat, but now they were closer, the bodies were harder to distinguish, shifting and merging in the flickering light of the flares.

She leaned toward Dalziel. "Can you see your man?" Her whisper was little more than a breath; they were sliding slowly in to the rocky point.

His gaze locked on the beach, Dalziel shook his head. "But he's there somewhere—they wouldn't be digging so assiduously otherwise."

Gervase tapped her arm, signaled to her and Dalziel to stop talking. Then he shifted forward to where an oarsman in the prow was checking the depth.

They were relying on the experience of the helmsman and oarsmen to bring the boat in smoothly and silently to the rocky point, close enough that they could slip over the side and wade to the beach. The sound of the waves breaking on the rocks and the froth and spume would give them cover, both for sound and sight.

Madeline looked again at Edmond. The man guarding him was relatively short, scrawny, not a local. The man's attention wasn't on Edmond, or on the stretch of beach beyond him, or the deeper shadows hugging the base of the cliffs at Edmond's back; like everyone else, the guard was watching the activity in the center of the beach.

Gervase tapped her arm again, then, like a seal, he slipped over the side and was gone. The boat bobbed, and there he was, standing, the water across his chest, below his shoulders.

Madeline gripped the edge of the boat, swung one leg over, then let herself fall. Gervase caught her, righted her before a wave could swamp her. He took a firm grip on her arm. Then Dalziel was in the water on her other side; he grasped her other arm. Each of them took the weapons the smugglers passed them, blades unsheathed, then they were moving, steadily wading to the beach.

Even in the water, both men moved with their customary animalistic, predatory grace; between them, Madeline was swept effortlessly along. She barely had time to register the water's coldness.

They came onto the beach among the rocks; crouching, they slipped undetected into the dense shadows at the base of the cliffs. They waited, watched, but the men on the beach had no inkling they, or the boats, were there. The group's attention remained fixed on their excavations; Edmond must have been entirely convincing.

Her lungs tight, every nerve stretched taut, Madeline glanced back; even though she knew the boat had been there, she could no longer see it. The five smugglers had slipped out beyond the first breakers as silently as they'd slipped in.

The oncoming storm and its elemental effects—the crash of the waves, the rising shriek of the wind—was now an advantage; it would mask their approach, the sound of their footsteps in the sand submerged beneath the unrelenting rumble and roar.

Gervase, ahead of her, glanced back and signaled. They straightened; in single file, hugging the cliff face, they moved stealthily, steadily, closer to Edmond.

Madeline gave thanks he was looking away from them, stoically watching the men dig. He seemed entirely unperturbed, as if he knew it would be only a matter of time before rescue arrived. A typical Gascoigne trait, that unshakable belief in his own invulnerability.

Gervase halted less than two yards from Edmond; she halted beside him, and Dalziel halted behind her. An instant later, she felt a touch on her shoulder. She looked around as Dalziel slipped past her, then past Gervase, to take the lead.

Dalziel's target—the traitor, their villain—was somewhere on the beach. Madeline stared, trying to see each man clearly, but again the shifting bodies defeated her. The man in the greatcoat she'd spotted earlier had merged into the melee.

This was their moment of greatest danger. Exposed, in the shadows yet perfectly visible if any thought to look their way, they had to wait until Charles saw them in position, then marshaled the boats for the beaching. How long that might take—

A sudden roar reached them, one that owed nothing to wind or water. Five boats came crashing onto the beach, carried on the crest of a single large wave. In the prow of one, his black hair in tight curls, a sword flashing in his hand, Charles looked every inch a pirate. The instant the keels grated on sand, men poured over the boats' sides, brandishing swords and long knives.

The wreckers, momentarily stunned—long enough for all the fighters in the boats to gain the beach—abruptly came to their senses and sent up an answering roar. There was a mad scramble for weapons, then the two groups clashed; sand churned and flew.

Madeline snapped her attention back to her own task—the sense of Gervase slipping away pulled her back. She saw him glide behind Edmond, enthralled with the battle raging before him, toward the guard, who was clearly dithering over whether to stay with Edmond or join the fray.

Dalziel had disappeared.

Gervase reached the guard, drew near. Sensing something, the man started to turn; Gervase struck him on the skull with his sword hilt. The man crumpled.

Seeing Gervase, Edmond struggled to his feet. Madeline caught him by the shoulders. "No—stay down!"

Dropping back to his knees, he turned wide eyes on her. "Maddie?"

"Yes, it's me. Hold still while I cut you loose." There was, she noted, not an ounce of fright let alone terror in Edmond's voice; he was excited, eager to join in. "Our job," she told him, sawing through the ropes, "is to guard Gervase's back."

"All right." Edmond was all but quivering with eagerness.

"There." Pulling the ropes away, she stood. She waited while Edmond rubbed his wrists and got to his feet. He turned to her, and she handed him the short knife she'd used to cut the ropes. "This is for you."

She knew her brothers very well.

Eyes shining, Edmond seized the knife. "Where—"

"You and I are supposed to stay here—me a little back

from Gervase's left, you a trifle further back, on his right."
Looking at Gervase's broad-shouldered back, Edmond
shuffled back a fraction. Madeline nodded. "Yes—like that.
Now we're in position to make sure no one attacks him
while he's defending us."

Edmond nodded, eyes on the writhing mass of bodies,
flailing and flinging themselves at each other. The clang of
metal on metal sang over the waves' roar; for a moment,
Madeline felt detached, as if the pitched battle were a dream
she was observing from a safe distance . . . then two men
staggered back from the pack.

Large, heavyset, they weren't locals. She saw them exchange a glance, a few snarled words, then they left the
group and came running up the beach, churning through
the sand toward her and Edmond, with Gervase ranged before them. The men targeted Gervase, focused their fury
and fear on him. They looked set to fling themselves, blades
flashing, on him—but in the instant before they did, he fluidly shifted; his sword swung out in a powerful arc, slicing
one of the men's upper arm.

The man yelped; both dropped back. Their eyes gleamed
as they took stock, licked their lips.

Crouching, they circled.

Gervase beckoned them forward. "Come on—don't be
shy."

Behind him, her own sword held out of sight parallel to
her leg, Madeline bit her lip; he sounded entirely relaxed,
tauntingly confident.

Another man fell back from the melee in the center. He saw
his two cronies, guessed their tack, and came to join them.

"Gervase . . ." Madeline warned.

"Yes. Time to change tactics."

That was all the warning he gave before launching a ferocious attack on the two before him, driving them back.

But other nonlocals had now seen. Understanding their

value—hers and Edmond's as hostages—in desperation they scrambled away from the fighting and came rushing to secure what might be their only way to win free.

She heard Gervase swear; with a swinging slash, he cut down one of the two he was engaged with, leaving him whimpering in the sand clutching his arm, and fell back. Poised with sword drawn, he stood between her and Edmond and the onrush of men.

Charles had seen but was surrounded by heaving bodies; he couldn't immediately come to their aid. Dalziel was far to their right; his task was to find the traitor and seize him, or, failing that, cut off all escape from the beach by taking and holding the only path up the cliff. Glancing across, she glimpsed him on the lower reaches of the path, sword slashing as he drove back men desperately seeking to flee. With nothing to lose, they redoubled their efforts, but the relentless ferocity with which he met them kept sending them reeling back.

Looking back at the men charging toward them, fanning out to come at Gervase from multiple angles, Madeline felt her heart thud heavily; her lungs had long ago seized. She swallowed, tightened her grip on her sword, drew her long knife from her boot, and edged closer to Edmond. "Follow my lead."

From the corner of her eye, she saw Edmond nod. Like her, he was watching the men advance; unlike her, there was not an ounce of fear in his heart.

The jackals circled, then two launched a ferocious frontal attack; Gervase met it, flung them back, but was immediately engaged by another. Meanwhile, two men slunk in, one on either side.

Seeing them advancing, Madeline stooped, picked up a handful of sand and flung it in the face of the ogre to their left; leaving him swearing and stumbling, pawing at his eyes, she stepped across Edmond, brought up her sword and thrust at the smaller man sneaking in on Gervase's right.

The man leapt back, eyes wide, his expression scandalized. "The bitch has a blade!"

Madeline wanted to follow him, but didn't dare leave Gervase's back unprotected—then Gervase shifted, engaging the smaller man. She pulled back, glanced to her left—in time to see the ogre lift his short sword.

He went for Gervase.

She got her blade up in time to deflect the thrust, gasped when the force of it reverberated up her arm; crossing her knife with her sword, catching his blade in the V, she heaved, and sent the ogre staggering back. Mean, piggy-bright eyes fixed on her; with a roar he lifted his sword high and came at her.

She got her crossed blades up, caught his—

Then he yelled and toppled sideways.

She glanced down to see Edmond—he was clutching the back of her jacket—pull his knife from the man's beefy thigh, just above his knee. She nodded in approval; as one they whirled away, leaving the ogre howling and cursing and rolling in the sand—he was large enough to effectively block others from rushing in from that direction—and swung to protect Gervase's other side.

Just in time.

Gervase had accounted for two more—all nonlocals—but three more desperate men had arrived, determined to seize them. Two had engaged Gervase, drawing him forward; the other waited, then rushed in from his left—

Again she swung her blade, caught the man's thrust and swung his blade over to lock between hers . . . but this time the man had the agility and momentum to turn with her—to shift his attack from Gervase to her.

She suddenly found herself face-to-face with a London bruiser, a heavyset man at least twice as strong as she. Her arms were braced, holding her crossed blades high, his trapped between . . . he'd ended standing firmly, legs apart, evenly balanced, hands locked on his sword hilt.

He smiled cruelly, and bore down.

Her arm muscles started to quiver, then shake.

Madeline stared into his eyes . . . then shifted her feet and kicked him, hard, between his legs.

His eyes bulged, his face contorted; uttering an inhuman shriek, he went down, dropping his sword to clutch himself— then he howled even more as Edmond darted out, stabbed him in the thigh, then darted back behind Madeline again.

She spared her brother only a glance—enough to see his eyes were alight; he was thrilled beyond description.

Dragging in a breath, praying her pounding heart would stay down in her chest, she checked that they were reasonably protected by the two fallen men on either side, then swung her attention forward—in time to hear Charles drawl, "Excuse me."

A second later, the last man facing Gervase crumpled to the sand.

Gervase was breathing a trifle rapidly; he studied the inanimate form at his feet, then looked up at Charles. "Spoilsport."

Charles shrugged. "You were taking too long." He peered around Gervase. "All well here?"

Lowering his sword, Gervase turned around; he knew both Madeline and Edmond were all right—he'd glanced their way countless times. He'd been so aware of them the entire time, he'd had to battle to keep his eyes and instincts focused on the men fighting him—had had to force himself to trust in Madeline's ability to defend Edmond. . . .

What he hadn't counted on was her defending him.

But she had, without hesitation. Although he'd known of each attack before she'd acted and would have done something to avert the worst, she—ably seconded by Edmond— had at the very least saved him some ugly wounds.

He met her eyes, saw concern in hers—and more. The

exhilaration of battle still rode him, familiar and potent, but tonight some other emotion was threaded through the mix. He found his lips lifting; raising an arm, he slung it about her shoulders, hauled her to him and buried his face in her hair. "Thank you." He whispered the words into her ear, hugged her close, then eased his hold.

Enough to look at Edmond; he nodded, still smiling. "Thank you, too—you did well. And you followed orders."

Edmond glowed. He brandished his knife. "We made an *excellent* team."

Gervase laughed, nodded. "That we did." He'd never fought as a team before, but he thought he could grow used to it.

Madeline's hands were pressed to him, splayed over his still-damp chest. They were both sodden and sand-covered to midchest, but a slow burn of elation was rising within him, obliterating any chance of a chill.

His arm still about her shoulders—with her apparently perfectly happy to remain tucked against his side—they turned to survey the beach.

Charles and Abel, assisted by the fighters from the boats, were dragging and pushing the vanquished, locals and non-locals alike, into a group a few yards from the bottom of the cliff path. None on their side looked to have sustained any mortal wound, nothing worse than slashes and cuts; some were nasty but none life-threatening. The same couldn't be said of the wreckers; at least two of their number lay unmoving in the sand, and two others were being supported by their fellows, unable to walk unaided.

As he, Madeline and Edmond walked toward the gathering, Gervase grew inwardly grim. There would be more deaths to come; regardless of what happened to the Londoners, the surviving wreckers would hang. Quite aside from the seriousness with which the law viewed the activity, here in Cornwall, where most families had a long association with the sea, wreckers were beyond abhorrent.

Madeline, no surprise, had been thinking along similar lines. She murmured, "We'll have to make sure their families don't suffer for their acts."

He nodded. Even close family members usually had no idea their loved ones had turned to the heinous trade. "John Miller will be shattered."

Soberly, Madeline nodded.

They circled the defeated, miserable men to come up beside Dalziel. He stood with his back to the cliff path, sword still in hand; no one had got past him. A sense of explosive, barely restrained frustration emanated from him as he studied the slumped, exhausted men.

His expression was set, beyond grim. He looked up, met Gervase's eyes, with his head indicated the clifftop behind him. "He's not up top. The roads are blocked. Christian's up there—he found a horse waiting and secured it. No curricle—he must have exchanged it for the horse during the afternoon."

Dalziel looked down at the men gathered on the sand before him, their vanquishers standing over them, awaiting orders.

Eyes bleak, he crouched before the ogre Edmond had stabbed. The man looked into Dalziel's face, and shrank back, small eyes flaring.

"Your master—where is he?"

A dark murmur rose from the group as others, along with the ogre, glanced around, and realized they'd been deserted.

The ogre hesitated, then spat, "Don't know—but he *was* here. He was pacing around, watching us dig, telling us to be careful—"

"You'd a known him if 'n you'd seen him," the scrawny guard piped up. "He looked just like you, a black-haired, smooth-talking devil."

"I saw one who looked like a gentleman," one of their young fighters volunteered. "Glimpsed him when our boat crested a wave, before we came in, but I didn't see him later."

"I saw him, too," Madeline said. "Earlier on, before we got to the beach. He was wearing a greatcoat, but I didn't see him later."

Dalziel rose. "So where is he now?"

Everyone, including the defeated men, looked around. Beyond the area lit by the flares, the night was a black velvet shroud.

Dalziel looked toward the northern end of the beach. "He didn't go up the path. He didn't reach the clifftop. What about that headland? Could he have walked, or swum, around it?"

"No," Gervase replied. "And he couldn't have slipped away to the south, either."

"He'd be dead if he tried," Abel opined.

"There's the caves." Edmond stared up at Dalziel; he hadn't met him before. "He might have hidden in them."

Swinging around, Dalziel stared at the deeply shadowed cliffs. "Can he get up to the clifftop through any of the caves?"

Edmond, Gervase and Abel all answered no.

Expression set, Dalziel nodded. "In that case, we search. Carefully."

He gave clear, concise orders, setting two of their band to hold the cliff path, and two more to watch over the villain's defeated crew; they roughly tied those of the vanquished men who might make trouble, before, in a group, the rest of them moved off.

Gervase led them to the entrance of the northernmost cave.

"We stay together, and search one cave at a time—no need to give him a chance to take any more hostages," Dalziel said. "We'll work our way down the beach, leaving two men outside to make sure he doesn't try to slip past us, back to a cave we've already searched."

It took more than an hour to search every cave.

Impossible though it seemed, their villainous traitor had somehow escaped the beach.

Leaving the last cave, trudging back up the beach, Gervase and Charles exchanged glances. They knew how frustrated Dalziel had to be feeling.

Reaching the bottom of the path up the cliff, Gervase stopped and straightened, stretching his spine. "What now?"

For a long moment, Dalziel made no answer, staring out at the waves rolling in, then he drew a tight breath. "I'll go up and join Allardyce. We'll search the coast and cliffs going north as far as Helston." He glanced at Gervase.

Gervase nodded, equally grim. "We'll head out on foot, doing the same in the other direction as far as the castle. He must have risked going around the rocks, either to the north or the south. If he's made it to the cliffs, one side or the other, we should find him."

That was the simple truth, yet he had a feeling in his gut that none of them—not him, Charles or Dalziel—held out much hope. Unbelievable though it seemed, their quarry had eluded them. Yet again.

Abel came up, saying he'd have his "boys" take their boats back up the coast to Helston, as well as returning the castle's two boats. "The lads will scan the coves as they row past."

He also offered to oversee marching their vanquished foes up to the cliffs, and then to the constable in Helston. He grinned. "That'll put me in good odor with the authorities—might as well get something from the night."

"You enjoyed the action, you old reprobate," Gervase said.

"True." Abel's grin grew wider. "But when you reach my age, you learn to make the most of what the good Lord sends you." With a chuckle, he stumped off to order his "boys" to their various tasks.

Taking Madeline's hand, collecting Edmond with a glance, Gervase started up the path. Charles joined them, along with those of their band who hailed from the castle, or had homes in that direction.

They reached the clifftop to discover Dalziel and Christian had already set out. Turning, they headed along the coast, following it toward the castle.

Drenched and shivering, the man they all sought clung to his refuge, wedged into a crevice in a clump of rocks out in the cove. He'd noticed the jumbled cluster some thirty yards from shore when he'd viewed the cove from the clifftop that afternoon. He hadn't given it a thought—not until, down on the beach overseeing the search, alerted by some sixth sense, he'd glanced across the ring of flickering light, and in the shadows at the base of the cliffs had seen the one man of all men he never wanted to meet while in his traitor's guise.

Shocked, mentally reeling, he'd known one instant of pure terror.

Then a second when he'd realized the three crouching figures were waiting for something—something that would come from the sea.

He'd turned, looked—caught one fleeting glimpse of a white face over the waves.

Desperate, mindless self-preservatory instinct had taken over. His only possible escape had lain in instant action. Attracting no attention from the laboring men, he'd walked unhurriedly the few paces to the sea, and kept walking, pulling off his muffler and hat, ducking beneath the waves as soon as he could, slipping out of his greatcoat, then swimming— battling, struggling, desperately fighting—against the swell and the treacherous currents to reach the rocks he'd known were there, but in the dead of night couldn't see.

If he couldn't see them, others couldn't either.

He'd thought he'd never reach them; he'd been flagging, wondering if, after all, his life would end like this—thinking that even if it did it was still a form of triumph, for Dalziel would never know, would be left forever wondering—when his hand struck rock.

He'd gripped, latched on; gasping, shaking—*praying*—he'd hauled himself into the lee of the rocks, then found the crevice into which he'd wedged himself. Submerged from the neck down, partially protected from the constant sucking surge of the waves, he'd clung, panting. Slowly panic had receded, and he'd regained his ability to think.

The battle on the beach ended. To his disgust but not his surprise, Dalziel's forces won.

For the immediate moment he was safe, but he had to get away—out of the area—cleanly. Leaving no trace. None at all.

This time, Dalziel had got far too close.

He didn't waste much time cursing, wondering how his nemesis had so unexpectedly and frighteningly appeared, all but nipping at his heels; the answer was played out on the beach before him. He hadn't recognized Crowhurst as one of Dalziel's men, but St. Austell he knew by sight. The way the three consulted made it clear Crowhurst was one of them—and the damn woman—Madeline Gascoigne—was equally clearly Crowhurst's. Which made her brothers far too dangerous to pursue. If he'd known the connection, he'd never have drawn so close.

He'd survived this long by avoiding Dalziel and his crew—always.

Now . . . now he had to cover his tracks and get out of the district quickly. If Dalziel so much as set eyes on him down there, he'd guess, and know it all in a blink. If that happened, he wouldn't see another dawn. Dalziel would act, and in the circumstances he'd be entirely without mercy.

If Dalziel saw him in the area, or in any way linked him with the traitor's enterprise, his life would be measured by the time it took for his nemesis to reach him. He'd known that from the first; it was now part of the thrill, the lingering satisfaction. Dicing with death and winning was exhilarating.

Reminding himself of that, that he'd thus far triumphed through every twist and turn, he watched Dalziel leave the beach, striding up the path to the clifftop.

Relief slid through him; he hated feeling it, yet he did.

Jaw setting, he determinedly turned his mind to his plans. He knew better than to leave anything to chance, to leave any thread leading back to him, however tenuous, unbroken.

Although chilled to the bone, he remained where he was, watched and plotted—striving to keep the fear that had earlier chilled his marrow from resurfacing and paralyzing his mind.

He saw them round up his improvised army, but none among it knew his name. No threat there. They were marshaled and led away under guard, toiling up the cliff path, some supporting the injured up the steep slope. Other men returned to the boats; he wondered if they might leave one until the morning, but all were pushed back beyond the breakers. Two went south; the others headed north, passing a mere ten yards away. He clung to his rock and made no sound, no movement; in the dark, they didn't see him, a dense shadow against the black rock.

He waited long after the beach was deserted—then waited still longer. He gazed across the waves at where he'd believed his lost cargo had been buried. Given the complete disinterest shown by Dalziel and his crew to the area lit by the now-guttering flares, and the caves lining the beach, he knew beyond doubt that the boys—both of them—had lied.

Ironic that he, who could lie so well himself, had so easily swallowed their tale. But they'd both looked so innocent, so incapable of guile. So young.

He'd like to get his hands on them and beat the truth from them, but he knew when to cut his losses and run. Even though some part of him presently submerged beneath the necessity of escaping, of staying unidentified and thus alive, howled and cursed and screamed at the loss of his precious cargo, his saner self knew that no amount of gold and jewels, of priceless ornaments and miniatures, would warm him if he were dead.

Would count for anything if Dalziel ever caught him.

He'd always viewed his collected prizes as tangible evidence of his victory over Dalziel, but the true if intangible measure of that victory was his continued existence.

He would, he told himself, make do with that.

After the beach had been deserted for hours and the flares had long died, letting Stygian darkness reclaim the scene, he hauled in a huge breath, eased out of the crevice, and pushed away from the rock. He struck out for the shore. The currents were no longer so strong; he reached the beach, managed to get his legs under him, and staggered up and across to the cliff.

In the dark, it took him a while to find the narrow path leading upward; he climbed it slowly, his boots squelching with every step. He shivered, but now the storm had blown over, the wind had changed; his clothes would dry soon enough.

Reaching the clifftop, he looked north, along the line of the cliffs, the edge of a dense shadow visible against the shifting gray of the sea. Far ahead, he saw a pinpoint of light bobbing, then it disappeared. They'd be searching the cliffs and the coves below, hunting him. He couldn't risk taking the cliff path, but as it happened, that wasn't the way he needed to go.

Head down, he struck out across the fields. After scouring the peninsula's beaches for weeks, he had a decent map of the area in his mind. He plotted a direct course that would take him inland, past several tiny hamlets and isolated farmhouses where he might find a horse. Even if he didn't, he could easily walk the distance and reach his necessary goal before dawn.

Then, after he'd dealt with the one last thread he had to break, he'd vanish. Once and for all.

Chapter 20

In the wee hours of the morning, Gervase, Madeline, Edmond and Charles trudged into the castle forecourt and slowly climbed the front steps. They'd followed the coast all the way from Kynance Cove, and as Gervase had prophesied, seen nothing.

Along the way they'd farewelled those of his workers who'd fought with them and who lived in villages they'd passed. On the top of the steps, Gervase turned to the small band remaining. Grooms and stablelads, they were wilting, feet dragging, but their faces stated they'd enjoyed being a part of the adventure, and catching the wreckers had been worth every rough moment.

He smiled. "Thank you for your help. We might not have caught our gentleman villain, but we've done well by the district in rounding up the wreckers. Off to your beds—I'll tell Burnham you're excused until midday."

They grinned sleepily, bobbed their heads in salute, then shambled off, some to the stables, others around the castle.

With Madeline beside him, her hand in his, Gervase

turned and followed Charles and Edmond into the front hall.

Sybil, Penny and Sitwell were waiting.

"Thank Heaven!" Sybil enfolded Edmond in a hug, then looked at Gervase and Madeline. "Just *look* at the pair of you—did you have to swim?"

He and Madeline glanced down at their clothes; once the storm had passed, the night had turned mild, but they were still damp and plastered with sand.

Tightening his grip on Madeline's hand, he met her eyes. "We'd better go up and change out of these clothes."

"Indeed," Sybil said. "We don't want any chills." She looked at Edmond, still within her arms. "And as for you, young man, there's a warm bed waiting upstairs—we'd best get you into it before you fall asleep on your feet."

Edmond grinned at her; the fact he didn't argue but allowed himself to be steered toward the stairs screamed louder than words that he was exhausted. He waved sleepily back at Madeline and the others. "Thank you for coming to rescue me. Good night."

Madeline and Gervase smiled, waved and echoed his good night.

Penny, meanwhile, had been welcoming, then inspecting, her husband. Finding a cut on his hand, she hissed in disapproval. "Men and their swords."

Charles chuckled and slung an arm around her shoulders. "Come on—if the dogs are in our room, we'd better get up there before they start barking. You can tend my injuries there."

Penny frowned at him. "How many are there?" But she consented to be towed to the stairs. She nodded a good night to Gervase and Madeline as they passed. "We'll see you at breakfast."

"Late." Charles didn't look back.

Gervase and Madeline grinned. He caught her eye. "We'd

better head upstairs, too." He lowered his voice. "And get out of these clothes."

They started toward the stairs. Behind them, Sitwell coughed. "I assume Mr. Dalziel and the marquess will be returning tonight, my lord?"

"They will." Gervase didn't halt. "They're mounted— they shouldn't be much longer."

"Very good, my lord. I'll lock up once they're in. I'll leave a message for Burnham that his boys should be allowed to sleep late. And we'll hold breakfast back until nine."

"Thank you, Sitwell." His gaze locked on Madeline's sea-green eyes, Gervase wound her arm with his. Slowly they climbed the stairs.

They reached the gallery to see the light from Charles and Penny's candle fading down one corridor. One candlestick remained on the side table; Madeline picked it up and sighed. "Dalziel's going to be disappointed, isn't he?"

Gervase steered her to the right. "I fear so. If they'd caught our villain, word would have reached here before us. I don't know how he got off that beach . . . perhaps he didn't, not safely."

Madeline studied his face in the flickering candlelight. "But you don't believe that."

His lips quirked self-deprecatingly. He met her gaze. "It's the logical, most likely explanation, yet . . . no. I think he managed to slip past us somehow. He's made a career of that—of slipping through Dalziel's nets."

"I can imagine that goes down well."

He grunted. "Indeed."

They strolled slowly along, then he said, "You called Dalziel fixated, and to some extent he is, but just like the rest of us, now the war is over he must have a life waiting for him, one he has to return to."

"You think after this he'll give up—resign?"

"Christian said some weeks ago that he thought Dalziel was 'tidying up.' This villain—our last traitor—is almost certainly the last item on Dalziel's list. If after everything else is settled that item remains unresolved, then yes, I think Dalziel will lay the list aside, walk away and get on with his life."

She considered, then murmured, "For one of his ilk, that will require considerable resolution."

He nodded. "Now you've met him, do you think he hasn't it in him to close the door and leave the past behind?"

She thought, then conceded, "No, but it won't be easy."

Gervase guided her toward the door at the end of the wing. "Agreed, but ultimately he'll have little choice. He's not a career soldier, like all of us were. He doesn't hold any commission. He was never in the Guards or any other regiment. Quite how he got to where he is, how he came to fill the position, we've never learned. But when he leaves it, he'll leave Whitehall altogether—he'll leave it all behind."

"As you all did—but it's followed you, hasn't it?"

He grimaced. "True, but when Dalziel walks away, I suspect that truly will be the end." He paused before the door, captured her gaze. "We've come close to this villain twice. The instant Dalziel appears, or as in the previous case, was about to appear, our villain drops everything, kills anyone who knows his identity, and vanishes. That's why I think he escaped us on the beach—because he saw Dalziel and did something so desperate none of us can even guess what. You saw him, one of the smugglers saw him. He was there—but then he saw Dalziel, and he wasn't there any longer."

"I imagine most villains would run from Dalziel. Whoever he is."

Gervase nodded. "That's why I think we won't see him again, and why it's unlikely Dalziel will get another chance to lay hands on him. He was here, in the district, to pick up his thirty pieces of silver, but by their nature and by his leaving them so long in France it's clear he doesn't need the money. Now he knows Dalziel knows of his lost cargo, he won't risk coming back to get it. No matter the attraction, it's no longer worth the risk. And that—taking possession of his thirty pieces of silver—was the last act in our villain's game. The war's over—there are no more moves to be made."

She frowned. "So Dalziel himself represents some special threat to this villain?"

He opened the door. "For whatever reason, for this man, Dalziel himself is the ultimate risk—the ultimate threat."

He ushered her into the room, closed the door, watched as, pensive, she walked to a chest of drawers and set the candlestick upon it. Stirring, he followed her. She turned as he reached her. Raising both hands, he framed her face, looked into her lovely eyes. "But now that's over for us, for all those here. The danger's passed—Ben's safe, Edmond's safe. . . ." He held her gaze. "Above all, you're safe."

She looked into his eyes, her own clear and unshielded, then she smiled, closed her hands in his jacket and tugged him nearer. "And you."

He lowered his head and kissed her—she lifted her face and kissed him back, generous, welcoming, infinitely giving.

Releasing her face, he reached for her, closed his arms around her and drew her flush against him. Angled his head, deepened the kiss.

And gave them both what they wanted.

Simply let loose the pent-up passion, the inevitable reaction to those fraught moments on the beach. Suppressed until now, passion became desire, and desire transmuted to need; it swirled up and through him, and flowed into her, welling, swelling, seeking release.

His unqualified surrender let her do the same, let her gift him with her passion, her desire and her need, in response, in reply.

For long moments, nothing else mattered but that simple

communion, that long-drawn-out kiss, that recognition, that savoring, that elemental understanding.

They needed this. For much the same reasons, they had to have this—this moment, this time, this reassurance.

This knowing. A primitive acknowledgment that they'd both survived, that both were there, whole and unharmed, triumphant and victorious.

That underneath all, regardless of all, each meant the world to the other.

Need welled, burgeoned, filled them.

Their lips parted; they caught their breaths, lips burning, lids lifting, eyes meeting from only inches apart, and suddenly, desperately, they needed it all.

Had to share all they were. Had to seize all, each heated second, each heartbeat, each touch, each burning caress.

Clothes shed, peeled from damp flesh, then let fall unheeded to the floor to scatter and heap as they would. Getting their wet boots off left them both laughing, an insane moment of indescribable relief before their gazes clashed, and hunger, both familiar and different, somehow edged with something finer, keener, some deeper shade of meaning, flared anew.

Took hold and drove them.

Into each other's arms.

Into heated nakedness where the only thing that mattered was to feel hot skin against skin, to grasp and caress, to touch, to worship—to possess.

To want.

Beyond words, beyond description.

Gasping, nearly blind, they tumbled onto clean sheets, onto a thick mattress that cushioned and cradled, amid pillows that tumbled around them.

She spread her thighs, clasped his flanks; he rose over her, reached between them and cupped, caressed, and she cried out.

Shifting, he bent his head, captured her lips, took her mouth, then with one powerful thrust joined with her.

Whirled them into the familiar dance.

Familiar, yet different.

Acceptance, a knowing; closeness, a giving. The moments spun out, spiraled, stretched.

Together they strove, together they gloried.

They reached the familiar peak and clung . . . until ecstasy shattered them, fractured them, fused them—left them floating, drifting as one, exquisite satiation flowing through their veins, the slowing thunder of their pulses a soothing rhythm in their ears.

With love, simple and pure, a shining magnificence filling both their hearts.

Dawn broke; about them, the castle awoke. Slumped amid the tangled covers of his bed, they slept on.

The sun was slanting in through the windows when Gervase awoke.

Even before he opened his eyes, even before his mind engaged, he knew. At some primal level he recognized, not just the warm body lying half over him, her breast pressed to his chest, his arm cradling her, her long legs tangled with his, but what had changed.

What had lent their familiar landscape that gilded edge.

His lips were curving even before he opened his eyes. He glanced at her, at the jumbled tumble of rippling locks that screened her face. Felt her stirring, as if sensing his wakefulness, she was waking, too.

Then awareness reinfused her limbs. Raising a hand, she brushed her hair out of her face and glanced up.

He smiled—at her, into her eyes. He couldn't recall ever feeling so joyous, let alone letting it so blatantly show.

Puzzled, she searched his eyes. "What?"

His smile only deepened. He looked up at the canopy to

hide any smugness in his grin. "You're going to marry me."

She didn't immediately reply. He glanced down—and saw it was taking her a moment to assemble a frown. She managed one, of faint disgruntlement rather than anger, and directed it at him. "Why do you think that? I haven't agreed to accept any offer, nor have you made one, if you recall."

His grin returned. "I know. But I will, and you will. You've made your decision. You've made up your mind."

Her eyes narrowed. "You can't know that."

Holding her gaze, he smiled, a softer gesture. Lifting one hand, he smoothed back her hair, but kept his eyes on hers. "I do know. You're in my bed. Naked in the Earl of Crowhurst's bed where only countesses of Crowhurst have ever lain."

Arching her brows, she struggled up; leaning on his chest, she made a show of looking around the large room.

He laughed, rocking her; he closed his arms loosely around her. "You knew that last night when we came in. You didn't bother mentioning it because in your mind it no longer mattered."

When she looked back at him, he tightened his arms in a gentle hug. "And you were right. You belong here. In this room, in this bed, with me. This is where you should—and will—spend your nights for the rest of your life. Here, with me."

She continued to look at him as if uncertain how to deal with him, with his sudden and absolute knowledge.

He arched a brow and tried for a vulnerable expression and tone—not easy at the best of times. "Am I wrong?"

Entirely unintentionally Madeline laughed. Still trying to narrow her eyes at him, and failing, she pushed back from his chest to flop on her back beside him, so she could stare at the canopy, too. "I do hope this isn't going to be a habit of yours—being so disgustingly all-knowing."

He chuckled; finding her hand with one of his, he linked his fingers with hers, raised them to his lips and pressed a lingering kiss to her knuckles. "Only with you."

She humphed.

After a moment—a moment in which they both, she was sure, looked ahead into the joint future that had, entirely unexpectedly, opened before them—he asked, "What persuaded you? What changed your mind?"

She was silent for a while, thinking back. Eventually, she said, "As you no doubt intended, it's been made transparently obvious to me over the past several weeks that you are truly in desperate need of a wife, not least to manage all the aspects of your life as earl that you are patently ill-equipped to deal with yourself, and that Sybil, your sisters, Muriel, my brothers and with few if any exceptions the entire local community—and even your ex-colleagues and ex-commander—believe that duty should fall to me."

"And that convinced you?"

She heard the surprise, nay, skepticism, in his voice and smiled; he did know her well. "No. That only made me more uneasy. Everyone here had viewed me as a lady who didn't need to marry, who'd been excused from marriage for over a decade, and then, just like that, they changed their minds? They might have been right, but what did they know of me?" She waved dismissively. "I'd never been a young lady looking for marriage—they'd never seen that side of me. I'd never put it on show. They'd seen me only as my brother's surrogate . . . what did they know of that other me?"

He waited a heartbeat, then asked, "So what tipped the scales my way?"

She felt her lips curve. "You . . . and in a strange way, our villain, or rather his machinations and how we dealt with them. *You*, in that you made the effort to see me, the real me. You never had before, but then you somehow stepped

back and gained a different, deeper and truer perspective . . . and once you had, you didn't retreat but instead
started to deal with me as me, not as who everyone else
thought I was. That was strange and unnerving and unsettling at first, but . . . in some ways it's been a freedom, a
freeing. With you, I can be who I am without any veil or
disguise—I can be the me I never thought I'd have a chance
to be."

His lips brushed her fingers again. "The woman you
thought you had to keep hidden, locked away, forgotten, in
order to care for your brothers."

No question, she noted. She nodded. "That was, and still
is, a strong point in your favor, but not the only one, not the
principal one."

"Not the one that persuaded you to change your mind."

Again she nodded. "My list of reasons for not marrying
you were in retrospect less revelant—important in their
way, but not the critical question. When I made that list, I
didn't truly know, didn't fully comprehend what that critical
question was. *Is*. But then you set about demonstrating that
my listed reasons weren't as I'd thought—which left only
that critical question unresolved.

"That was where we were when you told me you wanted
to—had from the first intended to—marry me." She turned
her head on the pillow, met his eyes. "That was the moment
when I suddenly found myself facing that critical question
and—so very unlike me—I discovered I didn't know the
answer. I didn't even know how to learn it."

She paused, studying his amber eyes. He didn't ask,
merely raised his brows and waited; she smiled. "There was
no single moment, no sudden revelation. Almost immediately Ben was kidnapped, and I didn't have time to think
about that question. But the answer crept up on me. It wasn't
what you did, the actions you took to get Ben back, and then
rescue Edmond, although I was grateful"—she squeezed his

hand—"more grateful than I can say, that you were there to help me get the boys safely back."

Drawing in a breath, she tried to find the words, the right way to explain how it was that, as he'd correctly divined, she now knew her path beyond question or doubt. "It wasn't *what* you did, it was *how* you did it. How you deal with someone is a reflection of how you see them, and throughout these last crazy days you've dealt with me in only one way—as if I were already your wife, as if you could no longer see me as anything else, as if the answer to my critical question was, at least in your mind, taken for granted."

She searched his eyes, then drew breath and said, "My critical question was whether you loved me. I knew I loved you, but didn't know if you returned my regard, not to that degree. But even if you did, I didn't know—couldn't see— how you could manage to convince me . . . but you did.

"You *demonstrated* the answer rather than gave it to me in words, and your actions spoke loudly and clearly. I understood what it cost you to let me go onto the beach at Kynance Cove alongside you—but you did. You accepted that, for me to be me, it had to be that way—you bent, adjusted to accommodate me, even though I knew that what I'd asked was one of the most difficult things for you, being you, to grant, to allow."

She looked into his amber eyes, clung to the understanding she saw there, exulted in it. "You showed me that despite being so alike, especially in that way, we could still have a life together, that we could be close, could share all the moments of a life, the difficult as well as the easy, that we could build a full life and enjoy it together while still being us—you being you and me being me. You showed me that your love and mine would allow that to be."

Smiling, she let her certainty show, let it light her eyes. "And that's what I now want—to spend the rest of my life with you, by your side, filling that space everyone seems so certain I was meant to fill, loving you and having you love me." Her smile eased; she felt it grow more serious, but no less sincere. "If that's what you want, then I want it, too."

He didn't laugh, didn't smile, although his lips were relaxed in an easy line. Shifting onto his side, he raised a hand and framed her face, looked into her eyes as though through them he saw her soul, as if he spoke to it. "That's what I want—that's the most important thing I would ask of life. I'll never be whole, never be complete, unless I have you as my wife, beside me, mine. . . ." He drew a tight breath. "Mine to love and care for, to build and enjoy a life with, to have at the center of my life, my heart, my soul."

He hesitated, then leaning close touched his lips to hers, then he drew back and met her eyes. "I haven't made a formal offer. What I would rather ask is that you be mine so that my life can revolve around you, now and forever. Will you marry me?"

She smiled, a trifle mistily. "Yes."

She kissed him, or he kissed her; it mattered not to either who made the first move. Wriggling her arms up, she wound them about his neck, held him to her.

His lips on hers, Gervase inwardly smiled, and locked his arms around her. He had her now, she was his and he would never let her go.

Two hours later they walked into the breakfast parlor to find everyone else had got there before them. Sybil, Belinda, Annabel and Jane called cheery good mornings. Returning their greetings, acknowledging others, Madeline was surprised to see Muriel and all three of her brothers seated at the table avidly chatting with Dalziel, Christian, Penny and Charles.

Muriel leaned back and caught her hand. "We had to come. Harry and Ben couldn't wait to hear what had occurred—and I couldn't either."

Madeline smiled, squeezed Muriel's hand, then followed Gervase to the sideboard.

They helped themselves to sausages, kidneys, ham, kedgeree and kippers, then Gervase held the chair beside his place at the head of the table for her; once she'd settled, he took his seat.

Edmond was relating what had occurred when he'd been seized. "The man—the London gentleman—told me he already knew that we'd found the brooch on Kynance beach. He told me so I wouldn't bother lying. All he wanted was for me to point out where on the beach we'd found it—so of course I pointed at the middle."

Christian nodded. "Very clever."

"What happened when they reached the cove and discovered the tide was in?" Charles asked.

Edmond explained, describing events much as they'd imagined them—that the man had cursed, then driven away with the lady, leaving his gathered crew hiding in a barn. He'd returned alone on horseback just before sunset. Later still, they'd stumbled into the arms of the wreckers, and, as they'd guessed, their traitor had persuaded the local villains to lend him their aid.

From Dalziel's and Christian's politely urbane expressions and the tiredness behind their eyes, it was obvious they had no good news to report regarding their London gentleman. Gervase caught their eyes, arched a brow. "Not even a sighting?"

Dalziel's lips turned down in a grimace. "He must somehow have slipped behind us."

Charles shook his head. "God only knows where he was hiding."

Madeline, studying her brothers with a sister's fond eye, noted the light—a light she knew to be wary of—shining in Edmond's and Ben's eyes. She followed their gazes . . . to Dalziel.

She glanced at Harry, but he hadn't been as exposed to Dalziel as the other two. Then she looked at Christian, Charles and Gervase . . . and fought against the urge to narrow her eyes. Dalziel, she suspected, was one of those men who too often proved to be a dangerous influence on a certain type of suggestible male. To her mind, all the males at the table, except Dalziel, fell into that certain suggestible class.

As for Dalziel himself, she doubted he was in any way suggestible; he was a man born to rule.

"If only there were some way to get just one good clue to his identity." Dalziel's eyes held a faraway, distant, predatory look. "It seems he doesn't want me to see him, which presumably means I'll recognize him . . . but none of you others will."

"None of the men he'd brought from London had any idea? An address? A way to make contact?" Gervase looked at Christian.

Who shook his head. "Not a clue. He walked into taverns in London, hired them, and gave orders to gather down here in a run-down cottage. He spoke to them there a few times. Other than that, they never saw him and have no idea where he might have been staying. He always wore a muffler and hat to shade his face, even when he was pacing up and down on Kynance beach." Christian looked across the table at Edmond. "Edmond's description was the same."

Edmond smiled shyly, shifting under their gazes, then he glanced at Dalziel. "Perhaps Lady Hardesty knows his name."

All conversation halted. Everyone turned to stare at Edmond, puzzled. . . .

Dalziel made the connection first. "The lady in the curricle?"

Edmond nodded, but the action was uncertain. He looked up the table to Madeline and Gervase. "I haven't met her but I think it was her. Tall, oldish, dark-haired—and she wasn't from around here. She was wrapped up in a cloak and kept the hood around her face most of the time, but she had a London accent, like the man."

Further down the table, Belinda leaned forward, peering at Edmond. "Did she have a mole—just here?" She pointed to a spot just above the left corner of her lips.

"Yes!" Edmond nodded. "I saw it. It was black."

Belinda looked at the others and nodded. "Lady Hardesty. Katherine and Melissa mentioned the mole."

Madeline recalled, nodded too. "She does have a mole there."

Around her chairs scraped as all the men got to their feet.

Dalziel set down his napkin. "You'll have to excuse us." He nodded to Madeline, then Sybil. "We need to reach Lady Hardesty as soon as we can."

Madeline remembered that their villain had a habit of killing all those who could identify him. She felt herself pale. "Yes, of course." She pushed back from the table.

Gervase had already sent a footman flying to the stables for four fast horses to be saddled and brought around. He exchanged a glance with Madeline, then led the men to the gun room for pistols.

The ladies looked at each other, then, breakfasts forgotten, everyone rose and went out to the front hall, milling before the open front door.

The men came striding back, each carrying two pistols, checking them while Gervase described the way to Helston Grange, Robert Hardesty's house.

Hooves clattered in the forecourt. Charles bussed Penny on the cheek as he passed. Gervase paused to brush his lips across Madeline's. "I don't know what we'll find, or when we'll be back."

She squeezed his arm, nodded and released him. "Go— and good hunting."

Dalziel heard and saluted her as he went past. His face was set.

The four checked saddle girths and stirrups, then mounted. In less than a minute, they were wheeling toward the forecourt's entry arch.

With Sybil and Penny flanking her, Madeline stood on the porch and watched them go. "I just hope they get there in time."

Sybil patted her arm, then gathered the youngsters and ushered them indoors.

Penny remained beside Madeline, staring at the dwindling figures of their men. "I hope they reach her before him, but from all I've heard of this blackguard, we're going to be disappointed in that, too."

Madeline glanced at her, met her eyes. After a moment, they turned and went inside.

They covered the distance to Helston Grange at a blistering pace. It was the first time Gervase had ridden with Dalziel; he wasn't surprised to learn his ex-commander was as bruising a rider as the rest of them.

They arrived to discover the majority of residents at the Grange had yet to rise for the day. When summoned to his drawing room, Robert Hardesty came rather diffidently in, puzzled rather than irritated by the intrusion.

"Lord Crowhurst." He smiled at Gervase and extended his hand. "It's been rather a long time."

"Indeed." Gervase grasped his hand, nodded curtly. "I apologize for the abruptness, Robert—we'll explain in a moment, but it's Lady Hardesty we've come to see. It's urgent that we speak with her."

His grim expression—and those of Charles, Christian and Dalziel ranged at his back—made Robert's eyes widen. Then Gervase's request sank in. "Ah . . . they—my wife and her friends—tend to keep London hours. I doubt my wife would be awake—"

"Lord Hardesty." Dalziel captured Robert's gaze. "We

wouldn't be here, making such a request at this hour, were the need not great. If you could send a maid to summon your wife?"

Robert Hardesty blushed. His gaze shifted away. It was apparent he didn't know if his wife was alone in her bed. But then he swallowed, flicked a glance at Gervase and nodded. "If you insist."

He rang the bell, gave the order.

Gervase was conscious of the urge to pace, something he rarely did; he could feel the effort Charles and Dalziel were making not to circle the room. Tension rode them all, unnerving Robert Hardesty even more than their expressions.

Then they heard the first scream.

Gervase pushed past Robert and headed straight for the stairs, Dalziel on his heels. He didn't have to look to know Charles and Christian had gone the other way, out of the front door to circle the house. Just in case.

There was no need to ask for directions; they followed the screams, gaining in intensity, rocketing toward hysteria.

Reaching the room at the end of the wing, they opened the door. A maid was backed against the wall a few feet away, her knuckles pressed to her mouth, her eyes huge, her gaze fixed on the bed.

On the figure sprawled across it.

The bulging eyes, the protruding tongue, the necklace of bruises ringing the long throat, the indescribable horror of what had once been a beautiful face clearly stated that life was long extinct.

Dalziel pushed past and went to the bed.

Gervase grabbed the maid and bundled her out—into the arms of the butler who had come rushing up. "Lady Hardesty's dead. Sit her"—he nodded at the maid—"downstairs in the kitchen and give her tea. And send for the doctor."

Although plainly shocked, the butler nodded. "Yes, my lord." He turned the now-weeping maid away.

Gervase went back into the room.

Dalziel withdrew his fingers from the side of Lady Hardesty's bruised throat. "Not cold, but cooling. She's been dead for hours."

He turned to the long windows giving onto a balcony; one was open. Gervase followed Dalziel out; the balcony looked toward a stretch of woodland bordering the Helford River.

Dalziel pointed to muddy scrapes on the railing. "No mystery how he got in."

They looked over and down. A gnarled wisteria with a trunk a foot thick wound up one supporting post to weave its tendrils through the ironwork railings. Gervase grimaced. "It couldn't have been easier."

Charles came out of the woodland along a path. He halted below; hands on hips, he studied their faces. "Dead?"

Dalziel nodded. "Anything down there?"

"He came up from the river." Charles waved at the path behind him. "His footprints are clear, definite—he knew what he was doing, where he was going. There's a rowboat drifting—he probably stole it from somewhere along the other side."

Dalziel exhaled. "I doubt there's anything left for us here, but in case anyone knows anything, we'll speak with all the guests."

Christian had appeared from the other direction; he and Charles nodded, and headed back to the front of the house.

Gervase and Dalziel reentered Lady Hardesty's room to find Robert Hardesty standing just inside the door, staring at his dead wife. His face was blank, empty; the expression in his eyes, when he looked their way, was lost.

Dalziel inclined his head and stepped past; at the door, he glanced back at Gervase. "I'll speak with the butler."

Pausing before Robert Hardesty, Gervase nodded. He caught Robert's bewildered gaze, and spoke calmly, soothingly. "The doctor's been sent for—he'll be here soon. He'll know what to do."

Dumbly, Robert nodded. He glanced again at the bed; his composure wavered, threatened to crack. "But *who* . . .?" He looked at Gervase, stricken and frightened. "People might think it was me. But I *didn't*—"

"We know it wasn't you. She was killed by a man—a London gentleman—we understand she was acquainted with. She was seen with him for a short time yesterday afternoon. The man is a known killer and a traitor—we believe he killed her so she couldn't identify him."

Robert Hardesty stared at him; Gervase couldn't tell how much of his words he was taking in.

Then Robert turned and looked again at the bed. "My sisters, and my aunt, were right. They said she, all her London connections, weren't . . . good. I should have listened."

Gervase gripped his shoulder. "When it comes to women, sometimes even young girls see more clearly than we." His sisters certainly had. He took Robert by the arm. "Come and have some brandy. It'll help."

Without resistance, Robert let Gervase lead him from the room.

It took them over two hours to interview all the guests at Helston Grange. All of them were accounted for; none of them was their villain, or at first blush knew anything of him.

Dalziel and Gervase handled the interviews while Christian spoke with the staff and Charles roamed outside, speaking with the gardeners, grooms and stable hands.

When they finally met up on the front steps, their expressions were unrelentingly grim.

"Our man never stayed here," Dalziel replied in answer to Charles's arched brow. "However, two of her ladyship's bosom-bows are certain she had a long-standing liaison with some gentleman of the ton, one that predates her marriage by some years. They believe the liaison continued, although very much more sporadically, after her marriage. The lady was free with her favors and had many other lovers, but the only lover she treated with absolute discretion, to the extent of not sharing his name or any detail of him with these two friends, was this old flame." He paused, then went on, "They believe he'd come down here, and that she'd been seeing him over this summer, but neither knows anything more."

Christian shifted. "Her maid, who's a local, thinks much the same—that despite the other lovers, including some of the men currently here, there was some man she knew from her past who she was seeing again clandestinely. According to the maid, he never came to the house."

Charles grimaced. "One of the gardeners thinks she and some London gentleman—tall, dark-haired, our usual suspect—have been using one of the old garden sheds down by the river for assignations."

"Which," Gervase said, "confirms that our man wasn't one of the guests, but very likely was this old flame."

"And," Charles went on, resignation filling his voice, "there's a horse missing. A nice chestnut gelding, plus a good saddle and tack."

They fell silent, then Dalziel quietly cursed. "The black-guard's escaped. He's gone."

For one instant, they all toyed with the notion of giving chase, then remembered in how many directions a man on a horse could have gone.

His face set, an impassive mask, Dalziel stepped down from the porch. "All that's left is for us to go home."

Epilogue

*G*ervase Aubrey Simon Tregarth, 6th Earl of Crowhurst, married Madeline Henrietta Gascoigne, of the
Treleaver Park Gascoignes, in the church at Ruan Minor
just over four weeks later.

The church with its strange serpentine stone was packed,
people standing in the aisles and overflowing down the
steps to fill the churchyard, all gathered to witness the joining not just of the two major local families but also two
people who were widely known and admired. Those inside
the church were mostly local gentry; the only outsiders
were Gervase's colleagues and their wives, Madeline's god-
mother and a few far-flung relatives. The day was one the
people of the peninsula weren't about to miss, and intended
to celebrate; the formalities were observed, but a relaxed,
joyous air pervaded all.

A stir went up when Madeline's carriage halted before
the lych-gate. Delighted exclamations rippled through the
crowd when she stepped down in a cloud of silk and lace.

Radiant, on Harry's arm she walked into the church and down the aisle to the strains of the organ.

Harry gave her away; he placed her hand in Gervase's, then stepped back to sit with Edmond and Ben. Charles and Gervase's cousin stood alongside him, while Penny and Belinda had followed Madeline down the aisle.

The service was short, uncluttered, direct. When the vicar named them man and wife, Madeline beamed, put back her veil and stepped into Gervase's arms. He smiled, kissed her, too briefly but they knew their roles. Turning, arm in arm, their faces serene, showing their joy, they walked slowly up the aisle accepting the congratulations of all who leaned close to kiss their cheeks and shake their hands.

Around them, the organ pealed in joyful celebration, almost it seemed in triumph. Certainly there was an element of that in the tenor of many of the congratulatory messages; it seemed plain that to everyone theirs was a union not just to be applauded but celebrated as an example that all was well in this corner of the world.

The wars were behind them; this was the future, one to look forward to and embrace.

It took nearly an hour for Madeline and Gervase to travel the distance from the church steps—where their assembled halfsiblings had showered them with rice—to the carriage waiting to whisk them to the castle; once inside, they relaxed with identical sighs, gently squeezed each other's fingers while they traded smiling glances, then sat back to recoup their energies over the short drive.

Gervase glanced at the brooch anchored between Madeline's breasts. "That piece may be old, but I doubt it ever looked so well." It sat perfectly nested amid the ivory lace adorning her gown's neckline.

Smiling, she looked down, tracing the worked gold. "It was nice of Dalziel to send confirmation that the brooch was officially declared treasure trove."

"Hmm." Gervase hadn't been surprised his ex-commander had thought of it; Dalziel rarely let any detail slip. The declaration had meant that the boys' ownership of the brooch had been recognized, and their gift of it to Madeline would stand.

"I had wondered," she murmured, "whether it was appropriate to wear it—something for which a traitor had sold information that hurt our troops." Looking up, she met his eyes. "But I decided that instead it was a sign he, our gentleman traitor, hadn't won. I have the brooch—he doesn't."

Gervase smiled back. "A sign of defiance."

Also, Madeline thought, a symbol, at least to her, of the events that had opened her eyes and brought her to this moment, to being Gervase's wife.

To having confidence in their love, to being able to say "I do" so sincerely.

Everyone had gathered in the forecourt and on the steps to greet them; the carriage rolled in and halted to applause and cheers. Gervase stepped down, handed her down and a roar went up—immediately followed by a deafening *boom*!

Everyone looked to the ramparts, then another of the castle's cannons barked. Madeline looked at Gervase, but he shook his head. Not him.

Charles materialized beside her, shutting the carriage door and waving them up the steps. "Your brothers," he told Madeline as the last of the cannons roared. "They thought it appropriate and conscripted Christian, Tony and Jack Hendon to give them a hand. Don't worry—they're safe."

Madeline laughed, relieved by that news and amused that Charles had been so quick to volunteer it. But then Penny was expecting their first child, so perhaps Charles was developing the sensitivity of a parent.

She made a mental note to mention it to Penny, then the assembled throng engulfed her with their smiles and congratulations; on Gervase's arm, she swept into the front hall, then they led the way into the vast ballroom, where the wedding breakfast waited.

The hours that followed were filled with happiness, pure, simple, a catalogue of relaxed pleasures, of those small moments that shine in memories ever after, a fitting accolade, she later thought, her gaze resting on Gervase, for a man who had selflessly served his country for so long.

She glanced around, at his friends and their wives, most of whom were in a delicate condition, saw the happiness they'd found shining in their eyes—other fitting accolades. Only Christian yet sat alone. She pondered that, then a bright laugh drew her gaze to Belinda—testing her wings with one of the younger gentlemen.

Looking swiftly around, Madeline located her brothers—all three, amazingly, were behaving themselves much as if their good behavior was their wedding gift to her. Her lips quirked, bittersweet; they would be returning to school in a few weeks, and when next she saw them Harry would be grown, with Edmond following closely. Her time to be devoted solely to them was at an end, but Gervase was now there to take them through the next phase, teaching them to be men, something she wouldn't have been able to do, and there was no man she more wished them to emulate.

In return . . . her gaze drifted to Annabel, and Jane, then back to Belinda, still smiling at the besotted young man. She would take the three girls in hand. Although she had no great liking for London, for them she would brave the ton and the Season and make sure they were presented properly. Sybil and Muriel would help, but Madeline accepted that, much as with her brothers the primary role had fallen to her, with Gervase's sisters she would be their mentor, their true guardian.

She wondered if Gervase would view her teaching them to fight and defend themselves, at least to a point, unladylike; regardless, she considered that a necessary accomplishment preparatory to their come-outs.

Life went on. One role ended, another began.

And yet another was developing, not here yet, which was just as well; by her calculations, she had eight months to get all the necessary arrangements to her liking before the next addition to their melded family made an appearance.

Her gaze drifted to Gervase; she smiled. She hadn't told him yet; she was saving the news as a surprise for later that night.

Gervase felt her gaze, turned and caught it—caught the secretive, madonnalike smile that played about her lips. She was so serene these days; she'd managed the organization of their wedding with an effortless ease that had left him amazed. The bombardment of decisions had left him reeling—had sent him slinking away to hide in his library. She'd smiled and let him go, and handled all with gracious aplomb.

Thank God he'd had the sense to marry her.

Leaving those with whom he'd been conversing, he strolled to her side, took her hand and drew her to her feet. When her brows rose in question, he smiled. "Come and waltz."

He led her to the floor, swung her into his arms, into the revolutions—and they both relaxed, let the barriers they deployed with all others, thin veils, true, but still there, fall. They smiled into each other's eyes, and simply shared the moment. That curious, fabulous, infinitely precious unity of feeling, of being.

They'd danced the first waltz long ago; there was little by way of formalities remaining. The musicians were supplying a steady stream of waltzes that a large number of couples were enjoying.

Following his gaze around the room, Madeline sighed, a contented sound. "It's gone well, I think."

"It has." He waited until she met his eyes. "But regardless of all else, I have all I need of the day. You."

She was already smiling, but her gray-green eyes softened, glowed with a serene light he was entirely content to bathe in for the rest of his life. He drew her closer, whirled her into a turn and gave himself over to the moment.

That sense of contentedness lingered, a gentle warmth about his heart.

Later, when he joined his ex-comrades and Jack Hendon at the side of the room in what had come to be something of a tradition, Christian raised a brow and asked after the traitor's cargo.

"The authorities in Falmouth sent a platoon of sailors the day after you and Dalziel left. They sifted the entire beach, and turned up three other pieces, all relatively small—a tiara, a necklace and a filigree orb. Once the platoon had retreated, the locals descended. They searched even more diligently, but found nothing more. The consensus of opinion is that heavier, denser items would have much less chance of being washed ashore, so most of our last traitor's thirty pieces of silver are almost certainly sitting on the ocean floor somewhere around the Manacles."

Tony Blake grunted. "At least he's been denied payment. That's some consolation."

Each and every one of them would much rather have seen him hang.

"If only," Charles said, "there was something distinctive about him. But a dark-haired, well-spoken gentleman who at a glance looks and sounds like Dalziel covers at least a quarter of the aristocracy."

"And we're unlikely to get another chance at him." Jack Warnefleet sipped the brandy he was nursing. "That's what irks most."

"Us, and Dalziel." Deverell narrowed his eyes. "I can't imagine he was happy, having got so close—on the same beach, in the same area—only to have the man slip through his fingers."

Gervase frowned. "Not happy, no. Strangely, however, I think he's resigned." He arched a brow at Christian.

Who nodded. "I traveled back to London with him afterward. By the time we reached town, I got the impression he'd shut the door on the last traitor and all his works."

"That meshes," Tristan said, "with whispers I've been hearing over the last weeks that he's expected to retire within the next month."

"He'd mentioned that he was tying up loose ends," Christian said. "There can't be that many more left."

Charles raised his brows high. "Which leads to a very interesting question—once he retires, will we finally be able to learn who he is?"

They all considered that.

"Unless he becomes a hermit," Tony said, "presumably we'll run into him as his real self—Royce Whoever-he-is, Lord Whatever."

"Curiosity is my besetting sin," Charles quipped. "I can't wait to fill in the blanks."

"I'll drink to that." Jack Warnefleet raised his glass.

They all did, then Jack glanced around their circle. "We seem to have made a habit of this, gathering at each other's weddings. As I recall, last time"—he nodded at Deverell—"at your nuptials, we all watched Gervase walk away, summoned back to his castle, and wondered what had called him back." With an expansive gesture, Jack indicated the rest of the room. "Now we know, and here we are, dancing at his wedding."

"This time, however"—Charles picked up the thread—"there's only one of us left to wonder about." He turned to Christian. And smiled. "You."

Christian laughed, entirely unruffled, but then, Gervase thought, he was the least ruffleable of them all.

He made them a mock bow. "I'm desolated to report, gentlemen, that despite considerable reconnoitering, I've as yet failed to discover any lady over whom I feel compelled to make plans. Much as I salute your endeavors and their exemplary success, as the last member of the Bastion Club unwed, I find myself in no great hurry to change my status. Aside from all else, you have between you set the bar exceedingly high, and I wouldn't want to let the side, as it were, down. I clearly need to polish my brass, as well as my address."

They didn't let it rest, of course, but teased and ribbed in a lighthearted, good-natured way. Christian, of them all, was the last man one would attempt to pressure—wasted effort. While he laughed and turned their comments aside with practiced ease, his stance didn't waver in the least.

In the end, Christian himself pointed out, "As both the oldest and the most senior peer in the group, my path to finding the perfect wife was always destined to be the least straightforward."

They all looked at him, trying to see past the comment, all sensing that it hid some deeper meaning. Whatever it was, none of them could fathom it.

Predictably, it was Charles who put their collective riposte into words. He fixed Christian with a wide-eyed look. "Whoever said falling in love was straightforward?"

Christian returned to London two days later. As he often did, he sought refuge at the Bastion Club. It was midafternoon when he climbed the stairs to the club's library. Closing the door, he crossed to the tantalus, poured himself a brandy, then settled in one of the comfortable armchairs by the hearth. And sipped. And thought.

There was no other member staying at the club; he was the last one unwed, with no lady waiting at home, at the huge house in Grosvenor Square.

He thought back to Gervase's wedding, to their gathering there, revisited the others' words, the advice they'd jokingly offered him; he smiled as he recalled, but then Charles's last words replayed in his mind and his smile faded.

Charles and the others had misinterpreted his earlier comment. He hadn't suggested that him falling in love would not be straightforward—he'd stated that for him, finding the perfect wife was not destined to be straight-forward. As it wasn't, for one very simple reason.

Whoever said falling in love was straightforward?

In that, he could prove Charles wrong. For him, falling in love had been the easiest, most straightforward and natural thing in the world. As he recalled. What, in his case, made matters anything but straightforward was the difficulty he faced in marrying the lady in question.

Not least because she was already wed.

Closing his eyes, he let his head fall back against the chair. A parade of memories flickered past his mind's eye—all the things that had happened, all the things he couldn't change.

In the distance, he heard the front doorbell peal; one part of his mind tracked Gasthorpe's footsteps as he went to answer the door . . . but then the past dragged him back, wrapped him in soft arms and the wreathing scent of jas-mine.

He was recalled to the present by a tap on the door, fol-lowed by Gasthorpe.

Christian opened his eyes.

The majordomo closed the door, then faced him. "A lady has called, my lord, asking to see you. She gave no name, but offered this note."

Christian beckoned. As Gasthorpe neared, he idly won-dered who in all the ton wished to converse with him, and about what—and how any lady had known to run him to earth there. His staff in Grosvenor Square knew better than to reveal his whereabouts, not to just anyone. He lifted the folded parchment from Gasthorpe's silver salver.

The sight of the script rocked him.

For a moment, he simply stared, then reaction rushed through him, jerking him free of all lethargy with a resounding mental slap.

His fingers shifted, fingertips tracing his name, not the one from long ago but the title he'd since acquired.

Even before he unfolded the note, the scent of jasmine reached him.

No figment of imagination or memory.

He fumbled, nearly dropped the note. His fingertips burned.

Drawing in a deep breath, slowing his movements, steadying them and himself, he smoothed out the note.

He read the few lines within.

Then he leaned back in the chair, his gaze rising, fixing unseeing on the hearth.

He didn't know what he felt; emotions careened through him, a jumble of reactions impossible to dissect. He breathed deeply, pulling air past the constriction in his chest; gradually a cool tension, an inward steeling, flowed through him.

Fate moved in inscrutable, damnably mysterious ways.

Gasthorpe cleared his throat. "My lord?"

Christian heard himself say over the pounding in his chest, "I'll join the lady in a moment, Gasthorpe. Tell her to wait."

THE SIXTH BASTION CLUB NOVEL,

The Edge of Desire,

tells the tale of Christian Allardyce,
Marquess of Dearne,
the last member of the Bastion Club yet to wed.

FROM AVON BOOKS IN FALL 2008

In the meantime . . .

STEPHANIE LAURENS'S CYNSTER NOVELS

continue with

The Taste of Innocence

AVAILABLE NOW

FROM AVON BOOKS

Following is an excerpt from *The Taste of Innocence,*
which is the story of Lord Charles Morwellan,
Alathea Cynster's brother
and Gabriel Cynster's protégé,
and the lady who, despite his resistance,
captures his heart.

THE NEXT CYNSTER NOVEL,

Where the Heart Leads

IS AVAILABLE NOW

FROM WILLIAM MORROW

He'd always enjoyed the boisterous warmth of those gatherings, yet this time . . . it hadn't been Gerrard's and Dillon's children per se that had fed his restlessness but rather what they represented. Of the three of them, friends for over a decade, *he* was the one with a recognized duty to wed and produce an heir. While theoretically he could leave his brother Jeremy, now twenty-three, to father the next generation of Morwellans, when it came to family duty he'd long ago accepted that he was constitutionally incapable of ducking. Letting one of the major responsibilities attached to the position of earl devolve onto Jeremy's shoulders was not something his conscience or his nature, his sense of self, would allow.

Which was why he was heading for Conningham Manor.

Continuing to tempt fate, courting the risk of that dangerous deity stepping in and organizing his life, and his wife, for him, as she had with Gerrard and Dillon, would be beyond foolish; *ergo* it was time for him to choose his bride. Now, before the start of the coming season, so he could exercise his prerogative, choose the lady who would suit *him* best, and have the deed done, final and complete, before society even got wind of it.

Before fate had any further chance to throw love across his path.

He needed to act now to retain complete and absolute control over his own destiny, something he considered a necessity, not an option.

Storm pranced, infected with his underlying impatience. Subduing the powerful gelding, he focused on the landscape ahead. A mile away, comfortably nestled in a dip, the slate roofs of Conningham Manor rose above the naked branches of its orchard. Weak morning sunlight glinted off diamond-paned windows; a chill breeze caught the smoke drifting from the tall Elizabethan chimney pots and whisked it away. There'd been Conninghams at the manor for nearly as long as there'd been Morwellans at the park.

Charlie stared at the manor for a minute more, then stirred, eased Storm's reins, and cantered down the rise.

"*Regardless,* Sarah, Clary and I *firmly* believe that you have to marry first."

Seated facing the bow window in the back parlor of Conningham Manor, the undisputed domain of the daughters of the house, Sarah Conningham glanced at her sixteen-year-old sister, Gloria, who stared pugnaciously at her from her perch on the window seat.

"*Before* us." The clarification came in determined tones from seventeen-year-old Clara—Clary—seated beside Gloria and likewise focused on Sarah and their relentless pursuit to urge her into matrimony.

Stifling a sigh, Sarah looked down at the ribbon trim she was unpicking from the neckline of her new spencer, and with unimpaired calm set about reiterating her well-trod arguments. "You know that's not true. I've told you so, Twitters has told you so, and Mama has told you so. Whether I marry or not will have no effect whatever on your come-outs." Freeing the last stitch, she tugged the ribbon away, then shook out the spencer. "Clary will have her first season next year, and you, Gloria, will follow the year after."

"Yes, *but* that's not the point." Clary fixed Sarah with a frown. "It's the . . . the *way* of things."

When Sarah cocked a questioning brow at her, Clary blushed and rushed on, "It's the unfulfilled expectations. Mama and Papa will be taking you to London in a few weeks for your *fourth* season. It's obvious they still hope you'll attract the notice of a suitable gentleman. Both Maria and Angela accepted offers in their second season, after all."

Maria and Angela were their older sisters, twenty-eight and twenty-six years old, each married and living with their husbands and children on said husbands' distant estates. Unlike Sarah, both Maria and Angela had been perfectly content to marry gentlemen of their station with whom they were merely comfortable, given those men were blessed with fortunes and estates of appropriate degree.

Both marriages were the conventional norm; neither Maria nor Angela had ever considered any other prospect, let alone dreamed of it.

As far as Sarah knew, neither had Clary or Gloria. At least, not yet.

She suppressed another sigh. "I assure you I will happily accept should an offer eventuate from a gentleman I can countenance being married to. However, as that happy occurrence seems increasingly unlikely"—she gave passing thanks that neither Clary nor Gloria had any notion of the number of offers she'd received and declined over the past three years—"I assure you I'm resigned to a spinster's life."

A massive overstatement, but . . . Sarah flicked a glance at the fourth occupant of the room, her erstwhile governess, Miss Twitterton, fondly known as Twitters, seated in an armchair to one side of the wide window. Now in middle age, Twitters's gray head was bent over a piece of darning; she gave no sign of following the familar discussion.

If she couldn't imagine being happy with a life like Maria's or Angela's, Sarah could equally not imagine being content with a life like Twitters's.

Gloria made a rude sound. Clary looked disgusted. The pair exchanged glances, then embarked on a verbal catalog of what they considered the most pertinent criteria for defining a "suitable gentleman," one to whom Sarah would countenance being wed.

Folding her new spencer with the too-garish scarlet ribbon now removed, Sarah smiled distantly and let them ramble. She was sincerely fond of her younger sisters, yet the gap between her twenty-three years and their ages was, in terms of the present discussion, a significant gulf.

They naïvely considered marriage a simple matter easily decided on a list of definable attributes, while she had seen enough to appreciate how unsatisfactory such an approach often was. Most marriages in their circle were indeed contracted on the basis of such criteria—and the vast majority, underpinned by nothing stronger than mild affection, degenerated into hollow relationships in which both partners turned elsewhere for comfort.

For love.

Such as love, in such circumstances, could be. Somehow less, somehow tawdry.

For herself, she'd approached the question of marriage with an open mind and open eyes. No one had ever deemed her rebellious, yet she'd never been one to blindly follow others' dictates, especially on topics of personal importance. So she'd looked and studied.

She now believed that when it came to marriage there was something better than the conventional norm. Something finer, an ideal, a commitment, that compelled one to grasp it, a state glorious enough to fill the heart with yearning and need, and ultimately with satisfaction, a construct in which love existed *within* the bonds of matrimony rather than outside them.

And she'd seen it. Not in her parents' marriage, for that was a conventional if successful union, one without passion but based instead on affection, duty and common cause. But to the south lay Morwellan Park, and beyond that Casleigh, the home of Lord Martin and Lady Celia Cynster, and now also home to their elder son, Gabriel, and his wife, Lady Alathea née Morwellan.

Sarah had known Alathea, Gabriel, and his parents for all of her life. Alathea and Gabriel had married for love; Alathea had waited until she was twenty-nine before Gabriel had come to his senses and claimed her as his bride. As for Martin and Celia, they had eloped long ago in a statement of passion impossible to mistake.

Sarah met both couples frequently. Her conviction that a love match, for want of a better title, was a goal worthy of her aspiration derived from what she'd observed between Gabriel and Alathea and, once her wits had been sharpened and her eyes had grown accustomed, from the older and somehow deeper and stronger interaction between Martin and Celia.

She freely admitted she didn't know what love was, had no concept of what the emotion would feel like within a marriage. Yet she'd seen evidence of its existence in the quality of a smile, in the subtle meeting of eyes, the gentle touch of a hand. A caress outwardly innocent yet laden with meaning.

When it was there, love colored such moments. When it wasn't . . .

But how did one define that love?

And did it mysteriously appear, or did one need to work for it? How did it come about?

She had no answers, not even a glimmer, hence her unwed state. Despite her sisters' trenchant beliefs, there was no reason she needed to marry. And if the emotion that infused the Cynsters' marriages was not part of an offer made to her, then she doubted any man, no matter how wealthy, how handsome or charming, could tempt her to surrender her hand.

To her, marriage without love held no attraction. She had no need of a union devoid of that finer glory, devoid of passion, yearning, need, and satisfaction. She had no reason to accept a lesser union.

"You will promise to look, won't you?"

Sarah glanced up to find Gloria leaning forward, brown brows beetling at her.

"*Properly*, I mean."

"*And* that you'll seriously consider and *encourage* any likely gentleman," Clary added.

Sarah blinked, then laughed and sat up to lay aside her spencer. "No, I will not. You two are far too impertinent—I'm sure Twitters agrees."

She glanced at Twitters to find the governess, whose ears were uncommonly sharp, peering myopically out of the window in the direction of the front drive.

"Now who is that, I wonder?" Twitters squinted past Clary, who swiveled to look out, as did Gloria. "No doubt some gentleman come to call on your papa."

Sarah looked past Gloria. Blessed with excellent eyesight, she instantly recognized the horseman trotting up the drive, but surprise and a frisson of unnerving reaction—something she felt whenever she saw him—stilled her tongue.

"It's Charlie Morwellan," Gloria said. "I wonder what he's doing here."

Clary shrugged. "Probably to see Papa about the hunting."

"But he's never here for the hunting," Gloria pointed out. "These days he spends almost all his time in London. Augusta said she hardly ever sees him."

"Maybe he's staying in the country this year," Clary said. "I heard Lady Castleton tell Mama that he's going to be hunted without quarter this season from the absolute instant he returns to town."

Sarah had heard the same thing, but she knew Charlie well enough to predict that he would be no easy quarry. She watched as he drew rein at the edge of the forecourt and swung lithely down from the back of his gray hunter.

The breeze ruffled elegantly cropped golden locks. His morning coat of brown Bath superfine was the apogee of some London tailor's art, stretching over broad shoulders before tapering to hug his lean waist and narrow hips. His linen was pristine and precise; his waistcoat, glimpsed as he moved, was a subtle medley of browns and black. Buckskin breeches molded to long powerful legs before disappearing into glossy black Hessians, completing a picture that might have been titled *Fashionable Peer in the Country*.

Irritation stirring, Sarah drank in the vision; his appearance—and its ridiculous effect on her—really wasn't fair. He knew she existed, but beyond that . . . From this distance, she couldn't see his features clearly, yet her besotted memory filled in the details—the classic lines of brow, nose, and chin, the aristocratic angles and planes, the patriarchal cast of high cheekbones, the large heavy-lidded, lushly lashed blue eyes, and the distracting, frankly sensual mouth and mobile lips that allowed his expression to change from delightfully charming to ruthlessly dominating in the blink of an eye.

She'd studied that face—and him—for years. She'd never known him to appear other than he was, a wealthy aristocrat descended from Norman lords with a streak of Viking thrown in. Despite his aura of ineffable control, of being born to rule without question, a hint of the unpredictable warrior remained, lurking beneath his smooth surface.

A stable boy came running. Charlie handed over his reins, spoke to the lad, then turned for the front door. As he passed out of their sight around the central wing, Clary and Gloria uttered identical sighs and turned back to face the room.

"He's really top of the trees, isn't he?"

Sarah doubted Clary required an answer.

"Gertrude Riordan said that in town he drives the most *fabulous* pair of matched grays." Gloria bounced, eyes alight. "I wonder if he drove them home? He would have, don't you think?"

While her sisters discussed various means of ascertaining whether Charlie's vaunted matched pair were at Morwellan Park, Sarah watched the stable boy lead Charlie's hunter off to the stables rather than walk the horse in the forecourt. Whatever Charlie's reasons for calling, he expected to be there for some little while.

Her sisters' voices filled her ears; recollections of their earlier comments whirled kaleidoscopically—to settle, abruptly, into an unexpected pattern. Leading to a startling thought.

Another frisson, different, more intense, slithered down Sarah's spine.

"*W*ell, m'boy—" Lord Conningham broke off and laughingly grimaced at Charlie. "Daresay I shouldn't call you that anymore, but it's hard to forget how long I've known you."

Seated in the chair before the desk in his lordship's study, Charlie smiled and waved the comment aside. Lord Conningham was a bluff, good-natured man, one with whom Charlie felt entirely comfortable.

"For myself and her ladyship," Lord Conningham continued, "I can say without reservation that we're both honored and delighted by your offer. However, as a man with five daughters, two already wed, I have to tell you that their decisions are their own. It's Sarah herself whose approval you'll have to win, but on that score I know of nothing whatever that stands between you and your goal."

After a fractional hesitation, Charlie clarified, "She has no interest in any other gentleman?"

"No." Lord Conningham grinned. "And I would know if she had. Sarah's never been one to play her cards close to her chest. If any gentleman had captured her attention, her ladyship and I would know of it."

The door opened; Lord Conningham looked up. "Ah, there you are, m'dear. I hardly need to introduce you to Charlie. He has something to tell us."

With a smile, Charlie rose to greet Lady Conningham, a sensible, well-bred female he could with nothing more than the mildest of qualms imagine as his mother-in-law.

*T*en minutes later, her wits in a whirl, Sarah left her bedchamber and hurried to the main stairs. A footman had brought a summons to join her mother in the front hall.

She'd detoured via her dressing table, dallying just long enough to reassure herself that her gown of fine periwinkle blue wool wasn't rumpled, that the lace edging the neckline hadn't crinkled, that her browny-blond hair was neat in its knot at the back of her head and not too many strands had escaped.

Quite a few had, but she didn't have time to let her hair down and redo it. Besides, she only needed to be neat enough to pass muster in case Charlie saw her in passing; it was too early for him to be staying for luncheon and there was no reason to imagine that her mother's summons was in any way connected with his visit . . . other than the ridiculous suspicion that had flared in her mind and set her heart racing. Reaching the head of the stairs, she started down, her stomach a hard knot, her nerves jangling.

All for nothing, she chided herself. It was a nonsensical supposition.

Her slippers pattered on the treads; her mother appeared from the corridor beside the stairs. Sarah's gaze flew to her face, willing her mother to speak and explain and ease her nerves.

Instead, her mother's countenance, already wreathed in a glorious smile, brightened even more. "Good. You've tidied." Her mother scanned her comprehensively from her forehead to her toes, then beamed and took her arm.

Entirely at sea, her questions in her eyes, Sarah let her mother draw her a few yards down the corridor to where an alcove nestled under the stairs.

Releasing her arm, her mother clasped her hand and squeezed her fingers. "Well, my dear, the long and short of this is that Charlie Morwellan wishes to offer for your hand."

Sarah blinked; for one instant, her mind literally reeled.

Her mother smiled, not unsympathetically. "Indeed, it's a surprise, quite out of the blue, but heaven knows you've dealt with offers enough—you know the ropes. As always the decision is yours, and your father and I will stand by you regardless of what that decision might be." Her mother paused. "However, in this case both your father and I would ask that you consider very carefully. An offer from any earl would command extra attention, but an offer from the eighth Earl of Meredith warrants even deeper consideration."

Sarah looked into her mother's dark eyes. Quite aside from her pleasure over Charlie's offer, in advising her in this, her mother was very serious.

"My dear, you already have sufficient comprehension of Charlie's wealth. You know his home, his standing—you know *of* him, although I accept that you do not know him, himself, well. But you do know his family."

Taking both her hands, her mother lightly squeezed, her excitement returning. "With no other gentleman have you had, nor will you have, such a close prior connection, such a known foundation on which you might build. It's an unlooked-for, entirely unexpected opportunity, yes, but a very good one."

Her mother searched her eyes, trying to read her reaction. Sarah knew all she would see was confusion.

"Well." Her mother's lips set just a little; her tone became more brisk. "You must hear him out. Listen carefully to what he has to say, then you must make your decision."

Releasing her hands, her mother stepped back, reached up and tweaked Sarah's neckline, then nodded. "Very well. You must go in—he's waiting in the drawing room. As I said, your father and I will accept whatever decision you make. But please, do think very carefully about Charlie."

Sarah nodded, feeling numb. She could barely breathe. Turning from her mother, she walked, slowly, toward the drawing room door.

*C*harlie heard a light footstep beyond the door. He turned from the window as the knob turned, watched as the door opened and the lady he'd chosen to be his wife entered.

She was of average height, subtly but sensuously curved; her slenderness made her appear taller than she was. Her face was heart-shaped, framed by the soft fullness of her lustrous hair, an eye-catching shade of gilded light brown. Her features were delicate, her complexion flawless—including, to his mind, the row of tiny freckles across the bridge of her nose. A wide brow, that straight nose, arched brown brows and long lashes combined with rose-tinted lips and a sweetly curved chin to complete a picture of restful loveliness.

Her gaze was unusually direct; he waited for her to move, knowing that when she did it would be with innate grace.

Her hand on the door knob, she paused, scanning the room.

His eyes narrowed slightly. Even across the distance he sensed her uncertainty, yet when her gaze found him she hesitated for only a second before, without looking away, she closed the door and came toward him.

Calmly, serenely, but with her hands clasping, fingers twining.

She couldn't have expected this; he'd given her no indication that marrying her had ever entered his head. The last time they'd met socially, at the Hunt Ball last November, he'd waltzed with her once, remained by her side for fifteen minutes or so, exchanging the usual pleasantries, and that had been all.

Deliberately on his part. He'd known—for years if he stopped to consider it—that she . . . regarded him differently. That it would be very easy, with just a smile and a few words, for him to awaken an infatuation in her, a fascination with him. Not that she'd ever been so gauche as to give the slightest sign, yet he was too attuned to women, certainly, it seemed, to her, not to know what quivered just beneath her cool, clear surface, the sensible serenity she showed to the world. He'd made a decision, not once, but many times over the years, that it wouldn't do to stir that pool, to ripple her surface. She was, after all, sweet Sarah, a neighbor's daughter he'd known all her life.

So he'd been careful not to do what his instincts had so frequently prompted. He'd studiously treated her as just another young lady of his local acquaintance.

Yet when he'd finally decided to select a wife, one face had leapt to his mind. He hadn't even had to think—he'd simply known that she was his choice.

And then, of course, he had thought and visited all the arguments, the numerous criteria a man like him needed to evaluate in selecting a wife. The exercise had only confirmed that Sarah Conningham was the perfect candidate.

She halted before him, confidently facing him with less than two feet between them. Confusion shadowed her eyes, a delicate blue the color of a pale cornflower, as she searched his face.

"Charlie." She inclined her head. To his surprise, her voice was even, steady if a trifle breathless. "Mama said you wished to speak with me."

Head high so she could continue to meet his gaze—the top of her head barely reached his chin—she waited.

He felt his lips curve, entirely spontaneously. No fuss, no fluster, and no "Lord Charles," either. They'd never stood on formality, not in any circumstances, and for that he was grateful.

Despite her outward calm, he sensed the brittle, expectant tension that held her, that kept her breathing shallow. Respect stirred, unexpected but definite, yet was he really surprised that she had more backbone than the norm?

No; that, in part, was why he was there.

The urge to reach out and run his fingertips across her collarbone—just to see how smooth the fine alabaster skin was—struck unexpectedly; he toyed with the notion for a heartbeat, but rejected it. Such an action wasn't appropriate, given the nature of what he had to say, the tone he wished to maintain.

"As I daresay your mother mentioned, I've asked your father's permission to address you. I would like to ask you to do me the honor of becoming my wife."

He could have dressed up the bare words in any amount of platitudes, but to what end? They knew each other well, perhaps not in a private sense, but his sisters and hers were close; he doubted there was much in his general life of which she was unaware.

And there was nothing in her response to suggest he'd gauged that wrongly, even though, after the briefest of moments, she frowned.

"Why?"

It was his turn to feel confused.

Her lips tightened and she clarified, "Why me?"

Why now? Why after all these years have you finally deigned to do more than smile at me? Sarah kept the words from her tongue, but looking up into Charlie's impassive face, she felt an almost overpowering urge to sink her hands into her hair, pull loose the neatly arranged tresses, and run her fingers through them while she paced. And thought. And tried to understand.

She couldn't remember a time when she hadn't had to, every time she first set eyes on him, pause, just for a second, to let her senses breathe. To let them catch their breath after it had been stolen away simply by his presence. Once the moment passed, as it always did, then all she had to do was battle to ensure she did nothing foolish, nothing to give away her secret obsession—infatuation—with him.

It was nonsense and brought her nothing but aggravation, but no amount of lecturing over its inanity had ever done an ounce of good. She'd decided it was simply the way she reacted to him, Viking-Norman Adonis that he was. She'd reluctantly concluded that her reaction wasn't her fault. Or his. It just *was*; she'd been born this way, and she simply had to deal with it.

And now here he was, without so much as a proper smile in warning, asking for her hand.

Wanting to *marry her.*

It didn't seem possible. She pinched her thumb, just to make sure, but he remained before her, solid and real, the heat of him, the strength of him wrapping about her in pure masculine temptation, even if now he was frowning, too.

His lips firmed, losing the intoxicating curve that had softened them. "Because I believe we'll deal exceptionally well together." He hesitated, then went on, "I could give you chapter and verse about our stations, our families, our backgrounds, but you already know every aspect as well as I. And"—his gaze sharpened—"as I'm sure you understand, I need a countess."

He paused, then his lips quirked. "Will you be mine?"

Nicely ambiguous. Sarah stared into his gray-blue eyes, a paler shade of blue than her own, and heard again in her mind her mother's words: *Think very carefully about Charlie.*

She searched his eyes, and accepted that she'd have to, that this time her answer wasn't so clear. She'd lost count of the times she'd faced a gentleman like this and framed an answer to that question, couched though it had been in many different ways. Never before had she even had to think of the crux of her reply, only the words in which to deliver it.

This time, facing Charlie . . .

Still holding his gaze, she compressed her lips fleetingly, drew in a breath and let it out with, "If you want my honest answer, then that honest answer is that I can't answer you, not yet."

His dark gold lashes, impossibly thick, screened his eyes for an instant; when he again met her gaze his frown was back. "What do you mean? When will you be able to answer?"

Aggression reached her, reined but definitely there. Unsurprised—she knew his charm was nothing more than a veneer, that under that glossy surface he was stubborn, even ruthless—she studied his eyes, and unexpectedly found answers to two of the many questions crowding her mind. He did indeed want her—specifically *her*—as his wife. And he wanted her soon.

Quite what she was to make of that last, she wasn't sure. Nor did she know how much trust she could place in the former.

She was aware that he expected her to back away from his veiled challenge, to temporize, to in one way or another back down. She smiled tightly and lifted her chin. "In answer to your first question, you know perfectly well that I had no warning of your offer. I had no idea you were even thinking of such a thing. Your proposal has come entirely out of the blue, and the simple fact is I don't know you well enough"—she held up a hand—"regardless of our long acquaintance—and don't pretend you don't know what I mean—to be able to answer you yeah or nay."

She paused, waiting to see if he would argue. When he simply waited, lips even thinner, his gaze razor sharp and locked on her eyes, she continued, "As for your second question, I'll be able to answer you once I know you well enough to know which answer to give."

His eyes bored into hers for a long moment, then he stated, "You want me to woo you."

His tone was resigned; she'd gained that much at least.

"Not precisely. It's more that I need to spend time with you so I can get to know you better." She paused, her eyes on his. "And so you can get to know me."

That last surprised him; he held her gaze, then his lips quirked and he inclined his head.

"Agreed." His voice had lowered. Now he was talking to her, with her, no longer on any formal plane but on an increasingly personal one, his tone had deepened, becoming more private. More intimate.

She quelled a tiny shiver; at that lower note his voice reverberated through her. She'd wanted to increase the space between them for several minutes, but there was something in the way he looked at her, the way his gaze held her, that made her hesitate, as if to edge back would be tantamount to admitting weakness.

Like fleeing from a predator. An invitation to . . . her mouth was dry.

He'd tilted his head, studying her face. "So how long do you think getting to know each other better—well enough—will take?"

There was not a glint so much as a carefully veiled idea lurking in the depths of his eyes that made her inwardly frown. She was tempted to state that she had no intention of being swayed by his undoubted, unquestioned, utterly obvious sexual expertise, but that, like fleeing, might be seriously unwise. He'd all too likely interpret such a comment as an outright challenge.

And that was, she was certain, one challenge she couldn't meet.

She hadn't, not for one moment, been able to—felt able to—shift her gaze from his. "A month or two should be sufficient."

His face hardened. "A week."

She narrowed her eyes. "That's impossible. Four weeks."

He narrowed his back. "Two."

The word held a ring of finality she wished she could challenge—wished she thought she *could* challenge. Lips set, she nodded. Curtly. "Very well. Two weeks—and then I'll answer you yeah or nay."

His eyes held hers. Although he didn't move, she felt as if he leaned closer.

"I have a caveat." His gaze, at last, shifted from her eyes, drifting mesmerically lower. His voice deepened, becoming even more hypnotic. "In return for me agreeing to a two-week courtship, you will agree that once you answer and accept my offer"—his gaze rose to her eyes—"we'll be married by special license no more than a week later."

She licked her dry lips, started to form the word why.

He stepped nearer. "Do you agree?"

Trapped—in his gaze, by his nearness—she just managed to draw in a breath. "Very well. *If* I agree to marry you, then we can be married by special license."

He smiled—and she suddenly decided that no matter how he took it, fleeing was an excellent idea. She tensed to step back.

Just as his arm swept around her, and tightened.

His eyes held hers as he drew her, gently but inexorably, into his arms. "Our two-week courtship . . . remember?"

She leaned back, keeping her eyes on his, her hands on his upper arms. His strength surrounded her. She felt giddy. "What of it?"

His lips curved in a wholly masculine smile. "It starts now."

Then he bent his head and covered her lips with his.

Don't miss any of the sensual, sexy, delectable
novels in the world of
New York Times bestselling author

STEPHANIE LAURENS

The Truth About Love
978-0-06-050576-9
Gerrard Debbington chafes at wasting his painting talents on
a simpering miss, only to discover that Jacqueline Tregonning
stirs him as no other.

What Price Love?
978-0-06-084085-3
Lady Priscilla Dalloway will do *anything* to save her twin
brother, including seducing Dillon Caxton.

The Taste of Innocence
978-0-06-084087-7
Charles Morwellan, eighth Earl of Meredith, is shocked when
beautiful, intelligent Sarah Cunningham refuses to wed him
for anything less than unbounded love.

Where the Heart Leads
978-0-06-124338-7
Barnaby Adair has made his name by solving crimes within the
ton. When Penelope Ashford appeals for his aid, he is moved by
her plight—and captivated by her beauty.

Temptation and Surrender
978-0-06-124341-7
Handsome, wealthy, and well-born, Jonas Tallent had everything
needed to enjoy life. Everything except the passion
he would find in Emily Beauregard's bed.

ALL BOOKS ARE AVAILABLE FROM AVON BOOKS.

LAU1 0809

Don't miss any of the sensual, sexy, delectable novels in the world of *New York Times* bestselling author

STEPHANIE LAURENS

Captain Jack's Woman
978-0-380-79455-3
Don't miss the story that informed and inspired the Bastion Club novels.

The Lady Chosen
978-0-06-000206-0
Tristan Wemyss, Earl of Trentham, never expected he'd need to wed within a year or forfeit his inheritance.

A Gentleman's Honor
978-0-06-000207-7
Anthony Blake, Viscount Torrington, is a target for every matchmaking mama in London.

A Lady of His Own
978-0-06-059330-8
Charles St. Austell returns home to claim his title as earl and to settle quickly on a suitable wife.

A Fine Passion
978-0-06-059331-5
Lady Clarice Altwood is the antithesis of the wooly-headed young ladies Jack, Baron Warnefleet, has rejected as not for him.

ALL BOOKS ARE AVAILABLE FROM AVON BOOKS.

LAU2 0809

Don't miss any of the sensual, sexy, delectable
novels in the world of
New York Times bestselling author

STEPHANIE LAURENS

Devil's Bride
978-0-380-79456-0

A Rake's Vow
978-0-380-79457-7

Scandal's Bride
978-0-380-80568-6

A Rogue's Proposal
978-0-380-80570-9

A Secret Love
978-0-380-80569-3

All About Love
978-0-380-81201-1

All About Passion
978-0-380-81202-8

On a Wild Night
978-0-380-81203-5

On a Wicked Dawn
978-0-06-000205-3

The Promise in a Kiss
978-0-06-103175-5

The Perfect Lover
978-0-06-050572-1

The Ideal Bride
978-0-06-050574-5

ALL BOOKS ARE AVAILABLE FROM AVON BOOKS

LAU3 0809

Don't miss any of the sensual, sexy, delectable
novels in the world of
New York Times bestselling author

STEPHANIE LAURENS

To Distraction
978-0-06-083910-9

Unmoved by the matchmaking "herd," Deverell,
Viscount Paignton, seeks help from his aunt to find a wife.

Beyond Seduction
978-0-06-083925-3

In a moment of recklessness, Gervase Tregarth swears
he'll marry the next eligible lady to cross his path.

The Edge of Desire
978-0-06-124636-4

Lady Letitia Randall is a woman like no other. The day
Christian Allardyce left her behind to fight for king and
country was the most difficult of his life.

Mastered By Love
978-0-06-124637-1

When the Duke of Wolverstone chooses
Minerva Chesterton for his bride, they will learn
who is master—or mistress—of whom . . .

ALL BOOKS ARE AVAILABLE FROM AVON BOOKS

LAU4 0809